Heaven AND *Hell.*
SIN AND
PLEASURE. THE
Devil SHE NEVER
SEES COMING...

Sin

BEAUTIFUL SINNER SERIES

ELENA M. REYES

SUMMARY

I am both heaven and hell.
Sin and pleasure.
The Devil she never sees coming…

Everyone knows that Malcolm Asher owns Chicago. Nothing—not a single move is made in my city without my authorization. I'm ruthless. Conniving. Worshipped by those around me, and yet, it means nothing the moment my eyes meet hers…

Clear blue and innocent, the delicate doll on this stage holds me captive against my will. She's decadence personified—a corruptible angel I want to own.

I'm hard for her. Starving for a taste. Eager for her to feel me.

This little girl has no idea of the danger she's in within my presence. How I will make her crave the darkness I control.

How I will make her…*Mine.*

SIN (Beautiful Sinner Series) #1
was written by Elena M. Reyes
Copyright 2019© Elena M. Reyes

Cover design by: T.E. Black Designs
Editor: Marti Lynch

Publication Date: April 29th 2019

Genre: FICTION/Romance/Erotica Suspense

I'M
MORE
BEAST
THAN
PRINCE
CHARMING.

Beautiful
SINNER

ACKNOWLEDGMENTS

Before we get to the book and its yumminess; I need to thank a few people that I adore:

C.M. Steele: You push me to be better. To work when all I want to do is be lazy. Thank you for everything. For letting me bounce ideas off you and for getting on my case when I fall behind. You've become such an amazing friend and I love you.

M. Robinson and Willow Winters: This blurb would've taken me a million years to write without your input. Thank you so much for taking the time out of your busy schedules to help me figure out the mess I had in my head. I admire you both so much.

K.I. Lynn: My Boo. My wifey. It's crazy how we met all those years ago and the paths our lives have taken. I know that I can always count on you to be there for me. To stop me from jumping off the ledge or when I threaten to erase over 45,000 words because I'm freaking out. You hold my hand and calm my fears. Thank you, babes. I love you with all my heart.

Marti Lynch: You have the patience of a saint and I love you! I thought for sure this time you'd kill me, but like always, you calm my fears and work with my crazy schedule. Thank you. THANK YOU. This book wouldn't be ready without your amazing work.

T.E. Black Designs: My babies have never been in better hands than with you. You are a true joy to work with, and I am so thankful for both your talent and professionalism. YOU'RE AMAZING!

Sansa and Aliana: Thank you so much for jumping in to Beta read for me on a moment's notice. I appreciate you both so much. I'm blessed to have you in my life as both readers and friends.

Elena's Marked Girls: This book is for you. You guys keep me going and always give me a reason to smile. Thank you for everything. For your unconditional support and love. Please know that I love you—that you mean everything to me.

Tiffany Hernandez: Girl, you came into my life about two weeks ago to be my P.A. and have made your mark. Thank you so much for all the hard work, for keeping me on track, and stepping in without prompting. It's because of you that I was able to focus all my energy on Sin and get it done on time. You ROCK!

Hubs and Kiddo: You are my heart. My entire world. Everything I do, I do it for you always.

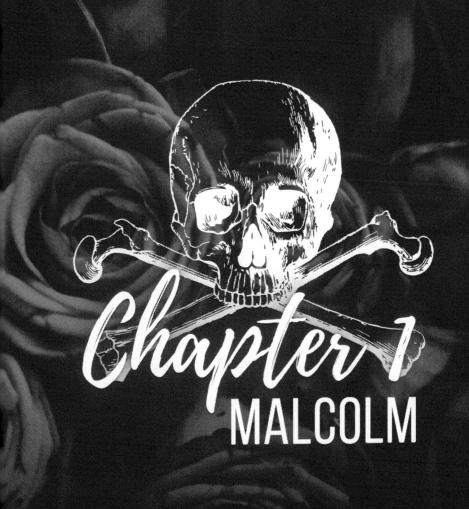

Chapter 1
MALCOLM

"M OTHERFUCKING IDIOT," I hiss out, letting the steel door behind me slam shut. My head is throbbing —muscles coiling—as the urge to break the neck of the *piece of shit* errand boy my father asked me to hire runs deep. Ire flows like lava through my veins, and I need to get ahold of myself.

Rash emotions lead to stupid decisions. Errors.

Like the one I now need to eliminate. It was a mistake, and I know better than to ever mix familial ties with business decisions. Nevertheless, I gave in when asked, and here we fucking are.

Millions could have been lost. Charges would have been pressed.

Now, I'm left with no choice but to right a wrong that never should have been.

The feds are now looking into the Jameson family and its ties to the dealing of stolen weaponry and narcotics. Because of a simple fuckup—something someone heard come out of *Michael*, a person under my employ, I'm making every tidbit of information on the Jameson account disappear.

Nothing stays on that file. Not so much as a single cent.

My IT department is making it as if they never existed. Moreover, in this country, they don't.

A few steps inside and the harsh scent of urine and perspiration invades my senses. My nose flares in disgust as I look toward the back—skipping over the three empty cells—and focus on the two near-naked men with their hands tied to a metal pipeline above their heads. Their feet are chained to the ground, limiting their movement.

They are the cause, and I am the effect.

Decisions have consequences. Repercussions. Rectifications that will appease the victims of their idiocy.

One spoke about things he doesn't understand, while the other tried to bribe the hand that feeds. Demanded that I kneel or else.

Because of that, tonight, I am their judge, jury, and executioner. The God each one will beg forgiveness to.

"Good evening." At the sound of my voice, one of the men looks up and his eyes widen. His bare chest is heaving with each rapid intake of air that does nothing to calm his nerves. Instead, his eyes lock with mine while a whimper leaves his split lip.

His fear is palpable, and it fails to move me. Motherfucking pathetic. *You knew better.*

My eyes flicker to the other man and take account of the few bruises already forming on his face. He seems to be muttering a low prayer under his breath, tears running down his cheeks while his eyes look toward the wall past me. Avoiding his reality.

No begging. No pleading for leniency.

They're smarter than I expect. Know better.

Nothing pisses me off more than someone who can't accept their fate with dignity.

"Evening, boss," everyone answers, a low rumble that reverberates off the walls. Unlike other men in my position, I don't wait for my clean-up crew to arrive. Instead, they stand at the ready wearing protective gear and white masks. Their faces are bowed, arms behind their backs as I pass them on my way toward the two men who've caused me this unnecessary headache.

"Any problem getting them here?" I ask Javier, the head of my security and right-hand man.

"None." He's watching the two squirm, smirking as he hands me my favorite knife.

"Thank you." Taking it from his hand, I flick my wrist and admire the sleek blade. This small token came from my father the day I took over. A sharp blade with a solid gold handle—the exact replica of the one he kept inside his desk upstairs when he was the CEO of Asher Holdings. Back when the bank played a smaller part in the underground world of money laundering.

A phone rings, and Javier is quick to remove it from his pocket. I recognize it, and know it belongs to the gossiping fuck. Both men cease all movement, their eyes on me as I accept the phone from Javi's outstretched hand.

I know who it is. I know what he'll say.

Pressing the green button, I put the call on speakerphone and wait. Silence looms, and the harsh breathing on the other end comes from a man I still admire. Someone who should've taught his son a few lessons early on.

"What is your decision, Malcolm?" Straight to the point, his tone not showing his true emotions.

"What do you want it to be?" I toss back, walking slowly over to his son. A son that reeks of fear and his own piss. Who couldn't keep his mouth shut after I gave him the opportunity to work for me. Work his way up the ranks.

"Family is the most—"

At my godfather's lame attempt, I laugh. It's harsh and sardonic, causing another scared whimper to leave the men. "Save that sanctimonious drivel for someone who buys it, Henry. We both know it's bullshit."

"Agreed, but he is my only son." That I can understand. The need for a man to have a male heir, someone to take over. "Spare him and I'll pay for the damages myself. Buy the forgiveness of your client."

"What else?" I take the few remaining steps between myself and Michael, his son. His eyes are on mine, throat bobbing as words fail to escape. True fear has a way of paralyzing people, and their basic motor functions become nonexistent. "Because you'll be paying *me* every last cent either way."

"What do you want?"

"Blood." My reply is automatic, and so is my hand as I lash out, cutting a jagged line down Michael's forearm. His scream curls around the room—penetrates every square inch and then breaks his father's heart. At once, my lips stretch into a wide smile as a soothing calmness settles over my limbs.

Their pain brings peace.

Beside him, the wannabe blackmailer fights against his bindings. He winces but doesn't stop moving as the steel around his wrist cuts the skin there. "This is a mistake! Please, I'll never say another word about—"

Javier backhands him with the butt of his gun. "Silence."

"Malcolm, please. Don't do this to our family." Henry's voice rings through, cutting off the pathetic pleading of his son's friend. Same low-life punk that thought he could blackmail me. "Discipline them, but don't kill my son."

"I've learned my lesson," Michael adds, face tight with pain. "I'll do whatever you want...fix this...but *please*...no more."

"Interesting." Blood flows from the wound, dripping down and onto the concrete floor. It pools near the center—follows the small slope down and into the drain I had the foresight to add into the room's design when I remodeled the bank. This is the lowest floor, two below what the actual building plans show.

"Okay." Once more, I punish him, this time sinking the blade of my knife deep into his thigh. My fingers manipulate the steel tip, twisting it as I tear through muscle. Crimson splatters all over my white shirt, ruining another garment.

Michael's sobs turn into a loud scream as I pull the knife from his flesh. He writhes, bowing as he tries to move away from me.

In the background I hear his father's outrage, revel in his pleading, but it's still not enough. I want more.

More blood. More destruction. More compensation for my time.

Within my rage, there is also the compulsion to teach this boy a lesson he will never forget. Prevent him from ever doing this again— save his family both the embarrassment and grief.

"Untie him, Javier, and bring over a chair," I instruct, taking a few steps forward and over to the other man. A man who's currently giving in to his panic. That fight or flight response that is coded deep into our DNA. That helps people survive disastrous situations.

He won't be as lucky.

Javi unlocks Michael's handcuffs and lets him fall to the floor: a crumpled, bleeding mess. The sound of a chair scraping against the floor follows, and it's loud within this space. Heightens the anxiety.

"Get up and sit," Javier instructs, standing over Michael. "Show some appreciation for Mr. Asher's hospitality."

A few men in the room chuckle and I hold a hand up, effectively shutting them up. While Javier's words are funny, now is not the time to give in to amusement.

"My leg—"

"Isn't broken," I interrupt, not bothering to look back. "Shut the fuck up and move."

"Michael, I swear to Christ! Do as he says," his father pleads, choking on his own desperation. That parental urge to take care of his offspring. It's instinctual. A deep-seated need that I can under-stand—respect—even if it means shit at the end of the day.

It didn't change the disaster his son's stupidity caused.

Leaving Javier to accommodate our guest, I focus wholly on the other one. "Name?"

"Please, I...son of a bitch!" he howls, body cringing back as I slice through the back of his right ankle, then his left. It's a shallow cut. Just the first of many.

"Name?" I ask once more, the tip of my blade slowly sawing back and forth over the back of each calf—going lower with each cut until the sharp edge slices over the first. Just enough to hurt. For him to slowly begin to drip down all over my floor.

"I told you my name that day inside your office." Another lie.

"This is your second offense. You get one more."

"But it's the truth." No, it isn't. His eyes shift downward and a shiver runs through him, giving away his nervousness. Fear.

Moreover, he has every reason to be scared.

"Last chance," I grit out, stretching my neck from side to side while my hand clenches around the golden handle. Adrenaline pulses through my veins—licks at the tips of my fingers as I drive the knife forward and into his stomach. Deep enough that I feel as it tears through flesh. Blood seeps from the wound, but I want more.

Twisting the blade, I pull it halfway out and take a step back—leave it right where it is below his belly button. "Are you ready to be honest with me now?"

"I'm telling you...fuck!" he yells out as the heel of my shoe kicks the weapon in deeper. I bury it—lodge it within his stomach where only half the handle is left visible.

Michael shifts in his chair, trying to stand, pulling my attention back to him. "Please stop."

"Why should I?" Another strike; this time I land a punch to the right side of his friend's ribs. He cries out a curse, body trying to fold into itself. It's a mistake, one that causes him to freeze when the pain magnifies.

"Please stop. I'm not lying."

"Boss, we're so sorry. It was a huge—"

Michael's word die as Javier places a gun to his temple. "Placing a bullet in you will be a pleasure, one that my boss won't begrudge me for. Keep testing his patience."

"Michael, please, son, stay quiet!"

With a smirk, I nod at Javi and watch with pleasure as he pistol-whips the idiot across the face, breaking his nose in the process. "Listen to your father, Michael."

"No more," he says, his tone tinged with pain. Regret.

I can almost taste his acceptance. Can see the glimpse of resolve in his eyes.

"That's up to you. If you sit there silently, things will progress without further incident. Talk, and…" I trail off as Javier lands a second direct hit, and a gash opens over the bridge of his nose. Rivulets of red pour down his face and neck, staining his chest with his life's essence. "Understood?"

With his right eye beginning to swell, Michael nods and looks back at the piece of shit still strung up. At the man who befriended him with one goal in mind: getting to me.

He's finally understanding that someone needs to pay, and it's either him or…

Grabbing the end of the knife, I pull out the handle, leaving the blade inside. At once he screams, the anguished sound rending the air as I slide it up his flesh.

More blood seeps from the wound; my hands are soaked. "Lying to me was your biggest mistake." His pain is not enough. Another inch up, and I stop. "Your second was not being smart enough to hide your tracks."

At this his eyes widen, lips parting to deny what we both know to be the truth, but I shake my head. Moreover, the idiot listens for once and closes his pale lips.

"Your name is Phillip Mitchell..." the knife slices upward a bit more and he strains to move away from me "...and you take on certain jobs for the head of EMB Financial Group. The same man I turned down three weeks ago, when he asked that we merge a certain department—the one you demanded twenty million dollars for in exchange for your silence."

I pause and look down, admiring the clean line that starts below his belly button and stops at the center of his abdomen. It's deep, but not enough to kill him yet, although the internal damage is done.

His life's essence is slowly bathing my floor with each drop that splashes below.

"End me already," Phillip groans, head lolling forward from the loss of blood. He's dying.

"Not until you tell me why Jonathan sent you."

"He didn't."

"Then who?" Because we both know he isn't working for himself. Phillip is nothing more than a low-level soldier—a follower —and this entire bullshit scheme didn't come from his simpleton mind.

I've read his rap sheet. Know where he lives and whom he associates himself with, and none have a position of wealth or power in Chicago. They're nothing more than thugs and "wannabe" gangsters that admire TV crime lords and wish to live a life of infamy.

"No one—"

"Bridgeport. That is where your mother lives...is it not?"

Phillip nods, tears running down his cheeks. "She has nothing to do with this. Please, don't hurt her."

"Then tell me who the fuck sent you," I snarl, lip curling over my teeth as I fight the instinct to strike once more. "Tell me, and she'll be taken care of for the rest of her life. She will want for nothing. You have my word."

Resignation flashes in his eyes, and they close. Another choked sob leaves his throat as his life slowly fades, each breath harder than the last.

"Tell her that I love her."

"Done."

"His name is Alton Foster."

I nod but say nothing. I knew this also, just needed confirmation before I rain hell on a man that doesn't respect our rules. Being somewhat new to Chicago, he is stupid and arrogant. A dead man walking, he has no idea the kind of war he just unleashed.

Before Phillip could take his next breath, I pull a gun from my back and shoot him once between the eyes. A mercy kill as two voices shout out—the one on the phone full of despair while his son fights against the hold my men have him in.

I'm done with the theatrics and put the gun back in its place. Everyone watches me as, with absolute calm, I pull the knife from Phillip's dead body and walk back toward my godfather's only child. My hands and knife are a bloody mess as I grab a fistful of his hair. "Hold your tongue out."

"Malcolm—"

"Be grateful," is all I say, grip tightening until his eyes water and I can literally feel as the strands break between my fingertips. "Now open and do as you are told."

"Anything but this."

"Would you rather join your *friend* in the next life?"

"I didn't know. You have to believe me."

"The sad part is that I do," I say, letting go and grabbing the handkerchief Javier holds out for me. He takes my place and digs his fingers deep into Michael's jaw, holding so hard that the latter gives way and opens. Michael's tongue peeks out, and with no patience left, I grip it using the small fabric square between my fingers.

Tears run down his face as I give it a harsh yank and then slice it clean off.

He sobs while his father is silent. Accepting.

I don't kill the dumb fuck, and both know that can change in the blink of an eye.

"Now you can never speak of that which you do not know. You

cannot put your life in danger or make friends with idiots that see you as easy pickings. Learn this lesson, own your mistake, and I will speak to you again in a month." Michael nods, whimpering in pain while my men help him up. Hold his weight. "Next time, I will not be so forgiving. Never betray me or this family again."

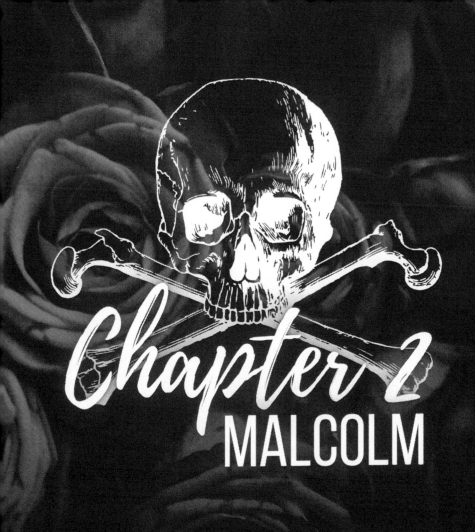

Chapter 2
MALCOLM

I'M PREOCCUPIED.

My mind is replaying the last line inside the email my informant—the FBI agent—sent over mid-afternoon. It flashes on a loop:

Eagle. Claw. Fly.

Those three simple words cause my hands to clench and the leather beneath my hands to groan in protest. It's been a few hours now since Michael was taken from here and his friend disposed of, and yet, as I connect more dots, the ire within me grows. Each tick of the clock throbs in time with the raging inferno rushing through my veins, and all because someone thinks they can take from me.

Because greed overrode common sense and they forgot their place.

Alton Foster made a move that will cost him. He ignores the rules.

In our business, discretion is law. You hear and see nothing.

I don't care who you are or how you came to have the capital you hold; my job is to move it around and turn the dirty money into clean. Untraceable.

Owning one of the largest banks in the world has advantages, and I use every fucking one in my favor. With facilities in almost every large city inside the United States, Europe, and Asia—the high volume of monetary transactions—we are untouchable. Not unless you want to disrupt the nation's economy.

Something no government can withstand, especially one that's one fuckup away from another recession.

Laundering is a skill set. A calling.

One that brings about danger—a danger that I welcome. It's a rush that satiates a need within. To these criminals, I'm their best friend until something goes wrong, and I've proven more than once just how dangerous I can be. How I am the one they should fear.

Taking a man's life doesn't keep me up at night. Instead, it feeds the darker part of my soul.

Swiveling around in my chair, I face the lit-up Chicago skyline from my office. The chair creaks, the leather protesting as I sit back and admire the city below through my floor-to-ceiling windows. This metropolis never sleeps. Never stops.

A never-ending chess game that I move at my discretion.

The phone atop my desk beeps, and I drum my fingers on the chair's armrest. Two hours until my appointment, and the darkness within me vibrates with need. With a depraved hunger—a different kind of yearning—that hasn't been fully satiated in a long time.

"Hey, Malcolm?" my cousin Mariah calls through the door,

waiting to be acknowledged before entering. No one enters this room without permission. They know better.

Other than myself and our security, she's the only person left inside the building, my cleaning crew and other employees having left an hour ago.

For a few beats I don't answer. Instead, I stare at the city below. It's ten p.m. and while the working class celebrates the end of another long week, I plot. Think. While the lights shine bright on this September night and bars fill up, I prepare.

Most people never realize that they walk past a killer several times in their life. That evil resides next door. No one cares. Most ignore the danger that lurks as long as the darkness never reaches their door. A common mistake.

Instead, the passersby below stop to admire the facade of my building.

Of the details carved in stone. Of the gold name stamped onto its front.

The Asher building is synonymous with money and decadence. All they see is sixty floors of opulence, and their greed blinds them from reality. Not a single person below would ever suspect the city's most eligible bachelor of being anything but perfect. That good looks and charms mean shit when you sit beside the devil and play in his backyard.

Just how I like it. This concrete jungle is unlike any other, and I own it. Every fucking single square inch of Chicago is mine. Run by me.

Not the mafia. Nor those that come from money.

No. Every move in this motherfucking city is made with my approval.

Mariah knocks this time; three quick raps against the wooden door. "Are you in here?"

Once more, I don't answer. Instead, I rise from my seat and take off my suit jacket. I lay it over the back of my chair and then undo the cuff links, tossing them next to a Montblanc pen my mother gave me on my last birthday.

My eyes survey the room, and a smirk crosses my lips. This office is so unassuming. So normal, and what you come to expect from a financial institution's CEO. Lavish, sleek, and nothing compared to the rooms just a few floors down.

Rolling the sleeves up to my elbows, I grab my phone and keys. My steps are slow as I make my way around my desk and to the door, pulling it open before she can try once more. "How can I help you?"

She rolls her eyes at my gruff acknowledgement, sliding the strap of her purse up her shoulder. "I'm heading out, *boss*. Do you need anything before I go?"

"Has the package been delivered?" I ask instead, ignoring the childish gesture. It's been a long day for everyone, and she's been on the clock since eight this morning. We're all tired—wound tight—and snapping at my little cousin won't help us get out of here any quicker.

"Dropped off an hour ago and is being treated by his father's private physician as we speak."

"Good." Giving her a gentle shove, I close the door behind me. "Any issues?"

"Other than Henry calling nonstop?" Annoyance crosses her features. "No, but the old degenerate has been at it every ten minutes for the last hour."

"What the fuck does he want?" At once, my ire returns in full force. Today, they were blessed by me—should consider themselves beyond lucky that Michael is still breathing. Something that I could still reconsider. A quick drive and a bullet from my gun could remedy that.

"Easy, cousin." Mariah lets out a giggle, her top lip curving up at the end. "He's just trying to kiss your ass?"

At that, I bark out a harsh laugh. "More like afraid of how many zeroes that bottom dollar will include."

"Do you need me to come in tomorrow? I will if you do, Malcolm." She pulls her cell from a pocket in her skirt and types something before hitting send. I'm not surprised by her offer. Both Javier and Mariah are always willing to step up when I need something taken care of in a rush.

"You just want to see him cry," I say, patting my front pocket. *I'm missing my keycard.*

"Guilty." No denying. No shame. Her phone pings then and she looks down, smiling as she reads the text. "I'm not the only one, either."

I know. "Is Javier waiting for you?"

"Yes, but that's not a definite answer. We can come in and fine-comb the system for any trace that could have been missed?"

"No."

"No?"

Smiling, I guide her toward the elevator and call for it. Being so late, the door opens quickly and I guide her inside. "It's taken care of, and I'm not accepting a visit from Henry until late next week. Get out of here and go enjoy your weekend with your boyfriend."

"Pity. Aren't you coming?" she says, her expression showing confusion.

Pressing the *Door Close* button, I shake my head. "I will, but I need something from my office first."

"GOOD EVENING, MR. ASHER," the hostess greets as soon as I step through the club's door. It's a private estate on Lake Forest with over five acres of privacy surrounding the twenty-eight-bedroom home. It's the perfect retreat for the rich and deviant—convenient at only a forty-five minute drive from my building at the heart of The Loop.

The clientele here is diverse. Those that like to succumb to their kinkier side without public knowledge. This mansion accepts everyone without judgement, and each floor handles a different kind of play.

I nod but don't say a word, my eyes giving her uniform a once-over. It's burlesque inspired today and leaves very little to the imagination. However, she does nothing for me.

Too much makeup. Hair overly teased and sprayed. Too easy.

I'm picky about who I fuck. Whose pussy I let tighten around my cock.

Used and abused will never be for me, no matter how hard they chase. Offer what they consider a valuable trade—something I could easily have delivered to my home at any given moment.

A man like me is very desirable to a gold-digging trophy wife. At six foot four, I exude dominance and power, and yet, it's the light green eyes that draw them in like a moth to a flame. My looks open doors, but no one has been able to fully handle my insatiable thirst for sex. My demand to take charge and own.

Not that I have wanted to find a woman, either. *Not since my one mistake.*

I want soft and sweet. Dependent and innocent.

The perfect little cock slut I can bend to my will, someone that I won't find here.

The women that work in this club are okay with being nothing more than a sexual object. They enjoy the attention. Get off on being used by every member who chooses to have a taste of the forbidden.

This place isn't about having an intelligent conversation or finding a deep connection.

People come here to fuck:

Each other.

The staff.

Or watch.

I'm here for the latter. I will never touch a whore, but watching is part of my religion, and this club caters to me, my needs, very discreetly.

There hasn't been a woman in over eight months worthy of my cock. My come.

"Will you be needing an escort to your room?" This girl is new. The last one knew not to speak to me. "Or do you have any last-minute requests tonight, sir?"

"No. Nothing else will be needed." I hold out the special black keycard with my name embossed for her to see.

"Of course, sir. Enjoy your—"

I walk away before she finishes, striding inside and into the main reception area. The music is loud and vibrates through every cell in my body. Heightens my cravings. All around me people are dancing —grinding to this deep and hypnotic bass—while giving in to their baser desires.

The room is dark and open with a winding staircase off to the left. It's all wooden floors and paneling, floor-to-ceiling windows, and the deep red drapes they use to accent them. It's high, stoned arches and intricate carvings—gold antique fixtures and expensive furnishings.

Old Victorian meets debauchery.

A few dominants, a group of three, stand off to the left of the dance floor with leashes in their hands and a naked submissive at their feet. Across from them, a couple is fucking while those on two long couches watch.

There are moans and whimpers. Commands and guttural growls of pleasure.

However, nothing calls to me outside of my destination. My oasis. A quiet room where a reward awaits me.

People look at me—some try to pull me into their conversations as I make my way through the crowd, but I don't stop. My body is wound so fucking tight, the blood in my veins a volcanic rush of hunger that pulls me deeper into the mansion.

I've never felt this kind of rush before, at least, not at this level, and it's euphoric. Almost maddening as I give in to the pull, an almost palpable magnetic chord that's guiding me toward my sanctuary.

I don't stop until I'm outside the door three floors up. There, I pause and take in a deep breath while reaching down to palm my cock. Give it a hard squeeze that does very little to alleviate my almost violent yearning to come.

Sliding the key into the door, I crack my neck while waiting for it to unlock. This room is owned by me. Never to be used by anyone else.

A private gift given by the asshole that owns the club to pacify a personal debt.

"Fuck," I spit out, teeth clenching as my dick throbs against the zipper of my pants. Another stroke of my hand, and the green light blinks to signal it's open.

A rough exhale leaves me as I turn the knob and open the door to a room the size of a master bedroom. Two steps and I'm inside. The lights are dim, and the heavy riff of a guitar plays in the background on low.

The large room is empty except for my chair and a small stage with a metal pole that runs from floor to ceiling. There's nothing sexier to me than watching a woman dance—lose herself in her movements while the tension mounts. Watch her become needy with each inhale, the shakiness of her limbs as I command her to spread her thighs and slip a single finger inside.

How her thighs quake.

How her pussy clenches in need of more.

How she begs for me to fuck her.

Something that will never happen, and it's in my denial that I find a release.

I'm a voyeur. A killer.

A depraved son of a bitch that can take a life with no regret, and then come from pulling pleasure from a willing whore.

Striding across the room, I stop at my throne. An antique chair with its intricate wooden carvings and velvet upholstering—it holds this dark tone of both goth and sex that I love.

The hint of depravity hidden behind an expensive price tag.

The music within the room grows louder and I turn, humming the tune as the stage becomes illuminated. Adrenaline—the high that comes from killing that asshole—and the anticipation has me throbbing.

Desperate for a release.

Taking my seat, I sit back and press the small red button atop a table to my right. Not twenty seconds pass when the door at the other end of the room opens, and then closes with a muted thud.

Picking up the bottle of gin from the glass table beside me, I pour a few fingers into the tumbler while ignoring the performer. There's an electrical current flowing through the room, an energy that unsettles me as much as it excites.

"Come forward," I demand, yet don't look up. Instead, I take a sip from my glass and enjoy the spirit on my tongue. Close my eyes as the crispness, with just a subtle hint of citrus, pleases my palate.

"Where do you want me?" a delicate voice asks, and my heart thumps harshly inside my chest. Tries to claw its way out as my eyes snap open.

"Fuck." It leaves me on a pained groan as the music fades and all I see is her.

She's not one of my regular girls.

She's young. No older than twenty.

She's breathtakingly beautiful and sweet.

My little doll.

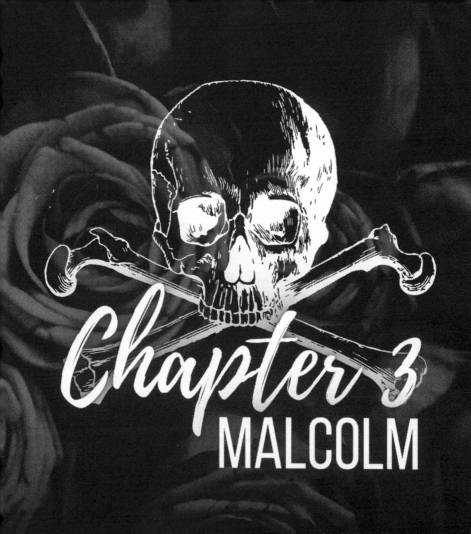

Chapter 3
MALCOLM

SHE'S DEFINITELY NEW and *innocent.*

I can almost fucking smell it on her. Can literally see the naivete inside those expressive eyes. Eyes that look away when mine bore into hers.

Something I find myself quite enjoying. That shyness. How lost she is.

It's there in the delicious touch of pink that sweeps across her cheeks and then down the soft curve of her neck. It exudes from her every pore as she nervously wrings her hands—the small hint of fear I took notice of before she began to avoid my gaze.

And fuck me if this doesn't both piss me off and turn me on.

While she takes in every detail of the room, I bask in the tension that's building between us; her uncertainty and my hunger.

Because there's no denying that I more than like what I see.

Unlike Michael's fear earlier tonight, hers makes me hard as fuck. Causes my entire being to pulse in time with each deep inhale she takes.

How the fuck did this delicate little thing end up working here?

She's not like the other women here. A blind man can see how out of place she is.

That she's more than likely inexperienced.

Not that it matters much. The journey is of no consequence to me when her destination is this room. With me.

I want her. Will have her. But more importantly, I won't share her with anyone in this place.

This little girl has no idea that I am the devil she never saw coming.

She will be for me alone. My personal tiny dancer.

That decision has me reaching down and undoing my belt. With a harsh yank, I toss it across the room. There's a clang—it's loud inside the quiet space—and she jumps. Finally fucking looks at me.

Bringing the glass to my lips, I take a sip and savor the herbal note of my gin, all the while my eyes roam her small frame. She has no idea what to do with herself, and for some reason, that pleases me.

I want to touch her.

Taste her.

Possess that genuine purity that causes an ache—an uncontrollable yearning to grow within me.

"Closer, sweetness." Neither of us miss the gruffness in my tone, how each syllable rumbles up my chest until it's a low and guttural growl.

"Yes, sir," she whispers low, taking her first step toward me. My eyes traverse her short frame, devour each piece of bare flesh I discover. Take in the rich, dark brown of her hair, and how each loose curl sweeps, then bounces around her bare shoulders.

This tiny morsel of sin is a natural beauty with wide, doe eyes in a rich cerulean tone. So expressive. Beautiful. She reminds me of a fairy tale princess. The kind that every dirty motherfucker covets and wishes to corrupt.

My gaze travels lower then, taking in her delicate upturned nose and the small smattering of freckles. Then to her bee-stung lips with the natural hue of a ripened berry that I want to see stretched around my girth.

Her skin is luminescent under the stage light. Soft, and with the barest hint of a tan. As if the sun kissed her skin. *My bite marks will look glorious on her.*

Next, I take in what she's wearing...

White and in soft lace. A short little dress that enhances her larger-than-a-handful-breasts—it's tight and revealing—displaying the sweet little tips that constrict under my perusal. She isn't wearing a bra, and my mouth waters while my cock gives a harsh jerk inside my pants.

Below her bust, the material flows out a tiny bit, but not enough to hide the flat of her stomach and wide hips. Her legs are long and toned, and her tiny feet bare.

This girl is petite, yet curvaceous. A tight little body meant to be fucked. Taken roughly.

Tilting my head, I watch her nervous habits take hold. How she leans most of her weight on her right foot. How she keeps biting that juicy bottom lip the closer to me she gets.

"Stop." At once she does as I ask a few feet away from me, eyes wide and staring into mine. Motherfuck, her shyness is delicious. Heady. "Twirl for me."

"As you wish, sir," she says, taking in a deep breath before letting it out slow. Her nipples are hard, pushing against the lace that leaves very little to the imagination. The sinuous curve of her body is

SIN

tempting, so delicate, and I watch, enthralled, as she closes her eyes
and performs a simple pirouette to please me.

"Again," I demand, voice rough and hands clenching. "Slower
this time."

"Of course." Once more, she rises onto the balls of her feet and
lifts one leg higher in what looks like a flamingo's stance. Her body
holds this position for a few minutes, head held high to elongate her
neck, before she slowly begins to spin. This turn is slow, a controlled
move that shows off every inch of her flawless form.

The way she moves, every minute shift, shows me that this
woman is a dancer. A trained one, at that.

What the fuck is she doing here?

Once more, that question floats through my mind and I know the
answer will not please me. Something about her is throwing me off,
and it's not my desire to own her soul. It's the sudden worry—that
gut instinct that I follow blindly.

If anyone's hurting her, not even God himself will save them.

"I'm going to own you, beautiful. Destroy what you know and
become your everything," I mutter low, rubbing a hand across my
jaw. Watching as my little beauty turns three more times before I
hold a hand up. "Stop." Again, she does, eyes shining bright and
cheeks looking flush. "Come pour me a drink. Three fingers' worth
will be enough for now."

A nod is all I get as she walks to me, hips swaying with each move.
She tries to step around my parted thighs, but as soon as she's within
my reach, I stop her. Fingers on her hips, I guide her closer—to take
her rightful place between my legs—while reaching over for the bottle.

And fuck me if the feel of her pliant flesh beneath my fingertips
doesn't cause me to shiver.

Limbs shaking, too, she follows my command. The bottle clanks
against the glass table as it almost tumbles from her grasp while I
lean forward. Pressing my nose against her midsection, I inhale deep,
pulling her sweet floral scent into my lungs and groan.

Fuck, I throb. Both hate and love how I react to her mere presence.

Her quick intake of air lets me know she isn't unaffected by me. Not that it matters much. I'll train her—overthrow her senses—into craving me.

"You smell like sin," I grunt against the fabric of her dress, nose skimming a tiny bit lower as my hand holds her in place. "But do you taste as decadent?" She doesn't answer. Doesn't so much as breathe. "What's your name, little Twirl?"

"My name?" she croaks, and it's hard to keep in my amusement. I also don't miss how she doesn't question the nickname.

"Yes. Your name..." I nip the fabric but keep myself from marking her "...full name."

Slightly shaking, she pours my drink and then sets the bottle down. "It's London—"

"London what?"

"London Foster."

That last name isn't very popular around here, but I do know one family with it. One that has been living in my city for eight months. Same one whose head of the family is an egocentric asshole who's made some bad investments as of late. Stuck his nose where it doesn't belong, and that idiotic decision will ruin him.

All of them. Her.

However, she might be the one to pay the biggest price. She's just become even more precious to me. London is collateral, but I'll take care of her. This doesn't diminish my hunger; if anything, it multiplies tenfold.

But I don't say any of this as my mind runs through different scenarios. No, instead, I give her a smile and a tap to the back of her thigh. "Beautiful name for a beautiful girl."

"Thank you, sir."

"Call me Malcolm." Something I've never done before, but I need to hear her say it. Say my name. Not "sir" or "Mr. Asher." I find myself wanting this to be personal. Comfortable.

That, and lowering her walls makes it easier to take ownership of someone who has no idea that a predator is hunting. Calculating. Taking account of every minute detail in order to win this dangerous game.

"Malcolm," she whispers a moment later as if tasting my name on her tongue. It's a sinful delight to hear her pronounce each letter —to take in how a miniature smile forms on her lips after. "Anything else I can do for you, Malcolm?"

"Dance for me."

"W-what?" It's a shaky exhale as I kiss the area beneath her belly button.

"Dance for me, London." I gift her a few more soft kisses. "Get up on that stage, eyes closed, and dance for me. Let me enjoy you just a little."

My eyes stay on hers as I give the request and then sit back in my seat. I eat her alive as she nods and takes a few steps, all the while facing me. It's almost as if she can't find the will to pull her eyes away, and I motherfucking enjoy watching her almost trip while making her way toward the stage backwards.

Once at the edge of the platform, she halts and gives me a soft smile. "Any particular request? Music you want me to—?"

"Slow." The word is out of my mouth before she finishes the question. "I want it slow, Twirl."

"Okay." She mouths the word *slow* and turns, giving me a small tease of the plump cheeks almost spilling from the dress's edge. It's ridden up, and with each move, I get a small taste of what will be mine.

"One more thing..." She pauses and tilts her head, listening to me. "Once the song finishes, you walk out without another word. Without looking at me." I'm hard. Throbbing. But instead of reacting like the animal she's making me feel like, I breathe in and take a sip of the drink she poured.

"Understood."

While London looks through the selection I have pre-approved, I undo the button of my pants and lower the zipper. While she nods to herself and hits play, I take my shirt off and toss it somewhere. While she shakes her head, tousling her hair, I pull my cock out and stroke myself once. While she gets up on the stage, back to me, and rolls her hips as the first strum of a guitar rents the air, I lick my lips.

I can't control my urges—this hunger that causes a hiss to escape through clenching teeth while she sways to the sensual beat. Can't stop myself as I swipe my thumb over the head, collecting the beads of pre-come there and spreading it.

This is foreplay. Makes my plans sweeter.

London dips low then, her knees spread wide apart while she arches her back. She bounces a few times, making the dress ride higher until the small string currently residing between two luscious cheeks becomes my focal point.

I fuck my hand with each gyration. With each arch of her back.

But nothing compares to the moment she stands, turns around, and with her eyes closed, skims a hand down the center of her chest. How she follows each beat—every single note in the song with absolutely perfection.

She's glorious in her element. Dancing as if no one else is inside the room with her, she rises onto the very tip of her toes while those hips sway. London's moves are precise. Like a serpent enticing—hypnotizing while she prepares to strike.

And fuck, do I love it.

My fist pumps in time with her every move. My hips rise, giving into the lust burning through my veins.

With her foot on pointe, she lifts the other leg straight in the air into a vertical split and I growl, the sound loud within the room. She hears it. I know it. Moreover, that second—the minuscule moment in time when she falters causes my stomach to clench.

Move my wrist faster.

Following my instruction, she twirls for me in a slow circle.

My little Twirl. My little ballerina.

London holds her poise with grace. She doesn't realize as she turns that the white fabric between her thighs stretches tight, giving me a small glimpse of the sweet pink I want to devour.

Her labia is visible. So is a small patch of wetness.

My orgasm is almost violent as I focus on the proof of her arousal. *Even the innocent fall.*

"Motherfuck," I grunt, grinding my teeth as the first rope of come shoots from the tip and onto my stomach. Pulsing—I'm fucking throbbing as the second and third follow, coating my hand and then abdomen. Every single nerve ending in my body is a live wire and breathing comes second to watching her move, oblivious to my actions.

London doesn't stop, and I don't ask her to. Instead, I continue to stroke myself softly as the song comes to an end and she leaves.

She doesn't look back, but my eyes follow her out.

She doesn't speak, but I whisper an *I'll see you soon.*

Her life will never be the same after today.

Chapter 4
MALCOLM

"SHE DANCES FOR NO one but me."

"Christ, Asher!" Liam yelps, jumping in his seat. He's been hiding inside this office all night, and as I walk in an hour later, I can see the why. He has a girl on his lap: late twenties, a redhead, and practically naked. The man is imbibing. Sampling what he perceives as his own merchandise. "You scared the hell out of me."

"Not my problem." Not waiting for an invitation, I take a seat across from them and lean back. Watch him squirm while the girl

SIN

begins to play with a loose curl around her bare shoulders. "Now, about London."

"Figures." His companion mutters low, something he ignores. Knows better than to acknowledge, but I don't miss her grimace when he tightens his hold on her midsection. "But it's true."

"Shut it, Stacy."

"No, Liam. Let her talk…" I narrow my eyes at her "…finish. Say what you need to say."

"She's too innocent for a place like this. Too inexperienced, and I worry certain clients will eat her alive."

I almost smile at her perceptiveness. She's right on both accounts, and I won't be the only one to take notice of Twirl's naïveté. However, I'll do more than that. I'm going to consume her and make her dependent on me.

Show her brother and father before they take their last breath that I own them. Destroy without a single repercussion. Alton chose their lives' path, and I'm now fate here to collect.

At my silence, Liam becomes nervous. Curious, while his body language shows discomfort. "I apologize if London ruined your night. Did she upset you?" His worry is almost comical—full of apprehension that I will lash out. *Pussy.* "She'll get better. It was her first day and dance."

His words please me. I was her first.

It's an egotistical response. Feeds my need as an alpha to dominate and conquer.

To own. Be everything she will ever need.

"This man is just going to use her," Stacy mutters under her breath, but I hear and so does Liam. It's obvious she isn't quite sure who I am and that she worries about London, so I let it slide this once.

However, how loud she's now popping her gum in a show of annoyance is downright disrespectful. *Motherfucking nasty habit.*

"Don't concern yourself with London. Just make sure she doesn't dance..." my glare settles on the redhead and she dry-swallows the gum "...much less goes near any of your other clients."

"I'll see what I can do." Sweat beads at his brow while he frowns. Thinking. "I scheduled her for one more client tonight. A friend of a friend."

Sitting back, I take a second to rein in my rage. Breathe in deep while looking around the spacious room. It's opulent, heavily furnished, and predictable in its display of wealth. The paintings alone in this room would set him back millions—stolen originals come with a hefty price tag.

And then there is him.

Heavier set, hair dyed to hide his greys, and an expensive Cartier on his wrist. A wife and a few teenagers at home while he fucks anything that walks. He doesn't discriminate. He doesn't care as long as his dick gets wet.

Be a real pity if he loses it all.

"Find her."

"I can guarantee her starting tomorrow?"

"She's getting ready for her next client now." They speak in unison, but my attention stays on her. That's when I notice a few things aside from her trashy appearance.

This woman doesn't look like the rest. She's fidgety; lipstick smeared a bit and pupils dilated.

There isn't a single doubt that she is high.

Leaning forward, I wave a hand. "Explain."

"Ummm..." she looks at Liam and he nods, squeezing her once more "...London's in the dressing room now; her next private show is coming up. Saw her there right before I came to bring Mr. Kravitz his coffee."

"How long ago was this?" Coffee my ass. I see the small mirror and blade atop his ostentatious desk. The white residue left behind on it. The small open bag. *Idiot.* "How fucking long?" I spit out, hand slamming atop the desk when they both go mute. "Answer me."

"Thirty minutes ago," she stammers while the color drains from

Liam's face. There's much he needs to account for, but not tonight. Tonight, he needs to stop London from getting up on another stage.

"If she makes it inside that room, I'll put a bullet in each of you." At my threat, she gasps while he nods. Knowing that I won't hesitate. Haven't in the past. "Find her. Pay her for the entire shift and then send her home with one of the many drivers here tonight."

"But, Malcolm—"

My glare cuts him off. "Let's hope for your sakes she hasn't stepped a foot inside."

IT TAKES another twenty minutes for them to find her, and it's pure luck that they do just in time. With her hand on the doorknob, and in another innocently indecent dress, Liam's plaything stops London.

Pulls her down the hall while I watch through a monitor in his office. Witness—hear as Liam greets her inside what looks like an employee lounge and asks her to sit. How he tells her that her second dance is cancelled, but that she'll still be paid in full. See him hand over the envelope I personally approved of, along with a tip.

A little something extra from me.

My little Twirl doesn't know how to react, her facial expression full of confusion, but she accepts with a nod. She doesn't argue. Instead, she heads inside the dressing room to change and grab her belongings. And in her normal clothes, London is exquisite.

Motherfucking...*cute.*

In a velour tracksuit with sneakers and her hair up high in a messy knot, she looks beautiful. Mouthwatering.

She has this girly innocence I crave to devour.

"Soon, Twirl," I say low, running a finger down the screen as she's being taken to the parking area set up for employees. "For the rest of our lives, I'm going to be all you know."

For as much as this girl brings out an animalistic desire in me, there's also an odd need to take care of her. It makes no sense. This sudden yearning to own her isn't solely brought on by her relationship to Alton, no.

I want her, and I'm not one to deny my instincts. My very nature demands that I make her mine, and I will.

And after I've satiated my lust and taken care of her family, I plan to explore these other *feelings*.

Later. Much later.

Now, my curiosity lies in a different area.

I make my move the moment the town car pulls up; my own vehicle awaits me at the mansion's doorstep. Grabbing the key, I enter and turn the fob just in time to see them drive down the driveway.

"Where are you heading, pretty girl?" I whisper, following behind them down a winding road. The highway is only a few miles away, and we merge left onto US-41 heading south.

For seven miles I follow close behind, only easing up a bit as traffic picks up while we get on the I-94. There're more cars than I expect for this time of night; a few semis and some drunken asshole yelling from the passenger side window about a basketball game we won.

And while the world around us zips by and the bustle surrounds me, I don't lose sight of her car.

They're heading straight for Chicago's downtown area, and it makes no sense. *Why are you here?*

The town car stops near my building, across the street and one over to be exact, at a garage meant for my employees. No one else is outside. No other car waiting for her.

"What the fuck is she doing?" Turning my headlights off, I pull over a little way down and watch her exit the vehicle. She says something to the driver and waves him off before turning around and walking up the small ramp where one of my security guards suddenly appears.

Someone who has been working for my family for over twenty years. Who I consider to be loyal, and trust.

Earl smiles and helps her with her bag, even says something that makes her throw her head back and laugh. A part of me wants to slam his head into the pavement for being so at ease with her, but I know him and his wife. A woman he adores.

From my position I can see that he's not looking at her with lust. No. There's something else there...

They disappear out of sight, and I'm tempted to follow.

Find out why Earl's letting her park here? Ask him how he knows—

Right then, a conversation we had three days back comes rushing to the forefront.

Sir, would you mind if a family friend parks here at night? She has a job that's far, and needs somewhere trustworthy to leave her own vehicle while she commutes...

Family friend. That's what sticks out the most since they haven't resided here long.

As more pieces come to light, something doesn't sit right with me. I don't know what Twirl's hiding, but I know Earl enough that he will never agree with what she's doing inside that club. He will borrow the money before letting her dance.

"Hurry the fuck up." The clock on my dash blinks with another minute passing, and I find myself growing anxious, my patience thinning.

A push of a button and my doors unlock. Hand on the handle, I'm pushing it open when headlights flicker near the building's exit. But then I am furious for a completely different reason.

"I'm going to burn that son of a bitch alive," I hiss, fingers clenching around the handle. A rusted piece of shit—what can barely be considered as a safe vehicle—passes in front of me, pausing at the corner to turn.

A thousand and one scenarios run through my head, and neither is better than the last. Why would a girl that comes from a somewhat affluential family sell herself for money?

Moreover, it's not for pleasure. Not because of a kink.

This is starting to smell like desperation, and I don't like it.

Within seconds, I am right behind her. Something she doesn't notice. Something I'll teach her to be aware of with time.

An old Toyota Corolla from the '80s with a muffler that's close to falling off and chipped paint isn't what she deserves. The more I see the car struggle to gain speed or change gears, the more my protective instincts grow.

Pressing the phone feature on my steering wheel, I hit number two and wait.

"Everything okay, Malcolm?" Javier asks after only two rings, sounding half asleep.

"Meet me outside of the Fosters' house."

"I'll be there in thirty." He doesn't question me. There's some rustling, and my cousin's voice in the background grumbling about the time. She'll get over it. "Are we going in together, or am I delivering a message?"

"*We're* delivering a personal invitation."

"A personal invitation?" he says slowly, sounding full of interest and confusion.

"That's it. Just a friendly visit."

"Something you aren't telling me here, Asher?" The man knows me, but now isn't the time to sit and discuss. We have tomorrow for that. Right now, all that matters is my little Twirl making it home safely.

That I assess her surroundings. Figure out her motives.

"I won't take *no* for an answer."

Chapter 5
LONDON

"WHAT DID I just do?" My legs are shaky, body trembling as I exit the private room. It's surreal. I feel lost, and yet, I won't deny that having his beautiful green eyes on mine made me experience the kind of excitement I've never been privy to.

Is that what having the attention of someone you find attractive feels like?

Even worse? I know what he did.

I could hear his grunts of pleasure while I danced for him. Know the exact moment he found his release, and I won't deny that my skin still tingles. That my panties are wet.

Does that make me sick? Weird?

With the cards I've been given, I should be running. And yet, here I am. Trying my hardest to calm down and move away from the corridor before he finds me a panting mess. A quivering ball of confusion that's using the wall for support.

Because he wasn't what I've been expecting. Not at all.

In my head, the men I've pictured since taking this job were bald, fat, and sexist.

Handsy. Disgusting.

However, what I got didn't fit the preconceived man in my mind.

Malcolm isn't any of that.

No. Not at all.

He's not the man the other girls told me is cold and distant. A dangerous animal that isn't to be trusted, but for some inexplicable reason, I do. Inside that room, I didn't experience fear or anxiety. Not once.

It's the opposite. With him, there's calm.

He didn't ask for extra privileges like the others. Like I know some of the other women here agree to. Enjoy.

Something that I might need to accept if the price is right. If my desperation sinks to a new low.

Malcolm's touch—I can still feel the possessiveness in his hold —was gentle yet firm. It didn't come with the repulsion I thought would accompany it. Not once did I feel like a whore.

Like the virginal idiot I am deep down.

The kind that in desperation ran to a total stranger's door asking for a chance.

The stereo clicks off then and I push myself off the wall, rushing down the hall before Malcolm opens the door. There's an empty room on this floor that Liam told me to use in case I want a breather, and right now, I'm needing more than that.

"Jesus, what is wrong with me?" I whisper, out of breath as I close the door and *his* opens a few doors down. My back to the wooden structure, I close my eyes and focus on his steps as he passes me and continues down the hall.

Heart pounding and hands clammy, I try and regain some semblance of composure, but it's hard. Too hard, when behind closed lids all I see is him.

That man is the textbook definition of tall, dark, and handsome. I'm petite against his harsher planes—soft curves to his muscular frame. The way he wore that suit, tailor-made to define every solid inch, is sinful, and yet the way he removed said jacket, rolled up his sleeves, and popped a button up top made my knees weak. Add to that the bold tattoo on his right arm, the skull with dark shadowing and bright blue eyes, and I'm left a literal mess.

And what's worse, *I* like it. Him. A lot.

His smile made me feel warm inside.

How his attention never left me still causes goose bumps to break out down my arms.

He's the kind of man no one survives from. A total destruction of one's senses; he's the hurricane I didn't see coming.

Jesus, London. Snap out of it.

Malcolm is a client. *A client.*

He's paying for a service, while I need men like him to reach my goal. He's nothing but a means to an end.

Shaking off thoughts of him, I wait another ten minutes before slipping out of the room and then taking the private stairway down to the employee area. It's a large space with three separate rooms attached; a locker area, changing room, and an employee lounge for a bit of relaxing.

Moreover, while Liam's a smooth talker with a penchant to come off as creepy, he's been very accommodating to my fears. To the years of distrust that have been scaring me.

My contract isn't like the others here:

No touching under my clothing.

No full nudity.

No sex unless I consent.

Liam knows who my family is. Why I'm here.

He's sticking his neck out by helping me, and that's something I appreciate. I know that having me dance for his clients will make him money, but he didn't have to hire me. Could just as easily told me to leave.

He doesn't have to offer me a way out. A possibility with hope.

This mansion whose walls hide secrets is exactly where my father and brother wouldn't be. I heard them one night saying as much, talking down the members and owner, making plans to out someone important.

They made the place out to be morbid and disgusting, while I find this a sanctuary.

Quick money. A way out from under my family's thumb.

My brother wants more than he should. Becomes braver with each night that passes, while my father sees me as a way out of his mounting debt.

They spend faster than either can produce and demand that I help maintain their lifestyle one way or another. I don't want to be a part of either of their schemes, much less what they are planning at the moment...

They want a war. Money. Power.

I need to be far away when that happens. They want to become what they will never be, and I refuse to become the casualty of their greed.

"So?" Stacy, Liam's assistant and a performer here, asks. She's by the small kitchenette preparing coffee, and she's not doing it right. There's splattering everywhere. "How did it go? Was he rude?"

"Not at all," I answer truthfully, walking toward her and shoving the cup deeper under the machine's percolator. No more splashing coffee.

"Thanks." Stacy gives me a sheepish grin. "I'm not exactly the Susie Homemaker type."

"Do you want to be?"

"That's weird, though." She waves a hand in the air, ignoring my question. But I see it in her eyes. Stacy wants to be, just in her own way. "All the girls complain he's a giant asshole. That he never let any of them physically near him. You dance, but don't touch."

That's the last thing I want to think about—someone else performing for him—but then the last part hits me. I did touch him. He initiated our contact.

Closing my eyes for a second, I relive the last hour and a half of my life. How reluctant he was to let me go.

Why am I different? Not that I say this aloud. Never. I'm new here and know how easily people can turn on each other. How someone can destroy who you are just because.

Instead, I find myself shrugging, opening the small fridge beside us to pull out a bottle of water. "Seriously, no complaints. He made me feel sexy, not stupid. I thought for sure I'd fall on my face and cry."

"Girl, that happened to me once. It's how I met Liam!" Her laughter makes me grin, the earlier tension dropping as we both fall into giggles. That fog he put me under starts receding and each breath I take is easier than the last. *I can still feel his touch. His warmth.*

"For real?" I ask, trying to act nonchalant, hoping she doesn't realize the sudden high pitch in my voice.

"Swear on my favorite pair of Manolos."

"That's one hell of a story to—"

"Take it from me, kid. Learn from my mistakes." Her mood change is instant. From happy to almost heartbroken. As if her uppers are making her crash. "Don't get attached. These men won't give you a fairy-tale ending."

Grabbing the now full cup, she places it on a tray with a sugar bowl and creamer. Not another word is said as Stacy walks out, leaving me in a state of confusion.

Why would she say that?

I'm not here looking for a man. I'm looking for an escape.

Besides, even if I did find him attractive, Malcolm has heartbreak written all over him.

———————

"YOU'RE HOME EARLY," I hear the moment I step in my father's house. Not that this surprises me, but it's wishful thinking that being early tonight would give me enough time to escape. To slip inside my room undetected.

It didn't.

Instead, I find my brother sitting inside the living room in his favorite leather chair with a glass of what looks to be cognac. His eyes are blue like mine, but a few shades darker. He's tall where I am short and muscular where I am slim. Our facial features differ, and personalities are like night and day.

Alton stares at me in a way that makes me feel uncomfortable. Makes my skin crawl.

"The diner closed early tonight," I say, letting the heavy wooden door close behind me. Even the low, muted thud it produces makes my body jump in place. "Bad batch of meat made a few people sick."

"Are you sure you weren't fired, Lola?" God, I hate that nickname now. Reminds me of Mom. She gave it to me, but now only he uses it, and each time it hurts. Cuts deep. Alton knows this, I've told him as much, yet the glint in his eyes tells me he doesn't care. He enjoys this sick game; there's a smirk on his face, a slow licking of his bottom lip before he takes another sip. "I'll be more than happy to hire you as my—"

"All is fine. I promise." The lie slips so easily past my lips as I walk deeper into the house. I have no choice. If they find out where I'll be spending my weekends and how much I'll be making, things will get worse. They'll take every dime, and Alton will demand that I serve him too. "I'm back on tomorrow for an overnight shift."

"Come here."

"Alton, I'm really tired. Can we talk tomorrow?" *Or never.*

Slowly, I edge closer to the stairs that lead up to the bedrooms. My bedroom.

"I'm not fucking asking you. Come. Here." The bastard pats his lap, spreading his thighs apart, and I freeze. It's not the first time he's tried this, demanded that I get close, but dodging is my specialty and this time my saving grace comes from our father.

"Why the fuck are you home?" He stumbles in, almost falling over the entryway's carpet. Dad looks unkempt and reeks of alcohol. The cheap kind. His hand snaps out, grabbing onto my arm to stop his fall and bruising me in the process. Fingernails digging in, he rights himself. "If you got fired, then you know the alternative. Get me that money, London."

Before I can respond, a hand slips around my waist, pulling me back. "Enough, old man. Let's not upset my little *Lola*."

"Of course, son. You're right..." he digs his fingers in deeper, making me whimper before he lets go "...marking her isn't going to help me."

A harsh shudder runs through me as I choke on a sob. Just feeling them close, much less touching me, makes me sick. They know this. Get off on my fear. "Can I please go upstairs now? I'm tired." Even I can hear the desperation in my tone.

Lips, Alton's lips, press against my temple as he squeezes me one last time. "Head on up to bed. We'll finish our—"

He's cut off by a sudden banging on our front door. Everyone stops, and I don't miss how fast Dad straightens himself. How he clenches a hand.

"Are we expecting anyone, Alton?"

"Not that I know of," he says, already pulling out his phone to check the front door camera.

There're cameras everywhere here. This isn't a home, more like a jail cell.

Whatever pissing game they are trying to play can end badly.

I'm not an idiot.

I know what they do and how much they owe a powerful family

in Miami; a debt they are forcing me to pay while they live their lives in peace. That my brother's thirst for authority will end bad. His greed will be their downfall.

There's one lesson everyone, no matter what walk of life you come from, has to learn.

Don't bite the hand that feeds.

And for people like them, the mob is their God.

"Son of a bitch," Alton spits out, hands clenching around his phone a second before his eyes flick to mine. There's something in his stare. A subtle hint of fear. "Get upstairs and don't come down."

"Son, what's going on?"

"It's Asher's right hand."

"At this time?"

"Who?" Dad and I speak in unison, and immediately I wish I kept my mouth shut.

"None of your business. Get the fuck upstairs." Alton's pissed, his nostrils flaring while he grabs my arm and pulls me in the direction of the stairs. His hold hurts. He doesn't care that I trip or that I crash into the banister; he wants me out of sight.

"Jesus Christ!" I yelp, trying to pull out of his hold. "Let me right myself." And as the last word slips past my lips, a gunshot is heard and a bullet lodges itself in the wall nearest to my brother.

No one moves for a minute. No one breathes.

"Open the fucking door, Foster. Don't force my hand," a man calls out, his voice deep with a hint of a Spanish accent coming through. "You have three seconds."

"Don't say a word," Alton threatens, pulling me behind him while nodding at Dad. And like the blind man he is, our father listens, opening the door to a man dressed in a crisp suit holding a gun.

"Evening." His tone is friendly, yet it's his eyes that let on to just how dangerous he can be. What he will do if push came to shove. "Thank you for accepting this early morning visit."

"What can I do for you, Javier?" Alton asks, shifting his body to

42

cover more of me. It has the opposite effect, because I see how this man's eyes slightly widen at the sight. There's curiosity there, and surprise, but no hostility toward my persona.

"I'm here to deliver a personal invitation."

"An invitation?" my dad asks, looking as confused as I am.

"Yes. An invitation." While this Javier talks, his eyes remain on mine, and yet I don't feel any distress. It's clear he is trying to make out my role here. Figure out who I am. Suddenly his phone chimes and he pulls it out, reading something and then answering. "You are aware of who Mr. Asher is, no?"

"Yes," Alton grits out, once more pushing me further behind him. "What does he want?"

"He requests your presence tomorrow for brunch at the Asher estate." There's a slick smile on his face. He's getting a kick out of how uncomfortable the men in my family are. "Eleven a.m. sharp— we don't take kindly to tardiness."

"My father and I will be there."

"All of you."

"She has nothing to do with—"

"Are you a Foster, sweetheart?" he asks, ignoring the men protesting.

I'm like a deer caught in the headlights.

If I lie, will it come back to bite me in the ass?

If I say the truth, will I get caught up in their mess?

"You don't need to answer—"

"The next time you try to intimidate her into not answering, Alton, we're going to have a very large problem on our hands. *She* can speak for herself."

Tensions rise. My brother's muscles coil tight and like an idiot, he reaches back and that's when I see a gun. More confirmation to set off my worries. Cements my rush to get the hell away.

The intent is there. Pure stupidity.

"I am," I say before things escalate further. "I'm the youngest child."

"Then I apologize ahead of time." Before anyone can blink, a second gun is in his other hand and he points them at my brother and father. My scream is loud. A natural reaction. "Hands off the weapon, Foster. Place them where I can see them."

He does along with my father. "Tell Asher we will be there. Tomorrow at eleven."

"All of you?"

"Yes." I'm the one who answers. Even if I catch hell after he leaves, I want this over with.

Whatever comes tomorrow, I'll get past it.

Working is all I have left, and it's my way out from underneath their thumb.

I just hope that this Mr. Asher understands that I'm innocent. That I'm not like them.

Chapter 6
MALCOLM

"WANT TO TELL ME why I left my bed to visit that asshole in the middle of the night?" Javier asks, slipping inside my car across the street from their house in Hinsdale. I'm all too familiar with this gated community, know people that live here, and as she showed her keycard and the gate unlocked to let her in, I followed.

He's waiting for an explanation, but at the moment my attention is on their house. All the lights downstairs are on, and I can just make out the form of a man pacing in front of the living room

He looks agitated, waving his hand angrily at something or someone.

"I don't like these fucks." Something isn't right with this family. Their arrival here a few months back made waves, but I let it slide as a favor to a friend. Same friend that he owes.

I've been patient while watching the recent boost in cocaine running through the southside, however, the Jameson situation is where I draw the line. Forcing me to make a phone call and change plans.

I'll pay Thiago the money in exchange for his life.

The oldest son of Marcus Foster is a fuckup. A pompous asshole who thinks he's invincible, and power should just be given to him.

A mid-level dealer with a death wish.

"Agreed."

"Was she in the room?" Stretching my neck, I lower the window and spark up another cigarette. The fourth of the night. I'm wound tight, muscles coiling, and nothing seems to calm me. Every cell in my body demands that I break down their door and take her.

Somewhere between the club and her house my thoughts have become clear. The voice inside, that animal I keep under control in front of the world, demands that I save her. Her innocence is titillating, exciting, and also London's downfall.

Why are they hiding her? That thought is churning within me. Bringing out a side that only the few women in my family ever see: a protector.

Deciding to stay inside the car was a last-minute decision. A hard one.

Tomorrow. But it made the most sense.

I'll deal my cards then. Twirl will be inside my home, within my protection, and I can control how and when I approach.

Her brother and father are full of envious desires; they'll be too busy plotting to realize that she's already met me. That I've already taken ownership of the youngest in the family. That they are dead men walking.

Getting her alone won't be a problem.

"She was."

"And…" Taking a deep pull of smoke into my lungs, I hold it for a few seconds before exhaling through my nose.

"His demeanor as he stood over her was possessive." For some reason, I am not surprised by this. I've been expecting this confirmation. Fire flows like lava through my veins as more pieces of this puzzle fall into place, and I have no doubt that my London is looking for an escape. To get away from them.

Question is, though, what do they want her for? How does she play into any of this?

Maybe she knows who I am and is… I stop that thought in its tracks. My Twirl is innocent, of that I have no doubt. Reading people comes with this line of work, and that girl is afraid of the world, not looking to dominate it.

There are two reasons why anyone, of their own free will, sells their body for profit. Desperation, or because you like it. You need the money, or get off on the depravity.

May God have mercy on their souls, because I won't. I want their blood on my hands, and nothing cements that more than seeing London's tiny figure standing at a small bedroom window upstairs.

The dim lights surround her like a warm halo. She's so fucking beautiful, and in that moment, I vow to protect her. Kill every single member of her family if they are the cause of her pain.

"What am I missing here?"

"Not now."

"Are we leaving?"

"Not now," I grit out, teeth grinding as London wipes her cheeks. She looks sad—pensive, while looking up into the night sky.

"This is about the girl." Not a question, and I don't answer. "Something isn't quite right in that house, Malcolm. The way they tried to keep her hidden, the fear in her expression…"

"What did Alton say about my invitation?" Twirl moves away

from the window, and after a few minutes, all goes dark. *Good night, baby.*

"They'll be there."

"Good." Nodding, I take the last pull on my cigarette and flick the butt toward the asphalt. "I want a file on London Foster on my desk by ten a.m. Everything on her."

"Just her?"

"She's the only one that matters."

"SIR, YOUR GUESTS JUST ARRIVED," my security at the gate announces through the intercom, and my eyes flick to the center screen across from me. I see the car. A shiny and new Mercedes in white that looks nothing like the rusty scrap of metal Toyota my Twirl drives. *Mistake number one.* "Do I let them pass or…?"

"No search. Open." I'm not going to scare London.

"As you wish." The gate opens and they drive up until they reach the roundabout where another member of security waits for them. You can see the looks of envy on the two males, while London looks uncomfortable. The worry is plain to see as it flashes across her delicate features.

I can't have that. After today, I want this to be where she finds safety.

Closing her folder, I put the information in the top drawer to my left and lock it. I've read enough to understand the mystery behind their actions.

What her miserable family fails to realize is that in my world, people talk. They are always willing to sell you out for a profit, something two of Alton's street pushers were all too eager to do.

My sweet little Twirl is nothing more than a pawn to the two Foster men, and it all stems from a lie. Something her mother took to her grave when she suddenly died four years ago, leaving a sixteen-year-old girl to fend for herself after a robbery gone wrong.

Or so the police report says.

One, to get out of a growing debt, he's been shopping around her innocence. Tempting the sick fucks he surrounds himself with into desiring the cherry between her thighs for a hefty price.

The other, he wants to dominate—intimidate her into becoming his whore. Alton wants an heir, but not from his fiancée, the submissive idiot that dotes on him because of his make-believe status. That gold-digger isn't good enough. He wants London. Wants to fuck her while parading the other around town.

Alton believes that London is his. His way into a hefty sum of money that she'll receive on her twenty-first birthday. A child will bind them together and is leverage in case she rebels.

Neither of these plans will come to fruition. I will never allow it to happen.

Two certificates have been signed, and I am the executioner.

"Malcolm?" Mariah slips inside wearing a huge shit-eating grin. I'm sure Javier has something to do with it. That she knows. "Magda's attending to them in the parlor, and Javier is standing like a pit bull guarding your package."

"Don't be obnoxious."

"Don't ruin my fun."

"You're lucky that I love you, little cousin. So very lucky." Pushing my chair back, I make my way around the desk and reach her at the door. "Make friends." There's no need for me to elaborate. She understands.

"Got it." Mariah nods with a smirk. "By the way, she looks sweet."

"She's untouchable."

"Thought as much," she muses, eyeing my black jeans, plain T-shirt, and boots. "Why aren't you wearing your typical overpriced suit? I approve of this, by the way."

"I want her to feel comfortable here." It's the truth. The last thing I want is for her to feel intimidated by me.

"Who knew you could be so sweet?" Slipping her arm through

mine, she tugs me down the hall and toward the voice of London's father, who is asking for a whiskey neat as I enter. No one notices me, but I see the dynamic. The men are in suits and sitting with a leg crossed at the knee, arms stretched over the back of the couch—a mimicking pose—while Twirl looks like she wants to disappear within the cushions of her chair.

She looks beautiful; there is no denying this as I stand and watch. However, the expression of distress and the way she tugs at the hem of her knee-length, bright pink bandage dress, tugs at my chest. You can see that she doesn't want to be here, and while it's my fault, I'll also be the one to right every wrong for her.

She's no longer alone.

My eyes skim down her sweet face and pouty lips to the decadence of her collarbones when I notice a discoloration mars her soft skin. Lower, I find a few more down her arms, and the growl that builds in my chest is unstoppable. It's loud and full of fury, shaking me where I stand as I catalogue every bruise.

"Don't scare her. She's good for you," Mariah whispers, passing me while making her way toward an equally-as-quiet Javi. His eyes meet mine and I nod, signaling the first move in this game.

"Hey, man. Good to see you again," Alton says, voice dripping in fake politeness. Hand outstretched for me to shake, he stands, completely ignorant to the nonexistent restraint I'm functioning under. "Thank you for the *sudden* invitation."

Taking his hand in mine, I squeeze hard enough to feel a knuckle buckle and dislocate. The pop is subtle, but no one misses his accompanying curse. "It's Mr. Asher to you, Foster. I won't correct you again."

"Understood," he grits out from between clenched teeth, rubbing his sore hand. "How can we help you, Mr. Asher?"

Fuck, I want to bash his skull in and watch the blood drip from every wall in this room. The carnal desire for retribution ignites within me and I want to feed the monster within.

Because everyone has one. That wicked urge to take matters into your own hands and right the wrongs you've been dealt, and while most people ignore that voice, I revel in mine. Need it.

The fingers of my right hand twitch as it lowers to my side, and the cold steel behind my back beckons me to end this bullshit game that he will never win.

And I almost do, until I hear the soft gasp that escapes her, and our eyes meet for a brief second. Her distress is clear to see, and so is the subtle blush that sweeps across the apple of her cheek.

My little Twirl doesn't know how to react. What to expect.

While her brother and father are looking at the dipshit's hand, I send her a soft smile. She returns the small gesture and then quickly looks down before anyone sees her.

I remind myself that his moment will come when my Twirl isn't here to witness. Never in front of her. She's not ready for my darkness...*yet.*

"Mr. Foster..." her father begins, standing up beside his son but he doesn't offer me his hand "...is there a reason for this sudden request? Have we offended you somehow?"

"Marcus, have you ever heard the saying: *no bad deed goes unpunished?*"

"I-I have." Marcus swallows hard while his eyes shift toward his son. "But what does it have to do with our being here?"

"Everything." Looking at Mariah, I hold up a hand. "Please give Miss Foster a walk through the gardens while I have a word with her family."

"Of course." Her smile is huge as she gives Javier's arm a squeeze and then walks toward a still-as-a-statue Twirl. "Let's leave the boring men to their business while we go grab a treat from Magda's kitchen. She makes the best double fudge brownies ever."

I can see that she's not sure what to do, and I'll be fucked if she asks for permission from these assholes.

"Go on, London. Enjoy the treat."

"Lola's fine, Ash—"

My glare shuts him up, and I also don't miss her expression of disgust at the nickname. "Did I ask for your opinion on the matter?"

"No."

"Then I suggest you learn to speak when spoken to." With that, I look back at Twirl and Mariah. "Enjoy yourselves, girls. This will be a little while."

"Of course, dear cousin. Take your time."

And it's as they walk out of the room that I catch a glimpse of the naughtiness she keeps under lock and key. There's a small smirk on her lips, a brightness in her eyes as she mouths the words *thank you.*

I am the sole person in this world she should ever fear, and the only one that will never harm her.

Chapter 7
MALCOLM

THE MOMENT THE LADIES leave, Alton shifts his angry glare my way. I know what he's going to say, but before the man further embarrasses himself, I walk over to my chair.

The same one that London was occupying a few minutes ago. I take in a deep breath, filling my lungs with her soft floral scent, and it takes everything in me to hold in the groan of pleasure.

There's a low chuckle that meets my ears a second before Javier takes a seat to my right, but I don't address his amusement. Instead, I arch a brow at my guest.

Two sit. Two stand.

"Are you waiting for an invitation?"

"How do you know my London?" Marcus asks, not moving to follow directions. He's fidgety, brow showing a hint of perspiration. Reeks of guilt.

"Sit down." I'm done with being pleasant. These two fucks need to understand just how vulnerable they are. "If I have to repeat myself, you'll each walk out with something broken. Understood?"

"Crystal." Marcus tugs on his son's uninjured hand to sit across from Javier on the opposite couch. For a few minutes we're quiet, my eyes on Alton while his grow uncomfortable with each second that passes. *Pussies.*

I have all the time in the world; my Twirl is safe.

A throat clears, and I shift my gaze to Marcus. "Speak."

"I'm sorry, but you must understand that as her father, I worry. How do you know London?"

Her father. Her father. Christ, this man is playing with the kind of fire that eviscerates, leaving no trace behind. It would be so easy. A flick of my wrist and two bullets is all it would take to eradicate the world of this filth.

"That's the wrong question, and we both know that." Leaning forward, I keep my eyes set on his. Let him see the fury burning behind this calm facade. "The correct one, is what *don't* I know?"

"Why are we here?" This time it's Alton who speaks up.

"Another stupid question." Standing up, I walk over to my bar and pour myself a few fingers' worth of gin. I can feel the stares on my back—the tension mounting—and I revel in it.

"Yet you give us no answer."

A chuckle escapes me, and I take a sip while walking back to my seat, savoring the crisp notes of citrus while the two asswipes squirm.

Another human trait that most cannot control: their nerves. Those ticks that are a part of our genetics—the makeup of our identities that controls reactions.

The shaking of limbs.

The twitch of a jaw.

The bouncing of a leg like the older man before me.

"Congratulations, Alton. You're as stupid as I thought you were."

"What the fuc—"

The click of Javier's gun stops him. "Try again, and be respectful. Do not mistake his generosity with patience."

"My apologies. No disrespect meant, I'm just..." He takes in a deep breath while shifting in his seat, using the same hand with the dislocated knuckle to push his weight toward me. He's in pain. Wishing he could retaliate against me—be me—but instead, is once again reminded to know his place.

I nod at Javi and he lowers his weapon. "Carry on."

"Please understand," Alton grits out, rubbing his hand, "I'm just concerned for my family. My sister isn't aware of our family's dealings, and yesterday's late-night visit has shaken her. I just want to make sure that everything between us is cool. That—"

"Save the bullshit spiel, Foster. We both know where your worries lie." I grab a small remote from atop a side table and point it toward the wall across from me. At once the whirling of a motor reverberates through the room as a faux wall moves up, exposing a hidden television screen above the fireplace.

Father and son look at the screen with trepidation that quickly turns to horror when a single image appears a second later. The color drains from their faces as reality smacks them.

It's his guy. The same piece of shit I personally killed less than forty-eight hours ago.

"Why are—"

"No more lies. No more playing dumb." The next photo is a close-up of his injuries. Each deep gash my knife made. Another shows his lifeless eyes and the gunshot wound that killed him. I leave the last one up. "Before you leave today, I want you to take a single lesson with you."

"Please let—"

"I know everything that happens in my city. Each move you make. Each breath you take."

"This is all a misunderstanding, Mr. Asher," Marcus begins once more while his son's eyes remain on the television. "Nothing that can't be talked over. We don't know why this young man involved us in anything."

Idiot gave himself away. *Fucking amateurs.*

"And who said that he involved you in anything?"

"But you said..."

"That I know it all. Take that as you wish." Standing up, I press a few buttons to hide everything again. Javier follows my lead, and we both walk to the room's entrance where I pause to address them again. "Today is nothing more than a friendly reminder. A warning, *dear friends.* Don't cross me, and mind yourselves—this isn't Miami. Thiago isn't who you should fear here."

IT DOESN'T TAKE LONG for me to find her.

She's alone and sitting on a small bench surrounded by roses. They're in full bloom, a small window of time here in Illinois that allows us to enjoy warm weather and the beauty of nature. It'll be gone soon enough; in a few weeks the temperatures will drop, and all this will die.

And yet, she stands out as the most exquisite flower of all.

Delicate and soft.

Decadent and sweet.

The innocence to my sins.

"I knew you would come," she says without looking up, in her hand a long-stemmed rose with a single petal still attached. The rest lay at her feet. "Mariah wasn't very secretive, nor was she a good actress."

"Is that so." I chuckle, coming closer. Just a few tiny steps separate us, and the fucking pull she holds over me is maddening.

An invisible cord that controls me. "I'll be sure to tell her as much."

"Why did you demand that we visit today? Are you going to tell them about..." she trails off, embarrassment coloring her tone. "This is such a mess."

"I'll never say a word." Seeing her in distress makes my hands clench, but if I touch her, this conversation won't happen. My need is too strong, and I have very little control left when it comes to her. "Trust me."

"But I don't know you."

"My intentions will be very clear soon."

"That's very cryptic, Malcolm," she sighs, shoulders dropping low. "Is this some kind of game? Because if they find out I work at that club, I'm dead."

"That's something I will never allow. Never." Taking the remaining steps between us, I lift her chin with the tip of my finger. Force her bright blues on mine. "This isn't a game, Twirl. To me this—"

"Why do you call me Twirl?" she interrupts, and if she were anyone else, that would annoy me. However, even while being inquisitive, I find her utterly adorable in her purity.

London has the upper hand here and has no idea.

"It's simple, really." My finger skims down her warm cheek, following the soft trail of flesh until I reach the edge of her dress. A dress that I know she hates; I fist the material and in a single tug, pull her against me. The material stretches, showing me her strapless bra and a peak at her flat stomach, but I focus on her reaction instead.

"What the!" London yelps, stumbling into my chest at the sudden move. Her soft to my hard. Her delicate to my animalistic desires.

"Quiet, sweetheart. Let's not attract the attention of my guards." Wrapping my arms around her waist, I draw her in close, run the fingertips of my right hand up her spine until reaching her nape. My fingers wrap around the base, tilting her head back to face me. "I just want a little more time with you. Just us."

57

"You're so confusing," she mumbles, but I hear her. I also don't miss the small shivers rushing through her. The goose bumps on her skin. How she never pushes me away.

"No more than you are." I dip low and place my forehead against hers, lips hovering. "I'm still trying to understand what this undeniable pull is. Why I can't keep my hands to myself when you're near."

"You can't?" Fuck, how naïve she is rocks me. Sends a shock wave of pleasure through every limb, and I can't stop myself when I pull her even closer. Let her feel me. And she does. Those doe eyes widen and her lips part, her breath coming out in small pants against my mouth.

"I can't stay away. Not even if you asked me to." That realization should rock me, but it doesn't. Instead, it pulls everything into focus. I will bring the world down to its knees for her if she so much as asks. I will kill to own her. "My intentions aren't noble, Twirl. I want you. All of you."

"I don't know what to say," she whispers, cheeks flushing as her eyes wander to my mouth. "My family will never allow us to—"

"They are for me to worry about, baby..." I lick my lips, a move she follows "...leave everything to me."

"I don't know how. I depend on myself." The heaviness in her words breaks something inside of me. They'll pay for her sadness with their blood.

"Past tense. I'm here now." Moving my lips slightly to the right, I kiss her cheek with tiny little pecks, each one lingering longer than the last, driving her own need to surface. Her huff of frustration when I nip her chin tells me as much.

"Okay." It's an unsure whisper. London has no reason to believe me, but right now she's being led by the yearning for human contact. Her desire for my lips mirrors my own, and I groan loudly when she connects her mouth with mine.

"*Fuck.*" My hands tighten their hold, cementing her body against me. Preventing her from pulling those plump lips from mine. She's soft and sweet; her taste sets off a chaotic explosion of hunger that shakes me, and I can't stop myself when I take a little more. My tongue parts her lips, sliding inside and entwining with hers.

Her touch is tentative, yet she doesn't back away. Instead, Twirl shows her own desire with little mewls of pleasure. How she fists her own hand in my hair to keep my mouth over hers.

London's acceptance of my dominance in this instance has me harder than steel. Almost demonic in my thirst to be buried deep inside her warmth.

"More," she moans low, a kittenish sound that shoots straight down to my cock, and I flex against her. Give a harsh jerk that brings me back down to reality.

I will have her, but not today. Not when we can be interrupted at any moment.

Slowing the kiss down, I embed my teeth into her bottom lip for a second and pull back. Her breathing and mine is labored, chest heaving as we slowly regain our composure.

"I'm going to need you to head back inside now, Twirl. Follow that path…" I point to the left of us "…and Mariah will be there. She'll take you back to where your family waits for brunch."

"What about you? Where will you be?"

"I'll be a few minutes behind, but I have eyes on you. Trust me."

She nods, gifting me a soft smile. "I'll try my best."

"Thank you, beautiful." Before she can take a single step, I press our mouths together once more and breathe her in. My nose skims the delicate skin from her lips to ear, where I pause. Kiss her pulse point. "I call you Twirl because you remind me of a ballerina. So pretty when you move, with the poise of an elegant swan. You're very distracting, London, and I'm enjoying each moment of madness."

Chapter 8
LONDON

"HOW WAS YOUR WALK?" Alton asks as soon as we enter the dining room, and I freeze up. His hand is wrapped in a dishtowel with what I can only assume is ice, and while his smile is friendly enough, I know better than to believe it. The truth is in the tightness around his eyes.

Did he notice my reaction to seeing Malcolm enter the room? Fear of his anger causes my hands to shake and for my body to want to withdraw into itself.

I couldn't stop myself then, no matter how hard I bit the inside of my cheek when Malcolm's eyes met my own. When his stare, so full of heat, ate me alive. Everything from last night came flooding back; his touch and the soft kisses he lay on my stomach while I poured his drink. How he took my scent into his lungs and groaned into my dress. All of it, every lustful moment hit me, while mixing with an uncontrollable horror that my family knew my secret.

But now, add to that my brother's calculating stare, and once more my panic ensues. I know him. Alton's thinking of ways to pin this disaster of a meeting on me.

Because with him, I am always to blame. Has been that way since Mom died a few years ago. If a glass so much as breaks in the house, even if I am not there it falls on my shoulders.

Their hate toward me makes no sense, but I no longer deny it. I've done nothing wrong except exist, and yet to them, it's reason enough.

Why weren't they like this when Mom was alive?

Why do I always feel like I'm missing a huge piece of a puzzle?

"It was a lot of fun," Mariah answers for me before I can come up with a lie, walking toward the side of the table where Javier is waiting. "Your sister has quite the keen eye for décor—colors, and I might need her help soon. Redecorating my loft will take some time, and another female point of view will come in handy. Don't you think, dear cousin?"

"I agree." Malcolm enters the room from the opposite entrance. Immediately the atmosphere changes once again. This time an electrical current of desire swirls all around me, and staying in place is difficult. My body throbs in his presence, while my levels of distress lower.

I feel weirdly...*safe*. Something that baffles me.

His presence dominates every square inch of this room while pushing my fear back. It loosens the tightening noose, letting me breathe.

Malcolm stops at the head of the table and looks at me, then at my father. The warmth from just a few minutes prior is completely gone. "Will that be a problem, Marcus?"

No one misses how he asks my father and not the head of our family. Something that infuriates my brother, and in a sick and perverse way, causes a smidgen of giddiness to flow through me. His lack of respect for the men in my family is clear to see, and I find myself delighting in the fact that the shoe is on the other foot for once.

That they'll experience inferiority like I do day in and day out.

"What do you think, Alton?"

"I didn't ask him for his opinion, Marcus, but yours. Now, answer the simple question."

My father nods his head, his lips thinning. "Yeah, that'll be fine. London could use new friend."

More like any friend. I'm a prisoner in my own home, the home my mother's father left her, and the only time I see the outside is when I work. No school. No fun. All I'm good for is to cook and clean—to bring home money so they can make payments to the Riveras.

Or spend it on some idiotic idea.

And let's not forget the poker tables my father frequents almost every other day.

We're lucky that Mom's family came from money and that our house is completely paid off. That when we came back from Miami after another failure from Alton, we had somewhere to live.

"Perfect." While Javier grabs Mariah's chair to pull it out, Malcolm does the same with mine, smiling at me, but then just as soon his eyes narrow. "Why are you full of bruises, Ms. Foster? Did you have an accident recently?"

Dad chokes on his drink while Alton looks at me, daring me to say anything. What's worse is that I know Malcolm saw these earlier, but why put me on the spot like this? Why mention it now in front of them?

"Just a minor slip last night," I lie, and he knows this. The way he glares toward the men in my family lets them know he isn't buying a single word coming out of my mouth. That he's doing this on purpose. That he's paying attention to even the most minute thing. "It's nothing, Mr. Asher. I'm clumsy."

I hate having to cover for them, but it'll be worse if I don't. Alton has never hit me, but I fear that day isn't too far into the future. The more I deny him, recoil from his advances, the angrier he gets.

Moreover, if he does, my father will never stop him. He'll never disagree or go against his prodigy.

Malcolm purses his lips, eyes hard. "No more clumsiness, London. No more bruises."

"Okay," I whisper, hating the way everyone stares at me. At the purplish marks left behind by the men who are supposed to protect me above all else. "I'll pay better attention to—"

Just then, a stomach grumbles loudly and Mariah laughs. "Sorry. I missed breakfast this morning due to work."

Thank God that works and the tension level drops as her boyfriend and mine—

No, not mine. I can't allow myself to get lost in him.

Malcolm asks me to trust him, and I'll try. However, my plans won't change.

He is a customer and a means to an end. My mind can't negate that. I'm so close to getting out of this clusterfuck, and it's the only thing that matters.

Their chuckles bring me back to the present and I know that I missed something, not that my brother or father notice the distress I am suddenly under. The confusion. Instead, they reach to serve themselves while Magda continues to bring in trays of food.

But *his* eyes aren't fooled. No, those deep seafoam eyes stare at me. See me.

Realize the danger I live under.

Moreover, it's in that dark stare that I get lost in once more. That

I find myself wanting to lean toward. My skin tingles and heartbeats accelerate—my body is in tune with his every exhale, and for a second, I give in and hope. Make believe that he's here to rescue me from this hell of a life.

Trust me, he mouths again, and God, I want to.

I just don't know how.

Chapter 9
MALCOLM

I ARRIVE AT THE office on Monday, the sun bouncing off the mirrored windows of the skyline while the streets begin to fill with morning commuters. It's early, but something doesn't belong in the picture before me, and I exit my car, making eye contact with a maintenance van across the street.

They aren't the best at hiding or looking for surveillance cameras —my guys had them on their radar within the first ten minutes.

Two of them.

The first is an older man, portly and with a mustache that hasn't changed since the seventies. He's someone I've dealt with before in the past and have a certain level of respect for. A man who still follows his moral compass.

A serious FBI agent. Has integrity.

Marcelles can't be bought and treats other with basic human decency. Even a motherfucker like me—a criminal—can appreciate that.

However, the other guy looks to be fresh off the Quantico farm. New in the field from the intel my own employees have given and the encrypted email my informant within the bureau sent a few hours ago.

No older than thirty, he's got sandy blond hair cut low and a medium build—average height and weight. Fidgety, he seems itching for action and can't stay still for long, which gives them away. You can't have a successful stakeout with someone leaving their post every thirty minutes on the dot to light up a smoke.

"I'm a bit insulted," Javier says, exiting the car behind me. He falls in step as we walk toward my building; neither the bank's lobby nor the offices above are open yet, but the financial district is full of nine-to-fivers arriving at work.

At that moment my all-black Navigator pulls away from the curb, merging into traffic and ignoring a horn. With the commute being horrendous Monday through Friday, a driver comes in handy.

"Agreed." I stop and turn, looking down at my watch. It's thirty to nine and I'm sure they'll be visiting before my ten a.m. coffee. I'm half tempted to wave just to move the process along; I have things to do and my girl to see. Being apart from her isn't sitting well with me.

I don't trust her brother or father to not do something stupid.

It's also why the man I have watching her has authorization to shoot first, no questions asked.

"Wonder why?"

I shrug. "To be honest, I expected more fanfare than this."

Not that they will find anything. The servers were wiped before the dawn of Saturday morning and the paper trails burned. Every trace of the Jameson name has been erased from our system in the aftermath of Michael's idiocy and Foster's greed, leaving nothing behind on our dealings or the physical money.

Money that I took ahold of and moved out of the States for security reasons.

No money. No evidence. No case.

"It's odd how very few have interest in that sale?" His phone pings then and he ignores it, which I raise a brow to. "It's an alarm your cousin set up on my phone. Woman is driving me insane with this multivitamin she wants me to take. Some crap she found in a TV informercial."

"And you aren't?"

"Nope. Just humoring her."

I shake my head at that with a chuckle. "Not surprised. You just can't say no to her."

"That word doesn't exist in her vocabulary, and I blame your parents and hers for that little gift."

The van's driver side window lowers a smidge then and the red tip of a cigarette becomes visible. We both look; I make it a point to let them know I'm aware they are there.

Marcelles has to be fuming inside that vehicle. Angry at the fact the moron he's working with doesn't understand the concept of being inconspicuous.

"Two, and one is green."

"Saw that." Javi brings his cup of coffee up to his mouth and takes a sip. For a man that holds no qualms in getting his hands *dirty*, he has an unhealthy love affair with whatever a caramel macchiato is. "For sale, though?"

Turning back to my building, I shrug once I reach the front doors of the Asher Building. "Possibly."

"Do we approach and make an offer on the land?"

"Not yet." They're listening. I know this. See the minute shift in a device they have hidden under a tarp and chain combination. What looks to be just sheet rock material being secured to the roof and side of the van. They went with blending in and not high tech, a mistake if you ask me. "Let them approach me first."

"MR. ASHER, YOU HAVE SOME VISITORS," Mariah says through the intercom a few hours later, her tone saccharine sweet—her way of addressing me when someone doesn't know who she is. "Are you busy, or can they pass?"

"Let them in." I sit back in my chair and make it a point of not shutting down my laptop. Let them see what I am working on; there's an architect's 3D model of my new bank in Shanghai on the screen along with the paperwork that gives away the logistics, cost, and timeframe for it to be up and running. I hide nothing, because by the time they always come demanding entry, the evidence they hope to find is gone.

"Of course, sir." There's no click from her side, letting me know she didn't disconnect, and I pay closer attention. "Right this way, gentlemen."

"Do you like working for him?" It's the younger one. Marcelles knows who she is. Knows better. "Does he treat you right?"

"Jesus," I mutter under my breath, amused by this.

"I hate it." And you can hear the pout in her tone.

"Why? Has he ever done anything to—"

"My cousin is forcing me to order his lunch every day. To file stuff in those big metal boxes with drawers." There's a cough, not sure from who, but it holds a hint of a laugh. "My nails look like crap at the end of each shift and my curls lose their volume. This is hell on earth."

"I'm so sorry you—"

"Christ, Shawn," Marcelles snaps, silencing his partner. "Mariah is Malcolm Asher's cousin and secretary. Whatever angle you're trying to play…just stop. We're not here for anything other than a word with the owner."

"Always a pleasure, Paul." Mariah laughs, the clack of her heels following her to my door. She pauses just outside and gives a knock. "May I?"

Brat. "Yes." The door opens and she enters first, walking behind my desk and taking her position to my left. They follow her in, stopping behind the two chairs on the opposite side. One looks normal and the other overexcited. "How can I help you, agents?"

"How did you know?"

"How are you, Malcolm?" they reply in unison, but my attention is on the older man. He extends a hand out for me to shake and I reach across my desk to do so, ignoring the now visibly annoyed toddler beside him. "How's your father?"

"Battling boredom at the golf course."

"Since when does Anthony golf?"

"Since my mother decided that they needed to be handier around the house in their old age. Her *honey do* list is a mile long, hence the new appreciation for golf." I can see that this small talk is angering the other man. Shawn doesn't like that a criminal—although I've yet to be indicted or convicted of anything—is acting as if their visit is of no consequence.

He doesn't appreciate that his *partner* isn't rude or demanding shit. He has a lot to learn. About me. About the way the world works.

Unless you have solid proof and come with an arrest warrant, you can't touch me or my belongings. And even worse, the fact that I'll never see the inside of a cell or receive anything other than a slap on the wrist grates on some people's nerves.

If I go down, so does the precious economic standing—luxuries—some high-ranking members of government enjoy. More money runs through this bank than any other in the United States, Europe, and China. Hurting my empire will crumble theirs.

No more hush money.

No more lobbying.

No more power.

ELENA M. REYES

Even if it tastes rancid in their mouth, I'm to be treated with respect.

Moreover, Shawn hates it. I see it in his face.

His eyes narrow and nostrils flare. "We need access to every deposit made into the United States from clients outside the country. Everything from late July to now."

"Is that so?" I scratch my chin, flicking my eyes from him to Marcelles. "His first job?"

"Yes."

"So, he knows procedure?"

"Yes." Poor man looks embarrassed.

"I'm right here," Shawn sneers, and it's hard not to knock his teeth back into his skull. "We have reason to believe that your bank is aiding in the illegal move of drug money."

"You're accusing me of a federal crime. Be very careful with that, agent. Your career can go—"

"Are you threatening me?"

"I'm stating a fact." I narrow my eyes, leaning forward in my seat with both hands flat atop my desk so I'm not tempted to reach for the gun. My eyes remain on his, even after Marcelles tries to intervene. With a single hand up, I stop him and direct myself solely to a now visibly uncomfortable Shawn. "I'm going to let your disrespect and unprofessionalism pass this one time. Take it as a will of good faith because you are new and clearly don't do your homework before throwing that badge around. What you're doing is overstepping the boundaries, the same laws you are pretending to uphold, yet feel as though you can now trample because of what? What is the point of this visit other than to harass and throw out weightless allegations?"

"We were told by an informant that this bank has ties to the Jameson family," Marcelles says then, his tone calm and without accusation. "We're just trying to follow up on a lead, Malcolm. Before a warrant is brought forth, we were hoping for your cooperation with this matter."

70

"Our conversation would've stayed on a friendlier note…" I tilt my chin in Shawn's direction "…had he not opened his mouth."

"Can we have a look or not?" Shawn tries to reinsert himself into our conversation, but I don't acknowledge him.

"How do you want to do this, Marcelles? Should I call my lawyer?"

"He will leave, and I'll handle this myself."

"I'm not going anywhere."

"If he does, then we have a deal." I nod, and the old man's posture relaxes a bit. "He needs to get off my property and not come back until he learns respect and how to follow protocol."

"It's a deal. I'll speak with my supervisor now and be back within the hour."

"Director Monahan will never agree to this," Shawn hisses through clenching teeth. "He'll never make a deal with—"

"Luther Monahan is someone I've known since I was a child and would not put up with his agents being obtuse and arrogant. Watch your tone and the way you conduct yourself." At my words, the cockiness in his stance deflates and worry seeps in. "You don't seem to realize just who you're dealing with here. Who I am. Look me up —learn a thing or two, and then when you're ready to apologize for basing your judgement on idiocy, you may come back."

"I'll never apologize to—"

"It's time for you to leave, agents. Follow me." Mariah, who's been quiet, interrupts Shawn. Our eyes lock for a second and I nod, fighting the smirk that wants to curl on my lips. "Mr. Asher has a day full of meetings, but I'll be available to handle everything with you personally, Marcelles."

"Agreed, and thank you." While I know Marcelles doesn't buy that I'm one hundred percent innocent, he still sticks to the rules. Doesn't overstep or accuse, because thrown-around insinuations can become defamation lawsuits.

"This is not how this works. You can't just kick me out," Shawn tries once more, his tone with Mariah a lot less arrogant. I also don't miss the appreciative looks he's giving her, ones that Javier will kill him for.

"Not up for negotiations." She walks around my desk and doesn't stop until reaching the door. There, she waits for them with a not-so-patient look and it's funny to watch how quickly they follow instructions. "Now, let's get you out and let Mr. Asher get back to work. He's a busy man and can't entertain nonsense."

And as they walk out and head toward the elevators, I only have one thought:

I'm going to enjoy watching the life drain from his body at Javier's hands.

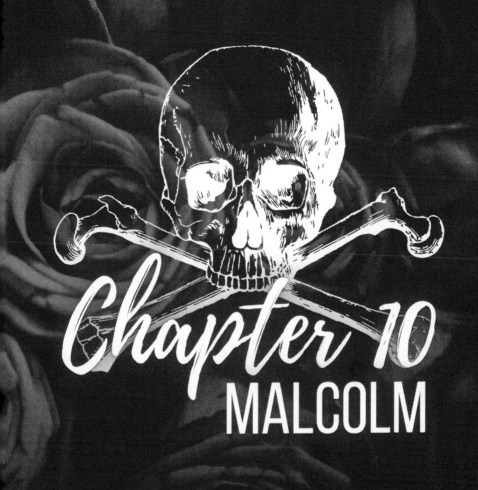

Chapter 10
MALCOLM

I FIND MYSELF standing over her bed two days later watching her sleep, the same way I've been coming into her home since Sunday night, using a copy of her key made with an imprint in clay, to be with her.

That very day I set a few plans in motion to protect her, the first being my entry and exit out of her home without detection. It didn't take much work to trip Alton's cheap system. Thirty minutes and a few Red Bulls later, my best IT guy hacked the system, putting the recording of a quiet house on loop and disabling the alarm.

No alerts. No proof of my ever being here.

To protect her while she gets some rest. Make sure that no one disturbs her.

She makes me worry. I feel protective— need to feed this uncontrollable desire to be close.

I tell myself it's because I want to make sure she's okay, but it's a lie. A poor one at that.

Every minute she's in this house, I'm restless. Worry.

Her family isn't to be trusted; the assholes disappear at night as they plot my end. Try to find anyone willing to take me on as a job. Offering money they don't have.

Alton doesn't understand that I have eyes everywhere. That for the right price, people are always willing to talk and sell him out.

London turns onto her back then, the thick comforter covering her from view falling down and exposing her chest. I count each rise and fall while contemplating how much my life has changed. Just how far I'm willing to go to keep her.

It's been five days since she walked into my private room and danced for me.

Four days since I've had some peace where she isn't invading my every waking moment.

Since that first night, I've become her stalker. Always just a few steps behind her in some way or another, gifting her the invisible space she needs to get used to the idea of me. Giving her the illusion that I'm not around when in fact, it's the opposite.

I'll always be here.

"Malcolm," Twirl sighs in her sleep, completely unaware of my presence. "So confusing…"

Son of a bitch. Even her sleep talk is adorable. Makes me feel like a king when it's my name that passes through those plump lips.

Leaning over her, I skim a finger down her soft cheek. Enjoy the way she turns into my touch so innocently. Her response is automatic. "Salvation comes with sacrifices. Yours will be in his blood." I press the tip of my finger to her lips. Linger there for a moment as her warm breath caresses my skin. "Sleep, knowing that you are protected. I'll always take care of you."

My phone vibrates inside my pocket, alerting me to the time. Pulling back, I reach over and pick up her older-than-dirt flip phone to dial mine—the call goes through and after I hit the end button, I erase it from her directory.

Walking to the door without another backwards glance, I exit the house through the back door. It's almost five in the morning, and I need to catch a few hours of sleep before heading in to work. There's a new position I need to fill and soon; a personal bodyguard for her. A female.

My men are good, but any male in her presence rattles the cage of my demon's jealousy.

Pushes me past what I am comfortable with.

I'm going to be the only man in her life.

THERE'S a timid knock a few minutes after one in the afternoon. "You wanted to see me, sir?" Earl asks just outside my open office door. He's waiting for me to let him in, looking tired and full of worry—the deep wrinkles on his forehead crease and his brows furrow. "Is everything okay?"

I offer him a small smile to ease the tension and wave him in. "Come in and have a seat, please."

"Should I close the door?"

"Not necessary."

"Okay." There's a tray Mariah left before leaving for lunch with a few bottles of cold pop, water bottles, and a few pastries. He eyes them but makes no move to take one.

"You don't have to ask or be offered one. Take whatever you want, Earl." For this conversation I need him to feel at ease, to relax enough to be forthcoming with the information I'm after.

"Thank you." He gives me a sheepish grin. "I've been so nervous after Mary relayed your message that I missed breakfast and lunch today."

"There's no reason for you to be nervous. None at all." Standing from behind my desk, I grab a Sprite and walk over to the small seating area across the room, taking a seat in a leather chair. I point to the small sofa to my right and against the wall for him to follow; he does so with his snacks in hand and waits. Looks at me without making a single peep. "Please understand that what we discuss in here today is a private and delicate matter. That I'm looking to help someone I think is in danger."

"Of course, sir..." I raise a brow and he chuckles "...Malcolm. Sorry. I'm just not used to addressing my superiors by their first names. It feels disrespectful."

"It's not when I'm asking you to. You've more than earned mine." Uncapping my drink, I take a few sips and set it down on a small glass coffee table beside a plain manila folder. "And it's because of that trust that I come asking for help.

"Anything I can do, I will. You know that."

"I appreciate that." Sitting forward, I let my hands hang between my thighs. "I need you to tell me the truth—everything you know about someone we both know."

"Who?" he asks, nose scrunching up before taking a sip from his drink.

"Who is London Foster, Earl?"

The man splutters, choking on his drink while the pastry slips to the floor. Earl wipes his chin with a handkerchief he pulls from his front pocket, his eyes wide as saucers. "Whatever she did, I'll take responsibility for. It's on me. I'll pay for."

"That isn't necessary. I assure you—"

"Please, Malcolm. She's been through enough." I'm not one to be cut off, but in this instance it works. He cares for her, sees what I do, and I have no doubt that he'll help me. "Give her a break. I don't know what she did, but her home life is shit and Mary and I do what we can to help without her brother or father knowing. Those two pricks use her—the money her mother left her—"

"I know."

"What?"

"Earl, I'm not going to hurt her. I'm here to protect every single hair on that pretty little head."

"But why?" He looks at me as if I'm the devil playing God, causing me to laugh.

"Honest to God, I want to help her," I say simply after a few minutes, my amusement waning. *Own her,* but I don't voice that part aloud. Instead, I relax in my seat—controlling the part of me that demands answers. That wants to reach across and force the information out of him.

What stops me from doing so is his honest affection for her. The fact that I know London would be angry, and to me, that's unacceptable.

"How do you know her? What did she do?"

"It's her brother's head I'm after."

Earl runs a hand down his face, a deep sigh leaving him. "That asshole is not Amelia's son."

"Amelia is their mother, no?" I'm baiting. Already know this. What I want is the details that aren't on a piece of paper. Firsthand accounts of how Marcus weaseled his way in. How he and his son came to hold Twirl's future in their hands.

"She is *her* mother." He takes another deep breath and lets it out slow. He's trying to figure me out and what to say. If he can save her.

"Earl, I'm not going to hurt her…" there's a small folder on the table that I push his way "…quite the contrary, actually."

"What's this?"

"Open it." Shooting me another questioning gaze, he takes the folder in his hands and opens it. His eyes skim across each page, taking in every single bit of information inside. The who, how, and when of the Fosters' operations. But more importantly, how they are funding their schemes.

ELENA M. REYES

Because that is what they are. A low-level operation running on one grandeur fuckup after another.

"As you can see, I've already done my homework. I know their plans, old man, but I need you to fill in the blanks. Help me end this for her."

"Malcolm, why are you doing this? What did Marcus and his degenerate son do?

"Hurt her." At my words his eyes snap to mine, and in them I see the same hate that's been brewing within me. I'm not the nicest man —being seen as an asshole doesn't hurt my feelings—but the one thing I will never do is hurt an innocent. Someone who has nothing to do with this life I've chosen. "He put his hands on that which is pure."

"You care?"

"I do."

"And she will be okay? No harm will come to her?"

"London will never know fear again as long as I have breath left in my body."

"Okay. Okay." Earl pulls his wallet from his back pocket and produces an old, worn picture from inside. It's the picture of two women about the same age as Twirl is now. There's no doubt that the one on the left is a younger version of Mary, his wife, but the other is the spitting image of London.

Or in this case, my girl looks just like her mother. The resemblance is uncanny.

It also proves that there's a connection between the families.

"How did you all know each other?"

"Mary and Amelia were best friends. They grew up and went to school together...Catholic school at that." He chuckles as a small hint of pink touches his ears. "They were beautiful, but my eyes have always been for Mary, even though she was completely out of my league. They came from a somewhat upper-class upbringing while I was poor, not that it mattered to me. One look at Mary and I was a

78

goner, something that amused Amelia. She didn't get it until she met Julian Conte her senior year of high school."

"Julian Conte? That names sounds very familiar."

"That's because he owned a chain of restaurants all over Illinois. Amore *was* theirs."

"Was?"

Earl nods. "He passed away when Amelia was still pregnant with London. Horrible car accident on his way home one night...he died on impact."

"Jesus." My poor Twirl's entire life has been filled with nothing but loss. Of her father. Of her mother. Her money and basic human rights.

"Yeah." Grabbing his drink, he takes a few sips while trying to gather his thoughts. "They fell in love. It was fast and hard and everything she ever wanted. Julian was good to her, there for her, and even in his death, took care of them. Everything he had was given to Amelia and at her death, it went to London."

Standing up, I walk over to the windows and look out at the Chicago sky. "However, it didn't go to her. Why?"

"When Marcus sunk his claws into Amelia, whose father left her some money as well, he adopted London and became the guardian of her inheritance until she turns twenty-one. He pushed and pushed and fought with her until Amelia took in his son and did the same. He manipulated her. Isolated her. Kept her from anyone and everyone that could see what was really going on."

"Where was her family? Why didn't anyone step in?" There're so many questions running through my mind. So many emotions.

I'm angry for her. For everything she was put through because of someone's greed.

Because that's what the fucked up situation my Twirl's in comes down to. Money.

"We tried," he suddenly snaps, but it's not at me and I don't interrupt him. You can tell he's angry at himself for not doing more, and I

79

want that. Let him talk. Get it off his chest while I get the info I need. "Time and time again, we tried to reason with her. Prove to her that she was better off without his toxicity."

Turning to face him, I lean back against the glass. Expression neutral. "And what happened?"

"Mary had a really bad fight with her the year before she died." For a few minutes he's quiet, breathing choppy while he looks down at the last sheet of paper in the folder. The private investigation into Amelia's death. "She begged her to leave him after a particularly bad fight. He was cheating and when confronted, smacked her around a bit. I fought him for her, beat his ass, and then went over with a few guys to get her out of that house until she could evict him through the courts. Everything had been set and bags packed, when the asshole decided to take London out of school for a father/daughter day." Earl looks up at me then, his eyes holding so much sadness. "You know what's the best way to win any mother over?"

"Love the child."

"Exactly. He knew that treating London like a princess would grant him forgiveness."

"I'm going to make this right for her. I'm going to take care of her."

"Amelia was a good mother that made mistakes, Malcolm, but I swear to you, all she wanted was for her little girl to have a family. The father that she lost." He stands and walks over to me, looks me in the eye. Pleading with me. "To the courts, he's in charge of her inheritance—the sale of the restaurant chain and her mother's money —and decides how her monthly stipend is spent until she turns twenty-one as per Amelia's will. All her life that little girl has been nothing more than a pawn in a game, and she needs someone to defend her. Care for her."

"I'm going to make him pay," I vow, extending a hand out, which he takes and tightens his grip. "Both of them will be avenged."

"Thank you."

"None needed." Just then my phone pings with a message from Javi.

> Breaking News on 32 ~Javier

Grabbing the remote from the coffee table, I turn on the large TV mounted on the wall. It's already on the channel when an image comes on, and I can't stop the smile that forms on my lips. There, in the middle of a quaint little shopping center's parking lot, is a white Mercedes Benz on fire.

Completely engulfed and unsalvageable. No victims or witnesses.

"Is that?"

"Yes. It's Alton's." The first of the many losses to come. This one is for the piece of shit '80s Corolla they have Twirl driving, while he leases a Mercedes on her dime. And if he gets another one, I'll burn that one and each that follows.

I'm going to take everything away from him. Slowly. Methodically.

"He's going to flip his shit," Earl snorts, smile as wide as mine. He's enjoying this as much as I am, but then turns serious. "Be good to her. Don't let them break her down like they did Amelia. Promise me you will save her."

"I'm going to do more than that." Taking my phone out of my pocket, I pull up her number and send off a quick text.

> Did you get my gift. ~Malcolm

It doesn't take but a few seconds for three tiny dots to appear letting me know she is responding.

> You are insane. ~Twirl

> How did you know I needed one? ~Twirl

I don't know if I can accept this. ~Twirl

My reply is just as quick.

You can and will. You deserve the best, sweetheart. End of. ~Malcom

Chapter 11
LONDON

THE MUSIC IS LOUD as I enter the employee's lounge on Friday, walls vibrating with each pulsing note that comes through each speaker. There's a party tonight, a celebratory function with a CEO of a tech company—a bachelor's sendoff that includes a free-for-all with the staff.

A bride and groom will each own a floor tonight to have what they call a last hoorah.

I've been dreading this night; I know I'm on the schedule for a group dance, and I'm not looking forward to it.

It feels wrong, Like somehow I'm cheating, which is ridiculous

That kiss is messing with me. His thoughtful gift throwing me for a loop.

He sent me a brand new iPhone when my old cell was about to crap out. But it was more than the thoughtful gesture—it's the text he sent after that gave my heart a jump start.

You deserve the best, sweetheart. End of.

The man is an enigma I want to solve, even though I should stay away. It doesn't slip my mind that his package arrived fifteen minutes after my brother and father left for God knows where. That he somehow knew that I've been eyeing a rose gold one, setting a small chunk each week outside of my moving fund to do just that.

My father doesn't know just how much I make. They have no idea that the waitress salary they think I have doesn't even make up an eighth of what Liam pays me.

The phone in my hand beeps with an incoming text, which I ignore. I can't give in. Must fight it, whatever this is, even though I want nothing more than to get lost in him.

It's a week later and I can still feel the ghost of his lips on mine; I can't get him out of my head. He's there and refusing to give me a single moment of reprieve. Swear I can smell his woodsy cologne inside my room when I wake up each day.

Feel his lingering presence.

I'm going insane.

Every single day since then, all I do is think. I let him steal my first kiss, and it's creating ideas in my head—wants that before meeting him never came to mind. What I didn't think is possible for me until I'm far away from this place: hope.

For more. For peace. For everything.

Back at his house, the way he held my brother under his control, was sexy. Made me feel safe and untouchable—they couldn't treat me like dirt. As if I'm their property.

Malcolm is powerful and rich. He commands respect by merely entering a room, which is something I never thought to find attractive in a man.

He's not like Alton and the idiots he associates with.

My brother and father haven't spoken a single word to me since that awkward brunch. A few glares from Alton, yes, but no reprimand or recrimination. Instead, they spend their days in my brother's office trying to figure out who stole and set his car on fire. There's been yelling, cursing—glass smashed, but all behind a closed door, and that was more than okay with me.

Those few days of calm were a godsend. While they slept, I took care of the house and their mess, staying out of the way the moment they rose from sleep.

"Get it together, girl," I whisper under my breath, trying to shake off this feeling that sits heavy in the pit of my stomach.

I can see Stacy inside the employee dressing room with another girl from where I stand, one that I met just briefly the day I came asking for work. Neither notice me, and that's okay. The last thing I need is another person asking me how my night with Malcolm went.

Each girl is wearing tonight's uniform, which consists of a ruffled pair of booty shorts, tassels, and stilettos, all in white. While the men on staff usually wear a variation of boxers or briefs depending on the request, I'll take a wild guess that theirs tonight will be all-black and tight.

Everyone that works here is beautiful, and so much more comfortable in their near-naked state than I will ever be. More uneasiness settles deep into my bones. More doubt on how I will get through the night.

You need the money. You need it to get out. It's my mantra. On repeat as I square my shoulders and take another step toward the room.

My plan of going unseen doesn't last long when my foot catches on the threshold, and at once, their low whispers cease. Both girls look at me.

One with amusement, the other like she's trying hard to figure me out. It's almost comical, and had I not been freaking out about getting up on a stage, my giggles would've burst forth.

"Hi." I give a small wave, walking over to the wall where our performance schedules are. Skimming the name list, I find mine, and pause. What the...?

London: Room 305
Private Dance

My heart takes off at a galloping speed and my skin prickles with excitement. He's back.

"Someone did a good job," Stacy sidles up next to me, speaking low. "I'm happy for you, sweetie. You're not meant to be downstairs with the rest of us."

"Why do you say that?" I ask, looking over at her. The thin strap of my shirt falls, and it's hard for me not to fix it, but I don't move. Instead, I keep my eyes on hers, begging her to give me an answer that makes sense. "Please give me something."

Our last conversation became weird toward the end, and the way she left, odd.

Suddenly, my strap is fixed and another shoulder bumps into mine. "You are too innocent for this kind of a job, sweetie. We like what we do, love sex, while you look afraid of your own shadow."

Turning my face, I scrunch up my nose. "I do not...do I?"

She nods, a hint of warmth in her stare. "Sorry, kid."

"Yes, you do, London." Stacy interjects, pulling my attention toward her. "And don't take offense, but Sila is right. You're a virgin..." she arches an eyebrow for confirmation, which I give with a nod "...then take this as the best thing that can ever happen to you and keep him happy. Come in, dance, and feel at ease that he's the look-but-don't-touch type of client. That you can still walk out of here when you are ready with that V-card intact."

But he does touch me. He kissed me.

Why am I so different? "I'm in way over my head," I mutter low, but not low enough as they both hear and laugh. "Not funny, jerks."

"A little," they answer in unison, and this time I join them in giggles. The world I'm suddenly in the middle of is out of my depth, should send me screaming, but instead, I am full of butter-flies in my stomach. A nervous excitement that I can barely hide from them.

And while they are right about everything they say; it doesn't quell my curiosity. The yo-yoing emotion dominating my body and mind.

I want. I don't.

Stay. Or run like hell.

Malcolm is like a roller-coaster ride. The kind that go up really high with a massive drop, and even though I'm scared of the unknown, getting on is all I find myself thinking about. Even when I know it's bad for me, that rush still flutters and tempts.

Confuses me.

"Your outfit for tonight is hanging next to your vanity, London," Sila says, bringing me back to the present. "It's per Mr. Asher's request." The look she's giving me—her grin—hints at something that I'm just not getting.

"Ummm, okay?" I shrug, not sure what this can mean.

"It's time to get ready."

"Still feel as if I am missing something."

"What Sila means to say…" Stacy rolls her eyes while also grin-ning "…is that you have a rack of clothing with dates for each beside your dressing area. All from him."

"All from him?" Are they messing with me?

Trust me.

Trust me.

Trust me.

"London, you only dance for him. Take a look at that schedule again."

My eyes shift to the wall and the piece of paper hanging on a cork-board. Finding my name doesn't take long, and neither does seeing what room I'll be in. Every night I'm scheduled says the same; he will own me every Friday through Sunday for the foreseeable future.

Throwing an arm over my shoulders, Stacy gives me a squeeze. "At least with him you'll be away from the craziness...no one will bother you."

Room 305: Private Dance

Why would he do that?

Or better yet, why do I like it so much?

Chapter 12
MALCOLM

TWIRL ENTERS THE ROOM five minutes before our time is set to begin. It's Friday night, and I need her, my body's wound tight from denying myself the pleasure of her touch. From only watching her through a small screen or sitting beside her a few hours at night when she's sleeping inside that tiny bedroom.

For her I've gone from voyeur to stalker, and I'm not the least bit ashamed.

And knowing what I do now, my killing of her family is a gift to humanity. They deserve the worst. Will receive a punishment befitting the crime.

"I can do this," she whispers then, pulling my attention back to her. For tonight, I vow to focus and make this solely about her. Give her something no one has ever before.

A choice.

London is stunningly beautiful; her steps slow while making her way toward the stereo and picking up the remote. That's when she notices the piece of paper there. A small note asking her to follow my instructions:

Hit play.

Face the wall.

Close your eyes.

Count to ten.

Fuck, I've missed her.

Miss her looking at me with sweet and curious eyes. Miss seeing the want reflecting back at me.

Her breathing escalates, and the remote in her hand slips to the floor as a shiver runs up her spine. This between us is palpable—an unstoppable force we can't control.

Can't deny no matter how much I know she's fighting it. Hearing her tonight while she spoke to the girls through a speaker inside Liam's office only confirmed what I already know...

Twirl is afraid.

Too pure for this son of a bitch that will break down every one of her walls. The more I see—learn about her—the stronger my urges become. The more the idea of us cements itself in my head.

"I'm going insane," she whispers to herself, oblivious to my presence within the room. Just how I want it. I'm hiding in the shadows. Nothing except her stage is lit up while I watch and sip from my drink. "Why am I letting him get to me?"

Because you want me. Because I'm as under your skin as you are under mine.

Twirl stretches her neck from side to side, shaking her limbs out to expel the tension. It's a waste of time; we're meant to explode. To burn hotter than the motherfucking sun each time we come together.

It takes her a few minutes, but London bends at the waist to pick up the small control. The little dress; a flirty light yellow number with a sweetheart neckline and short hem rides up, giving me a peak of the silk panties underneath. The ones that carry my initials at the upper right hand corner.

A guttural growl builds in my chest at the sight, but I fight it. Swallow my desire while palming my hard-as-steel cock, the thin dress pants doing little to contain the visible bulge—the throbbing against the metal zipper.

I want to fuck her. Own her.

Bury myself so deep within her pussy that she'll feel me for days after. Ride her so hard that the imprint of my dick will forever be etched into her walls. Mine will be the only cock she'll ever know. Ever want.

Closing my eyes, I take in a deep inhale. Try to regain composure when the music begins. A slow and sensual beat meant to entice the senses. That blatantly expresses my desires.

The hunger to taste every single inch of her.

My eyes snap open as the first riffs rent the air. I wait for her next move.

Her acceptance.

London takes her time, and I am in no rush.

I count down the seconds until I see her turn and give me her back. Another harsh exhale leaves her, arms shaking, and I quietly stand.

Another minute and she tips her face down. I follow her move with one of my own. Then another, and it's when I'm halfway across the room that I hear her.

"One, two, three…four," she whispers to herself, and then pauses. London tilts her head as if listening for my entrance. *Tsk, tsk, baby. Come on. Finish for me.* Holding my position, I wait for her to begin again. Sixty seconds pass, the intro for another song begins, and she gives in. "Five, six, seven…"

Before Twirl can say eight, I'm right behind her, her back to my front, and my hands clench as she whimpers out a shaky *nine.*

We both need this. To be close. To touch, and before she utters the next number, my lips are at her ear. Kissing the shell, nuzzling her fragrant skin. "Ten."

"I knew you were here." London's skin breaks out in goose bumps, a tiny map of sensitive flesh that I nip as I follow the path down to her collarbones. Nipping her there, I soothe the sting with my tongue. "F-felt you."

"Is that so?" I ask, wrapping my arm around her midsection. The stomach muscles clench beneath my hold as she gasps at the sudden movement. "Why do you think that is, Twirl? Why can you feel my presence?"

"I don't know."

"Don't lie to yourself." At my words, London turns in my arms, eyes slightly narrowed. And fuck me if I don't like this glimpse of fire. "Something you want to say, Ms. Foster? Any questions?"

"There is."

Dipping down, I nip her bottom lip. "And?"

"Why am I different? Why are you doing all of this?" There it is. What's eating her.

Curiosity is a bitch and one people don't quite know how to tame. That inquisitiveness gets them into situations they have no business digging into. Or in this case, it will open a box she isn't quite ready to receive.

The attraction is mutual. Our desires match evenly. However, the life she's been given has created this defense mechanism she can't help but hide behind. It's easier for her.

"Are you sure you want the answer?"

"Yes." The pleading in her eyes—the desperation in her voice dictates my next move. Before she can protest, I grab a thigh in each hand and lift her up, wrapping them tight around my waist. A small squeak escapes, but there's no protest as I carry her back to my chair.

Instead, she wraps her arms around my neck and holds tight. Presses her cheek to mine while her lips whisper something that's too low to hear but end with *dangerous*.

Taking a seat on the wide chair, I tap the table and the bottom stand illuminates with a low light. There's just enough room for her to straddle me comfortably, and I push her back a bit so I can focus on her flushing face. On the brightness in her eyes.

On every fucking question and doubt that I'll erase—decimate in order to own this precious doll.

"This is better." Not a question, a statement. Being close is right. The only way this talk will work.

"Agreed." London moves her upper body back, but her hips stay just a few inches from my cock. So fucking close that I can feel her heat. Her thighs are exposed, the dress riding up just enough to give me a glimpse of her sweet, virginal pussy. "But my face is up here."

There's a hint of amusement in her tone, and I shrug. "Not going to apologize, Twirl. I find you utterly perfect."

"You're a smooth one, aren't you?"

"I don't lie." Bringing both hands to her hips, I bring us flush while spreading my fingers wide over her lower back. She's heat. Softness. Feels like the perfect sin, and I've yet to have a taste of her decadence. "With me, you will always know where we stand. What I am thinking. There will be no secrets between us."

"Why do you keep saying there's an 'us'? I don't know you." As she says this, there's a minute shift of her hips. It causes my cock to flex against her, to throb, while those cerulean eyes become heavy. "Tell me."

"Ask me the right question," I grit out, fighting my own desire to devour her.

London stares at me, swallowing hard as she finds the right

words. And the moment she does, it's a glorious sight. Her back straightens, the subtle shift pressing her core harshly against my girth while she licks her lips. I groan at the natural sensuality she displays, not holding back—wanting her to see just how much I desire her.

"Tell me, Malcolm." Her hand, small and soft, cups my chin. "I need to know why I'm suddenly feeling as though my freedom is within reach." London's exhales are heavier, soft little pants over my lips. "Who are you? Why are you here for me?"

"You want to know why I always want you close?" My right hand leaves her hip, fingertips skimming up the center of her back until I reach her hair. Hair that I grab a fistful of so I can tilt her head back enough to lick a path from her neck to chin. "Why I can't stop reaching out for you?"

"Yes," she mewls out, hands moving down to my shoulders— grabbing onto *me*.

"Are you sure you're ready for that answer, sweetheart? Because there's no going back after I say the words."

"Please. I need to understand."

Nodding, I tighten my hold and appraise her. Rejoice in the mirrored hunger I see reflecting back at me. "What would you say, Ms. Foster, if I told you that I want to own your soul? That I want to make you mine. Tie you to me in every way a man can."

A whooshing breath leaves her. "I'd say you are crazy and that we don't know each other. My family isn't going to allow this."

"So, you have already said," I hiss out when I feel her thighs clench.

"Because it's the truth. My brother—"

"I'm more of a monster than prince charming," I interject, putting a stop to that idiotic thought he's put in her head, "but it doesn't change our reality."

"And what reality is that?" Another song begins, a heavier beat that pulses through the room. It sexy. Enticing. "You haven't even asked me what I want yet."

"Because I already know." With my other hand, I grab onto and stop the slow roll of her hips. The unconscious dancing she's been torturing me with. "You want out from beneath your family's thumb, London. To feel safe again and free-fall into this explosiveness between us."

Her entire body freezes. "How do you know?"

"You're running, and that stops here." With a soft touch, I run soothing circles over her skin with the pad of my thumb.

"Still doesn't explain how—"

"Sweetheart, there isn't a single move made in this city that I'm not aware of. That doesn't reach my ear."

A slight flash of fear passes through her eyes then. "Then you know that...?"

"That your father and brother are scum? About the money they owe the Riveras back in Miami and their plans here?" My fingers dig a bit into her hip, but I release her before their imprint appear on her skin. I'll never mark her out of anger, only pleasure. "Yes, I do. And mark my words, baby...they will pay." *For everything they've stolen from you.*

"But how?" With her hands on my chest, she tries to stand but I hold firm. "Why are you doing this? I have a plan. My mind was made up."

"*Was* being the operative word." Bringing her face down to mine, I kiss those bee-stung lips with a bit of the manic hunger I possess. My tongue seeks hers out the moment she groans against my mouth, prying her slightly parted lips apart and taking what belongs to me.

She's tentative in her own exploration, slowly running her hands up my chest and then neck, until she finds purchase at the nape. There, she embeds her slim fingers into my hair and tugs, creating a shooting rush of pleasurable pain that settles on the tip of my dick.

I flex against her, and she whimpers.

I press her down harder, and her thighs tremble.

I want to come all over her softness, but before that can happen, I'm going to gift her tonight.

Slowing the kiss down, I suck the bottom one between my teeth and bite down. "Tell me you want this? Admit it to yourself that you want me."

Heavy-lidded eyes stare at me, so open and honest. "I do."

"Thank you," I say, pressing my lips to hers once more. "Twirl, I need you to know that I'm not a good man. That I have and will do things that you won't agree with, but I promise you one thing...you will never fear me. The world might see my wrath, but you never will."

"I don't know why I believe you, Malcolm, but I do."

"Good." Grabbing her hips, I stand her up between my spread legs and sit back. Scratch the stubble on my chin as she squirms before me. "But enough with the heavy for now. We'll come back to this another day."

"Another day?"

"Yes, and we will finish this..." I give her a pointed look and she nods "...but right now I have a present for you."

"A present? More than the phone and all the clothes you had delivered to me?" She's baiting. Wanting me to admit my possessiveness.

"I'm not going to apologize for monopolizing your time here. You dance for me." It's not a request, and this girl just smiles. Not at all upset, which makes me happy. "But yes, I have a small token, just so you see how serious I am. That this is about more than getting between your thighs."

"Are you saying you don't want me?" The playful tinge to her tone makes me chuckle. London is more relaxed in this moment than I've seen her to date. Like a weight has been lifted from her shoulders.

"Baby girl, my biggest wish is to impale you on my cock. To watch you choke on a scream as I split you in two." Her mouth drops open and those soft cheeks flush. She's not put off by my words; the way she shivers and comes closer is evidence enough. My girl likes a dirty mouth. "But not tonight. Tonight, I want you to choose. We do what you want."

"What I want?"

"Anything and everything. Even if that means you walk out that door and go home to bed."

Chapter 13
LONDON

WHAT I WANT?

What do I want?

It's a question that no one ever asks me anymore. Well, not since Mom left this earth to find peace in heaven. I see now that she was the only one that cared for my well-being. The one that taught me to dream big and fight for my happiness.

It's why I am trying so hard now. Why I'm willing to sell my body if it comes to that.

Things weren't always the way they are now. I remember days of warmth and happiness. When money was the last thing on anyone's mind.

But then she died, and so did the peace I had. Working here to find my freedom is all I have left. It's my last promise to her memory.

However, looking into his green eyes, my metaphorical walls crumble. They don't stand a single chance against his devilish grin with just the right amount of sweet that causes my thighs to clench. A subtle movement he doesn't miss.

Fighting my desire for him isn't working; it's the true meaning of a losing battle. He makes me want more. Makes me want to let go and live.

"Tell me, Twirl." Malcolm sits up, running the tips of his fingers up each leg. "I'll give you anything you want." Slowly, he finds his way to my waist where his fingers almost encompass my abdomen— all the way around with little room left between his fingertips, show- casing how tiny I am.

Something else I like about him. Find attractive.

Malcolm Asher is the epitome of all things male. The literary equiv- alent of what I've read about in books when describing a true alpha.

He's dangerous, and from what I have seen, those around him show nothing but respect in his presence. And yet, with me he's shown another side; it's still rough, yet not intimidating. He's not trying to force himself on me, but instead, make me want him.

And I do. God, I do.

The man is handsome, dominant, and pushes every single one of my buttons. Gives me a boost in confidence—makes me feel comfortable in my own skin.

I'm beautiful to him, but will I survive if things blow up in my face?

"I don't know how to answer that, Malcolm. What I want isn't going to suddenly appear."

Those fingertips dig in—the small bite of pain feels good. "Don't fight it, baby. Just let go." He makes it all sound so simple. Like my wishes are his command, and that's very dangerous for me.

However, the more his stare penetrates mine, I find myself unconsciously moving. Straddling his thighs once more, my dress bunches up around my midsection as I press our bodies close. No room between us.

"I want my freedom, Malcolm." Laying my forehead against his, I give in. Saying aloud what I've kept hidden for years. "I want to feel alive."

"Then it's yours." He groans, flexing his hips against the shallow roll of mine. And *Christ,* I feel every solid inch. How thick he is. How much he wants me.

Wants this between us, and more so because I'm the one who's initiating this contact. Because I want him too.

Seeing his physical desire—the hunger in his eyes creates a heady reaction in me. It's freeing. No pressure whatsoever as I give in to my own wants.

Just let go.

He's in my head. Under my skin.

Prickling at my senses and chipping away years of repression.

"That's it, beautiful. Take what you want," he groans, tightening his grip, yet it's my hips that move above his. It's my control that keeps us at a torturous pace.

Everything in this room disappears. Consequences have no meaning; where we are or how we met. That no longer matters to me. I don't care that he's a client, is dangerous for me, and hates my family.

All I can concentrate on is what he makes me feel, and I let my instincts guide me.

"You make me want things, Malcolm. Things I shouldn't think about until—"

He crashes his mouth to mine before I can finish. It's urgent and rough, a raping of my senses that shreds the last bit of sanity I'm holding on to.

This time when my hips buck against him, its hard and fast, sending a lightning bolt of pleasure through every limb. A feeling I chase with another gyration, more closeness.

I want to feel his skin on mine. Every solid inch, so I settle for unbuttoning his shirt. "Get it off," I whimper into his mouth, trembling as the last button slips free and the shirt reveals a strong chest below.

That's when I see it. He has another tattoo.

On the right side of his chest is the large image of an owl in black and white with an all-seeing eye held tight in its claws. It's beautiful, with bold lines and its intricate shading. The entire thing stands out against his slightly tanned skin, and I'm not the least bit embarrassed by my reaction to this.

It's visual. It's automatic. It's instinctual.

I rub myself against his cock with hard little bucks of my hips while pushing the offending fabric back over his shoulders. My thighs clench with each roll, fingers tracing over his hard pecs and lower, over each solid indentation of his abdomen.

He's strong. Defined. All man.

"Fuck," he grunts out then, and it's the sexiest sound I've ever heard. His hands wander lower to my bare thighs and flex over my skin; he's fighting back his own need to take over. To touch me where no other man has. To claim what he believes is his. "Corrupting you, sweet girl, will be my greatest achievement. I'm going to enjoy watching you become my beautiful little slut. My every-fucking-thing."

Those words on anyone else's lips would incense me, but with him, I shiver with pleasure. Become wetter, the proof of my desire coating the front of his pants.

"I'm so close," I breathe out, choking at the end on another moan as one of his large hands pushes me back to sit up, changing the angle. Thick and throbbing, he takes over my movements, arms flexing as he guides my body over his.

"Come for me, Twirl. Let go."

"Please," I beg for more. My limbs are thrumming with pleasure and my heart is racing. A delicious orgasm licks at my senses, almost there, when he releases my hip and brings a hand to my throat. "What are—"

"I'm not going to ask you again." His fingertips trace my neck; his thumb, with the symbol of a cross tattooed on his skin, settles on my lower lip. Just sits there, while the rest of his hand spreads, caressing my neck. "Come for me."

"I-I... oh *fuck*," It leaves me on a cry that borders on painful. I'm gone. No longer in control over my body as pleasure zips through me. Burns me.

Nothing has ever felt this good. All the others given by my own hand now fall under the mediocre category.

"I can feel you clenching, baby. Seeking my cock," he grits out, stilling beneath me. "Son of a bitch, you're going to feel so good taking every inch of me as I claim you. When I finally steal that gift you've kept for me."

Even as he twitches, pulses, Malcolm's eyes stay on mine. And it's the animalistic hunger in them that takes the very breath from my lungs.

Another rush of pleasure takes over me and I fall forward. I can't breathe. Can't move.

Yet his hands are everywhere, slowly bringing me back down with every caress. It takes a while, but when I find my breath again, I look up and find him smiling down at me. It's a soft look, one that tugs at my heart.

That I'm not prepared for in the least.

"You okay, sweetheart?"

Blood rushes to my cheeks, and I bury my face in his neck. "I have no control with you."

"That's not a bad thing."

"It's a dangerous thing for me."

At that, he pulls me from my hiding spot to face him. "What are you afraid of? I'd never hurt you."

"My family—"

"Has no place in this conversation, London. It's about me and you." He leans in and presses a featherlight kiss to my right cheek and then left. To my forehead and then chin. "Don't fight me, baby. Don't fight us. Let me take care of you."

Christ, I don't know what to do.

I'm attracted to him. Feel safe.

"This is crazy. I don't know you, have no idea how any of this will work." Everything he says is exactly what I want to hear, but is it the truth? Or is it what he *thinks* I want? Because I feel a little caught in the middle of whatever is going on between him and Alton. "Give me a little bit of time. Give me a reason to stay."

"Okay."

"Okay?" I ask, a little confused at how easily he gives in. "Just like that?"

"Yes, just like that." Malcolm taps my thigh, signaling for me to get up. Immediately, I panic that he's leaving. It comes out of nowhere, overwhelming me as I stand with shaking knees. He sees this and follows me up, wrapping an arm around my waist to keep me steady. "I'll give you what you want, but I'm always going to be one step behind. Chasing you. I'm not giving up, just letting you catch up." His head dips down, lips brushing my own, once, twice, before he nips the sensitive skin. "Now get dressed. I'm taking you to pick up your car."

"How do you know my car isn't here?"

"Better question is whose building are you parking at?"

THERE'S noise coming from the kitchen area when I enter the house a few hours later. It's past my usual time of return—the sun is up and the streets full of people on their way to church for Sunday mass.

Blaming Malcolm for this would be easy. For taking me to breakfast and spending an hour and a half doing nothing more than sitting beside me at some small café inside his building, but I won't. Truthfully, I don't remember the last time someone made me feel this way.

At peace. Comfortable.

I ate while he watched, a sinful smirk playing on his lips each time I bit into the heavenly strawberry pancakes the cook made. The one instance he spoke outside of crooning about my beauty or to tell me he hasn't been with anyone in more than a year—his refusal to accept mediocrity—was to ask if my family said anything after we left.

Did they give you crap over me? Question you? He worries, and I find that sweet.

No one so much as looked at me when we got home. I was told to disappear.

That didn't relax him. Instead, he grew pensive. Picking up his phone a few minutes after, he sent out a text before returning his attention to me. And even as we said goodbye beside my car, because of his refusal to let me walk in alone, there was something in his eyes that made me shiver.

Not because I fear him. Not at all.

It's more of an *I see him.* Know that he's capable of anything to be the victor in the end.

My ears are on high alert as I close the door with a muted thud. So low, I doubt they know I'm home. No one's yelling, which is a good sign, but for some reason my defenses are on high alert.

I know them. Know how they function.

Last Saturday's brunch with the Asher family is still on their minds. How he made them look weak, churning within their gut as hatred flows through their veins.

Toeing off my shoes, I pick the sandals up and walk toward the staircase. I don't want them—Alton—to come and find me; avoiding him is for the best right now. What I did a few hours ago with Malcolm is dangerous for me—I'm playing with fire—and I don't know if I can hide it. The unadulterated happiness he brings.

Because he does. He's giving me a small semblance of hope.

Tells me that I am not alone anymore.

My bare foot hits the landing when a hand grabs my arm. "What the?"

"About time you showed up to make breakfast," a woman I've never seen before says, her acrylic fingernails digging into my skin right where my father's marks are fresh. "Hurry up. We've been waiting."

"Get the hell off me." Without care, I swing my arm out while trying to shake her off, and she teeters on what are ridiculously high heels.

"You bitch!" she shrieks, breaking skin as she holds on tighter.

I'm falling backwards and I grab onto the banister to keep myself up, smashing my elbow into the wood. "I'm not warning you again." I can feel a few drops of blood weep down my arm where she's tearing the dermis. "Let. Go."

"You need to learn some respect."

Cocking my other arm back, I move to strike when another arm appears, halting mine before it connects. "We don't hit our guests, Lola," Alton tsks, looking at me with disappointment. "Especially one that is family."

"Family?" I'm ignoring the other comment; it's hypocritical and a bait. He's looking for a fight. "Your conquests are nothing to me."

"Brittany is my fiancée, and you will respect her."

"Goes both ways."

"Don't push me, kid. Know your place and shut your mouth." Taking a step closer, he bends a bit at the waist, putting his face a hair's breadth from mine. "Better yet, I need you to talk. You need to answer a few questions for me."

"Tell that to your—" His hand wraps around my throat, silencing me. Alton's grip is tight, nothing like the pleasurable one of Malcolm's, and I'm panicking. My body thrashes against his, and I claw at his hand in desperation, something that amuses him by the grin on his face.

"Don't get brave, little girl. This is my house, and I own you," he spits out, pushing me backwards. There's a step behind me and I tumble, the edge of the second and third landing digging into my back while the room grows quiet.

This is a first, and it shocks more than it hurts. I'm angry, my body visibly shaking as he towers over me with the smug rat he calls a fiancée smirking.

"I won't tell you again." Alton spits out, his hand coming down to cup my cheek, but before he can, I pull back. Stand up before he tries to touch me again, ignoring the shooting pain traveling up my backside. "We need to talk, London. Now."

"Not interested. Good night." Turning, I give him my back and place my foot on the next step.

"We aren't done," he thunders, while his girl laughs as if this is the funniest things she's ever seen. Makes me wonder if she's high herself.

"I am." Another step. If I can take two more up without him following, it'll give me the space I need to sprint up. However, his next words stop me in my tracks and a whooshing breath leaves me.

"How the fuck does Malcolm Asher know who you are?"

"I—"

"Answer me, Lola. Are you fucking me over with him?"

"Please, as if a man like that would ever look at her," Brittany interjects, venom coating each word. There's a hint of jealousy there that I just don't understand.

For exactly thirty seconds I pray to come up with an answer that will save me. That he will believe.

It doesn't come, but the sound of a knock on the door makes everyone pause.

Chapter 14
MALCOLM

I'VE GOT HER. ~Mariah

Javier looks over at me, and I nod. He grabs his phone, sending a text to the car in front of us with three of my men awaiting orders.

I heard enough a few minutes ago to burn this entire house down with its occupants inside.

Fuck, do I want to end this shit. Kill every single one of them, but I need to handle things in a way that benefits Twirl. That takes back what has been stolen.

They are lucky that I now know what I do.

That my P.I. gave me new information corroborating what Earl said before I left for the club last night. Not fifteen minutes after reading, I found myself rushing to meet her while spitting out orders for my men to be here this morning. We were just a few minutes away, and two streets down waiting for Mariah, when things escalated.

Whoever put their hands on her will lose the use of said hand.

Even though the biggest infraction of all is mine by leaving her alone for the twenty minutes between her arrival and my cousin knocking on their door. Everyone was with me awaiting orders. No one watching her home.

Eyeing the folder on my dash, I take a deep breath and center myself while the girls leave the area.

What those papers prove is the only thing stopping me.

My wrath has no mercy when it comes to her, and those first few documents sent me into a blind rage. A fury I still feel pumping through me but had to rein in while with my girl.

Because she's just that. Mine.

The second I saw that innocent face and sinful body; I gave in to the desire she brought forth. This need to protect and devour. Break and hold together.

I will make her crave the darkness I control. Accept her own demons.

This house and the belongings inside, what's left of her mother and father's estate, belongs to London. Everything, and it's all she has left of them. She's the sole heir as per the will and testament, something that these two have lied about. Misused. Stolen.

And while memories carry people through grim times, the value of a physical reminder is priceless. I won't take that from my girl.

"Baby, who was that?" Alton's fiancée's voice carries through the small listening device Javier left behind on his visit. It's by the front door where this whore decided to stake her bullshit claim of hierarchy over my Twirl.

That's going to cost her. Them.

"What the fuck was his cousin doing here?" Marcus asks, a slight slur to his speech.

Without saying a word, I flick the headlights on and off. Within fifteen seconds five car doors open and each one disperses to a different area of the house.

One at the front.

One on each side.

And the one that walks with me as I enter the house through the unlocked back door. He'll wait for me there until I exit or give my second signal.

Their home is a nice two story with brickwork facia. It's over 3500 square-foot design has five bedrooms and three bathrooms with the smallest of all being London's. The back of the house is where the spacious kitchen resides, and it's filthy.

Empty beer cans litter every available countertop space and the overflowing garbage bin. The eat-in nook area has a few stacks of cash, an open bottle of prescription pills, and a blade beside it. There're plates in the sink, pots with something charred, and cigarette butts all over the floor.

It's disgusting, and if they expect for Twirl to clean this up, they have another thing coming.

Grabbing a barstool from behind the island, I place another listening bug underneath and then take a seat with my Glock on my lap. Right in the middle of the room, I wait while listening to them talk in the distance. Mumbling about her leaving and the state this house is in.

That they are hungry, and don't like my family close to her.

Marcus is the first one to enter and at the sight of me, he freezes. He doesn't fully step in, more like stops at the entrance and looks at me. Just stares.

Holding a finger up to my lips, I tell him to keep quiet.

The other two take their time to follow. They're kissing, stopping a few steps behind the father and their focus is on each other. On wandering hands and swapping spit.

They sicken me.

"What can I do to calm you down, baby?" Brittany croons, her hand moving down his chest. "Prove that this isn't a big deal. Malcolm Asher would never—"

"Can answer for himself," I interject, and their two heads snap my way. Marcus isn't moving, and his son and whore aren't very hospitable either. "Do come in."

"H-how did you get in?" Marcus asks, his eyes shifting around the room, looking for either an out or a way to defend himself.

"We've had this discussion before, Foster. Don't ask stupid questions."

"As you wish, Mr. Asher. Why are you here, then?" There's an expensive-looking knife set a few feet from him and he shifts, moves closer. I see the intent and on my next inhale, I raise my gun and release two bullets.

One blows away the knife set.

The other goes in and out through the old man's shoulder.

"Fuck," he yells out, staggering back while holding his arm. The sleeve of his light blue, unkempt dress shirt is quickly becoming saturated. Rivulets have become one large spot as blood runs down to his fingertips and pools on the floor below.

His wide eyes are on mine while I just raise a brow. "Be grateful this one missed my target."

"Oh my God!" the woman screeches, her tone grating on my eardrums and I am tempted to shoot her.

"Silence her." Alton doesn't move and I fire another shot, this one right by his head. This time they both flinch; an inch or two to the left and his earlobe would've been taken clean off. Or worse. Either would work for me. "That is my last warning."

"Brittany, go upstairs and lock—"

"Wrong. She doesn't leave." Bringing my other hand to my face, I scratch my jaw. I'm tired and in need of a shave, but that will all have to wait. There's a small field trip we will all be taking this morning before I can enjoy the rest of my day.

"I have nothing to do with this," she whimpers a second before Alton smacks his hand across her mouth, silencing her. He leaves it there for good measure while pulling her by the waist closer to his body. Tears run down her cheeks, leaving tracks of her mascara and liner in their wake, and I don't feel sorry for her. Not one bit.

Brittany looks pathetic and weak, just like Alton wants her to be. A whore for his pleasure, while London evades his every move. She's aware but doesn't have a lick of remorse. She's here for the money.

The lifestyle.

"Oh, but you do." With that, I stand and head to the door. Opening it, I stop at the threshold and look back over my shoulder at the three idiots. "You have thirty minutes to clean this shit up. All of it. If you are late a single minute, I will let one of my men collect a finger for each consecutive sixty-second period. Understood?"

"Malcolm, what—" At my glare, Alton swallows hard and nods, his eyes shifting between his injured father and me. "I apologize, Mr. Asher, but I have to ask…what's going on? Why are you here?"

"The clock is ticking. Hurry up, and you'll receive answers."

Twenty-nine minutes later, we're on our way across town toward the Washington Park area. The guests inside my car are semi-silent as I drive with Javier as my passenger; the Fosters are looking out the window while the woman cries, muffling her low whimpers with a hand over her mouth.

Not a word since Carmelo, my guy watching the back door, gave me the all good. The room was clean, and they were ready to leave.

Now, though, as I take the scenic route toward the self-storage units they use for business purposes, I find myself tensing. Full of this adrenaline—a demand from my body for retribution. There's this thirst for blood that I can only fight for so long as my muscles strain against my rigid composure.

The more I think about everything they've done, the angrier I become. The more my pulse rises, I feel a red haze fall over my senses. Every cell in my body thrums, and I flex my hands on the steering wheel as I park in the empty lot.

No one's here except for the owner, a man who for a few bucks sold me the three units full of merchandise: coke and electronics.

"Get out," I say and step out myself. The early morning sun feels good on my face, but you can already feel a small chill in the air. Autumn is slowly creeping in, and with it, the change in seasons can be drastic. From one spectrum to the other.

Without looking back, I walk toward the unlocked front door and open it. There's no one inside as per my request, and the office door is wide open so I can shut down their security feed myself. Not that I completely trust them, but I accept the gesture with as much good faith as I can muster.

Javier walks in behind me and takes charge of their system, turning the power off and also using a signal scrambler for added protection. What happens here will stay between those in attendance.

Leaving him at the front, I make my way toward the storage units with my men and the Fosters in tow. Theirs are in the row second to the back and on the left; the sole occupants of that space. Secluded and with minimal foot traffic.

However, more importantly, what greets me makes me smile.

Each one is open, and the merchandise inside being accounted for by other members of my staff. The heads of my auditing department have things in crates with the quantity, product name, and the street value already on a neatly written note.

"You can't do this," Alton thunders, his hands clenching at his sides while his girl and father just look. Mouths open and eyes wide, they watch as their investment—the buy-in being part of my girl's monthly stipend—is being confiscated, and the three million they were counting on making disappears. Her brother's face turns red

112

and his chest heaves with anger. "My business has nothing to do with yours, Asher. I don't owe you anything."

"That's where you're wrong."

"What the fuck—" Every man on my payroll pulls out a gun and points it at their heads, silencing his rant before it begins. He pales and shrinks bank, bumping into an annoyed Carmelo who shoves him off.

"Can I shoot him, boss?"

"Careful, Alton," I hiss, ignoring his request for now and take a step closer, and then another. I don't stop until I'm right in his face, hand snapping out to wrap around his neck. Similar to how he held London. "You're treading on thin ice as is."

"This is all a misunderstanding." His bullshit words fall on deaf ears. Alton thrashes and I tighten my hold, pressing on his trachea. Enjoy how with each breath his body fights to get free but can't.

"Be grateful that I'm starting off slow. That retribution will come in steps." The longer I hold him, the weaker he becomes, and when his knees buckle, I push him back toward Carmelo. "Help him find his footing."

"Please stop," Brittany whimpers, face splotchy and nose running. "Can we all just stop and talk about this. I'm sure that—"

"Why?" Marcus cuts her off then, finding his voice, his tone is low, but it carries a hint of rage. His eyes stray toward his son. You can see that he's full of worry, but the man is smart enough not to move. He doesn't even try to comfort the fiancée who looks close to passing out.

"*Why, he asks?*" Looking toward this hall's entrance, I nod at Javier and not ten seconds pass when the entire place goes pitch black. The woman screams, and a few muted thuds follow.

The sound of bodies hitting the floor.

In my head, I count to sixty and then clap once. The sound is loud, reverberates around the large space and bounces off the metal doors. A click is heard, the kind of noise that comes from the flipping of an electrical breaker, and then section by section comes back on.

A smile crosses my lips at the sight that greets me. Three people are on the floor, kneeling a few feet apart. Two males and one female; each one has a guard.

She's crying.

Alton is fighting to regain his composure.

Marcus is holding his arm tight to his chest as the wound once again seeps blood. My eyes shift to the guard standing behind him and zero in on the red-stained skin of his thumb. I don't say anything, but my smirk gives away to my pleasure.

From the corner of my eye, I see Javier hold out five fingers letting me know how much time I have left. Other guests are due to arrive soon, and there are a few things to discuss before then.

The Fosters' first locker has a chair inside, and I grab it. Place it in front of Alton. "Look at me," I say, and with the tip of my shoe push his face up. You can see the anger boiling within—feel his hatred of me. "Keep them here and pay very close attention. Do you understand?"

"I do."

"Good." With a swiftness he isn't expecting, I pull out my knife from a small holster on my ankle and slide the smooth steel across his cheek. Press just deep enough to leave a superficial wound from his cheekbone to the corner of his bottom lip. Blood seeps to the surface and a few drops glide down his face. "Don't ever fuck with what's mine again."

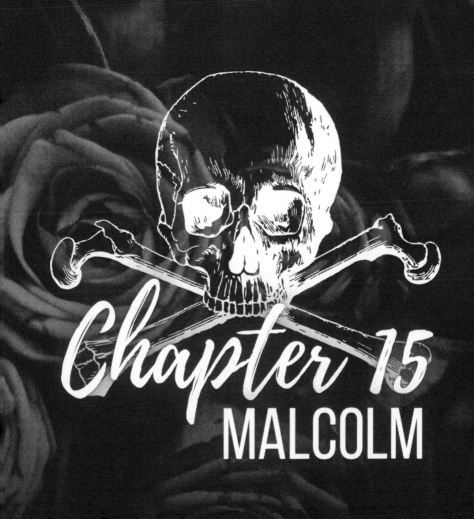

Chapter 15
MALCOLM

"BUT I HAVEN'T DONE—"

My hand across his cheek, the same one I just cut, silences him. "Speak when spoken to, not before." Gathering some of the red on his cheek with the tip of the blade, I rub it into his skin, letting the sharp edge scratch at the cut. "We had this same discussion a week ago, and yet here we are. Going over the same bullshit. Wasting my time."

Javier comes over then to drop a folder with both information and a set of pictures in front of him. Every single one has a date and time stamp on them. They show a blatant disrespect for my personal belongings.

I sit back, crossing my arms over my chest. "Go on. Look at them."

Alton does as I tell him, picking up the paperwork first with shaky hands. He flips through each page, face pale and head shaking back and forth. "No. No!"

Those papers hold the transcript of a conversation he had three nights ago with a buddy of his and mine. Someone I use from time to time to deliver verbal messages to clients in the business of importing drugs into the US. To Alton's bad luck, this man owes me a favor after I took care of his mother's hospital bills, and he recorded their talk.

A call where London's *brother* asks him to help him both rob and kill me, the latter by cutting the brake line to one of my vehicles. More than likely, the SUV my driver uses.

"Yes. Now, pick up those pictures."

"Mr. Asher, you have to believe me. This is all a lie. I don't understand why I'm being framed or…" His father's scream of pain cuts him off, and he looks over to see my guy dig two fingers into the wound this time. Marcus is sweating, shaking as the shock of pain ripples through his body.

"Pick up the photos."

"Please, son," he begs right before another scream rips from his throat. More blood. More pain. His father's body trembles as the finger imbedded into his flesh is taken out, and staying on his knees is no longer an option. Marcus falls forward, the cold cement cushioning his fall as he lies in a fetal position.

"Please, Asher. No more."

"Listen to your father, Alton. Look. At. Them."

Trembling fingers drop the papers in hand and pick up the photographic proof of his idiocy.

There's ten of them in total, and each show different moments

116

within the last few weeks where he stuck his nose where it didn't belong. Where he made a move to inconvenience me.

The first few are nothing special, except for the third, which shows him paying off Phillip. How they stupidly made this transaction while standing outside of my building in the middle of the financial district two weeks before his death. Three in the morning and within the shot of my security cameras when no one is around to question them.

Which also begs the question of where my men on the clock were?

A large metal door at the end of this hallway opens and closes with a loud bang. A group of people enter, two with hoods on their heads, but my eyes are on the man at the center.

"Good morning," I say, standing up to greet my guest with my hand out toward him. He's the main victim in the giant mess of a hindrance. "How are you, my friend?"

"Could be better, mate." Casper Jameson grips my hand tight before pulling me into a hug. "Bloody traffic here always gets me in a mood."

"You're a native, Casper. You should be used to it by now."

"Semi native, thank you very much." He's the only person I know whose accent is a crazy mix of British with hints of Chicagoan. His family and their operations are run out of the UK with connections all across Europe and the east coast of the United States. Guns, marijuana, and cocaine are his favorite poisons, and I am the magician that makes all profits look legal.

Strip clubs.

Laundromats.

Car washes.

All businesses that deposit quantities in cash day in and out.

This last run should've been simple. It wasn't, and I now need to make reparations.

"Four months a year is enough to qualify."

"Fuck you, and never." He laughs, slapping my back. Others

around us chuckle, but just as soon it all dies down. "Now, how are we going to fix this, Malcolm? Cause we have a lot of money being held up by—"

"I have it all," I interrupt, and he raises a brow, his questioning gaze set on mine. "Before the feds got ahold of it or put a pause on the transaction, I froze everything. Moved the capital offshore, and my guys did what they needed to do to make everything disappear."

"So we're good, then?"

"No. Not in the least." Tilting my head toward Alton and his father, I sneer. "We won't be okay until I make an example out of this asshole and his family."

"Who are they?"

"The orchestrators." At once he pulls his gun out and points it at Alton, but before he shoots, I push his hand down. "They are mine, Casper. All three."

"Then why tell me, arsehole?" he hisses, nostrils flaring. "This delay is costing me a shipment coming in tomorrow night. With the heat on my operations, the weapons supplier isn't feeling comfortable."

"Because I want them to watch you leave this warehouse with every single *ounce* of their merch." That's when he sees the bricks wrapped in plastic; barrels upon barrels of Columbian pure snow. "The coke and electronics are yours to do with as you please. Dump them in the river for all I care, but they won't make a fucking cent in profit."

"Apology accepted, bloke." Walking over to one of the containers, he pulls out a small knife from his jeans and rips a brick open. With the tips of the blade he takes a small amount and tastes it. Nods to himself in approval. "I'll take it all."

"Done." Looking at a very quiet Alton, I smirk. "Load it up. Three trucks are outside waiting, and Casper's men will drive them away."

"Understood." Javier whistles and within minutes, everything is gone. As if it was never here.

"Thank you, Malcolm. I know my business is always safe with you…"

"But?"

Casper looks pensive as he walks back to me, his eyes shifting between the men with hoods and the three on the floor. "How will we make sure this never happens again?"

"Like this." Carmelo comes forward then, a box in his hands. "Go on. Open it."

"If it's a bloody snake, you arse, I'll shoot you."

"Open it." I laugh, knowing how much of a pussy he is when it comes to reptiles. Goes to show that no matter how dangerous or big you are, everyone has a weakness.

He does, and then looks at me. "What the pissing hell is this?"

"Two tongues. One for each man that played a part in this."

"Michael?"

"Knows to never betray his family again. Losing his was his penance."

"He's family…no?"

"Then he should know better. They all do now."

"And the other?"

"Belonged to Phillip Mitchell. A low-level criminal that he…" I point at Alton "…paid to try and extort me. His idiocy cost him his life."

"Thank you." He tosses the box toward a still-crying Brittany who scrambles back with a shriek when they land a few feet from her leg. "When can we continue with the transaction? Will it be while I'm still here?"

"Give me three weeks to make some moves."

"Done." Casper extends a hand for me to shake. "I'll be heading out, mate…I'm hungry and need to make another pit stop before heading home."

"Of course, but before you go…" Javier lowers the hood from the two men and stands back while I pull out my gun and fire two shots. One in the neck and the other in the chest. The men fall to the ground and no one moves; all eyes are on me. "They weren't very vigilant during their shifts and let people make illegal deals on my property. For that they paid the ultimate price."

I still have one more rat to deal with…

"What's fair is fair." He turns to leave, but before he does, I speak again, halting him mid-step.

"There's a simple request that I want witnesses for."

"Of course, brother," Casper says with a nod, turning back to fully face me.

With my eyes set on Alton's, I walk over and pick up the last two photos in the bunch I gave him. It's of my Twirl. In the first, she's smiling wide while looking up at the sky with her eyes closed. However, the second is of her inside Mariah's car where she fell asleep. The one my cousin sent me seconds after I walked out of their home so they could clean.

Her neck is red, fingerprint marks visible across her sensitive skin.

Skin that should only bear my marks. Only my teeth and fingertips marring her flesh as I enjoy her body.

He looks down at them and then back up to me. He's catching on. My message is clear, but just in case, I crouch down to his level and meet his hard stare. "If you ever lay a finger on her again…" I grab his, the one with the dislocated knuckle, and hold it against the cold concrete. With the butt of my gun, I slam down on the bone. Four solid blows and there's a crack; I'll give him credit for holding his scream in. "Touch her— fuck with her—and I will dispose of you a small cut at a time. Filet your flesh and then feed it to your dear old father while you watch. It'll be a slow death. Agonizing. One that I will take immense joy in, Foster."

"I love my sister," he chokes out as I slam the gun down once more. I don't buy the concern.

He wants her under his thumb. To control. To use her as he pleases.

Over my dead body. "As of today, she's mine. I'll be taking her, moving her in with me as part of my payment."

"My daughter is innocent...please don't do this, Mr. Asher."

"Save the fake concern, Marcus. You're just upset I'm removing the cash cow from within your grasp." Standing up, I take a few steps back, ignoring his shocked gasp, and right my clothes—wipe my hands on the wet towel Javier hands over. "It's a done deal. Come near her...hurt her again...and what happened today will seem like a happy memory." Flicking my eyes to my men, I give them a nod. "Get them up and out of here. Clean it, and then close shop. For today we are done, and I have somewhere to be."

"Are you really letting us go?" Brittany asks, voice low.

"Because you're a woman, I've been extremely nice to you. Don't push it, Brittany...because a piece of shit like you doesn't deserve to breathe the same air as her." With that I walk out with Casper, and after agreeing to meet sometime during the week, I get into my car. They can handle everything from here; I need to get home. Need my own reward.

Chapter 16
MALCOLM

"**S**HE'S UPSTAIRS SLEEPING," Mariah says from her seat at the breakfast nook inside my kitchen. She brought her here at my request. To my house outside of the city. To rest. To relax so I could attend to her. "Poor thing is exhausted. Her neck and arms, Malcolm…fuck…tell me you broke theirs?"

"One has a bullet hole in the shoulder, while the other has a mangled hand. Will be quite useless from now on." Walking over to the counter, I drop my keys and phone after shutting the latter off, something she notices and raises a brow. "No interruptions until Monday morning after eleven. The meeting with Jameson was held today, instead, and the one with Benjamin from accounting needs to be pushed back until one."

"Anything else, *sir*."

"Is Magda here?"

She snorts, the sound so unattractive. "I already gave her a paid weekend off. Give me some credit here."

"Then no. Not a damn thing other than you leaving." *Not until after I speak with London about moving in.*

"I love you too, grouchy. Consider it done." Picking up her coffee cup, she walks to the sink and leaves it inside. "I'm happy for you, cousin. Enjoy the time off and be good to her."

"I will be." Leaning back against the counter, I wipe a tired hand down my face. "We both can use some rest after I shower. Unfortunately, I'm wearing some of their sweat and blood. It was profuse."

"Better than Michael who peed himself inside of Carmelo's jeep. Idiot thought they were taking him out to kill him," she says with a laugh, walking past me while her hand shoots out and connects with my arm. "Is Javi outside? Because I don't feel like driving."

"Brat." It's my mature reply before I pick her up and carry her toward the front door. A quick press of two fingers on the push release, a kick with my foot, and the door opens.

"Put me down, jerk! I'll call aunt—"

"There you go." Literally deposit her outside. "And to answer your earlier question, when isn't Javier waiting for you?"

"Touché." Her smile is beaming.

"Goodbye."

"Be patient."

"You have ten seconds to leave my property before I—"

"I got her, man. Go get some rest...it's been a long morning." Javier takes over and throws his personal headache over his shoulder. He strides off my front porch with her cursing our names while wearing a smirk—the woman is certifiable and I love her, but right now, I want everyone gone.

Slamming the door shut, I toe off my shoes and then slip the shirt over my head. My pants drop next, and I pick everything up while making my way upstairs and toward a special laundry chute. One that leads to a small incinerator inside my basement which deals with these kinds of messes.

The moment I open the small door behind a painting, everything whirls to life and heat sweeps across my face a minute later. Ten minutes and all is gone. Mere ashes that no one can decipher.

I am left in nothing but a pair of grey boxer briefs in the middle of the hallway when I close the latch and the machine turns off. My sole focus now is finding Twirl and wrapping myself around her. Enjoy every single second of peace we have together before I flip her world once again.

But first, I need a shower.

SHE'S THE SWEETEST VISION. Perfection in its purest form.

Twirl's laying in the middle of my bed when I enter the room twenty minutes later fresh out of the shower. She's cuddling my pillow, hair fanning out like a halo around her while a few drops of water roll down my chest from my still somewhat wet hair.

The towel in my hand doesn't bother to stop a single one as I focus on her.

How soft she looks.

How warm she must be.

How perfect she's going to feel against my body when I finally take her.

It's been a long twenty-four hours, and while I'm bone-deep exhausted, my cock still throbs beneath my sweats at the sight of her. Find her utterly delicious while her plump lips part and she tightens her hold on the pillow, choking the fluffy material.

"Need Malcolm. Stay," she sighs in her sleep, shifting her arm.

I've never wanted to be the victim of a headlock more in my life.

"How can she be so sinfully sweet?" I ask myself, shaking my head as I drop the towel and fully enter the room. The door closes behind me and I press a button beside it that darkens my windows another few shades.

However, I can still make out the feminine curve of her hip as she shifts onto her side. London is sinuous. Decadent. And the closer to her I get, my body comes alive.

I feel her all around me. Her soft floral scent fills every single inch of this room, while the sight of her here, in my room, my house, fills me with warmth.

She brings out emotions in me that make no sense. That I've never thought to experience. Didn't care to because the women around me were all after two things: my cock and money.

The notoriety that came from having my name attached to theirs, something Twirl doesn't care about. I truly doubt she knows who I am or what I own.

She's refreshing. Sweet.

I always want her close.

My last relationship was a disaster waiting to happen.

A slap in the face. A lie.

And at the end, when I put an end to us, I didn't feel anything. I didn't love her. Never did.

Love: a word that didn't fit my life outside of family members. Those that hold blood ties to me, and yet, no one brings out in me what London does.

With her, I crave a bit of tenderness. To fuck her raw and then cuddle her close.

Somehow, she's broken down walls made out of reinforced steel, getting under my skin.

Placing a knee on the bed, I climb up, careful not to shift too much and wake her. The mattress distributes my weight as I lower myself beside her, slipping beneath the comforter to move closer.

Even the simple set of pajamas Mariah put her in feel sinful.

Her body heat sears me in the most delicious of ways. Slowly, and even though I should wake her—let her know she's with me, I wrap an arm around her midsection instead and pull her closer. The second her back meets my chest; I feel the tension drain from me. My entire being sags into the mattress while my lips press a soft kiss to the back of her neck.

This is enough for now. Just holding her and knowing she's safe is enough.

London startles at the move, shooting up from the bed while trying to remove my arm from around her. "Don't touch me, Alton," she whimpers, and my heart breaks. My entire being freezes as her fear rocks the both of us.

She needs me. Those words are the sole reason I stay in this bed instead of heading out once more to hunt her pig of a brother down. To dismember her father.

"Twirl, it's me," I croon low, flipping her onto her back so she can see my face. However, her eyes remain closed as a tear slips down her cheek. Her bottom lip trembles. "Please, open those gorgeous blues and look at me."

"Malcolm?"

"I'm here."

Her small body stills and after a few deep breaths, she meets my stare. A heavy sigh—relief settles in as she realizes that she's not at home. That she's safe. "How?"

"You okay now, sweetheart?"

She nods, but then her brows furrow. "What are you doing here?"

"What's the last thing you remember?" Keeping my tone soft, I lay beside her but keep an arm around her midsection. Nothing inappropriate, just letting her feel me. Get used to my touch.

"Telling Alton I was heading to bed after he..." Trailing off, Twirl brings a hand up to touch her neck—grimacing at the tender flesh there. That's also when I see the angry lines down her arm, the hint of blood near the edge of broken skin.

My eyes move back to hers. If I see those marks again... "What did he do?"

"I don't want to talk about that." She shakes her head, eyes pleading me to drop it. London opens her mouth a few times and then closes it while her eyes survey the room. "How did you know where I…did Mariah call you? Because she appeared out of thin air, telling everyone we had an appointment with a designer that I never agreed to. She all but pushed me into the shower, gave me fifteen minutes to change, and I don't remember much after that."

Her rambling is adorable.

"That was all me." With my forefinger, I run soothing circles over her stomach. "I sent her."

"Why?"

"Because I don't trust those assholes, and I was right." I'm not telling her about the small listening device or the men that have been watching. Not yet. Because there is a small part of me that needs to deal with the guilt I feel for being late. "Wish she would've gotten there sooner. That I drove you home instead of letting you go alone after breakfast. I'm sorry."

"This isn't your fault." Turning to face me on her side, she cups my jaw while her thumb sweeps across my skin. "None of this falls on you. Please believe me."

"But it does." Nuzzling her palm, I turn my face and kiss the center. "You can't change my mind on that."

"Agree to disagree for now…" she shrugs "…I guess."

"You're cute."

"You're handsome," she counters, and a ghost of a smile curls up at the corner of her mouth. "Still doesn't explain why I have a half-naked man trying to seduce me? Or how you got into my room without me hearing you."

"Afraid I'm going to bite?"

"Not one bit, but that doesn't answer the question."

"Through the door for that last part." I let out a low chuckle at her glare. Can't help myself and I lean forward to nip her chin. "And for your information, this is my home. I told her to bring you here. To me."

"Why?" Her body stiffens for a second, head shaking. "I'm not ready to have sex," she blurts out, "It's too soon and contrary to what happened last night I'm—"

"We need sleep, London." Pressing my forehead to hers, I stare into her eyes. Let her see the truth in my words. "I brought you here so we can rest without anyone interrupting. Just rest."

"Really?"

"Yes. Just sleep." I lay back to prove my point.

"Thank you." Two simple words, but they hold so much weight behind them. So much gratitude as she settles once more, and of her own accord moves closer, settling next to me with her head on my chest. She melts into my gentle touch, each stroke of my fingers up and down her side, soothing figure eights that soon have her closing her eyes, a serene look on her face. "Can we talk some more later?"

"Anything you want."

"A girl can get used to this."

Kissing the crown of her head, I let my own eyes close. "Sleep now, Twirl. I've got you."

That's my last thought as sleep takes me under; *I've got you.*

I'm never letting her go.

Chapter 17
LONDON

FIVE YEARS AGO...

"YOU'VE GROWN UP so fast, Lola," Mom says out of nowhere, startling me.

"Quit sneaking up on me, old woman!" I shriek, a high-pitched sound that only teenage girls can reach, and it makes her laugh. Me, not so much as my heart tries to beat right out of my chest. "Or do I need to buy you one of those bracelets with the tinkling charms? Maybe a cowbell?"

"Brat." Still smiling, she shakes her head. Yet those blue eyes continue to appraise me.

"You suck." Moving away from the vanity, I grab my phone and close it before she sees the beauty website I'm looking at. Or worse, reads the article giving advice on something she has no business knowing.

"And you're spending far too many hours looking at yourself in the mirror, young lady. What gives?" Walking inside, she follows me until we reach my bed. Sits next to me when I refuse to answer. "Something you want to tell me?"

"Not really. Nope." That's my first mistake. You never answer too quickly. "Everything is fine, I swear. Was just looking at a new braiding technique I want to try out."

"Cool…" Mom sweeps her long brown curls over her right shoulder "…let me see. I'm always looking for ideas."

She's not buying it.

Crap.

Double crap.

"How about we do this later? I'm supposed to meet Kristine—"

"What's his name and age, London."

"What are you talking about?" Avoidance is key in this situation. Last thing I need is for her to tell Dad, who will tell Alton, and then I am left to deal with his wrath. He hates all of my friends—forbids me from ever dating anyone. "It's just a simple hairstyle."

Mom purses her lips. "And I was born yesterday."

"More like a hundred years, but…"

"Funny." Wrapping her arm around my shoulders, she pulls us back so we're lying down with our legs over the edge of the mattress. For a few minutes we stay silent, just looking up toward the ceiling, when she lets out a long and tired sigh. "I've let that crap with your brother go on for far too long. I've always chalked up your bickering to sibling antics and paid no mind because once he got older, his attention would shift. Marcus says it's nothing when I bring it up, that with age he'll stop picking on you, but you're hiding things from me because you're worried—"

"I'm not, Mom. I swear."

"Then tell me what's going on? Why the sudden swoony smiles when you get a text or—"

"His name is Santiago, and he moved here from Spain a month ago," I whisper while my face heats up, eyes refusing to meet hers. "He's cute and all the girls are crushing hard. We've never spoken until last week when he invited me to sit with him at lunch. That's it."

"And..."

Turning my head, I scrunch up my nose. "And what? Not following."

"Child, I swear to God." Mom mutters something under her breath that I don't hear before grabbing my hand and giving it a squeeze. "Did you have lunch with him or not?"

"Once. Yeah."

"Did you have fun?"

"He's pretty awesome."

"Then that's all that matters," she deadpans; the look she's giving me all knowing. Aware of my worry when it comes to Dad saying I'm too young to date and Alton being an even bigger jerk. "One day, baby, a man is going to come into your life and sweep you off your feet. He will become the center of your world, as you will be his. Don't hold back because of fear or what someone will say. When that moment comes, years from now, you promise me to hold onto it with both hands and never let go. Savor each moment you have together because tomorrow is never promised."

"Mom, I'm only fifteen and it was just lunch. Not that serious."

"I'm not talking about today, Lola. But one day it will happen... trust me."

PRESENT

"...HOLD onto it with both hands and never let go. Savor each moment you have together because tomorrow is never promised."

I awake with a start, but don't move. Her words come back, and I can't help but question if this is what she was talking about. Is Malcolm my person?

However, that question will have to wait since I notice something else...

There's a weight against my back, yet it's not crushing.

A warmth surrounding me, yet it's comforting.

I've never slept so at peace. Happily. Completely letting my guard down with not a single bit of fear over what could happen when my defenses are down. No one here is going to harm me.

I know this, Malcolm showing me as much with every single one of his actions.

His respect for me. For not taking advantage of me.

For once, that little voice deep inside that always warns and keeps me alert is silent. Resting. Free.

"Feel so good," his sleep-roughened voice murmurs, arm pulling me tighter to his chest. I don't know how long we've been like this, but the proof that we haven't moved much is in the position we still lie in—my back to his front with his arm beneath my head. "How are you feeling?"

"I'm good." More than, and I almost say this when a human need presents itself. My bladder is full and unwilling to wait, so I push his arm up and squirm to the edge of the bed, when he tugs me back.

"Where do you think you're going?"

"Bathroom," I say, turning to look at him from over my shoulder. "Point me in the direction, and I'll be back in three minutes."

"Can I count you down?" Another tug and I'm face to face, lips an inch apart at the most. "Do I win something if you take longer than that? I think I should."

"Aren't you playful in the...what time is it?" The way he stares at me causes my face to heat up.

"Who cares, and only with you." His lips ghost mine, soft little pecks that melt me in place. "The door right across from us and hurry up. I'll make us something to eat."

"You can cook?" This surprises me, and it also doesn't stop me from stealing one more kiss before I pull back and slide off the bed. I don't pause to look back at him until I am on my feet and a few inches away, out of reach. "Or are you going to ask Magda to whip something up while you take the credit."

"Being sassy looks good on you." Malcolm scratches his bare chest, a move I follow. "Eyes up here, sweetheart."

"That's my line." Where these bold replies are coming from, I have no clue, but I like how freeing it is to be around him. How I don't feel like I have to walk on eggshells around him.

Malcolm is powerful, and yet I am not intimidated. Never have been.

With me he is different, and I like it.

"First of all, the bathroom is right behind you," he drawls, eyes roaming my body and pausing at the two hard tips I'm trying to ignore. The second I slid off his bed, I realized that my thin lace bra hid nothing. That the cool air over my skin while a hot guy—*he* looks at me—is a very bad combination for my modesty. "And second, Magda has the rest of the weekend off. It's just us here and I want to keep it that way."

"Just us?"

He sits up, abs tensing as he holds himself up with one hand. "Problem with that, Twirl?"

I swallow hard. "No. None at the moment."

"Good." Malcolm scratches his jaw. Same jaw that has the most mouthwatering five o'clock shadow I've ever seen on a man. It makes me want to lick him. "Now hurry up before I pick you up and steal a sample of the sweetness between your thighs."

Those words don't register at first, but when they do, I turn around and all but run into the bathroom. Lock the door as his laughter follows me inside and my cheeks heat up. It's not the first time he's implied this. Making me his.

Voicing what I know he wants, and I'll be the biggest hypocrite if I deny wanting it too.

Because I do. I want more. So much more.

However, at the moment it isn't right. There's something I want from him first.

He's earning my trust.

"Girl, get it together," I whisper, looking at my expression in the mirror of his vanity. What I see staring back at me in the mirror is surprising; I'm smiling, and my eyes are bright—cheeks flushing because of his words and the truth behind them. Because for the first time in a long time, someone cares.

I'm not one hundred percent ready, but the same want is there chipping away at my fear.

With him, I'm not afraid or focusing on the finger-size purplish marks my brothers left on my skin. I'm not obsessing over the way Alton let Brittany treat me—the broken skin she left behind when she dug her nails into my skin. Malcolm doesn't feel like the stranger he is for all intents and purposes, and while the man isn't shy about voicing his wants, his actions are showing me he also cares.

It's because of him that Alton wasn't able to do more damage.

He's making me want to stay.

Shaking the thought from my mind and the dangerous road it will travel down, I begin to disrobe, dropping the pajama set Mariah shoved into my hands as soon as I set foot inside this home. They were new, with a tag, and in my size. Made me suspicious, but exhaustion made me compliant and I changed out of my clothes.

The light blue romper set with flowers and my tan sandals are somewhere in his room. At least, I hope, because his wall-to-wall shower looks so inviting and I plan to relax for a few minutes inside.

The bathroom is spacious and white. Every surface, even the décor is white—expensive, with subway tiles throughout and a very spacious custom claw-foot tub.

It's modern and clean. Beautiful.

Too much for a single man.

Its showerhead system reminds me of the one Alton has in his shower at home. Not as fancy, and I know which knobs to turn. Three separate heads come to life at once, and the bathroom fills with steam pretty quickly.

It's an open concept with just a half wall of glass at the end where the water pours from, and I step inside. The hot water feels amazing on my tired body. A moan passes my lips when I turn around, giving the jets on the wall beside the nozzle my back. Tension drains, and yet there's a new kind of energy buzzing around me.

More so when I grab his shampoo to wash my hair. His scent, so masculine and all him, surrounds me. Embeds itself into each one of my pores as I wash off. Massage the lather into my hair and then let it run down my body; a gentle caress that only heightens my need to have his hands on me once more.

I want him to win me over.

Grabbing a bottle of conditioner from the same brand, I pour some into my hair and let it sit while I lather the rest of me. Touching myself inside his shower creates images of us. Where it isn't my hands but his, where he's whispering filthy things in my ear as I shatter in his arms.

The first swipe of a finger over my clit sends a shock wave of pleasure through my body so strong that my knees shake. Every muscle contracts, and on the second, I rub harder, tiny little circles over my trembling bundle as my walls pulsate and throb.

I'm so close, and I've barely touched myself.

This is all over him. His face and voice.

An image of him pushing me up against this very wall with a leg over his hip.

My fingers travel lower and to my opening. I'm wet, and it has nothing to do with the water pouring down my sensitive skin. Circling my entrance, I slip a single digit inside to the second knuckle.

"*Fuck*," I whimper, body almost shaking from the need to find a release. Slowly, I push my finger in and out of my tight hole. Four pumps, and then I push a little more, adding a second. Walls locking down, I press the palm of my hand against my clit and shatter. Come apart with a silent scream and panting breaths.

It's the most I've ever done sexually.

At home, I've never felt comfortable enough to explore. Always afraid of Alton finding me.

Or worse, wanting to touch me.

But here, I let go and as I slide to the cool tile floors, I find myself smiling. Body limp and at ease.

What this man does to me. What I know I'll let him do in the future causes another rush of pleasure to zip through me and I close my eyes—focus on my breathing when I hear his voice coming closer. Calling something out to someone five seconds before his hand knocks on the door.

"Did you finish, Twirl?"

"Yes," I manage to squeak out, and the door handle jiggles.

"Babe, can I come in?" There's a hint of amusement in his tone.

"I'll be out in a minute." Scrambling to my knees, I rinse the evidence of my private desires and shut the water off. "Give me ten…just need to get dressed—"

"I'll gift you twenty. Your outfit is on my bed."

"Okay." Grabbing a fluffy white towel, I wrap it around myself and open the door. "Can you pass me my clothes?"

His throat bobs harshly as he swallows. "I am completely fucked when it comes to you, and I'll never complain over it." Malcolm turns then and walks back to the door, almost crosses it when he pauses at the threshold to look me up and down once more from over his shoulder. "You are simply mouthwatering, sweetheart. Makes me hate my parents for interrupting the quiet morning I had planned for us. I don't want to share you with anyone, not even them."

"Your what?" His words make my heart beat fast and palms sweat, but his parents being downstairs is going to cause me to pass out. "Repeat, please."

"My parents, Ms. Foster. Hurry up..." he licks his bottom lip, eyes on my bare legs "...I want them to meet you and then leave. In and out. I don't think I can handle more than a thirty-minute visit right now."

Chapter 18
MALCOLM

W E'RE SITTING AT the breakfast nook area of my kitchen when she comes downstairs wearing her cute little outfit. It's short and flowy and she looks beautiful. My mouth waters as her hips shimmy with each tiny step closer.

Beside me, my parents are oblivious to her entry. They continue talking about a week-long trip to the Dominican Republic they've been wanting to make, that Mom almost has him ready to book. She wants my input—to agree with her—and I'm ready to offer them my jet if they leave now.

To get out so I can enjoy my time with London.

"Son, are you even…" Mom's words trail off, and I can only guess why. Twirl is standing beside me, her hand on my shoulder, squeezing, silently asking me to help her figure out what to do, but I won't. With me, she is fucking free to act as she wishes. To fit her own mold and not the preconceived bullshit someone else pushes on her.

Dad clears his throat then, a small smirk on his lips. "Want to introduce us, son? Cause if you don't, I can't be held responsible for your mother's next action."

That seems to snap my mother out of her gawking; she turns and smacks him in the arm. "Don't be an asshole, dear. First impressions matter."

"Yes, *sweets*." He winks at London, and it does the trick as a low giggle escapes her. "Much better. No need to be nervous around us."

"Sorry. I just wasn't—"

"We crashed your lazy afternoon. No apologies needed…" she waves her off, and then raises a sharp brow at me "…where are your manners? Name, Malcolm. Introduce us the correct way."

"This is London Foster." They know the name and what their greed almost cost the business. "This is new, and we're taking it slow."

"Is that so?" Dad's eyes meet mine, and the softness from a moment ago is now gone. There's only a reprimand and anger. At what? I have no clue, nor do I care.

"She has nothing to do with her asinine family's affairs," I hiss from between clenching teeth, hands in a fist. "Quite the opposite, really."

"Malcolm!" Mom yells out, eyes wide and bouncing between a now-stiff London and my father. "And really, Anthony? When have you known him to be anything but diligent."

"I'm sorry my family is an issue for you. They are for me too, and I'm working on moving away as we speak. Fearing for your life isn't fun, sir." My girl tries to take a few steps back, but I don't let her. If anyone leaves, it will be him. "Let go, Malcolm."

"No." This is her first lesson. An introduction into my world, and she will rise above it.

Fuck whoever points a finger. Even if it's someone in my family.

Since her mother died, all she's done is let others step on her. Manipulate and mistreat; it ends now.

My father has never been a saint and needs to remember that. Just because he's retired now, it doesn't mean that the sins of the past are now null and void. Much less would he be okay with anyone pinning those on my mother's head.

"I'm leaving, okay? This is just another reason why—"

"Stop. Breathe, sweetie." The words don't come from me, but my mother who is now standing beside London and giving her a hug. Her green eyes, a few shades lighter than mine, glare at my father until the man shrinks back in his seat. "He's an old grouch that seems to have forgotten to take his anti-asshole medication this morning. If my son says you're one of the good ones, then that's all I need."

"What did he do now?" Mariah calls out, entering the kitchen with an amused Javier in tow. In his arms are two pastry boxes from a Ukrainian bakery in town. "I swear, lately you've been on a roll, old man. First with Dad yesterday, and now London. *Tsk, tsk.*"

I'm not going to question why everyone's here, although I know it's my cousin's idea. She wants them all to meet. To see me falling for a slip of a girl with more honor and pride than anyone I've ever met before.

"Why am I being ganged up on?" Every eye in the room except London's turn to look at him. His indignation almost makes me laugh. Almost, because if she leaves, father or not, I'll kick his ass. "I did nothing wrong. Wanting an explanation isn't a federal crime; I'm on her side here. If I'm looking at anyone with questions, it's my son. Doesn't anyone else see the issue here? The bruising and deep scratches?"

"Watch it." Narrowing my eyes, I lean forward in my seat. "I've never hit a woman, much less hurt someone important to me. Don't criticize what you don't know when you have no right. You have no moral high ground to stand on."

"Why else would she be here?"

"What the hell is that supposed to mean?"

"Welcome to the family, London." Mariah pulls her from my mother's hold, shaking her head while navigating an in-shock Twirl out of the room. My mother, on the other hand, is glaring at my father and Javi remains quiet. He's used to our craziness. To the fights and loud voices.

They make it to the entrance before my girl stops abruptly. Watching her turn with fire in her eyes is thrilling. Makes my cock throb at the sight of her anger. "You know nothing about me, and yet you judge. You know your son, and yet don't trust his decision to have me here or his motives. Malcolm," she says, a dainty finger pointing straight at him, "has been nothing but kind to me when my own family hurts me. Respectful and even sweet within his own gruff personality. He's given me hope that I'll be more than okay."

"Anything else, *Dad*?" I sneer while my chest fills with pride at her words, her defensiveness making me feel like a motherfucking king. As much as I don't like seeing her uncomfortable, anything that awakens her passion—that tiny demon fighting to be set free—is a blessing.

No more hiding. No more fear.

"Yeah. Just one more thing." Anthony Asher stands from his seat and walks over to her, his gait slow and without aggression. When he reaches her, Mariah moves to step between them, but then moves to the side at the last second. Before London can flee, or I can lay his ass out, he's hugging her tight. Whispering something in her ear that only she can hear and then nods. When they pull back, she's smiling. "Hungry?"

"Kind of." She steps out of his embrace, kisses his cheek, and then walks back to me. No one speaks. No one even questions what he's doing. Instead, we watch as she takes her rightful place, standing beside me, and entwines our fingers together. Gives them a small squeeze that pulls the tension right from my body. "Can I help with anything?"

"No can do, Miss London. You're a guest." Javier smiles at her while placing the two boxes of pastries on the counter. "Sit and enjoy yourself."

"But, I can—"

"Hey." Turning her face to mine, I tip it up with my finger and lay my forehead on hers. Ignore everyone's looks while keeping my voice low so only she can hear. "Are you okay? If you want them gone, say the word and it's done."

Because even a murderer like me has family issues. Boring and mundane ones. Ones that make a member look like an asshole, but in the end it's swept under the rug because it comes from a good place. We'll never be angels, but we do care.

You fight and make up because you love them. Forgive and forget because those closest to you will do the same when you fuck up. Kill those that have done wrong toward them, and then come home to a mid-afternoon brunch or a late dinner with all the fixings.

This is my normal, the side of me I want her to see the most of.

Because money and blood take up a substantial portion, but they're not the entire pie. A life with me will be insane, dangerous, but will have moments like these to fill the void of normalcy even the most depraved need.

Even if Dad's behavior came at the worst time, I know it's not malicious. Not that I'm going to let this go. He has some explaining to do, but for now I'm shifting my focus back to her.

"It's fine. Promise."

"Swear it."

"Scout's honor." She holds a pinky up for me, those sweet lips curling up at the corner. Lips that I can't help but nip.

"Fine," I grunt against their plumpness, "but they get one hour before I kick them out regardless. Today is about me and you. You're not working this weekend..." *or ever again* "...Liam agrees that you need some time off and you will be paid by me."

"But," she splutters, not knowing how to answer.

"But nothing." Another bite. "Agree with me, Twirl. You know you want to."

"You're so stubborn."

"And?"

"Fine. One hour."

"One." Nodding, I pull back and direct her toward the seat next to mine. "Sit down, babe."

And just like that, it's back to normal. The late lunch my parents had catered is set on the table, chairs are brought close together, and everyone digs in. No one cares about the mini showdown or how much more comfortable we would be in the dining room.

We eat. Talk. And I enjoy the softness of her upper thigh underneath the table.

"Your family is not what I expected, but I like it…them," she says later in the evening, head on my thigh while we watch some poorly made horror flick. The kind that goes straight to DVD and only a sub-culture of people like. Everything is bad, mind numbingly so, but she loves it. Finds some of the "morbid" scenes funny. "Especially Javier. He's hilarious."

"He's a trip when we're together like that. At work he's a different person, so please don't get offended if he's ever short or serious. It's not personal. He just has to be as the head of my security."

"Is that his official title on paper?"

"It is."

"Hmmm." Twirl nods, mulling things over. "And what is it that you do, Mr. Asher?" Those big doe eyes watch me, lip caught between her teeth. She's looking for a lie that isn't going to come.

"I am the owner and CEO of Asher Holdings Bank here in Chicago. We're the second largest bank worldwide, with the one at

The Loop being our home base. We have financial centers all across the United States, Europe, and Asia who deal within four business groups: commercial, investment, wealth management, and private global banking."

"Wow."

I laugh. "It's boring, really."

"Sure, it is. Boring…" she rolls her eyes at me, reaching up to flick my lip "…my brother just loves to associate himself with the most monotonous people—those that have never so much as gotten a parking ticket are his peeps."

"You are something else, Twirl."

"And I need the truth. I'm not dumb."

"Then how about a tit for tat. I've shared something with you, and now it's your turn." Grabbing her finger, I bring it up to my lips and bite the tip, soothing the sting with my tongue. "Tell me something."

"Anything?" Her mock glare only makes my cock jerk.

"Anything."

"Okay. I'll play." She turns on her side to face me better, the low lighting in the room dancing across her soft features. It also accentuates the smattering of bruises on her neck, and it takes everything within me not to go after Alton again and break his. *Soon. Very soon.* "I've been a dancer for most of my life…" I open my mouth to say I know as much, but she makes a *zip it* motion "…talk and I stop."

"So bossy." Slowly, I stroke the marks on her neck with my thumb. Just gentle sweeps as to not distract her, but to soothe, and then lower to her arms where the deep scratches are red.

"Get used to it." *That mouth is going to earn her a few spankings in the future.* "As I was saying, Mom put me into ballet classes when I was around four, and I did well, stuck with it for a few years, but that kind of dancing wasn't my passion. I just went along with it until I stumbled, literally, into a lyrical class down the hall from mine. It changed everything for me. The way they moved, the graceful lines of their bodies as they told a story, was eye opening."

"How old were you then?"

"Almost twelve, and I nagged Mom to death until she gave in." Pain laces her every word.

"So, you are telling me ahead of time that you're a nagger?"

That did the trick; the sudden sadness in her eyes is gone as she smacks my chest. "Jerk."

"Never said I was a saint."

"I don't need this abuse. Maybe I should head...shit." London sits up suddenly, panicking, trying to right her clothes and smooth down her hair. "I need to go. Marcus and Alton are going to kill me."

"They can never touch a pretty little hair on your head again."

She pauses her frantic movements to look at me. "What does that mean?"

"You no longer live there, London," I say, pulling her back to sit beside me. "After what happened and the enemies they've gained, I can't let you live there any longer. Not when you're in danger and they will sell you to protect themselves."

"But where will I go? I have no one and—"

"You have me. My family." She lays her head on my shoulder, and I kiss the crown of it. "I'm here and not going anywhere. This is fast and sudden, but stay with me. You can have your own room if you want...just know that I expect nothing in return."

"That doesn't sound right at all. I know them, Malcom," she says instead. "Alton wouldn't allow it."

I shrug, and she looks up at me. "He gave in with no problem."

"You did something...didn't you?" Her tone isn't accusatory. If I'm reading her right, she just might be a tiny bit relieved to leave that hellhole. "Tell me."

"Broken hand and a gunshot wound."

"Funny, Malcolm. Real funny."

"More like well deserved, but okay."

"You're serious." Still no anger or worry; she just wants clarification.

"As a heart attack." I steal a quick kiss. "Another movie?"

"Why am I not bothered by this?" For some reason, *that* seems to bother her. The lack of emotion. Empathy when it comes to her abusers. "Does it make me a horrible person to be kind of happy about this?"

"Does it make me a monster for pulling the trigger or smashing the hand?"

"Not at all."

"Then fuck it." Grabbing the remote, I pass it to her. "How about that next movie…"

"In your bed? For some reason, I'm really tired." As if to prove her point, a deep and long yawn escapes her. Also don't miss how she chooses my bed over the others. "Whatcha say?"

I'm not the least bit surprised by her exhaustion. It's a lot to take in and she'll need time to process, which I'll give her. What I won't allow is for her to ever feel bad for them. Whatever lot they receive in life, it's well earned.

Instead of answering, I stand and sweep her off her feet. Pull her close to my chest while walking to the steps and up, and it's once I'm there that I remember something I wanted to ask earlier. "What did my father whisper in your ear in the kitchen? Did he apologize?"

Her head snaps up from its place at my neck, her smile cheeky. "Better than. He said, and I quote: *This one's going to keep you on your toes, kid…*" I almost laugh at how she deepens her voice to mimic his "*…I'll shoot him and anyone you ever need me to.*"

Chapter 19
MALCOLM

"WHY ARE YOU up so early?" London asks shyly from the entrance to my office. Sleep rumpled and in just my T-shirt, she looks delicious. Warm and soft. It's why I left the bed shortly after she fell asleep. Each sigh from her lips made me throb.

The remnants of pre-come on my pajamas is the proof of my desire for her tight little body.

I want to fuck this little doll. Break her.

But I want her desperate and ready for it. Begging me to.

And she will. That's why I'm not rushing it.

Instead, I savor every single piece of concrete that deteriorates from around her mental walls. Last night is evidence of that. How she turned toward me, body molding to mine with a leg thrown over my hip. How she asked to wear a shirt of mine instead of the sleep set that Mariah gave her.

Every single move she's made since realizing that this is my home has been with me in mind. Touching me. Sitting beside me. Even the food she served me when everyone else made their own plate was without conscious thought.

It's a natural instinct. That desire to take care of me, just like I'll always do for her.

And even though she hasn't said anything about moving in, I know she's staying.

"I had an email that needed my immediate attention." Also not a lie. However, what's inside that correspondence will have to wait. I have more important plans. "And it's not early, Twirl. It's twenty to twelve."

"Everything okay? Do you need me to…wait, it's almost noon?"

"No and yes?" I push my chair back and pat my lap.

Rolling her eyes, she takes her time walking around my desk and coming to a stop between my legs. Twirl leans back against the desk, her expression showing amusement. "That made no sense, Malcolm. Give me full sentences, please."

"Brat," I playfully growl at her, taking ahold of her hips and pulling her closer. Close enough that I can sit up and press my nose against her stomach. That I can wrap my arms around her and nip the skin above her belly button. "Yes, it's almost noon. And no, you aren't going anywhere."

"Okay." She rakes her fingers through my hair, and my eyes close. "So, what are the plans for today?"

"First, I want you to never stop doing that." It feels so good, soothing, and when she gives the strands a not-so-gentle tug, I almost fucking attack. The little shock of pain settles on my already hard cock, and I pulse. My entire being tenses while the minx giggles above me. "I'm tallying every single infraction for a later payment. Keep testing me, sweetheart."

This time, her blunt nails scratch my scalp. "Pay attention, Mr. Asher, and answer the question. Plans?"

"We have a date."

At that, she pauses. "Do we, now?"

I nod, nuzzling her abdomen while one of my hands skims down her thigh and then calf, only to follow the same path up. Two times I do this, each one stopping at the hem of my shirt. "The entire day is planned and set to begin after you have breakfast. I'm going to spoil you a tiny bit today."

"Do I get a say?" She's trying hard to sound put off, but I can hear the smile in her voice.

"You get to say *yes* and *thank you*." Propping my chin on her skin, I look up and catch London fighting back a grin. "Want to start now or when we get there?"

"Instead of being a jerk, why don't you feed me or point me in the direction of the kitchen? I got lost three times trying to find this room, and it's on the first floor."

"As you wish," I say, standing to my full height and pressing every inch of my body against hers. My fingers at her hips dig in and hoist her up, causing her to wrap those perfect thighs around me, bringing her core to rub against my cock with each new step I take out of my office and to the other side of the house.

Bright blue eyes look at me with a spark of desire I want to feed. Nurture.

I don't pause or fuck her against my walls like I want to. Instead, I bring her inside, place her atop my granite countertop, and step back. "I made waffles earlier and left them warming, but if you want something else, just say the word." My voice is gruff, a literal expression of how wound tight I am.

Feet dangling over the edge, she looks at me with wide eyes. "Waffles sound good." London licks her bottom lip, and I follow the move with hunger. With a throbbing cock.

"How many do you want?"

"How many are left?"

Parting her thighs, I step between them and her heat sears me through layers of clothing. It's taking every last ounce of strength to not push her shirt up and exposed her panty-covered cunt. "As many as you desire."

"Two will do for now." Her tone is breathy, and I also don't miss the way her chest expands with each deep inhale.

"Okay." Leaning forward, I nip her chin. "Coffee or juice?"

"Orange juice now and Starbucks later?"

"Absolutely." Taking a step back, I run my fingers down her thigh and to her knees. "I'm going to get your plate and step back into my office for a few minutes. You have two hours to eat, shower, and do whatever it is women do to get ready."

"But I have no—"

I quiet her with a finger over her lips. "Already taken care of. Everything you need is in a bag on my dresser. Trust me."

"Is THE BLINDFOLD REALLY NECESSARY?" she asks from beside me, mouth in a pout while I drive to our destination. It's been like this for the past twenty minutes, and I find myself enjoying her petulant act.

Because it is one. Showing just the barest hint of a smile when looking ahead.

Or when I answer with a playful grunt.

Something that a few weeks back would've annoyed me, I now find entertaining. The reactions she pulls from me are different, possessive, and full of contentment.

A balance I didn't have before.

"We have fifteen hours left in this trip," I say just to fuck with her and almost laugh when her head snaps in my direction. "Catch a nap, Twirl. It's going to be a while."

"You can't be serious?"

"And if I am?"

"The scary part is that I'd still want to go." There's so much heaviness in those words. Truth.

There's something between her and I that while I still don't understand completely, I can't deny, and neither can she. We fit. Work in a way that brings out the best in each other.

She brings equilibrium, while I give her confidence.

She calms me where I give her freedom.

I protect and offer a chance to reclaim her life.

She gives me her. A chance at an honest love.

"Why is it scary?" I ask, pulling into the parking space designated for special clientele. The place is somewhat empty now, only a few spots in use as people leave to beat traffic. Putting my Maserati in park, I take her small hand in mine and intertwine our fingers. "Do I scare you?"

At my words, the slight tightness around her mouth loosens. "Not at all. Why would you even think that?"

"Curiosity." Turning her face to mine, I slip the blindfold off and then wrap my hand at the nape of her neck. I bring her face closer to mine. "Because even at my worst, London, I will never hurt you. The world could burn to the ground and it wouldn't faze me, yet you— you I would kill for. Trust me."

She licks her lips, eyes on mine. "You say that a lot...*trust me*... and the thing is that a large part of me already does. More and more every day."

"Good." A rough exhale leaves me at her words, but there is one thing I need to make clear. "The only time I will ever break you is with my cock, and I'll make sure you love every single second. That you beg me for more."

"My being a virgin doesn't bother you?" she asks, stammering as her face turns pink with embarrassment, once again reminding me just how innocent she is.

"The opposite, really." Leaning over the center console, I kiss her. Part her soft lips with my tongue and steal the very breath from her lungs. "Knowing I will be your first and last is... *Jesus,* London, I feel like a conqueror acquiring the world's greatest treasure. You are my reward in this life, and I plan to keep you happy. You will never want another man, and it won't be based on threats or bullying, but because no one will ever treat you like I will."

The next kiss is more possessive than each before, giving her a glimpse of the animalistic hunger I'm keeping under a tight control for her.

Fingers flexing over the back of her neck, I tighten my hold and tilt her head. Angle her to my liking and kiss her like I haven't before. No control or slowing down, I want London to accept this part of me and yearn for it.

To know that while she is my equal in our day to day, in bed I will own her. Will possess her with each touch.

And then, when I feel her body tremble, I let her go.

Releasing my hold, I sit back and watch her squirm for me. Take in a few deep breaths while gathering her composure, but I see the effect.

The outfit I bought for her is simple and comfortable, but at the same time hides very little from me. A pair of black yoga pants that molds onto her every dip and curve, a white tank top with a matching lace bra that shows how hard her nipples are, and a pair of low UGG boots to keep her feet warm.

It's not cold outside, not the near freezing temps we're used to, but the evening air still has a small bite to it. Enough that I gave her an old hoodie of mine to use if she needs it.

One that has my name on the back. A gift from my mother I never put to use, but now I appreciate.

"Wow," she whispers low, almost to herself.

"You're perfect." My eyes flicker to those kiss-swollen lips and then to the time on my dashboard. "However, if we don't stop right now, I'm taking us back home and locking the door."

"What?"

"We're here." Turning the car off, I get out without replying,

SIN

adjust my cock, and walk around to her side opening the door. "Come along, Miss London Foster. We have a date to begin."

Twirl puts her hand in mine, letting me pull her out. She stands a few inches from me. Looking at me. "It's getting harder and harder to pull back from you, Malcolm Asher. Very hard."

"I've never had a choice when it comes to you." A click of my fob and then I find myself walking with her hand in mine. We make it just outside the parking area when she stops, finally realizing just where we are. "You okay?"

Her mouth is gaping, and her eyes show excitement. "Oh my God! Which one are we doing?"

"Both."

"You brought me to the Planetarium and the Aquarium. Malcolm..." my name is a sigh on her lips "...you're killing me. I never stood a chance."

"Does this mean you approve?"

"This means... *I love it.*" And this time, she controls me with her lips.

Chapter 20
LONDON

THERE ARE A FEW moments in your life that mold your future.

Losing someone you love.

Becoming an adult.

Then, there is that split-second where your heart and mind connect. Where it recognizes a significant shift and the happiness a new arrival brings. Where you feel the worry you carry slip through your fingers, and the world around you fills with brightness.

That perfect instant is where I am right now, watching as Malcolm slips his fingers below the surface of a shallow tropical pool. He's wiggling two digits as a stingray comes close enough to touch. His face is calm as the animal pauses just beneath his hand, letting him pet it with soft strokes. It's the most serene I've seen him, and I'm enjoying every single second.

From the different attractions—mammal or reptile exhibits—he's been attentive and informative. Sharing with me what he knows, how he's secretly an animal documentary lover, and how it's his go-to when he wants to decompress.

How much he admires snakes but hates them close unless it's behind a glass enclosure.

How Shark Week is something he never misses and wants to share the next one with me.

It's a normal conversation. Not what I've come to expect from a man like him.

From the men my brother associates with.

More so, after he confessed to hurting Dad and Alton. That my home now is with him.

What should've been shocking isn't, and I'm finding myself being swept away by a deep sense of relief. I'm not upset with him about either one. It's the opposite.

With my hand over my heart, I can say that I'm happy right where I am. With him.

I'll even confess to wishing I'd been a fly on that wall when it happened.

What does that say about me?

I can't think about that now because what comes to mind is worrisome. I've never been a vengeful person, but ever since meeting Malcolm, it's something that comes to mind from time to time. A churning thought that fills me with the need to see them pay.

If I go back home, how long would it be before Alton's abuse turns sexual?

Focusing on Malcolm again, I push the fear of that thought away and shake off the darkness it brings. Instead, I admire how casual my date's dressed. Not that I don't appreciate him in a suit, but there's something extra sexy about a man in joggers and a T-shirt combo. For some reason those grey sweatpants he's wearing have become a weakness.

It's sporty, yet accentuates his solid form. That, and each time his arms wrap around me from behind, I feel him. Every solid inch.

Thank God the area we're in is almost empty and he's staying close. Because for as much as the man is possessive of me, I find myself feeling the same.

"Aren't you going to try?" His voice is sexy. Smooth as whiskey.

"I like watching you instead."

His eyes meet mine, and there's a hint of something dangerously provocative flash in them. "You like to watch?"

"You?" I give him a coy look from under my lashes. "All the time."

"Dangerous creature," he mutters, but I hear. Also notice the flex of his cock when he turns to me, wet hand at his side while taking the remaining steps between us. Malcolm presses the entire front of his body to mine, and the room becomes hot. An inferno of desire only he can bring forth.

"I'm not the dangerous one here." It sounds needy even to my own ears.

"You know, one day I'll forget the definition of the word slow and just take you."

"I never said we had to go at a snail's pace, if you...Malcolm!" I find myself with my back to his chest and a secure arm around my hips where he lifts me with ease. My feet are a couple of inches off the ground and I can't help the giggles coming out of me.

We look ridiculous.

The few people mingling around just look at us while he not so casually walks me out of the aquarium without another word. He doesn't stop, not when someone recognizes him and asks to have a word, nor when the pathway from the aquarium to the planetarium fills with people.

SIN

He's like Moses and the sea of people make room for the rich lunatic holding his date like a toy down the pathway.

It's not until we come to the Adler entrance that I sober a bit. It's closed.

"Hey, you can put me down now. I can walk back to the car."

"Back to the car?" Instead of releasing, he just turns me around in his arms. Like a ragdoll, he manipulates my much-smaller frame to his liking, and I find myself enjoying it. Feeling delicate and at his mercy is sexy. "Are you ready to call this date over?"

His brow creases, and I reach up with my thumb to smooth it out. Don't like him upset. "Not at all, but we can go somewhere else too."

"I'm so lost, Twirl."

"The sign says closed for the general admission crowd."

"Oh, that. Fuck, you're adorable." A soft smile graces his mouth and I can't stop myself, pressing mine to his for a small kiss. "Can I get another?"

"After you explain why we aren't leaving."

His arms tighten their hold on my hip and lower back. "Because we aren't the general population, sweetheart. I bought out the After Dark show tonight so it's just you and me."

"Are you serious?" Tears spring to my eyes. The gesture is more than sweet and totally unnecessary. "You don't need to spend money to impress me, but the thought you put into this is appreciated. Thank you."

"None needed, sweetheart." He sets me down, sliding me over his rigid length and then offers me his hand. Ignores the small whimper I let out. "Ready to have your mind blown by my chivalry?"

I laugh at that, wiping the one tear that escapes. "You and chivalry don't belong in the same sentence."

"So little faith," he admonishes with a tsk from the back of his throat while placing my hand at the crook of his elbow. When I turn my attention to the entrance again, there's a man now around

157

Malcolm's age waiting for us with a smile and tray with two champagne flutes.

"Welcome to the Adler After Dark experience, Mr. and Mrs. Asher." Extending the drinks toward us, he waits until we each take a glass before speaking again. "We're so thrilled to have you with us tonight."

"Thank you," is all Malcolm says. No correction on the names or the title, which isn't mine. Instead, the man looks a bit smug about it. While I, on the other hand, don't know what to say because the way his last name and my first sound together isn't unappealing. It's too soon to think about it, but not off-putting. "Everything set up...?"

"My name is Dean, sir, and yes. We are ready to proceed as you please."

"Perfect. I appreciate that."

"It's our pleasure." Once inside the Rainbow Lobby, he takes us toward the center and stops at the crossroads that lead to two separate exhibits. Dean turns to face us in front of two signs, each pointing in a separate direction. "Do you wish to dine with the moon first or peruse the stars?"

I'M NERVOUS.

Excited.

Out of my mind for what I'm going to do but can't stop myself. Control this need that's been burning—being fed by his attention all day. A never-ending game of foreplay.

It's been a constant bout of attention and lingering touches. Playful one moment and then sinful the next. Roguish smiles thrown my way, and then ice-cold glares toward anyone that tried to get close. If the guide at Adler's Planet Nine Show or the waiter's eyes strayed my way for too long, I was pulled closer.

He's possessive, and I like it. More than.

It's ludicrous that he gets jealous because I can't stay away. No one registers when we're together, and even when not, my mind is always on him.

Why does everything with him feel so right? Makes sense?

Even now, as he walks around the bed to turn down the sheets, I can't help but find the action sexy. Perfect. Full of those little gestures that people overlook but to me are everything.

"Are you going to stand there all day watching me? Or is this a new habit we are forming?" Malcolm asks suddenly, a hint of amusement in his tone. I notice how much he does that with me—laugh, he lets go of that rigidness that scares the hell out of people; with me, there's none of that. "Not that I mind."

The muscles in his bare back flex as he tosses aside another decorative pillow, while his low-slung basketball shorts give me a small peek at the deep V of his hips. I can also see how much he likes my attention. The outline of his cock is unmistakable, and my mouth waters just a tiny bit.

I wonder how he tastes. Will I be able to handle him?

And while the fear of pain is still there, that he won't fit, I want him.

"I'm just admiring the view." Malcolm Asher is built like a baseball player: tall, strong, with well-defined muscles. His tattoos stand proud against his fair skin with a hint of a tan, colorful details with dark edges that tell a story. Gives a warning.

Every single one I have seen has a matching theme that is quite clear; I see all. The eyes in their bright blue, an almost identical shade to mine, are a reminder that he has people everywhere, just watching. The owl on his chest stands for intelligence—Malcolm is wise and attentive to details; he doesn't make mistakes. Dangerous.

"Want to do so from a better vantage point? Or are you scared I'll bite?" Smug bastard.

"Please do." The words are out of my mouth before I can stop them, but it's the truth. If my reply surprises him, he doesn't say anything. Instead, he just looks back at me from over his shoulder with a smirk. It's almost as if he can read my thoughts.

All day—since I met him—I've been more vocal with my thoughts. What I like and don't want. There's a certain level of ease that's been missing since Mom died.

With him, I have no fear. No repulsion or wanting to get away.

It's the opposite. I want more.

Closeness.

Touches.

To fully live my life.

"I've told you that sassy mouth is going to get you into trouble."

"So you've said, but…" Trailing off, I push off the door frame and take two steps inside. I do test his control. Push him into taking things a little further than some cuddling or kissing.

To play a little. Touch a little and explore.

"Last chance to get in this bed, say sorry, and get some sleep." It's a barely controlled growl, and my thighs clench. His fists are at his sides when he turns to face me fully, matching my two steps. Closer. "I want you, London. Fucking hunger to taste that sweet little pussy between your thighs, thighs that tremble at the mere sound of my voice. Don't tempt me, sweetheart…I'm trying here for you."

I swallow hard, shivers running down my spine. "Maybe not all the way, but a sample…shit!" Before I realize what's happening, I'm airborne one second, and on my back the next. Pinned beneath him from head to toe, his larger frame hovers over mine while those piercing green eyes roam.

He doesn't speak. Just looks. Takes inventory of every single inch of flesh on display.

The shirt I'm wearing is his. My panties are another pair he bought for me. My breasts are free and nipples tightening under his hungry gaze.

"You need to be honest with me, London." Jesus, the roughness in his voice causes goose bumps to rise on my skin. I'm sensitive. Aching in a way I've never experienced before. "Tell me what you want from me. What do you need."

Chapter 21

MALCOLM

"Y OU." SHE DOESN'T hesitate. Not for a single second. "I want you to touch me."

It's her truth. She needs this. Me.

No matter how crazy—the fast pace of our relationship—we both want this. Accept the cards fate has dealt.

"*Fuck.*" It's a groan of mercy from my lips. Embedding my right hand in her hair, I angle her head to my liking before slanting my mouth over hers. Savor the top before tracing the bottom with my tongue. "I'm going to enjoy you slowly. Taste every single inch of this beautiful body."

"Please," Twirl whimpers, spreading her thighs to cradle my hips. She's soft and warm. Her heat sears me through the thin layer of my shorts, caressing my cock. "More...I need more."

My kiss is possessive, yet worshipping.

My hold dominant, yet loving.

Her taste is decadent, an addiction-inducing pleasure that pulls a growl from deep within my chest. It's loud and almost feral, shaking me while her thighs tremble—tighten their hold to try and keep me from pulling away.

"So fucking sweet. Addictive." Nipping her bottom lip, I travel lower, licking a path down her throat and to the neck of my shirt.

A shirt that's ridden up, exposing her legs and panties.

A shirt that's doing very little to hide her lack of bra.

A shirt that I rip right down the center with one harsh tug.

"Oh my God," London moans as I pull the tatters of cotton away from her skin, tossing it somewhere behind me. Her back arches off the bed, offering what's already mine, while goose bumps dance across her skin.

"Not God, baby. Just this motherfucker who owns you." Sitting back, I take in her wanton form. The softness of her skin and the gentle slope of each breast. How mouthwatering her small nipples are; a light pink tip that tightens under my perusal. "So pretty."

"I need you to touch me." London sits up, grabbing my wrist and pulling. And I let her. Let her guide me to her right tit that fits perfectly in my hand; she's just a bit more than a handful and perky.

I take her hard little bud between two fingers and pull.

A pink flush sweeps down her face and neck. It covers her upper chest, and the color is beautiful. I want more of it. A deeper shade, and I slap the very top of her breast, catching the puckered flesh with the tip of my finger.

Three smacks and I attach my lips to her nipple, flicking the sensitive skin as a grunt rips from my throat. Her smell is intoxicating, her skin soft as a petal.

"Malcolm." It's a cry, a low, keening sound full of a need that fuels mine.

"What do you need?" Pulling her in deeper, I flick the tip before biting down, then lick a path across her chest to the other breast. Her hips buck beneath me as I suckle her, but she doesn't answer and that won't do. Pinching the nipple hard, I lift my head to stare down at her. "Answer me. What do you need?"

She's breathless and panting and lost in her arousal. "For you to own me."

Good girl. I hum against her skin and suck a path down her breast and ribs, leaving small reminders of my hunger. Tiny bruises that mark my conquering.

Her stomach clenches the lower I go, a sweet giggle escaping as I reach her midsection, and then a groan when my lips caress her hip.

Taking the waistband of her panties between my teeth, I pull the material. White satin and with my initials at the upper right hand corner, I revel in their stretching and the small peak of smooth skin beneath. In her wetness seeping through.

My mouth waters and I release the fabric, letting it snap back against her skin. Nuzzle her. "How do you want to come, London? My mouth..." I lick the satin over her clit, and she cries out "...or my fingers?"

"W-what?"

"Pick one." This time I tap her tender bundle of nerves with two fingers. "Mouth or fingers?"

"I can't pick. No one has ever touched me," she hisses out, sucking in a deep breath as I smack her pussy once more.

I know she's a virgin. Love the fucking fact that the tight little hole between her thighs will only know me.

"So innocent, and yet you're greedy." Lowering my body to the mattress, I place a leg over each of my shoulders and inhale her sinful scent. She's so fucking wet and I've yet to touch her, the crease of her thigh glistening. "Are you willing to let me do as I please? Give you what I know you need without a single complaint?"

"Yes...anything. Just help me find—"

"Move your panties to the side and show me your pussy." Wide blue eyes meet mine, but she follows my instruction. Slow, and with a hint of excitement, her hand comes down to the edge of her panties and fingers the fabric.

Watching her dip a single digit beneath the silk is downright sinful.

With the patience of the saint I am not, I wait for her to show me. To open herself to me.

To trust me.

Because intimacy is just that, trust between two people that care about each other. Anyone can fuck, but sharing private and personal moments carries weight.

However, nothing could've prepared me for the rush of animalistic greed that rushes through me at the sight of her. *She's mine. No letting go.*

London is pink and glistening with her arousal, clit throbbing beneath its hood. Her scent surrounds me, a heady and saccharine smell that is uniquely hers. She's perfect, and with my eyes on hers, I take a lick from her opening to clit, laying a tender kiss on her mound.

Christ, she tastes like heaven and hell. Like she will be the end of me and then the rebirth.

And if I wanted to hurt Alton before, now I want him to die a slow and agonizing death. To watch her flourish at my side as he loses it all. While I place the world at her feet and worship this altar every fucking night.

Because I am. Before I pull the trigger, he will know that I own her. *Love her.*

"Son of a bitch." I drag my teeth across her clit as the reality of that thought slams into my chest. It's fast. Sudden. But the truth is there and always has been. I just never put a label to the emotion.

This tiny beauty beneath me is my person.

SIN

"*Fuck.*" At once, her body arches up, back bowing as a moan leaves her. She's writhing—hips lifting toward my hungry tongue.

With two fingers, I part her lips and pull back to watch how her hole clenches. How the wetness gathers at her entrance and then slips down to the crack of her ass. An ass I want to bite.

And I do just that, right at the tip. I embed my teeth and press down hard enough to leave a mark and then soothe the sting with my tongue, loving her flesh with slow licks as I follow the path back to her pussy.

She swollen for me. So wet. And seeing her lost in the pleasure I give makes me feel like a motherfucking Titan. All powerful and indestructible.

Sliding my tongue through her slit, I eat her like a man possessed. Sucking. Biting. Devouring every drop of wetness she gifts me.

London fights against my mouth, wanting to move her hips, but I hold her down with a forearm across her hips. "My pace. My rules."

"Need you, please!"

My reply is a smack to her inner thigh and a quick flick to her clit. Then another. Taking the throbbing bundle of nerves between my teeth, I slip a single finger inside to the second knuckle. She's so fucking tight, walls gripping as they pulse—try to pull me in deeper.

Her innocence is there against me, and I don't want to break it. Not with my hands.

That treasure belongs to my dick.

"I want to fuck you," I grunt against her clit, and she claws at the sheets. "My cock aches to be inside you. To claim you." At my words, London's hooded eyes meet mine, her panting breaths accentuating the heaviness in her breasts. Her hard nipples and the slight sheen of perspiration that covers her skin.

She's a goddess. *She'll be my queen.*

"So good, Malcolm. God, that feels so good," she cries out when I pump in and out at a faster pace. Five rapid little jabs, before I pull my finger out and circle her clit, rubbing her in tight little circles while my tongue laps at her juices.

Fucks her entrance.

Blue eyes roll back, and her mouth drops open. Chest heaves as breathing becomes difficult.

Her reaction feeds my need to see her come. To have her bathe my face.

"Come for me, Twirl. Give me what's mine." And then I pinch her clit.

"I'm almost...*fuck*!" London comes with a scream, muscles clenching as her wetness drips down my lips and chin. It pools on the sheet below as I continue to love her, slowly bringing her down after a minute.

She's limp in my bed, but her smile is wide. Tired but relaxed.

Leaving her in the morning is going to be hard.

WE'RE SITTING at the dining room table when London finds me the next morning. She's fresh out of the shower and wearing a ridiculous pair of wide-leg pants and crop top in a light grey cotton. They look cute, but on anyone else the bottoms would look funny.

Yet, on her thick hips, they work. Accentuate that perfect body.

Pausing at the entrance, she toes the floor, looking a bit unsure. "I'll be in the kitchen..." Twirl points in the general direction it's in "...anyone need anything?"

Shaking my head, I crook a finger. "Come here."

At my words, a tiny smile crosses her lips. "Yes, sir." However, the mock salute I'm given before she comes causes my dick to harden. *Sassy little thing.*

There's a natural sway to her hips that I can't help but watch. It's sensual. Coquettish. A cock-teasing quality that she can't control and isn't aware of.

London isn't conscious of her own appeal. Of her control over me.

A throat clears to my left, but I ignore the assholes and continue my perusal.

We've been working for a few hours now, preparing for the next few days and what I expect to be done while I'm gone. How they will handle the FBI agent lingering around my building downtown.

Vital information—both customer and transaction details, along with a few photographs of Shawn at a strip club—sit in front of me, and yet, the only thing I can focus on is my hunger for her. The desire to sweep everything off this table, witnesses be damned, and spread her out for me to enjoy is almost maddening. I'm not leaving without eating her pretty little cunt once more.

Getting on the plane with her taste on my tongue and scent on my lips.

However, it will have to wait, and instead, I'll settle for a kiss on the mouth. Once she's close enough, I reach a hand out and grab hers, pulling her down to my level.

Those blue orbs hold a hint of mischief—relief and happiness—when I press my lips to hers. "Good morning, beautiful."

"Hi."

"You sleep okay?" I ask, nipping my way down to her jaw where I take the skin between my teeth. "Feel rested?"

"I did and do." She brings a hand to my hair and scratches the scalp, tugging on the ends. London does this a few times, eliciting a hum of approval. "Very warm and comfortable."

"Good." With the bottom of my foot, I push out her chair to my right. It scrapes against the wooden floors as I release her tender flesh and sit back. "Please join us."

"Are you sure?"

"Absolutely," Mariah answers for me, a hint of amusement in her tone. "Besides, you need to know what's going to occur over the next few days."

A lot is going on, and unfortunately, my plane leaves in a few hours.

Magda walks in then, a platter of bacon and eggs in each hand. She looks over at Twirl, her eyes lighting up. "Lovely to see you, Miss Foster."

"You too." London sits, grabbing the carafe of coffee and pouring a cup. "Thank you for breakfast."

"My pleasure, sweet girl." She leaves and comes back a few minutes later with some waffles and cut strawberries, the syrup and butter already on the table. "I'll be in the kitchen. Let me know if you want or need anything."

By the time she leaves, London has my plate ready and almost overflowing with food. She places it in front of me and then fills her own. "Eat."

"Yes, boss," I say with a chuckle, and Twirl rolls her eyes. The other two follow her lead, silently piling on food, and then digging in as we ignore the paperwork in front of me.

I can tell that she's curious, but I'll give her credit for waiting. She's giving me the chance to explain. Giving me a chance to prove that she can trust me.

Once my plate is pushed forward, Javi and Mariah do the same, waiting for my next move. My eyes remain on hers, though. There are so many questions in them, a small hint of doubt that I'll erase.

"Twirl, I'm going to be leaving the country for a few days."

"What? Why?" There's a hint of panic in her tone. Her eyes look sad, but she'll understand that it's a temporary thing. I'll always come back to her. For her.

"There's a business meeting in Costa Rica I must attend, but I'll be back in three days." Beside me, Mariah pushes a piece of paper toward her. My itinerary. "That's the information on my flight, where I'll be, and how to contact me. Don't hesitate to do so if something happens...I don't care how small or inane you think it is...call me."

Grabbing the paper, she looks over every single line on the sheet. It takes her a few minutes, but once she's satisfied, London places it to her right and looks at me. "What am I supposed to do while you're gone? Do I move back and wait—"

"The fuck you will," I interrupt, my discontent clear. Leaning toward her, I take her chin in my grasp and hold her stare. Make sure that her attention is on mine and she doesn't misinterpret my words. "Your place is with me. In my home. Never, not for a single second, think that being anywhere but beside me is acceptable."

"But—"

"No." I shake my head, caressing her cheek with my thumb. "And I want you moved in when I get back. Everything you own and want to bring needs to be incorporated with mine."

"Okay, but I'll need some help."

"That's where I come in, Miss London," Javier says before I can. Her eyes are on mine, though, never wavering. "Your bodyguard and I will be here to get you moved in. You'll meet her tomorrow. Gina has been assigned to you, and while Malcolm is gone, so am I."

"New bodyguard?" She's lost and doesn't know how to assimilate everything we're saying. The concept of someone taking care of her is foreign.

It's new and scary.

Especially after what we did yesterday. The new intimacy.

And while breaking the news gently would've been ideal, I don't have the luxury. Her neck and arms bear the evidence of their mistreatment. I know their plans. Know how much they want her back, and I wouldn't put it past them to try taking her by force and making a run for it.

"Yes, and don't argue with me on this. You won't win." Bringing her closer, I brush my lips against hers as I speak. "Your life is about to change drastically, sweet girl. This is for your safety and my peace of mind. *Trust me.*"

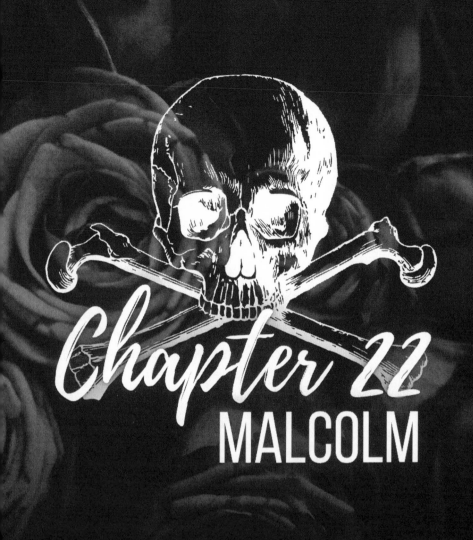

Chapter 22
MALCOLM

"**A**FTERNOON, SON," MY father says taking a seat across from me. He's smiling, looking a little cocky, and I put my newspaper down, placing it beside my drink.

He's a last-minute addition to this trip, and by the look on his face, he knows why he's here.

Father or not, the shit he pulled with my girl a few days back needs an explanation.

I'm not London, and I don't have a heart of gold.

"Thank you for joining me last minute."

"I've been expecting your call." Dad takes his seat, and a second later the stewardess places a whiskey neat in front of him. "Thank you, Ellen."

"Let me know if you need anything else, sir." And then just like that, she disappears from sight. The in-flight crew knows to make themselves scarce unless we call upon them after the doors close and the engines turn on.

My men are a few rows back and watching a basketball game while Carmelo studies the information Javier gave him before this flight. He knows the drill, what I expect, and takes it seriously, which I appreciate.

"Get it off your chest." Dad's voice pulls my eyes to his.

"I will in a minute. Go ahead and get your story together." Grabbing my phone from the table, I swipe my finger across the screen and send Twirl a quick message.

> Taking off. Behave while I am gone, and I'll have something sweet for you when I get back.
> ~Malcolm

Her reply is instant, and it's hard to keep myself from smiling.

> I've always been an angel. ~Twirl

> Promises. Promises ~Twirl

My mind immediately goes back to just before we left for the airfield and I had her bent over the bathroom sink, legs spread, with my face buried between her thighs. To the way she whimpers every time I rake my teeth over her clit. The way she trembles when I dig my fingers into her hips, holding her in place.

I can still taste her decadence on my tongue.

See the fire in her eyes when she begs for more.

An attachment comes through, and it's a picture with some sort of filter that adds wings and a halo to her. She's glowing in it. Beautiful. Wearing the sweetest grin, with a small hint of the blotchiness from the few tears that fell when I kissed her at the security gate.

It's perfect. She's perfect.

Another text comes in just as I'm going to respond.

> Is it weird that I miss you already? You just left and I feel off without you here. ~Twirl

> Not at all when I feel the same. Call you when I land. ~Malcolm

"Happiness looks good on you," Dad says, pulling my attention away from her messages. "And your mother adores her, by the way."

"Why?"

His smile drops, and he gives me a grimace. "Shit didn't look good, Malcolm. That's the God's honest truth." Dad rubs a tired hand down his face. "Look at it from my point of view; a pretty girl, her last name is Foster, and she's wearing bruises on her neck and deep scratches down her arm...wouldn't you be concerned?"

Nodding, I pick up my glass and drain the rest of its contents. "I agree that it looked bad, but you made her feel unwelcomed in *my* home, and that's unacceptable. Pull me aside. Question me where she can't hear, but never in her presence again. Understood?"

Ellen appears then with a new drink for me; a gin and tonic with a cucumber and lemon slice, setting it on the table beside a cheese plate.

"Thanks."

"You're welcome, sir." Once more she disappears inside a small area up front for the staff.

"You're right. How I handled it was wrong, and I apologize."

"Accepted."

"I know you'd never hurt someone who's an innocent, son. More so, someone we both know isn't involved in her family's schemes, but I couldn't in good conscience not ask—"

SIN

"Wait a minute." Holding a hand up, I stop him. *We both know...* "What do you mean by that? You know her?"

"No." Dad picks up his drink and takes a sip, then another before putting it down again. He's not looking at me; his stare is on the round ice cube inside the glass. "I don't know London, son, but your mother knew Amelia."

"Through Earl?" Because that's the first thing that comes to mind. A few muffled curses come from a few of my men. They're yelling at the TV, and when I hold a hand up, they quiet down at once. "Is that how you knew London's mom?"

"That, and Julian Conte, her spouse, did business with us." Dad reaches into the messenger bag he brought onboard and pulls out a picture. He places it face down and pushes it toward me. "We ran in the same circles and did a few social functions together. They were a very nice couple who had shit luck with the *company* they kept."

I don't miss his emphasis on the word "company." Picking up the photo, I bring it up to my face and study the people in it. Mom and Dad are to the left, with Amelia, and the man I know to be Julian, in the middle. They're laughing at something, having a wonderful time at what looks to be a Christmas function of some sort.

However, my eyes focus on the last person in the group. His face is familiar, just younger in appearance. An angry asshole putting up the front of a good friend and enjoying himself while his date looks to be bored.

Marcus Foster looks the same.

Same miserable expression.

The devil in me recognizes the malice in him. His thirst for money and power. His willingness to kill everyone in his way to obtain it.

He's pulled the tail of the wrong demon this time.

"He knew her father." It's a statement, not a question.

"Yes."

"There's more to this story, isn't there?"

"That's what Earl believes, and so do I."

Placing the photo down, I look at my old man. "He came to you for help?"

"About seven months ago. He's worried about London's safety."

"Is that why...?"

"I reacted?" Dad nods. "In part, yes."

"You knew who she was?"

"Your mother wasn't sure—a lot of time has passed since we saw Amelia—but I knew immediately. Aside from the pictures Earl has shown me, she's her mother's spitting image." Leaning forward in his seat, he lowers his voice. "Malcolm, you have to know that my surprise wasn't at her being there, or not approving, but the shape she was in. Those women have been through enough, and I wasn't about to stand back and let her pay for a crime that isn't hers."

"Why didn't you come to me the moment Earl spoke to you?" I can't disguise the bite in my tone. The anger at knowing I could've saved her sooner.

"Because you made a deal with the Riveras."

Understanding dawns on me. "And they should've been dead by now."

"Exactly," he says with a heavy sigh, shoulders drooping a bit. "The last thing we wanted was for them to run, or worse. They'll kill her out of desperation, and then Marcus will gain total access to her inheritance. We couldn't run the risk of word getting back—"

"There's a rat," I deadpan low enough so only he can hear.

"You know?"

"I have my suspicions, and I'm letting the scum trap himself."

He rubs his jaw, eyes shifting to my men behind us. "You've always been ten steps ahead of everyone."

"Paying attention to details is my job."

"And yet something is bothering you."

"I failed her."

"No, you—"

"I did." Sitting back, I close my eyes and picture her face. That sweet smile and the soft expression she gets when I call her Twirl. "I should've never accepted the deal with Thiago and shut them down the moment they stepped foot in my city. I should've just paid the debt they owe and put them down like the vermin they are. There's a lot of *I should haves,* but I didn't, and now that's a wrong I'm going to rectify. London will never know pain again. Never feel fear. They will die so my girl can reclaim her peace."

"What are you going to do?"

"I'm going to paint a beautiful picture with their blood."

"Welcome back, Mr. Asher," Maria and Juan greet me in the driveway of my vacation home in Costa Rica, their accents heavy. They've been with me for a few years now; a trustworthy, older couple that lives here and takes care of the property year round while I'm away.

They're here to cater to my guests and never ask questions.

They've never been reluctant to clean up a mess if things turn south.

But more importantly, they've never said a word about the business that's transpired.

"Happy to be back," I say, extending a hand out to Juan and then Maria. They each shake it, and then get right back to work on unloading the back of the rental. The men traveling with me are already taking their luggage down and heading toward a separate home, a smaller structure to the right of the main house, where they'll stay while we're here.

Except for Carmelo and my father. They will be with me.

"Has anyone else arrived?" Dad asks, exiting the SUV with his phone in hand. He's reading something on it, chuckling to himself, before typing a reply. "Or do we have time to relax for a bit?"

Maria pauses on the second step and looks back. "You're the first to arrive, señor."

"Perfect." Dad follows her up to the house while I survey the area. I'm sure he wants to call Mom and then rest for a bit, while I'm feeling restless. A bit edgy.

You miss her.

I do. Not going to deny it.

Being with her these last few days—having her close and drowning myself in her scent—was heaven, but I couldn't bring her with me this time. Not when she isn't ready to deal with assholes that walk around thinking women are here to only serve one purpose.

To be on their knees.

In time, she won't cower from those men. She won't so much as blink when they make a comment. London will know how to protect herself. She'll shoot first and let me worry about the consequences for her later.

That the only man she will ever kneel for is me, and that's because she wants to. Craves it.

Carmelo's voice meets my ears then and I tilt my head, catching the end of his instructions. He's walking my way with four others; two of them will man the security kiosk and the others will handle perimeter checks around the clock during our stay.

No one gets on this estate without my knowing. No one leaves without my permission.

This property is nestled on a private stretch of land between a waterfall and the dense Costa Rican jungle. Its lush vegetation surrounds the back, while the ocean is visible from the front because of the high vantage point of this cliff. The warm waters below and white sandy beach, with miles upon miles of solitary beauty, is only accessible by foot or short motorbike ride down a hidden trail that a select few know about.

It's beautiful, peaceful, and I have no neighbors for a few miles. The perfect place to host a man with just as much blood on his hands as I do.

He's one of the world's richest; a modern-day narco. A man that resides at the very top of every most wanted list in the world.

Someone who values his privacy and ability to fly under the radar above all else.

Roberto Castillo is rich, smart, and someone who moves a lot of money through my bank. A loyal customer from a secluded mountaintop in South America who owes me a favor.

One I plan to cash today.

Chapter 23
MALCOLM

"SO, YOU FORESEE NO future delays after the Jameson issue?" Roberto asks, sitting back in his seat out on my lanai, an ice-cold beer in his hand. His right-hand man nods beside him, yet the move is a bit sloppy. A bit drunk. He's sipping on his fourth serving of rum while Carmelo and my father don't move an inch.

Don't show any emotion.

Blank faces greet Roberto's question, and I bring my own drink to my lips, savoring the orangey hop flavor. "This business has no guarantees, yet I've never failed you. My record speaks for itself."

The smell of an open flame and meat permeates the air. Juan is at the grill while Maria prepares a few typical dishes for our guest; a few salads, rice and beans, fried green plantains and empanadas. It's been hours since my last meal and I'm starving, feeling a bit agitated by his lack of faith.

"It's not you I'm worried about per se..." he trails off and I tilt my head to the side, raising a brow. "There's been a few rumors. You know people talk—"

"About what?" No one misses the bite in my tone and his men tense, two reaching back to grab the guns tucked at their waistbands. *Idiots.* What they fail to realize in their cockiness, the bravado that anyone with power suffocates in, is that no one is invincible.

It's the most obvious that gets you killed.

Danger is always in front of your face, not hidden.

Like now, I scratch my chin and two of my men get into position, the scopes at the end of their semi-automatics barely visible from the roof's edge. A dangerous scenario for anyone that pisses me off.

Those snipers are on my payroll. Are loyal to me.

Roberto shifts his eyes to Carlos, who's busy laughing, not a single care in the world while I break down their actions. Mannerisms.

"Who's talking?" my father asks, his own hand clenching once before he grabs his own beer. "Please share."

"They're saying you're distracted by a woman."

"Is that all?" I laugh, a harsh, sardonic sound that fills the now-quiet space. And just as soon as it starts, it stops when I turn my hard eyes on a still-chuckling Carlos. The man is oblivious to my mounting ire.

"No disrespect meant, my friend." Roberto is a smart man. It's why he's still alive when so many have fallen before him. He thinks. Plots. Makes the right investments.

I recognize in him what he sees in me: no remorse.

In this business he needs someone to trust with his assets, and I make a fortune from each transaction. It works, until it doesn't.

At this moment, it's becoming a failure.

"I fail to see how my private life holds weight over my business."

"This came from someone close to you. A Jimmy Cross?"

His noose just grew tighter. "I know the name, yet it still doesn't answer why it should matter to anyone."

"To me, it doesn't. I just wanted to address—"

"See, boss." Carlos slaps a hand down on the table. The impact causes his drink to spill, and the asshole has the audacity to snap a finger at Maria to clean it. She makes a move to do so, but the shake of my head stops her in her tracks. Something he doesn't notice. Nor does he realize that three hands on this table have moved beneath the wood. "I told you Malcolm doesn't let a meaningless fuck control him."

"Enough, Carlos," Roberto hisses from between clenching teeth, a hand up but no call to action. To remove the asshole.

Shaking his head, Carlos grabs Roberto's bottle and drains what's left in two deep pulls. Once it's empty, he slams it down with a sneer on his face. "Pussy is a dime a dozen and most come attached to a whore—"

His head flies back from the impact of my bullet, blood splattering his boss and Carmelo. Neither so much as flinch. No other guns go off.

Instead, we watch as Carlos's body slumps with his head hanging at an awkward angle, red dripping from the exit point at the back of his head. It pools on the floor below and then spreads along the grout lines of my terra-cotta tiles.

There are small bits of flesh and bone fragmented by the force, sticking to the pillars and walls near his body. The scene is gory and a bit gruesome, and yet, I feel a sense of relief settle deep into my bones.

My agitation is somewhat sated. At once, I'm a little calmer.

"Thank you for that." That comes from Roberto; he's wearing a tiny grin on his face. "Motherfucker was driving me insane."

"Why didn't you just put him down?" I place my gun atop the

table, and then pick up my drink to take a hearty sip. "The man was obnoxious."

"Idiot was my wife's cousin." Roberto shrugs, pulling a handkerchief from his pocket to wipe the few splatters on his face. "You know…" he waves a hand in the air "…family and all that shit."

"And this won't cause an issue?" Snapping my fingers gets everyone moving. Roberto's men take the body into a large storage I have in the woods, while mine will assist in preparing the corpse for transportation back to whatever family he has. Maria's already cleaning, abandoning her cooking for the moment, while her husband goes around the table refilling drinks and then replacing the ruined chair.

"Not at all, since he died at some bar with his hand between the legs of another man's wife."

"Poor guy." Carmelo lifts his bottle in the man's memory.

"He was a nuisance who took liberties which weren't his to take. I put up with him for my wife who took pity because he has no wife or kids. No one who really cared." Roberto sits back, nodding to himself. Thinking. You can tell the exact moment his attention shifts back to what's important; business. Why he needs me. "However, I have more important things to worry about than what story to tell my lady. We need to move the equivalent of half a billion dollars in six months, Malcolm, all in Mexican pesos this time. Five transactions coming from different states within Mexico starting in two weeks. It's going to an offshore account in Barbados, and then from there to Switzerland."

"Consider it done, but…" I pull out my phone and cross-check his last choice with an email from my informant. "Not to Switzerland. We're going to split the final destination between Uruguay and somewhere East."

"Uruguay works, but where east?"

"China. Shanghai, to be exact."

I'M on my plane back to the US the next day around midday. Roberto left early this morning after a late dinner and then a few friendly games of pool, needing to reach the Panama Canal and ensure that a shipment of drugs passes through without incident.

He has men in that port, but one can never be too careful when money is involved.

Money moves the world, and it's the reason why so many illegal businesses exists. One hand washes the other, especially when a few bills are thrown at any complication that can arise, but people get greedy. Want more.

And the problems lie with that *more*. With the opportunity, those idiots make mistakes, and in his business, that's more common than one thinks. Even those at the top have to watch their backs of thieves.

Because everyone has a price. That golden number which makes them willing to take a life.

"We'll be landing shortly, Mr. Asher," my pilot announces, and I buckle myself in. This is a short pit stop that's unavoidable before I head home. To be honest, I should've made the trip the moment I found out he was released.

My eyes stray away from the TV in front of me and over to the window. The sun is high, and the waters off the Florida coast glisten in its light. The city of Miami is beautiful, loud, but hides a danger beneath its golden surface that many fail to see.

I see it, though. The allure. The mist of sin and carnal desires that turns people into criminals.

The wheels touch down on the tarmac, and I turn my phone on. Immediately it pings with three text messages; two from Twirl and one from Gina.

The woman has been with me for a little over six months, working as a daytime guard inside the Asher building. She's diligent, an ex-military medic who came home to nothing. Her family died, and the law failed to find their killer.

Javier knows her from when they were kids, vouches for her, and I've promised my help.

That alone has made her loyal to Twirl.

> They're both here just as you predicted. Cemetery entrance and waiting to approach. ~Gina

My fingers fly over the keys of my phone as the unbuckle seatbelt sign flips on and the pilot maneuvers the plane to the disembarkment point.

> Call Javier and have him meet you there. ~Malcolm

Three little dots appear on the screen before her reply comes through.

> Already done. I'm at one end of the road and he's at the other watching. ~Gina

> Approach made. Looks tense but the older Foster spotted Javier. ~Gina

With her response comes a photo of the three of them standing at a gravesite. They're too close, and my girl looks uncomfortable. She's wearing all black, a shirt and pants, and her face is half hidden beneath a large pair of sunglasses. The other two are of no importance, but I do smile a little when I see the bandage on Alton's hand and the sling on Marcus's shoulder.

> Good. They don't go anywhere with her. Keep close and alert at all times. ~Malcolm.

> Understood, sir. ~Gina

> Keep me updated. ~Malcolm

Giving her one last look over, I put my phone away and stand.

My guards have already gotten off and are waiting for me just inside the private gate area. The plane will refuel here, and the crew will take a break while I meet up with an old friend.

The terminal is full of travelers as I make my way through the vast number of gates and restaurants. All overflowing, but even through this maze of faces, I spot Thiago Rivera easily.

He's alone, sitting at a table in one of the more upscale bars inside this concourse and nursing a drink.

The man looks different. He's bulked up and his features have hardened while in jail paying for a crime he didn't commit.

"I'm not surprised by your call," is his greeting, a small smirk on his face.

"Good. Then you know why I'm here." I extend a hand out for him to shake, and when he does, I pull him up into a man hug. "Happy to see you out, Rivera. That was a shit case and setup."

"I know." He nods, squeezing tight and then letting go to take a seat. "It's cost me something far more valuable than time."

"Then I won't take any more of it." Carmelo hands me a folder then and walks away. He'll wait outside along with the other two that stayed with me. Dad left for Chicago straight from Costa Rica via first class with a few bodyguards. "I want to liquidate their debt. The Fosters will owe me."

"Why?"

I slide the folder to him. "Open it."

Thiago flips it open and his eyes harden. Fingers twitching. "That poor girl is innocent. She's nothing like them."

"She's mine." At my words, he looks up and realization hits. Understanding, because he would kill anyone that touches his Luna. "Their lives will end by my hands. Agree or don't, Thiago, it makes no difference. This is a courtesy visit because of our friendship, but my compliance with our agreement died the very minute they touched her."

"Fuck the money." His large frame sits back, jaw ticking. "Keep it, burn it...donate it for all I care."

"Then what do you want in exchange?" I ask, mimicking his actions. My eyes are on his. Unwavering. "If not money...?"

"I'll be there to witness."

I nod. "Done."

"Good." He stands and I follow, walking out after tossing a few bills to cover his drink and tip. "Are you heading back home or staying in Miami for a few days?"

"My flight leaves in half an hour."

"Mom will be sad she missed you." He chuckles, and a bit of the man I knew before he took the fall for his brother seeps through. "She's been cooking all day for the party tonight."

"Wish I could, but London needs me."

"Say no more. Next time." He gives me one last slap on the back before pulling me into a hug. "Be good to her, Asher."

I pull back and match his shitty grin. "Are you going after Luna?"

"I am." His phone beeps then, and he pulls it out to read the message. At once his features darken, and the plastic in his grasp groans under the pressure of his hold. "Call me when you're ready to proceed."

"You okay?"

"Just have a girl to reclaim and a motherfucker to kill." Thiago turns around and leaves then, merging into the crowd while I make my way back to my gate. The plane is ready for take-off when I arrive, and I approve the change.

I'll be home in a few hours.

Hold her sooner.

Kiss those lips.

Pulling out my phone, I send her a short message.

I miss you, Twirl. ~Malcolm

Chapter 24
LONDON

I T'S BEEN SIX HOURS since he left, and I miss him like crazy. In a way that makes no sense. As if a piece of me is gone, and to be whole I need him back.

It's his cocky grin and smoldering green eyes. His filthy words and possessive touch. The way he commands respect by simply entering a room or how he treats me like I'm a precious doll.

Like he needs me just as much as I do him.

This is crazy—we're insane—but it works. We click. Connect on a level that I've never experienced before.

Mom's words come to mind then:

Hold onto it with both hands and never let go. Savor each moment you have together because tomorrow is never promised.

The two sides of him draw me in, pull, until my will becomes his. Because I find myself *wanting* to please him. Make him happy.

"Where do you want us to put these boxes?" Javier asks, pointing at the man named Jimmy that works for Malcolm. He's serious and a little weird, looking at everything and keeping tabs of the expensive items inside the living room.

He makes me feel uneasy—looks at me as if he knows me, or something that I don't. But instead of saying something, I don't.

For now, I'll pay attention to my surroundings and count down the minutes until he leaves. Until I can speak to Javier or Malcolm about the emotions he evokes.

My gut doesn't trust him, and Gina doesn't seem to either. I've caught her looking at him a few times, eyes narrowed and body tense.

Always standing closer to me when he's in the room. Like now, she moves to stand in front of me while speaking with Javi, blocking me a bit from view.

She did this at my father's house.

Never leaving me alone. Always near and alert, even though no one was home. No signs of Dad and Alton as I took my belongings and we drove away without a backwards glance.

I force a smile and point at the corner near the back. "It'll be fine over there. Actually, put them all there."

Not that there's many. Six boxes and once suitcase is all I packed, grabbing what's important and irreplaceable.

The money I've been saving that I hid beneath an old floorboard under my bed. A few photo albums, Mom's old jewelry box with what's left inside—what Dad hasn't been able to sell and gamble away. My clothes aren't much and take no space, while my books fill two boxes.

Everything else are things that Mom left behind for me.

Mementos, a box that's taped up, and in her handwriting, with knickknack she saved from each one of my birthdays. Almost a life-time worth of memories. It's been in my closet for years, from the day I found it in our attic underneath a blanket and beside the chest with my old baby items.

"That's all for tonight," Javier says then, bringing my attention to the three of them. "Jimmy, take the night off. I'm going to need you tomorrow morning."

"I don't mind staying. Help Gina with—"

"I'm not repeating myself." Javier's tone doesn't leave room for argument. It's final, and I watch how Jimmy forces a neutral expression on his face. "Report downtown at nine. I'll be there to grab you. We have an order pickup for the boss."

"Understood. Have a good night." With a final glance my way, he walks out with Javi following behind him. We don't say anything as we wait for Javier to come back; the feeling is mutual.

Something is off with him.

Instead, I busy myself by opening the first box, which has books. I pull them out one by one, stacking them atop a table until I can figure out where to put them.

Hopefully Magda can give me an idea in the morning.

"Want some help with that?" Gina asks after a while, coming to stand beside me. "I'm an amazing unpacker."

I smile at her. "How about organizing by color? I've always wanted to put them on a shelf in a gradient style; lightest to darkest."

"Sounds good to me." Gina starts with the ones on the table while I inspect a small book of poems that Mom always kept on her nightstand. There are scribbles in her penmanship, little notes on how a specific line made her feel. How beautiful they were.

"And that one?" Javier's voice cuts through my memories, bringing my focus to him. He's pointing at the small book in my hand. "Is that one going to the library like the rest? Or will they go in the office?"

"I was thinking about getting them sorted while he gets back. I'm not sure where to—"

"Sweetheart, he wants you to mix your things with his. Put them in the middle of the staircase and that man wouldn't care," he says, tone gentle. Javier walks casually to my stack and picks up an old copy of *Emma* that's been in my mom's family for years. "Or better yet, why don't I show you."

"What're you talking about?" My interest is piqued.

"Ten bucks says I can find the most out of place for it, and he'll love it."

"I want in on this." Gina wipes her hands on the black slacks she's wearing. "However, this needs to be ridiculous. Somewhere that'll leave him scratching his head."

"You're both crazy." I'm shaking my head, a giggle bursting through. "I'm in. Double or nothing."

"Done. Now..." Javi scratches his jaw "...where to put this?"

"I'm leaving that up to you. Just make it good."

"Or, you can both be neutral and let me?" Gina interjects, a wicked glint in her eyes. "Whatcha say?"

"Go for it." Taking the book from him, I hand it over. She walks away and toward his office, leaving me with the perfect opening to address my concern. "Javi?

"I know."

"Something isn't right."

"You have a good eye." He bumps his shoulder with mine. "Don't doubt yourself. If someone gives you the creeps, nine times out of ten, they are one. An off chance isn't worth the risk of your safety."

"Does Malcolm know?" Because I don't see him letting someone untrustworthy work for him.

"He does. Trust us."

SINCE LAST NIGHT I've been feeling off. As if I'm missing something —forgetting something important—and this morning at eight a.m. it finally hit me.

Mom died five years ago today. Taken from me by some asshole that only cared about the money she had inside her wallet that night, his next high, or God knows what, because to this day, he still hasn't been found.

Not a single trace. No one cares to look.

One minute she's here, and the next gone.

Moreover, that night I lost my entire family.

Dad hates me, and Alton no longer pretends to see me as a little sister.

At sixteen, I became an orphan. I was lost and desperate until just recently when Malcolm came into my life. And while a part of me mourns Mom all over again today, the larger part of me just misses *him*. Today, I just need *him*.

He's been in my life for such a short period of time, and maybe the rest of the world will think I'm insane for moving in with him, but deep down it feels right. Like I belong here.

"Are we stopping for flowers," Gina asks the closer to the cemetery we get. I've been quiet. Lost in my head as I try to fight the guilt for being more torn up by his absence than this anniversary.

Maybe it's because of how many years have passed.

Maybe it's because I don't want to spend the day alone like all the years prior.

Looking out the window, I shake my head. "I always pay for year-round service. The cemetery puts fresh flowers in my name, because I never knew when they'd allow me to come and do so."

For a second, I feel her eyes on me. Hear the sadness in her tone. "Is there anything you need from me? For me to do?"

Not unless you can magically make him appear.

"Just drive down to the end of this road and turn left. The second row after is where the family's mausoleum is." The cemetery is almost empty when we arrive around mid-morning on Tuesday, most people coming to see their loved ones over the weekend. It's an old and very large park, accommodating the affluential and rich. Those that can afford large buildings to house the final destination of the entire family.

Funny, it also serves to show me a cold, hard truth I've been neglecting up until this very moment. The women of my family are the providers. First Mom, and then I took up the slack when they didn't lift a finger to cook a single meal, and then there's the odd jobs to help pay bills.

"This one?" Gina points to a large structure, the only one near the end of this road.

"That's the one," I hear myself say, but I'm on autopilot now, literally asking one foot permission to move the other. "Right here is fine." My body feels heavy as she parks and I exit, and yet, I manage to hold a hand up when her car door opens. "I'm going to need some privacy, please."

"Completely understandable, London. I'm just going to stand beside the car and get some air."

"Thank you." I don't turn back to look at her, though. My eyes are set on the entrance to her resting place. One foot in front of the other, I walk closer with tears brimming. My chest feels tight and breathing becomes a bit choppy.

Being here. Entering this space and finding that it looks the same hurts for some reason.

Maybe it's because I'm the only one that cares.

Maybe it's because I feel like a failure for not standing up for myself.

Maybe it's because a part of my soul wants to unleash years of anger on the world for the unfairness of it all. And while I know it's not her fault, the pain still lingers.

I feel abandoned.

"Why?" I'm choking, emotions bubbling to the surface that for so long I kept hidden from everyone. From myself. "Why, Mom?"

"It was just her time, Lola," Alton answers out of nowhere, and I freeze. Where did he come from? How didn't I hear him enter?

"What are you doing here?" There's an edge of panic to my voice, my fight-or-flight instincts kicking in. *Calm down. Gina is close and nothing will happen.* "Did you know I would be here?"

Chapter 25
LONDON

"SHE WAS MY MOTHER, too." His tone is softer than I ever remember him using, and I'm taken aback by it. It throws me off. Turns my sudden fear into annoyance.

Since when? That retort sits on the tip of my tongue, but instead I step around him. He's misconstruing my question earlier. I'm not asking why she died; it's clear to me that life has a beginning and end that no one can predict. No matter how unfair it is, how much I miss her, it is what it is.

What I want is answers.

Why do they treat me like crap?

Why is Alton fascinated with me?

Why does Dad threaten me every time he can?

Just fucking *why*?

"I'll leave you to your visit, then," I grit out, waving a hand in the air before turning to leave.

"Wait." His hand shoots out to stop me—it connects with my arm and he winces, bringing my attention to the bandages around his hand. To the purple and swelling around his wrists. Alton notices where my eyes are and pulls it away. "That's a gift from Mr. Asher himself."

"Kind of like the ones you and Dad left on my arm and neck? Or how about the scratches your fiancée took immense joy in making down my arm." With the tip of my finger I point to each one, waiting for some bullshit excuse or one of his threats. It doesn't come this time, and I'm not ready for the regret in his eyes as I look at him once more.

"I'm sorry," he says, his voice hoarse and low. "There's no excuse for my behavior, London, and I'm truly sorry."

"I don't know what to say." It's the truth, and I also don't feel comfortable inside this enclosed space alone with him. "Maybe I should come back later. Go ahead and have your visit—"

"No. Take your time...you were here first." Alton gives me a sad smile, and it throws me off. This entire change of behavior isn't like him at all. *Did Malcolm hit his head?* He only mentioned a broken hand and bullet to a shoulder; did I miss him giving this man a personality transplant? "...Dad and I will wait outside. Please, just give us a few minutes of your time before you go."

"Again, why are you doing this?" I say, exasperation coloring my tone. "You don't care. Never have."

"That's where you're wrong, sis. You're everything to us." With that he walks out, leaving me alone inside the mausoleum, feeling lost and unsure. The sole thing giving me comfort is that Gina is nearby, keeping an eye, and she won't let anything happen to me. *None of them will.*

"This is such a mess, Mom." Taking the steps to where her plaque is on the wall, I lower myself to the floor right in front of it. I sit crossed-legged and look at her name, trace each letter with the tip of my fingers and then check the water level inside the metal vase. "What are they playing at? They've never come here. Not once since you died."

Silence. Not that I expect anything different, but outside the wind picks up and the stained-glass window above the entryway rattles a bit.

At this, a small snort escapes me. "Is that your way of saying run? That you're not buying it either?"

A memory hits me then, something she said to me on my fifteenth birthday. Dad fought with her that night. He was so mad over my gift; a girls-only weekend trip to California we never took because he forbade us from going alone.

"Apologies are empty when the actions prior hold malice. One thing is making a mistake, Lola, but when a person hurts you because they can—to make you feel small—that's not love. Never give someone the power over you to do so, baby." Mom cups my face, her smile sad. *"Don't make my mistakes."*

"I promise I won't." Leaning forward, I place my forehead against the cool marble. Lower my voice so Alton can't hear me outside. "Besides, Malcolm won't allow it. You'd love him, Mom. How he is with me. How he defends me."

The heaviness I've felt since last night lightens with each word I share. With how I gush like any woman my age would with her mom when she falls...

Christ. That train of thought stops me.

I can't lie to myself. Can't deny that I feel something special for him.

"I think he's my one. The guy you told me would come into my life and change it all." A shadow appears at the doorway but doesn't enter. Just stands there. "There's so much I want to share with you, and I will...soon. For now, please know that I'm happy—that I've found peace away from Dad and Alton. I love you so much, Mom. Always."

A few stray tears fall from my eyes, and I wipe them away. It's always hard to leave here, but today there's also hope blooming in my heart because for the first time in a long time, I'm not alone.

Standing from the floor and with one last touch to her grave, I walk out to face Alton and Dad. The two are standing close, whispering and looking like utter crap. *How did I miss this when Alton apologized?*

Their clothes are wrinkled. Unkempt.

Their hair is greasy and skin a bit pale.

Once I'm near, they stop talking while my brother gives me that pathetic look once more. "Can we go home and talk? I'm late for my next dosage of pain medication."

"No." Lowering my sunglasses over my face, I shrug. "If you need to go, then go. We can have this chat another day."

"Don't be difficult, London. We just—"

"Dad, stop. Not this time." My eyes shift toward Gina and notice her hand at her side, how her eyes are on the men of my family. Alton notices her, while Dad looks toward the other end of the street and I'm not the least bit surprised when I spot Javier there. He's casually leaning against the side door of his car, a grin on his face. It also explains why they didn't barge inside and forcefully remove Alton. "I'm not interested in going to the house, but I'll give you the chance to speak with me if you want, and I'll give you plenty of time to go and get your meds. Meet me at Rojo's today around five. Google it if you don't know where it is."

"Why can't—"

"That's perfect. See you there." Alton gives Dad a hard look and reluctantly, he nods. They walk away after a few minutes of my silence. I'm sure my attitude is throwing them off, and it surprises me too, but feeling safe does that to a person.

If only this didn't feel like a mistake.

Or worse, how do I get Gina and Javi to agree?

THEY'RE ALREADY HERE when I enter the Mexican restaurant at 4:45 p.m. on the dot. Sitting at a table near the back, they spot me, and the company I keep, the moment we enter.

It's the compromise Javier gave me.

They'll sit away from us, but within visibility. I have to be easily reachable.

That, or it's a no-go, and I agree with him. Alton's apology isn't making much sense—it goes against everything he stands for. In his egotistical mind, he's never wrong, so saying the words *I'm sorry* causes a danger sign to flare across my processors.

It's fake, no doubt about that, but why?

I slip into a chair across from Alton and Dad, giving them a tight smile. "Have you been waiting for long?"

"Just a few minutes," Dad answers, picking up his drink of what looks to be pop, and taking a sip. "We got drinks but were waiting on you to order."

"Have you eaten here before?" Alton opens his menu, flipping through the few pages in the binder. "Anything you recommend?"

"No, but I've driven by it a few times and it caught my eye."

The waiter appears then, in his hand a tray with fresh chips and a couple small dishes with salsas. He places them in the middle of the table. "Hi, I'm Miguel and I'll be your server today. What can I get you to drink, Miss?"

"An horchata is fine." He nods, and before he can ask me what I want to eat, I hold a hand up. "I'm not going to eat here; I'll be placing my order to-go a few minutes before I leave. Thanks."

"Of course, you just let me know when you're ready." Turning his attention from me, he looks at them. "And for you two?"

"Why aren't you eating with us? You chose this place." Alton ignores the waiter, directing his attention to me. A flash of annoyance crosses his features, but he hides it quickly.

"Please choose something, London." Dad isn't happy either, he's looking down at the menu, lips in a thin line as he makes his plea. A plea with a hidden edge of *do as you're told.*

"No, thank you." They hate my talking back. They hate anyone that challenges them.

Like Malcolm, who doesn't take shit and won't hesitate to let you know how beneath him you are.

"We don't want to argue. That's fine," Alton says then, his expression back to that sad look he gave me at Mom's grave. "I'll have the chef's taco tray; the six count is fine. Bring extra lime and another Modelo with them."

"Of course, and for you, sir?" he asks, not looking at my father, busy jotting it all down.

"I'll have a large chicken tortilla soup. That's it."

"Perfect. I'll put this in now and be back with your drink, Miss."

Once more the table goes quiet after the waiter leaves. It makes me wonder what's the point to this. Why ask to talk and say nothing?

I take in a deep breath and let it out slow. "Why am I here?"

"We wanted to talk with you away from *his* influence. Try to make you see reason, Lola." Dad shifts in his seat, grimacing when his arm hits the table's edge. He pulls it toward his body, the sling digging into his shoulder—a shoulder where a small piece of bandage peeks out from the collar of his pullover. "He's using you to get to us. It's not love or whatever bullshit Asher said to turn you against us. Your family."

"Really?" His words sting, but I keep my expression neutral. With them, I expect the attack. They want me to doubt myself. "Is that the best you can come up with?"

"London, he told us as much." Alton grabs my hand atop the table, giving it a squeeze, and my body wants to recoil at his touch. I try to remove my hand from his grip, but he holds tight. "You have to believe us. You are nothing but a pawn in a sick game."

"Let go of my hand." I keep my voice strong. I'm a bit louder than usual so Javier and Gina can hear me. And they do. A chair scrapes against the flooring with the sound of footsteps following, getting closer to our table.

"London, a word please." Gina leaves no room for argument as she reaches for my hand in Alton's, and with a flick of the wrist, releases his hold.

I'm quick to stand, taking a few steps back while avoiding their gaze. "I need to visit the restroom anyway. Let's go." The bathrooms are across the restaurant, and we bypass an angry-looking Javier as we do. His phone is in his hand. Once inside, I turn to face her and let out the breath I've been holding since Alton touched me. "Thank you."

"None needed." Gina wets a wad of paper towels in her hand and places them on my forehead. "Next time your brother so much as breathes wrong, I'm shooting him. Anyone with a working neuron can see how uncomfortable you are with them."

"I'm more upset by the crap they are trying to pull. The things they are saying about Malcolm."

"Please tell me you don't believe—"

"No, I don't." Giving her a soft smile, I turn around and open the faucet to splash some water on my face. The coolness feels amazing against my flesh and it calms me. Helps re-center me. After a few more minutes of quiet, I dry my face and neck. "Come on. Let's get this over with."

"You don't have to. We can leave...just say the word."

"I know."

The restaurant is a bit fuller when we step out, with a large group blocking my way as I go back toward Alton and Dad. It forces me to walk around the group and staff helping them sit, putting me right behind their table where the two are oblivious to my presence.

"Fucking asshole has sunk his claws deep into her," Alton spits out before taking a deep pull from the beer he was nursing. "She's going to make this hard, and I'm taking it out on her ass the moment I get my hands on her. No more waiting."

"Calm down, son." Dad scratches his jaw, tilting his head toward an angry Javier watching them. "We can't act now...they have her under tight surveillance."

"Then when, old man? Because the longer we wait, the harder it will be."

"Eyes on the prize. Remember that." Marcus reaches over and grabs my drink, taking a few sips without shame. When the contents are halfway gone, he places the cup down, and turns to look over at the family with two screaming kids. "With the older cunt gone, the younger one won't be a problem. Stick to the plan, Alton. We sell her virgin holes, take her inheritance, and keep the pathetic bitch as a personal slave to bring in money."

"She's mine." Alton nods while it feels as though the floor beneath my feet has been taken from me. How can they be so cruel? How could I be so stupid to come here?

"Word." It slips past my lips in a low whisper, almost drowned by the busy restaurant, but Gina hears. Without asking any questions, she walks with me to the table and helps me grab my purse from its place on the chair beside mine. She guides me out of the place, ignoring their protests and the call of my name.

Nothing registers as we make it outside and continue toward parking.

Not when we pass our car. Not when another door nearby opens.

Nothing, until a pair of arms I know pull me inside the backseat of a large SUV and settles me on his lap. His touch awakens me then. Breaks down every fucking wall that once stood around my heart, protecting me.

The moment he whispers in my ear *I've got you*, I break down.

Chapter 26
MALCOLM

S HE'S SHAKING. SOBBING.

Pouring out years of pain and anger caused by two assholes I'm going to kill. A slow death. Agonizing as I repay them with the same kindness they've given her.

The anger flowing through my veins is blinding. Consuming me while my limbs feel tight. Muscles tense—clenching as my desire for violence grows. It's been building since I landed, and Javier told me where they were. Why they were here.

I tried being civil for her sake. They should be thankful to still be alive.

Yet, the moment I step out of town, the lowlifes came out to play. Whatever they said, hurt her. Broke down that final reinforced-steel-wall she hid behind to escape this pain.

And on the anniversary of her mother's death.

"I'm sorry, Twirl. So sorry I didn't make it back to you earlier," I whisper into the crown of her head while wrapping my arms tight around her small frame. She's against my chest, burrowing her face into my neck as the tears soak my collar. Her small, nimble fingers cling—hold on to the fabric of my shirt in a death grip as more teardrops flow. "Please don't cry. Seeing you this upset is killing me."

"No one dies from tears," she mutters low, then hiccups. The sound is cute. "And I can't stop them. Just so much—"

"I know." The car slips into traffic easily, taking the route toward my home. There's a minute nod against my skin and then a long, shuddering sigh. We don't speak as my driver maneuvers around cars or when the occasional horn is honked.

We just stay as we are while I run my fingers up and down her spine in a gentle motion. It takes a while for her sobs to calm and for her breathing to even out, letting me know she fell asleep.

London is clinging to me while I offer her support. I inhale her soft scent, pulling the floral smell deep into my being as I try and keep my composure. The more she relaxes, the more my ire burns bright.

Knowing she's resting gives me a chance to speak with Javier. He's sitting in the front passenger seat and fuming. He cracks his neck then knuckles, body shaking a bit.

"What the fuck happened?" I hiss out from between clenching teeth, my jaw ticking as I fight to keep my voice low. The last thing I want is to wake her up.

"Alton grabbed her hand and wouldn't let go..." he pauses, looking back at her with regret when she whimpers "...when we saw that, I got up and Gina took her to the bathroom. My eyes stayed on them the entire time after I sent the message, but they wouldn't look at me. By the time they came back, London heard something, and Gina took her out. When the Fosters stood to follow, I threatened to shoot, and they sat back down. My focus was on removing her at all cost."

"Okay." Shifting her a bit so she's more comfortable, I lay a kiss on her forehead. Then add another to her cheek that's still wet with tears. "In forty-eight hours, I want everything back in her name. Enough with the childish games."

"Consider it done."

I give him a nod and then look back down at the gorgeous girl in my arms. Skin blotchy and a slight mess, she still takes my breath away. Stirs in me a protective side no one, not even my mother, has ever seen.

"I'm going to make this right," I whisper against her temple. *They're going to pay for this in blood, and it's time I start collecting.*

"Welcome back to the land of the living, sleepyhead," I say, startling her just inside the kitchen entrance, causing her to squeak. It's a high-pitched sound that I find...*cute*. Makes me want to bite her just a little bit. "Are you hungry?"

I've been awake for hours thinking now, weighing my options. However, after speaking with Gina and knowing what she heard, it's time we talk. No more waiting.

London needs to make a few tough decisions today. The first comes in signing her name on the dotted line of a few sheets of paperwork to regain the power over her future. I'll always support her, but as my equal and not someone who lets fear dictate her life.

However, I know that will come with time. With my patience and helping her see that what they did—how they treated her—isn't normal.

London narrows her eyes at me and huffs with a hand on her chest. "What are you doing hiding in corners?"

"It's hardly hiding when I'm sitting here finishing my breakfast out in the open." Pushing out a chair with my foot, I point to it with my fork. "Join me."

Her fake annoyance melts and the pain resurfaces. "I'm just not hungry."

Dropping my fork, I push my chair back and open my arms. "Come here." Her bottom lip trembles, and she comes to me with no other prompting. With her in my lap, I take her chin with two fingers and turn her to look at me. Let her see the honesty in my words. "Please, let me take care of everything. Let me help you fix the mess they've made for you."

"You spoke to Gina?" I nod, and she wipes away the two tears that have fallen. "How much worse is it than what I heard? How much do I need to prepare myself to hear?"

"I'm sorry, Twirl. I really wish it wasn't this way."

"Not your fault." London leans into me, forehead on mine. Her exhale is sweet and minty on my lips. "To be honest, Malcolm, you've done more for me than I can ever repay and—"

"I take care of what's mine. End of." Taking her bottom lip between my own, I suck on the tender flesh before releasing. "Your happiness is what I'm after. It's what gains me entry into my heaven...it gives me *you*."

"I've been so lost...scared." My girl takes a deep breath then and lets it out slow. The heavy sigh makes my own chest ache for her. For the weight those two assfucks are placing on her head. "Deep down I've always known something was off. With the way Marcus treated Mom. With Alton's sick fascination with me. That's not love. That's a mixture of hate and gaslighting—machismo at its finest. They just wanted us to be subservient and docile so they could do as they pleased."

"You're brilliant, sweetheart. I have no doubt that you'd be long gone by now."

Her small fingers play with the bottom of my shirt, absentmindedly swiping her pinky across my lower abdomen. My reaction is automatic, muscles clenching beneath her touch. "Do you think we would've met otherwise?"

"Of that I have no doubt."

"Yeah?" Her watery eyes lighten a bit, and a small grin curls at her lips.

"Yeah." Lowering my hand to her ass, I pat the luscious flesh so she stands. "Now, let's get you fed and caffeinated before we continue with this talk. And before you say you're not hungry...humor me."

"Do I have a choice?" I'm happy to see that even with the world she knew crumbling around her, my Twirl still has her sass. That she's not pushing me away.

She's hurting, and before the day is over, it'll only get worse. Today I'm staying home to show her what they've done—stolen from her. She'll learn that her father isn't Marcus and that Alton is a depraved son of a bitch.

They both are.

To free her, I have no choice but to break her heart.

I don't answer her. Instead, I pick her up by the waist and I stand us up, only to place her in my seat. There's a small huff, maybe even a slap to my shoulder, but she doesn't fight me when I prepare her coffee or when I place a plate of cheesy eggs and toast in front of her.

"Eat, and come to my office when you're done. I got a few emails to look at."

"Eye, captain." Twirl even gives me a mock salute.

"So bratty."

"You like it."

"I love it." The words slip, but I don't take them back. I do love her mouthiness and playful nature. Her positive outlook and hunger to experience everything life has to offer. "Now, eat up. You have thirty minutes before I come looking for you."

"How can they live with themselves?" London asks me thirty minutes later; the evidence I've given her so far lies on the floor where the folder landed after slipping through her fingers. She's shaking, begging me to make it go away, but I can't. I'm going to do what no one else had the decency to do, and tell her the truth. "My life has been nothing but a lie. One on top of another while the castle they built is now drowning me."

"It was never your mother's intention to hurt you, sweetheart, but she made bad decisions." I bend down to gather the folder and its fallen contents before taking her hand and walking us to a small seating area inside my office. Waiting for her signal to continue isn't easy when all I want to do is break those chains holding her down.

After a little while, London holds out her hand for the information again. "They're not my family."

Not a question. It's a statement, and I nod beside her. "No. They aren't."

"Okay..." she swallows hard, lip trembling "...how do I find out who my biological—"

"Already done." Pulling out the second sheet inside the file, I hand it to her. Just stay quiet as she reads every line with precision. I've seen the photos of her mother, and while they hold a resemblance, there's also a deep connection to her father's Italian roots. Her complexion, hair color, and even the slightly fuller lips come from his side of the family. His mother and sister were the same.

"Julian Conte," Twirl says the name slowly, tilting her head to the side. Thinking, the deep furrow of her brows and the faraway look in her eyes tell me as much. "I've heard that name in passing all my life. *Julian Conte.*" Closing her eyes, she sits back against the cushions. Two tears fall, and she doesn't wipe them away. "You know, most fights between them ended with his name being shouted out by Marcus, and all this time, I just thought it was some model or actor from their youth that Mom had the hots for and he was jealous of."

SIN

London's sad eyes open and land on mine. "How did you find all of this? Why?"

"Beside my own concern for you?"

"Yes."

"Earl and Mary are terrified you'll end up like your mom. A shadow of herself."

"They know?" she gasps, sitting forward while I nod in confirmation. "Why the hell didn't they tell me anything? Why stay quiet all this time?"

"Because Marcus threatened to move you far away and cut all contact. With hurting you physically, and neither was willing to take that chance. They had no help, London, and did the best they could to be there for you."

"Jesus, this is..." she trails off, and I wrap her tightly in my arms as the first sob breaks free from her chest. Just hold her to me while the reality of what could've been seeps through, and we're not even at the worst. Where my suspicions lie.

Seeing her tears feels like a dagger to my chest. It hurts.

Caring for someone does that to you. Their pain is yours, and you will tear the world apart to take it away. Nothing has proven this fact to me more than seeing her this distraught.

The way London clings to me so desperately further ignites my need for their blood. I want her gripping me from pleasure, never pain.

Kissing her forehead, I breathe in her sweet scent. It helps calm me. Keeps my focus on her and not ending them. I made a promise that their end will be slow, and it will be. Each strike from me will leave them reeling—crying for a mercy I will never grant.

"They both love you but couldn't take on either of them. Not without help, because sadly, they know someone in the Chicago PD that covers for them."

Her head shoots up at that, blue orbs wide with fear. "Lieutenant Bristol. That's who they know...he and Alton went to high school together."

207

"Thank you, sweetheart." Slowly, I wipe the dampness from her cheeks. "I knew the whom, just needed confirmation on the connection."

"He's a cocky jerk. The guy has always given me the creeps."

"Did he ever touch you?" There's an unmistakable bite to my tone. If he has, the Lieutenant will be dead by the end of the night.

"Was he creepy? Yes, but never moved past a leer or comments on my looks. I swear."

"Okay." I'll leave it at that for now, but something still doesn't sit right with me about this man. Especially if he's covering for the Fosters because no one does anything without some sort of personal gain. His job is on the line and so is possible jail time if found out.

What did they offer him?

London grabs the file then and continues to look over each document, pausing on a particular one detailing the Conte family. The one she will never get to meet. "They're all dead?"

"All except for your cousin Aurora who lives in the Lincoln Park area. She's the daughter of your father's sister who passed away a few years ago due to complications from a kidney transplant."

"I have a cousin," she breathes out, and for the first time since we started this talk, Twirl smiles. It's a curious one with just a hint of excitement. "Mom was an only child and my grandparents died when I was small…I've never had anyone outside of the Fosters."

"Well, now you have my family, and we're crazy enough to keep you entertained for years to come."

"You'll probably give me greys early." And it's that comment that lets me know she'll be more than okay. The sadness lingers, but it won't be permanent. This opens the doors for her to another world, and I think that gives her hope.

"That mouth of yours." I give her a playful growl before leaning over to nip her shoulder. "But there's more to discuss, and I need your attention for a minute."

"What else?" There's trepidation in her tone.

"You're the sole beneficiary in your mothers will, London. Just you."

"That can't be right...they...Marcus told me...*fuck!*" She rubs a hand down her face. "It's mine?"

I get up and kneel in front of her, bring our faces level, and I'm proud to see some anger in those expressive blue orbs. "Say the word, and I'll proceed with getting everything handed back to you. The house is yours and so is the monthly stipend you get—and they've been misspending—until you turn twenty-one and receive your inheritance from Amelia and Julian."

"And the Fosters?"

"Karma."

"In that case...*word.*"

Chapter 27
LONDON

FOR THE LAST THREE days I've been under a fog. Just going through the motions as I make peace with what I now know to be the truth. Everything I knew is a lie. A tiny fib that at first seems innocent—a man finding love with a widow, wanting to take care of her and her small child as they navigate through their new normal. It has all the makings of the perfect daytime movie on one of the popular channels women fawn over.

But it's not like that in reality. This story is a nightmare that I have not fully awoken from.

How can I? For years, I was nothing more than a servant to those two men—the same two that were supposed to be family. My protectors.

I did everything they told me to. Have been working to help pay bills and fund their vices so I could escape their threats for another day.

I'm a joke to them. Nothing but a pawn.

Truth is that the more I read, the more it stings. The angrier I am.

"Sick assholes," I hiss out, putting my hair up in a loose bun before grabbing the next paper in the file Malcolm gave me. This one has Julian's information, and I read through it for the thousandth time. Seeing in bold black ink where he's from and the dynamic of his family makes me both happy and melancholic.

Happy because I can see they were good people. Sad because I will never have that with them.

You have Malcolm now.

And I do. God knows he's been a saint as I sort my head.

I'm safe because of him. Because he cares.

I want to stay for him. Make him happy.

However, right now my focus is on my father's life story on these next few pages:

How his parents were from Rome and came here when Dad was three.

What schools he went to, where they lived here in Chicago, and the pictures of my parents on their wedding day. The smiles on their faces brings one to my own, and how he looks at her reminds me of the way Malcolm gazes at me. It's that same sweet and unguarded expression that makes my skin flush and heart beat fast.

Then there's the knowledge that my father's buried in the same mausoleum as my mother. That they're resting together, and that every time I visit, he's there listening too. Dad's ashes lie in the space beside my mother's. Something she did without anyone's knowledge—without Marcus finding out—so she could be with him again someday.

The last few pages in this file explain the financial situation I'm in. What has been taken; the sale of Dad's restaurant chain, and how at his death, everything he owned went to Mom and then me. The details of two hefty life insurance policies are here too, and while the amounts surprise me, learning that Marcus knew my father before his death doesn't sit well with me.

A horrible feeling I can't shake churns within my gut the more I think about it. The more I stare at the few pictures that Malcolm put inside the folder.

Why would my father associate with a man like him?

My guess is that it all comes down to money.

Back then it was his or hers, and now it's mine. The Fosters want and have plans for it.

Knowing all these minute details helps me put together the pieces of a puzzle that were missing. Things that now make sense the more I think about it.

All my life I've thought that Alton and I are nothing alike. We differ in both personalities and looks. No resemblance whatsoever outside of our blue eyes, and his are a darker shade than mine. For years, I just thought that each kid took after one parent, but it's so obvious to me now how wrong I was.

Mom wouldn't hurt a fly, while Marcus doesn't care about anyone other than himself. She was selfless to his selfish.

"I've been so blind," I mutter to myself and rub my left eye. I'm tired. Just plain ol' exhausted but can't stop re-reading what these papers say. "How could Mom let him—"

"Breaking News," comes from the TV then, stopping my train of thought. The local anchor is on the screen and tilting her iPad toward her. Her face shows no emotions while her eyes are wide, looking at someone beside her and then at the monitor. **"An explosion occurred a few minutes ago at a warehouse near the South Side now known to be the headquarters of a local prostitution ring. Luckily, no one was on the premises when the blast occurred, and the authorities are searching for the identity of the owner."** She pauses and looks toward another camera. **"We'll**

have more for you soon as our team arrives on the scene. If you or someone you know has any information that can help arrest those responsible, please call the number on your screen."

Doesn't Alton rent a building in the South Side? I know I've seen the rental agreement for it.

I HAVEN'T HEARD a peep from the Fosters in five days now.

Not from them. Not from my Malcolm about them.

Nothing. Not even confirmation of my suspicions about the explosions that took out a large building on the South Side.

It's almost as if they don't exist, and I like it. Love the peace and normalcy I'm experiencing.

Things that to other people are boring, I'm enjoying—from doing laundry to watching a cooking show during the middle of the day—there's no rush in my schedule or fear of someone's wrath. I'm just being me. Thinking. Figuring at my pace what I want to do with the rest of my life.

For the first time, nothing's off the table and everything has possibilities.

My life at the moment is domesticated bliss, while tomorrow I could go back to school and he'd be just as happy for me. He enjoys my cooking, more than Magda's, but will adjust if that's what I need. I am falling for this man more and more every day.

His generosity. How sweet he is with me.

How safe I am because everyone around us respects him.

The small things he does to let me know he cares.

Like now, I'm at the stove finishing our dinner as he walks through the door that connects the garage to the house. He's smiling at me with a long-stemmed rose in his hand. It's a light blush and in full bloom. "Honey, I'm home," he croons with this handsome-ish, cocky grin on his face that only he can pull off. His strides are long as he walks over, the dark pinstripe three-piece suit he's wearing looks delicious on his body. This man is perfection. "Miss me?"

"Someone's in a good mood." Taking the flower from him, I crook a finger, so he crouches a bit to my level. Without any kind of heels, it's hard to reach him even if I stand on the tip of my toes. When he does, I don't hesitate to kiss his smiling mouth. Just a quick peck, then nibble. "And thank you."

"I'm in a great mood." Malcolm wraps his arms around my body, pulling me closer. Chest to chest. "You're here, and the food smells delicious. What're you making?"

"Enchiladas two ways." My own hands explore. Caressing his arms and then shoulders, I dig my fingers in a bit on my way to the nape of his neck where I embed my fingers in his hair. "Then for dessert, I made my very first flan."

Making our dinner has become my thing. Gives me a chance to spoil him a bit.

Magda gave me complete use of her kitchen, and I gave her the afternoon off. She's been here for years and I didn't want to step on her toes, but when I mentioned wanting to do this, Magda just gave me a huge hug and told me to go nuts and have fun. That this is my house too.

"Fuck, I'm a lucky son of a bitch," he groans and then slants his mouth over mine. This kiss is hungry, a full possession of my senses as his tongue meets mine—caressing and tasting me. His body is wound tight against mine. Muscles clenching, Malcolm picks me up and places me on the countertop beside the stove, stepping between my parted thighs and pressing his throbbing length against my cotton-covered core.

The thin material of my shorts lets me feel him. All of him.

His slacks do little to hide his desire for me, and I want more.

To explore, and I almost say this when the timer goes off.

"Don't stop," I beg, but he pulls back. Just a few steps, but it does nothing to cool the need burning through my veins. "Ignore the food. Come back."

Malcolm shakes his head, that same shitty grin is back. "No."

"Why?" I pout, eyes wandering down his body and settling on the thick outline of his length. "I'll leave it in the warmer and—"

"I'm going to run upstairs and take a shower..." my mouth opens to protest, but the predatory gleam in his eyes shuts me up "... behave, and I'll eat you for dessert later, instead."

***

"Have I thanked you for dinner yet?" His lips skim my ear, causing goose bumps to break out across my skin. His breath fans across my neck and then lower when he nibbles on my shoulder. "Told you how fantastic it was?"

"Only about a hundred times." I'm sitting between his spread thighs on the living room couch with my back to his chest. His bare chest. There's some thriller movie playing in the background, based on a book he seems to love, but for the life of me I can't concentrate. I'm tense. Aware of every solid inch of him and this overwhelming need to please him.

Maybe it's because of how gentle he's been with me or the way he helps me sort through my thoughts. How he never fails to ask me what I want or what plans I have for us in the future.

How proud of me he was when I told him my desire to open a foundation that helps women escape violent situations. Victims— women and children—who have no way out of the nightmare they live in. People like myself; who escaped because someone cared enough to save them.

Malcolm inserts himself so flawlessly into my tomorrows, and I don't find myself minding his company one bit. I value his opinions. His intelligence.

Everything about him drives me crazy in the best of ways. I want more.

More time. More of his touch. More of these drugging little flicks of his tongue over the area right beneath my earlobe.

However, every time I try...he puts a stop to my advances.

He's waiting on me to heal from the lies that broke my heart, but what he fails to realize is that he put me back together again that same night.

"Well, it was amazing, and I appreciate the effort." His fingertips skim the edge of my loose tank top, dipping beneath the hem to caress my stomach.

"You're welcome, and none needed." It's a low keening sound that escapes without my permission. Slowly, those same hands wander high, over my torso and stop around my neck. One alone takes up the entire expanse, and I'm distracted by how unafraid I am of him.

His masculinity calls to the inner slut in me. How much bigger he is—his hardness to my petite form is a turn-on. It makes me think of more intimate moments where he could easily dominate me. Take me.

I want him to claim me.

"I'm going to enjoy spoiling you, Twirl," he whispers, tightening his hand so I can feel the thin metal chain he's holding against my throat. Where he's hid it all this time, I have no clue, but then again being distracted does that to a person. The charm digs into the skin a bit. It's cold, small and round, a delicate piece that he brings up to my face after letting go. "My tiny dancer. So beautiful and devilishly sweet."

"Malcolm," it's a breathless sigh. My eyes are on the thin, gold chain with a vintage locket hanging from it. The intricate design on it is beautiful, but what stands out is the delicate ballerina in an en pointe pose. "It's so pretty and too much. You've already—"

"Arguing with me will get you nowhere, London." Large fingers open the clasp and show me an old photo inside. "Do you like it?"

"How did you...?" My eyes water, and I turn to look back at him with a huge smile on my face. So thankful for this man. "Where did you get this picture?"

"I have my ways." His smirk is so sinful, his body mouth-watering.

"Put it on me." He does as I ask when I turn back around to face the TV. The fact that he went looking for a picture of my mother and me as a baby leaves me without words. And while there are three that I want to say, they evade me at the moment.

I might not have any experience when it comes to sex, but I know what I want. And I want him.

Not because I need to repay this kind gift, but because nothing will please me more than loving him. Showing him with my actions what I can't verbalize just yet.

Before he can protest, I stand and turn to face him. On my knees and between his, I place my hands on his thighs and squeeze the now tense muscles. Massage him slowly, all the while my eyes are on his.

His wander, though. From my baby blues, to my lips, and then to the now beautiful gift he's given me. Malcolm looks me up and down in this position; I can see the want in his eyes. Almost touch the fire that burns between us.

Our need is palpable.

Combustible.

And I'm tired of the words *no* and *slow*.

"London, you don't have to do this." He swallows hard when I bite my bottom lip. "My gifts don't come with any expectations."

"All the more reason to act on my own wants. This isn't for you..." walking my fingertips up his gym shorts, I pause at the waistband and pull the fabric back, exposing him "...this is for me."

Chapter 28
LONDON

MALCOLM DOESN'T MAKE A single move to stop me. Doesn't so much as breathe when I wrap my hand around his girth, fingers not fully touching as I pull him out. He's thick and long, absolutely perfect with velvet-smooth skin and a drop of clear-like fluid at the tip.

There's a part of me that's scared. It's my first time touching a man like this, and yet excitement wins out. I'm curious.

I want to explore him. I want to taste him.

Enjoy the more intimate part of a relationship between a man and his woman.

Because that's what this is. It's clear to me that he is mine and I am his.

My mouth waters at the sight, and I lick my lips. "Show me, Malcolm. Teach me how to please you."

At my words, his entire body shakes. A deep rumbling sound forms in his chest, and I pull my eyes away from the perfection throbbing in my hand to meet his eyes. They're hooded, and the hunger in them causes my core to clench.

"That's a dangerous offer, Twirl." His hand comes over mine and strokes twice, the grip tight. "The way I want you is dangerous. Perverse. If you're not ready for all of me...want this, back off and head upstairs. This is your one out."

Mimicking his fluid motion, I pump him once on my own, causing him to groan. "Please."

"Are you sure?" It's a hiss, his hands clenching at his sides. He's holding back for my sake, and I don't want that. "I'll never hurt you, but I won't be gentle. Can you handle all of me?"

Instead of answering him, I do something that seals my fate. Ties me to him.

I lean forward and kiss the very tip of his swollen head, rubbing my lips back and forth once and then lick his essence from them. Then, just to push him further, I place him back inside his shorts and sit back on my calves, meeting his stare. Let him see in mine how serious I am.

How ready I am for every single part of him.

Malcolm gives me a nod and then that sexy grin I like. "Lose the top, Twirl. Show me those pretty tits." Without a second thought, I lose the simple cotton shirt and toss it somewhere behind me, followed by my bra. He sucks in a breath but doesn't say anything, his eyes roaming, caressing the curves of my breasts. "Come closer and arch your back. Tell me to touch you."

That gravelly voice is a weakness of mine. Something so natural and raw, the tone of his voice—the hunger in it—send a shiver down my spine.

"Please," I whimper as my nipples tighten to almost the point of pain. Pain at being denied what I need.

Him. From that very first time inside the room at Liam's club, my world has been revolving around his. I belong to him. He's my happy place.

"*Fuck*, the neediness in your tone is delicious." Malcolm brings a hand up to my chest and cups my right breast, weighing it in his hands before pinching the tight little bud. He gives it a harsh tug, but instead of cringing away, I welcome the new sensation. The sting of pleasurable pain causes my core to clench and clit to throb. "You want this," he croons before giving the same treatment to the left. "Want me."

"Yes." I arch further, inviting him to take more. "It's you. All of you."

"Good girl." With the hand on my chest, he pushes me back a bit, and I scoot two steps back. He stands then, over six feet of solid muscle hovering over me, the outline of his thickness at my eye level. "Undress me."

My hands tremble. The thrill of the moment travels through my body, goose bumps rising as I use his thighs as leverage to stand to full height. My face to his chest, I step into his space and lay a tiny kiss over the place where his heart is, then across his other pec as I work my way up.

I nip his collarbone, standing on the tip of my toes to reach his chin where my teeth dig in just a tiny bit. "I trust you, Malcolm."

"Say it again." His hands take hold of my hips and lift me off the floor so I can look at him in the eye. "Tell me."

"I trust you," I whisper before kissing him. Hungrily. Needing him to accept that for as much as he wants me, I can't be without him anymore.

His tongue in my mouth is demanding and I gladly submit to him, soaking up his every grunt for more. How his hold on me tightens when I swipe my tongue across his bottom lip. "Addictive little thing. So fucking perfect."

"We are. Perfect for each other." Slowing us down to a few soft pecks, I wiggle in his hold. Malcolm pulls back to look at me, but I arch a brow. "You might want to put me down."

"Do I?"

"You will if you want me to use my mouth in a more productive way." I make a show of licking my bottom lip in a slow swipe he follows. That causes his dick to flex against my hip.

Malcolm leans forward and takes the still wet lip and bites down hard enough for it to sting. "As you wish, sweet Twirl." He lets go after a quick kiss and lowers me, my body sliding against his until my feet meet the floor.

Once I have my balance, he steps away and sits down, the expression on his face similar to the very first time we met inside the club.

It's a bit of an angry hunger mixing with his natural edge that makes him dangerous for me.

And I'm wet for him. Soaking my panties and the thin boxers I stole from him.

Knowing that I want to feel all of him, I take in a deep breath and shimmy out of the shorts. My panties too.

Humming his approval, he makes a turning motion with his hand and I give him what he wants. Taking my position with one foot slightly back, I gift him three slow twirls and then on the last, drop back to my knees.

I crawl the few steps between us, coming to a stop between his parted thighs. "Lift," is all I say as I give his bottoms a tug. On the next pull, he does as I ask and rises just enough so I can take both items covering him off.

Our eyes stay connected as I toss his boxer briefs and shorts somewhere behind me. What sounds like glass crashes on the floor, but neither of us stops to look.

Instead, I lower my lips to his skin, trailing open-mouthed kisses up his right thigh. Let my instincts guide me. "I've never done this before, Malcolm. Never thought much about dating or sex. With you, though..." I nuzzle the soft hairs on his leg "...with you I want it all. Want to give you all my firsts."

"I'm going to cherish you, London. Give you the motherfucking world on a silver platter if that's what you wish for." His fingers thread through my hair, pushing the long strands back off my face before wrapping it around his fist. A tug has me hovering over his cock. "Now kiss it. Show your appreciation."

My tongue darts out, swiping over the slit before I lay tiny kisses from tip to base. "Show me how to please you."

"Open your mouth, baby." It's a hiss, his fingers tightening their hold as I follow the instructions, sliding his length through my parted lips. "*Damn*, you look beautiful like this. Worshipping my cock with those plump lips like the good little slut I knew you could be."

His words should offend me, but they don't. I enjoy them. Let them travel across my senses as this part of me I didn't know comes alive. Thrives beneath his touch.

"More," I say around his shaft, pressing my tongue against him before taking the tip between my lips and sucking. His hips buck before he pulls all the way out. He holds me above him, hard eyes on mine as a whine leaves the back of my throat. "Don't stop."

"Beg me," he growls, fingers tightening, and the stinging bite settles on my clit. "Beg me to suck my cock."

"Please let me suck your cock, Mr. Asher."

"Motherfuck." Slowly, he lowers my mouth down his shaft, rubbing the underside on my tongue as I hollow my cheeks. It throbs, his pre-come coating my lips when he pulls me up and off, rubbing himself over my lips with each pump of his hips.

I lick them. His taste off them. "More."

"My naughty little girl," he grits out, pushing in deeper, and my first instinct is to pull back. I gag as he touches the back of my throat, but his hold keeps me in place. "Relax, sweetheart, and breathe through your nose. Yeah...just like that...*fuck*."

He thrusts his hips a few times and stops, pulling me off so I can catch my breath. "Ready?" he asks.

I nod, not entirely sure what he means, before he guides me down again and I take him between my lips. The thickness of his cock makes me ache with the desire—with the need to feel him filling me, and my thighs rub together in search of the friction I crave.

"Let's see how much you can take." I barely get in a deep breath before his hips flex up and both hands push on the back of my head. The moment I begin to gag again, he holds me still, instead, giving short little thrusts into my mouth. "Swallow." It's a difficult task, one that earns me a deep groan before he begins pushing again. "I'll get this mouth trained. One day you'll take it all."

I gag again and attempt to breathe through my nose, and he pulls me off, leaving a string of spit connecting my lips to his cock. Once I get control of my breathing, he repeats, sliding to the back of my throat and holding me there as I acclimate to the sensation.

This time, when he thrusts up, I don't gag. Knowing what to expect calms me, and I look at him from beneath my lashes. Four quick pumps and I'm moaning around him, sliding my teeth over his skin on each exit.

"Fuck, Twirl," he groans before letting go of my hair, arms stretching out. "So wet and hot. That mouth is the definition of sin."

I pull back and take in a deep breath. "Did I pass, Mr. Asher?"

"You did, and you've earned a reward. One that you will swallow all of."

"Yes, sir." It's a whimper. A plea. I ache for him.

"How wet are you?"

I bite down on my bottom lip as I nod, my hand slipping between my thighs. I let out a shaky moan as my fingers swipe across my swollen clit. "Soaking and needy."

"Show me." Gathering up some of the wetness, I pull my fingers up to show them glistening. He grabs my wrist and pulls my fingers to his lips, his tongue lapping up the juice before sucking them into his mouth. "So juicy."

"Please."

"Rub that pretty little kitty while sucking my cock, London. Make me come." I love the commanding tone, crave it, and obey, because it's something I want just as much as he needs.

I wrap my hand around the base and take him into my mouth again. This time there's no instruction, no guidance. He wants to see how badly I want it, and I'm about to show him. Instinct and desire mingle and intensify, and I find myself moving up and down his length, sucking and lavishing the hard flesh with my tongue. "That's it, beautiful. Take me deeper, Twirl...let me fuck that mouth."

In that moment I realize another truth. There is nothing sexier than a man's moan. His pleading for your touch.

Taking him all the way back, I fight the urge to pull off and breathe through my nose. "Mmm," I hum and then rake my teeth down his length. The muscles of his abs contract and he throws his head back, closing his eyes and biting his bottom lip.

It's that sight right there that brings my hand back between my thighs, and I rub myself while working my mouth up and down his length at a rapid pace. I'm so close, thighs trembling. All I need is a little more to find my own release when he breaks me.

"Don't fucking move, and swallow every drop," Malcolm all but snarls, lip curling just a bit, and I pause. Follow his instruction and suck, hollowing my cheeks as the first stream of come coats my tongue. As the second follows, my own orgasm tears through me and I tremble, riding my fingers as he gives me every last drop.

When he's done, I lick him clean and lay my head on his thigh. My jaw hurts a bit and my body still tingles, but that is an experience I want to do again. And again.

Before I can fully catch my breath, Malcolm lifts me up and into his arms. Cradles me against his chest while tipping my face up to meet his. "Hi."

The softness in those gorgeous green eyes and the sexy grin cause me to giggle. "Someone's happy."

"Someone isn't ever letting his precious gift go."

"Is that so?" I nuzzle his cheek. "Because no one asked me if I agree to this."

"Babe, the moment you walked into my room that night, you lost all rights." Then, he surprises me with a quick and passionate kiss. Tasting himself on my lips, he groans and pulls back so I can see just how serious he is. "You're mine."

Chapter 29
LONDON

I 'M IN BLISS. A wonderful period of my life where everything feels right, and I have no worries. It's like being a kid all over with the added bonus of having adult privileges.

In the last two weeks I've come to terms with the lies and betrayal. I've forgiven my mother because when all is said and done, she did the best she could. She stayed with a monster to give me the best life possible with the cards she was dealt. Out of her love for me, she endured so much pain with the Fosters.

I remember the shouts. Her cries. Her wanting to leave but staying because we were a family.

Losing my father must've been hard. I can only imagine the emptiness she felt, because I now understand what love does to a person. What you will do for them.

I'd kill to save him if it ever came to that.

Being with Malcolm, seeing his own feelings for me come to light with each action he takes, is humbling. Fills my once-beaten heart with joy. I'm in a better place because of him.

I love him.

His easy smiles. His charming disposition.

Even the darkness he tries to hide from me.

Every single facet of his personality calls to mine, and I accept him as he comes.

Dangerous and sweet. The perfect deadly concoction.

"We're here, London," Gina says, bringing me back to the present as we park in front of a Starbucks. "Are you coming, or do I get you the usual?"

"Nah. Give me a moment and I'll come in." Pulling my cell from my small purse, I send him a text.

> Getting coffee, and then heading home after a stop at the paint supply store. What do you want for dinner? ~Twirl

Putting it away for now, I exit the car and walk toward the entrance. Gina is just past the threshold when someone pulls on my arm.

"What the...?" My eyes shift toward the person; the curse on the tip of my tongue dies at the sight of Brittany. She looks just like the last time I saw her. Angry and overdone in the makeup department. Desperation swirls all around her.

"Aren't you going to say hello to your brother's fiancée, Lola?" Another tug, her hold painful, and I yelp. "Come give me a hug."

My head shakes, and before I can call Gina, the click of a gun is heard. She's right beside me, her Glock pointing at Brittany's chest. "Remove your hand. You have three seconds before I shoot."

She lets go and holds both hands up. "I'm just saying hello. No need for the hostility."

"Bullshit, and you know it." Gina steps between us further, pushing me back, creating distance between us. "Leave."

"This is a public—"

"Mr. Asher will be in touch," she spits out, interrupting Brittany who looks toward a store across the street. My eyes follow and meet the ones of a man I hate. Alton stares at me, then looks to Gina, and you can visibly see his disdain for her.

He mouths the word *I miss you* slowly then gives me a wave, and I shudder. I'm so caught up in my disgust that I miss the rest of their conversation. All I manage to catch is the sight of Brittany walking past us.

She's at the curb's edge when she turns to look back at me from over her shoulder. "I'll be seeing you soon, dear little Lola. Oh, and tell Asher he's welcome."

MY ARM IS a little sore after we get home. Her hold had been painful and my old fading bruises become a little red.

"Fucking great," I say, rubbing the area of my forearm when my phone beeps from somewhere in the foyer.

Forgetting the coffee, we came straight back. I tossed my bag on a table while Gina left to find Magda and some ice for my arm. After, she left to go and pick up the painting supplies which were my last stop for the day. I want to change the color of our bedroom walls from white to a grey-ish mauve color that caught my eyes on a design show.

That was an hour ago, and I'm still in a daze.

My vacation from them has come to an abrupt end.

Another beep and I follow the sound, finding the small device on the floor of all places. Picking it up, I swipe a finger over the screen and find ten texts and four missed calls. All from Malcolm.

> Something simple is fine ~Malcolm

> Or how about I bring dinner, and you wait for me naked on our bed ~Malcolm

> I want you to sit on my face tonight and ride my tongue ~Malcolm

A few others go on like that until the last one a few minutes ago.

> I'm coming home. ~Malcolm

Touching the small picture of him I have at the top of our message thread; I press the call button and wait. It barely rings once when he answers, the harsh rustle of wind on his end lets me know he's outside—more than likely heading my way.

"Are you okay?" There's some bite to his tone, but I know it's not with me. A car honks near him and then another. "Tell me you are okay?"

"I'm fine, babe. A little shook up, but fine...I promise." Opening the front door, I walk down the steps and down his driveway. My mind is racing, trying to fight off the fear seeing *him* brought on, and I need to keep moving. Put one foot in front of the other as I fight to find my calm.

"They should have never approached you. I'm sorry—"

"Not your fault." And it isn't. However, it does make me think. Makes me wonder what it'll take to rid myself of the men I thought were family. "Actually, I'm safe because of you. Because you care."

"I more than care. Never doubt that."

His words bring a smile to my face and I close my eyes, soaking in the meaning behind them. "I more than care too."

"I know." Cocky man. "Maybe we can call it a Netflix and Chill day?"

"Get back to work, Mr. Asher."

"London—"

229

"Chop *chop*, mister." The leaves to my left rustle, but I pay them no mind. This property is safe. "Go wrap up whatever you need to and then come home. We'll order a pizza and eat it in bed while watching that boring movie you had on last time."

"So bratty."

"You bring it out of me."

"Are you sure? I can come back with no problem."

"Positive. See you soon, babe." Disconnecting the call, I open my eyes and realize that I'm at the end of his long driveway. At the entrance and staring into the eyes of a man I've never seen before. "Who are you?"

"Are you a Miss London Gabriela Foster?" The way he says my name, as if he knows me, isn't sitting well with me. That, and how does he know my middle name? I never use it. "Please don't be alarmed, ma'am. I just want to talk to you."

I take a step back from the closed gate. "How do you know my name?"

"Can I come in and speak to you? I'm with the FBI and have some questions."

"Show me your I.D." *Where the hell is security?* I know someone is always guarding the entrance and back of the property. "If I do, can I come in?"

"You need to regardless." His eyes tighten at my answer, lips thinning, but he schools the expression quick enough. Back is the smile he gave me when I first noticed him standing here. It creeps me out. He creeps me out. "Never mind. Whatever it is, I'm not interested."

"Did you know that the man you're sleeping with is a killer?"

That makes me pause and step back, my anger rising. "Why would you say something like that? Show me your badge, or my next move is to call security and the cops."

"As you wish." He pulls out a small manila packet from inside his suit jacket along with a bifold wallet. Flipping it open, he holds it to the bars so I can read his name. The first thing I notice is he's part of the Federal Bureau of Investigations and his name is Shawn Hayes. "Satisfied?"

"Not really." Some would think this should put me at ease. It's the opposite. Makes it worse.

Why would a member of a government agency be here?

Why would he avoid showing me his credentials until I mention calling the police? If he's here under direct orders, he wouldn't care. He also wouldn't be fidgeting and looking back every few minutes.

A true professional wouldn't be skulking in a corner or giving me leering looks.

"Look, I'm not here to make you uncomfortable, Miss Foster." Agent Hayes comes closer to the gate, shifting his eyes to the area behind me. "I'm here to help you. Get you out of a situation that could end with your body in a morgue."

"What the hell is—"

"Malcolm Asher is a killer."

"Leave. Go before I scream."

"He killed his last girlfriend, London." Shawn opens the manila envelope and pulls out what looks to be pictures. His jaw ticks as he looks at the first, his expression full of ire as he tosses them at my feet. I don't look down. I don't move. Whatever is in those photos I have no doubt will haunt me. "Go on. Look down."

"Leave."

"Fucking look before I jump this fence and make you." The warning in his tone, the way his hand goes to his side makes me bend slowly, following orders. There's a glint that comes from his weapon as he pulls it out. "Look at what he did to her. Karina Hughes is dead because of him."

A loud gasp leaves me and my stomach heaves; what's in the pictures below is haunting. Will forever be etched into my mind. "No. No." I'm shaking my head, hands trembling as I flip to the next. A beautiful girl.

Vacant eyes.

A bullet hole right between the eyes.

Her body with a bluish tint in a morgue, bruises littering her body.

Blood. So much freaking blood.

It's everywhere. Splatters. The floor and the wall behind her.

"He killed her. Took her from those who love her. Still mourn her."

"Leave," I say, my voice shaking, but get no response. When I look up, he's gone and I'm alone.

My body begins to shake, and breathing gets hard. Those empty, blank eyes are all I see.

Every image rushes across my mind in a fucked-up reel, a tiny horror movie that holds my life hostage. Fight or flight kicks in, and all I want to do is bolt. Run away from it all and never look back, however, I can't.

Maybe I'm crazy, but accepting this at face value feels wrong. Off.

Malcolm would never hurt someone he cares about. You know this.

"What're you doing, London?" a voice calls from the other side of the gate, the engine of a car running. "You okay? You're shaking."

My eyes leave the pictures and lock with Mariah's. "Help me."

Make sense. Tell me it's wrong.

Whatever she sees in my expression puts her in panic mode, and she runs back toward the gate's access panel. Her fingers work fast to push in the code, but to me everything seems to be happening in slow motion. Each breath is harder than the last.

This has to be an error. Please, God. Let it be wrong.

"What's got you so scared, sweetie. What're you looking…" Mariah trails off now, seeing what I am. She takes the pictures from my hand and pulls me with her toward the still running car, placing me in the passenger seat and even buckling me in.

I'm on autopilot, and it isn't until we pull into traffic down the street that I react. "Where are you taking me? What the hell is all this?"

"Who gave you those pictures?" she asks instead of answering me, making a right turn toward the expressway. "Please, London. It's important that I know where these came from."

"An FBI agent—"

She cuts her eyes to me. "A Shawn Hayes?"

"Yes, but why?" We're on an expressway with the signs indicating that The Loop is our destination. "What's going on? Why are you even here?"

"My cousin gave me the afternoon off and I decided to spend it with you. Was hoping we could get some lunch or watch a movie, but now that won't do." Cutting off an older man in a large SUV, she presses down on the gas of her BMW coupe. "You doubt him."

"My rational side is telling me to run, but my heart doubts what that agent said. The man I know, and the one Hayes painted, are not the same. Can't be."

"And what if he is?"

"Then there has to be a very good reason behind his actions." That's the God's honest truth. Deep down I know Malcolm is dangerous, my fam—the Fosters wouldn't fear him if he wasn't, but I still need an explanation. *I need him to make this right. Give me back the feeling of safety taken from me today.* "All I know is that right now, I'm scared."

"Of him?"

"Of everything." *Of knowing that either way, my feelings for him won't change.*

"All the more reason to go see him." With a high arch in her brow, she looks at me for confirmation.

"Would you take me back to the house or elsewhere if I say no?"

"Would I agree with it? No, but yes, I would."

"Thank you." I believe her. Just like I know that rash decisions can lead to catastrophes. That he's never been anything but good to me, and I have to believe in that if nothing else. "Now, take me to the Asher building. He needs to see these photos."

A small smile crosses her lips and she takes my hand in hers, squeezing. "Don't lose your trust in him, London. Not everything is as it seems."

Chapter 30
MALCOLM

EARLY THAT SAME MORNING...

"YOUR UNEXPECTED IS HERE," Mariah announces around ten thirty through the intercom. I've been expecting this visit.

Have seen him skulking around; at the airport and outside my building. He's following a dead-end trail that will lead to nowhere.

"Let him in." I grab my cup of coffee and sit back in my chair. Waiting. There's a ping on my computer, an incoming email that I've been waiting on all morning from the developer in Shanghai, but it'll have to wait. The construction of my building is ahead of schedule and will be completed within the next eight months versus a year.

I'm happy with that. Opens the door for more business.

"Good morning, Mr. Asher." Shawn enters my office sans Marcelles. His cocky gait and grin—that *I know something you don't* attitude doesn't intimidate me in the least. However, I'll give it to him for having enough balls to continue his pursuit.

"Drop the polite act and get to the point."

"Is that how you want to play?" Shawn eyes the documents on my desk, trying to read something he'll never understand. It's in Mandarin and from the office of a powerful organization requesting my services.

To this agent's detriment, I've read his file. Know his strengths and weaknesses. While the man prides himself on his brute attributes, the skill of speaking several languages evades him. He understands some Spanish and Italian, but that's it. There's no fluency.

"Curiosity is killing you, isn't it." Not a question. And while he will like nothing more than to take a picture or the paperwork itself, that would be breaking the law. No warrant, and it's an invasion of privacy.

Inadmissible in court with the right amount of money thrown at it.

"One day you will fall, and I'll be there to expose you. Walk you out of this building in handcuffs."

"Is that right? Keep talking...please." With my cup, I point to both a camera and the intercom system that's still on. "Threatening a highly respected man, harassing him, won't look good for the agency."

"People like you make me sick. You have no right to record me—"

"This is not a public domain, Agent Hayes." Standing from my chair, I walk around it and lean back on my desk. Wave a hand around. "It's my building. My property, and I can surveil anywhere I wish to."

"Why were you in Miami recently?"

"Are you following me, Agent? Have I become an obsession?" I counter. If he thinks that knowing my travel itinerary will scare me, once again he put the eggs in the wrong basket. Had he been paying closer attention, my meeting in Costa Rica should've been the priority. "And to answer your question; we needed to refuel. I never left the airport."

"Where were you prior?" He's getting agitated, face red. "What are you hiding?"

"Am I under arrest? Do you have a court-issued warrant?"

"No, but—"

I silence him with a hand held up. "Get out, and quit wasting my time."

Hayes puts his hands inside his pockets and rocks back. "It's in your best interest to cooperate with me."

"Is that right? And why is that?" Javier and Carmelo appear at the doorway to escort him out, but I give a minute shake of my head that stops them. "Please tell me why that is."

"Think of those you love."

"I'd take that same advice, Agent Hayes. Be very careful who you threaten." Looking back at Javi, I signal him to come in closer. "Get him off my premises, and tell Mariah to get me in contact with Director Monahan. I'm done playing games."

"Consider it done, boss." Carmelo places a hand on Shawn's shoulder. "You can leave two ways...escorted, or on your own. Choose wisely."

Hayes shrugs his arm off, all the while his glare is set on me. "You'll be very sorry soon enough." With that he leaves, and both men follow. One to make sure he leaves, and the other to tell his girl to contact the FBI director.

This man is going to be a problem.

I can already see it.

Another loose end that needs to be cut off from this thread.

PRESENT...

AFTER MY TALK WITH LONDON, I'm calm enough to head back upstairs and get a few last-minute items done. With everything happening, I'm going to take a few days off and surprise her with a small vacation.

She needs this, and so do I.

I also need to feel those juicy lips wrapped around me. On a tropical island where it's only us and naked, the sun bathing her skin while I fuck her mouth. Take her innocence and claim it.

My mind revisits how well she took me down her throat a few days ago—how easily she gave in to her needs and handed the control over. Since then, I've eaten her out a few times and then came in her mouth as I stood above her, jacking off to the sight of her satiated face. It's done the job of calming me down, gave her the chance to embrace who she really is, but the wait is over.

"What do you think, Mr. Asher?" Li Qiang, my oversight director, asks. He's been working with the developer and a P.R. agency—transferring over to this location from North Korea to keep us on this new schedule. If we lose the momentum, have to change things again to accommodate a new completion date, it'll cost me more than the money I'm spending.

Customers, my clientele, don't trust those that are late. Constantly change times and dates.

"Contact Mariah tomorrow, Li. She's handling the final decisions regarding the grand opening and its guest list. What she says goes."

There's a knock on the door, and I hold up a hand for them to give me a moment. "That's right. Okay, I'll let her know." Another knock, a bit more persistent, and I look up to find my girl and Mariah, both wearing matching expressions. He says something else, but my focus is on an upset Twirl. On the hold she has on an envelope in her hands. "I got to go. Call her at some point tomorrow and figure it out."

"O—"

I hang up before he finishes, already making my way to her. When I reach her, I take London's hand in mine and ignore the slight flinch. Whatever happened between our phone call and now has her scared.

It's like seeing that lost little lamb all over again from the first night at the club.

Shifting my eyes to Mariah, I level her with a hard stare. "What happened?"

"She had a visit to the house."

The moment those words seep through, my vision gets hazy and red. Anger rushes through every limb, and I have to take a few steps back. I don't want to make things worse, but the way I feel right now is nothing less than murderous.

"Shawn Hayes was at the house?" It's a barely contained snarl, and Mariah is smart enough to close the door to my office. She nods in confirmation. "What did he do?"

My eyes are on my cousin, but it's London that answers, pulling my attention toward her. She takes a few steps my way with a look on her face that I can't quite decipher. "He gave me these at the gate, and before you ask, when we were on the phone, I took a walk down the driveway, not really paying attention since I feel safe there. When I hung up with you, there he was. Looking at me and quite honestly, giving me the creeps."

"Show me." Yet I make no move to touch her. I'm shaking. Hands clenching.

"I'm not looking at those again." When I make no move to take the envelope, a flash of hurt crosses her soft features. She hides it under a mask of indifference, but I see it. All of her, while with trembling hands, she places them atop my desk. "Please look and explain, Malcolm. All I want is an explanation of why that man did this."

Nodding, I walk to my desk and open the now-worn manila packet. The second the first photo falls into my hand, I have to take a moment to breathe. That son of a bitch has no idea what he's just done.

"Empty this floor and the three beneath, Mariah. No calls or interruptions for the rest of the day," I say with my back to them, leaning with my palms flat on my desk. The pictures scatter in front of me, yet it's the one with her face, bullet wound on display, that I focus on. There's an eerie calmness taking over my body. Scenarios playing out and plans forming.

Shawn Hayes just signed over his life to me.

"Of course. I'll be with Javier downstairs if you need us." The door opening and closing follows, leaving just the two of us inside my quiet office. Her breathing and mine are the only sounds within.

On my next inhale, she's behind me. Close, her hand presses against the center in a supportive gesture. "Talk to me. Don't shut me out."

Not moving. Just touching. Her warm touch begins to thaw the ice flowing through my veins, but it's not enough. I'm going to kill this motherfucker myself. *My face will be the last he sees.*

"Before I explain, I need to know—"

"For a few minutes, yes, I did." Her tiny fingers move up my back, digging a bit into the tense muscles. "But I'm here, Malcolm. I'm here, so you can explain to me why this man sought me out. Why no one at the house...why security never came to remove him."

At her words, I turn around and lock eyes. Green on blue. "You're not upset about the dead woman?"

"Oh, I am." Her eyes flicker to the photos and then back at me. There's fear in them, but for some insane reason, it's not with me.

"Something happened with her and you were involved, there's no denying that. Your reactions confirm it, but my question is *why*? Why did he personally deliver these? Why did he say that you took her from those that love her? Not past tense, but present."

Holding a hand out, I give her the option to take it and follow me. When she does without a second of hesitation, I feel some of the tension leave my body. With her hand in mine, I walk us to the seating area and sit with her beside me.

London makes a noise of disapproval at the back of her throat and lifts my arms so she can crawl into my lap. "Much better. Now talk."

Chuckling, I shake my head. "You're one of a kind."

She shrugs. "I am."

"Okay, before I explain, I need to know a few things."

"Shoot."

"What were his exact words, Twirl? When he showed you those pictures, what did he say word for word."

She takes ahold of my hand and begins to play with my fingers. "He said you killed your last girlfriend. That you, and I'm quoting him here…"

"Go on."

"Look at what he did to her. Karina Hughes is dead because of him," Twirl whispers, pleading with me to set things right. "Now, my question is quite simple. Did you—"

"I did." I'll give her credit for not getting up and running for the door. Instead, my girl gave a nod and kept her eyes on mine. Waiting for the rest of this story. "The girl in those photos is someone I dated for a while. It wasn't love or anything special, just a companionship based on our mutual needs. Hers for money and mine for appearance sake."

"So, you didn't love her?" Her question is so low I almost miss it.

"Not at all." I push back a stray piece of hair behind her ear, giving her a soft smile. "Karina was superficial and made a mess of everything she touched. While I did give it an honest try with her, nothing was there. No love. When I ended the relationship because quite honestly, I was tired of the bullshit and fake tears she used to manipulate those around her, it never crossed my mind that things would go so far."

London turns in my arms and straddles my thighs. Leaning forward, she presses her forehead to mine. "What happened to her. What happened to you?"

"I wouldn't take her back, and she got desperate. Angry with me and my family." I close my eyes, seeing that moment all over again. Reliving Karina's last moment alive. "Somehow she convinced my mother to have lunch with her at their home. The staff there found it odd, and Magda, who was filling in for the cook on vacation, called me to let me know. You can imagine I rushed over, London, and what I found put me in a blind rage."

"Tell me." Her lips ghost mine, just a soft caress. "I'm not going to judge you."

"Karina held my mother at gunpoint, making demands about money owed and wanting to be paid. She threatened her life. Held the gun, dug it deep into her temple while my mother sobbed. To this day, I hold no remorse. None. I didn't think twice about shooting her then, and I would all over again to save someone I love."

Wetness coats my cheek before I hear a sniffle. When I open my eyes, what greets my line of sight is comprehension and respect. Not a single ounce of judgement.

"You did the right thing, Malcolm. Had it been my mom, I would've done the same without a doubt." My girl swallows hard, lip trembling as her emotions pour out. It's been a crazy day for her. "I'm so sorry I ever, even for a second, doubted you."

"Thank you." I kiss her soft lips then, tasting her tears. It's slow and gentle as I wind my arms around her back and pull her in close. This kiss isn't like the others that overpowers and destroys our senses, where time seems to stop, and nothing but the other person remains. No. This kiss feels like coming home. Like acceptance and understanding. "And I'm sorry that he sought you out. That you felt alone in that moment."

"Something isn't right with that man or his visit," she says then, sitting back as a heavy sigh leaves her. "What a coincidence that I see Alton, Brittany, and this man all on the same day?"

Indeed.

Picking up the locket on her chain, I finger the ballerina. "This chain can never come off you, Twirl. It has a small tracking device inside, and until I put an end to the Foster men, I can't take the chance of something happening and not being able to find you."

"Say what?" Then, for some reason, she starts to giggle, her body shaking in amusement. That is, until she notices I'm not joining her. "You can't be serious...are you?"

"I'm not joking, London. Promise me you won't take it off."

"Do you think it's necessary?"

"Yes."

"Okay."

"Okay?" Hands on her thighs, I caress the soft skin in gentle strokes with my thumbs. "That easy?"

"Pretty much." She shrugs then, shifting a bit in my lap to get more comfortable. Her heat sears me through my pants, but for the moment, I have to ignore my desire for her. Have to pretend that I don't see how hard those little nipples are or how my mouth waters at the sight. "You've done nothing but take care of me without crowding, and I appreciate that, Malcolm. The things with my father...finding the truth for me...I can't thank you enough for that. I trust you, and if you say it's needed, then I'm following your lead."

"All I want is for you to be safe and happy." *And you will have that soon enough.* Taking a pause, I choose my next words carefully. Since we met, I've done my best to not push too hard and let her make up her own mind, but what's coming next isn't a request. She needs this. "That's why you and I have a date tomorrow at a shooting range and then some time at the gym after for sparring lessons. It's going to be our thing at least three times a week for the time being."

"We are?" Twirl can't hide her excitement at the idea, and that pleases me.

"Yes." With two fingers I grab her chin and bring her lips to mine. Peck them once, twice, and then stare deep into those beautiful blue eyes, wanting her to see the truth in my words. "I never want you to feel fear again."

Chapter 31
MALCOLM

"I WANT HIM IN a cell within the hour. Presidential treatment," I hiss out, eyes on the screen in front of me, watching as the dumb fuck walks away from his post. The door to my office closes just as Jimmy looks past the camera and toward the gate, while on another screen, London opens the front door with her phone in hand.

She's not paying attention to her surroundings. It's something we'll address soon in training.

I'm happy she feels safe at our home, but in this world, you can never truly let your guard down. Being able to protect yourself and knowing what to do are things that'll come natural to her once I'm through. I've seen the gleam in her eyes—the hint of her own darkness below—and I'm going to nurture that tiny demon. Sharpen her claws.

On the monitor, she's just talking. Her lips curling a bit when she pauses near the end of the driveway, closing her eyes with a small smile on her face as the last bit of sun caresses her skin.

Beautiful, and you can see the appreciation for her looks on the leering look Shawn gives her. *He's a dead son of a bitch.*

My phone pings then and I pause the feed, flicking my eyes to the device. Twirl's name flashes with a message attached.

> We're home. Please don't be too late. ~Twirl

My girl left about thirty minutes ago after Gina came for her. While I love and trust Mariah, right now she needs protection. More than one available gun.

I'm past being civil or being rational. They've been poking the wrong beast, and I'll show my next hand soon enough. My ducks are in a row, and the last piece is about to make an appearance.

> Promise to be home before your show starts. Wouldn't dream of missing an episode of the cheesy goodness you love so much. ~Malcolm

Three small dots appear on the screen. Then they disappear. Then start again.

This goes on for a few minutes. However, once her reply comes through, I can't stop the laughter from bubbling out. That, or the way my cock twitches at her words.

> Was that sarcasm I detect in your letters? ~Twirl

> Are you being bratty, Mr. Asher? Do you need a spanking? ~Twirl

The thought of *my hands* reddening those luscious cheeks is very appealing. A cock-throbbing little fantasy I'll make a reality soon enough. I'll push her boundaries a bit. Make her crave more.

After the way she perfectly worshipped my cock, I know her desires match mine. That she's the one the Lord above used my rib to mold. For me.

London's been saving herself for me without knowing.

But more importantly, there's another truth I uncover with each passing day. My own confession.

This cheeky little thing means everything to me. I love her.

> Careful, little girl. This man does bite. Spanks too if you want. ~Malcolm

Her reply is instant. And so is the shiver than rushes down my spine and then settles on the tip of my dick.

> Promises. Promises. ~Twirl

At six on the dot, I find myself walking down the stairway toward the holding cells a few floors below the bank. The lighting is low, and it takes me a moment to adjust as I cross the threshold and into a very interesting show.

They don't notice me, and that's okay. I prefer to watch for a few minutes.

Undoing my jacket, I lay it on a chair near the entrance as a laceration appears on Jimmy's brow. Next, my fingers undo the buttons of my shirt, one by one, and then leave it atop the jacket as Javier delivers another bare-knuckle blow to Jimmy's midsection.

Closely followed by two more, and the prisoner's screams mute the sound of the large door closing.

The air meets my chest while the energy within the room flows around me, taunting, igniting my need for blood.

For a few weeks now, I've been playing nice. I've been under-standing.

That ends here.

Today, I begin my reign of justice.

Carmelo steps back from Jimmy, letting the man go so he can swing on the chain. He's bloody and crying, begging them to stop. Each of my men shake their heads, knowing that what comes next is the kind of mindfuck most can't handle.

"Shut the fuck up," Javier growls, fist connecting with Jimmy's jaw. The man's head snaps back as blood splatters the ground below and Javi. "Why did you vacate the security kiosk without letting anyone know? Why did you let Agent Hayes come and go as he pleased?"

"I was calling my pregnant wife back. She's been feeling off?" A lie. *Stupid, stupid man.* "Swear it, Javier. You can call and ask her."

"Bullshit." Carmelo walks toward a small table nearby and picks up a gun—he cocks it back and points it straight at his chest. "I'm going to give you one more chance to—"

"Enough." Everyone stops and looks at me. Two with a bit of mirth, and the last, Jimmy, with fear. A fear that manifests itself in perspiration and tears. To a rapid growing wet stain that appears at the front of his pants the closer to them I get. "He's telling the truth."

Relief, pure unadulterated relief pours out of him in tears. Pathetic.

"Oh, thank God," he whimpers, falling to the ground as Javier releases the locking mechanism on the pulley system for chains. "Mr. Asher, I don't know what's going on here. I've never done anything to jeopardize the business or those you associate with. I'm a worker. Just a foot soldier."

Another lie. Besides, no one ever mentioned him hurting my business. He gave that up himself with that comment. Not that I didn't already know this, but like every other fool, you give them leeway and eventually they'll hang themselves.

Jimmy Cross has been selling me out to the Fosters for a while now. He met with Alton just before they made the move to extort, and again just recently, running his mouth about London. He's one of the reasons why Roberto's wife is grieving the death of her cousin.

I nod, hand coming up to scratch my bare chest right over the all-seeing owl. "It's been a huge misunderstanding, Jimmy, and I apologize. Please let me compensate you for this unfortunate event."

"Only if that pleases you, boss." He looks up at me from the floor, the right side of his face swelling. "I'll be okay with a few days off just to rest."

"Consider it done." Turning to Javier, I give him a hard look. "Help him to a seat. I want him to witness how I deal with traitors. How I skin a rat and the man responsible for his beating."

"That's okay, boss. I just want to clean up and go home."

"Take a seat, Cross. Sit and enjoy the show." There's no room for argument, and he nods, letting Javier help him. Once he's comfortable to the right of the room, I walk to the door and open it, revealing a man on the floor with a guard holding a gun to his head.

The cleanup crew is silently awaiting orders too.

There's a gasp, but I ignore it. Instead, I raise a hand and snap my fingers once. The boys know what to do, and without a word they carry the asshole inside while Javier keeps Jimmy in his seat. His hold is firm, and while the fight or flight kicks in, my now-freaking-out employee can do nothing about it.

He knows the man as the owner of a bar he frequents. Someone he places bets with here and there over the season of our Chicago Bulls. To whom he lost a lot of money not long ago on a rigged poker night.

Jimmy doesn't consider him an enemy, but I do.

What they didn't consider into their equation is my finding out. People talking.

Frank Lewis is a personal friend of Marcus, one Lieutenant Bristol's uncle from his mother's side, and the man responsible for the meeting between the Fosters and Jimmy. For luring my employee away with the temptation of a paid debt and enough money to walk away from everything, including his wife. For planting ideas in his head that were never set to become a reality.

Marcus and Frank would kill him if their plan came to fruition.

Unfortunately for Frank, I need Jimmy alive for just a little bit longer. He's the head of the snake I must cut to terminate easy communication, to scramble their piece-of-shit wannabe network, and send them into hiding.

I want them desperate.

Afraid.

Crazy enough to make a few stupid moves.

My men drop his near-naked form between me and the ash-white security guard before taking their places once again. Frank's body hits the cold concrete hard and he groans, head bouncing off the ground as he tries to get into a fetal position but can't. It's slow. His limbs aren't cooperating.

Consciousness seems to be slipping, eyes rolling back, and I bring him back with a kick to his midsection. He cries out, shifting onto his back, choking on air while his body stiffens—trying to breathe through the pain.

Still, I land another. And another.

Each hit is direct and now aimed at his ribs. An area that is quickly turning an angry red while a welt appears from the tip of my shoe, the hard leather marking his skin as blood begins to pool at the surface. Bruising.

"Please stop," he begs, coughing. Frank moves a hand to block my next direct kick, but I move last minute, landing the blow to the side of his leg. "Let's work this out. I'll tell you anything you want."

"Anything I want? Is that right?" Kneeling, I grab his face, forcing his focus on mine. "What could you possibly say that will change the outcome here?"

His eyes flicker to Jimmy. "I know a few things."

"Humor me." I stand up and as I do, Carmelo and the other guard do the same with him, holding him up a few steps from me. "Tell me a story."

"Marcus Foster isn't your girlfriend's father. It was all a lie."

"Tell me a better story. Be original." Shaking my limbs out, I stretch my neck.

He eyes me with distrust, fear radiating off his shaking form. "Alton wants her for his own—" I cut him off with a right hook to his jaw. At once he goes stiff and begins to fall back. The sole reason he doesn't hit the ground again is my men.

"String him up." Jimmy's stench hits my nostrils, more potent now, and I turn to look at him. "Want to get cleaned up?"

"Yes, please." His voice is low. Meek.

"I'll take care of it." Javier moves to the wall behind him where there's a knob and he turns on the overhead irrigation system for this section. This one works with stinging pressure, pelting the walls and ground for cleaning purposes, while the dirty water flows toward the center of the room where a large drain sits.

When the four of us step back, Jimmy gives us a perplexed look. It doesn't last long when that first jet of cold water hits his beat-up face—the pressure stings—reopening the cut above his eyebrow—causing blood to flow down his face in rivulets. His companion in idiocy screams, now awake and freaking out when he realizes that he's strung up and without an escape.

We let them cry it out until all that's left are shaking bodies and weak pleas.

Carmelo looks at me then, and I give a minute nod. He leaves the room to retrieve something for me.

"Please make it stop."

"This is a mistake." They speak in unison, tones hoarse.

I step beneath the water and head straight toward Frank's body. Look him in the eye. "You want it to stop?"

"Yes."

"Then tell me a story."

"What kind?" You can see it on his face. The resignation. He's realizing that this is his end.

That his only choices are brutally or quick.

"The kind that'll make your last minutes on this earth bearable." If it weren't for how angry I am, I'd find this somewhat amusing. Walking over to the switch, I shut the water off and then level Jimmy with a glare that dares him to move. "Can you do that, Frank? Can you surprise me?"

"Yes."

"Good answer. Now, once upon a time…" I trail off so he can continue.

Fat tears run down his cheeks, his lip trembling. "Can I please have a mercy kill?"

"That's up to you."

Frank takes in a deep breath and lets it out slowly. "Once upon a time there was a young innocent girl who was hurt by the men in her life. Those men wanted the riches that belonged to her by birthright." His eyes remain on mine as I circle his body, listening to the bullshit I already know. What I want is confirmation to my investigator's findings. To get the answer to the last piece of this puzzle. "Her evil stepfather and brother were planning to…what's that?"

"What's what?" I say taking a syringe from Carmelo and removing the cap. Since he's taking his time, I'll force his hand and speed this up. "It's a special cocktail I have just for you. You see…" I sink the needle into his thigh and press down so every last drop enters his body "…when I met up with an old friend in Miami not long ago, he gave this to me when he hugged me goodbye. A token, if you will."

"What is it? Why does it burn?"

"It's rattlesnake venom. Raw and pure from a milking farm in Florida." At my words the panic begins. The more agitated he becomes, the faster the toxins travel through his bloodstream. Soon, he'll begin to feel some numbness in his limbs and begin to sweat. There might be some nausea or loss of sight…maybe even some bleeding as his organs begin to shut down. An unattended rattler bite is deadly. "Now, what were you saying about her twenty-first birthday? What are they planning to do?"

"Kill me," Frank slurs a bit, some spit escaping from the right side of his mouth. "Please. Just end this."

"Tell me what I want to know, and I'll gift you some mercy."

"What about my wife—"

"She'll keep the bar and be taken care of. Not that you ever gave a shit about her to begin with."

His head lolls back. "Tell her I am sorry."

"Done. Now say it."

More tears fall, and he has a tough time swallowing, so I offer him water from a bottle Carmelo thought to bring with him. The hemotoxin is working faster than I anticipated. That, or he's having an allergic response to it. Either way, I'm getting what I need from him.

"Thank you."

"None needed. Carry on."

With difficulty, he brings his head up and focuses his stare on me. "They're going to sell London's virginity to the highest bidder on the night of her twenty-first birthday. They want to break—pass her around to anyone willing to pay the fee—until nothing is left but a shell of a woman. Then, when his control is obsolete, Marcus wants to kill her after she signs everything over to him and Alton."

There it is. The ultimate goal.

His next intake of air is difficult, and I notice his face swelling.

Pulling my favorite knife from my back pocket, I flip it open and let the steel blade reflect a bit of the light in the room. "Anything else I should know?"

"You have a—" He doesn't get to finish as I bury my knife up his skull via his chin. The long blade lodges itself, and I twist the handle to make sure he's dead.

Frank's body sags against the chains and his breathing is no more.

"Clean this up, and take Jimmy home," I say while removing my knife. "He can thank me another day for killing the scum responsible for his pain."

Chapter 32
MALCOLM

WHEN I WALK IN the door a few hours later, I find London asleep on the couch. There's a repeat of her favorite show playing, the women fighting about something that no one cares about, yet my girl finds amusing. The trashier the show, the more she loves it.

Taking the control from her hand, I turn the TV off and set it aside. My eyes stay on her beautiful face and pouty lips. On how she's smiling a tiny bit.

That innocence in her kills me. Makes me throb.

It reminds me of her inexperience, yet how eager to learn she is to please me.

"Sorry for missing it, pretty girl," I whisper, leaning down to nuzzle her soft cheek. "I'll make it up to you. Promise."

Being late tonight was inevitable. After disposing of Frank and having Jimmy taken home to his not-pregnant wife, I sat down to have a conversation with Javier and my lawyer.

Amelia's home is back in the legal possession of her daughter. A judge sided with London over the contest of the will, seeing that several changes were made the day of her death and the filing signature was wrong. As of today, at four thirty in the afternoon, she no longer has a guardian. The accounts are hers and the stipend will be deposited into an account I made for her in my bank.

No one has the right to touch a single cent of hers.

The Fosters will be served with an eviction notice tomorrow, and she won't be in Chicago when it happens. I'm taking her away. Giving us a break.

Javier has his instruction, and Mariah will hold the fort down, emailing me only when it's an emergency they can't handle.

"How do you plan to do that?" One eye is open, and she looks adorable in her fake annoyance. "Cause the episode you missed was epic."

"Is that so? Who fought with whom this week?" Slipping my arms beneath her body, I pick up her grumpy form off the couch and carry her into our room. Not once since moving in has she slept anywhere but beside me. "Or did the dude go to the strip club? Was he caught getting friendly with a dancer?"

"Neither." There's a pout in her tone, and I kiss her. Nip the plump bottom lip while she rolls her eyes. "The mother was tripping on his girl and they fought over dinner. Food and cheap wine went everywhere."

I lower her down to the mattress, laying her back so I can crawl over her body. "How can you watch those shows?"

Boggles the mind how much she enjoys these things.

"Cheesy goodness, boo. It's all in the cheesy goodness."

"Do you think you can give those up for a few days starting tomorrow?" I kiss her chin, then neck, licking a path down London's throat toward her chest.

"Why?" She arches to give me better access. "What's going on?"

"Nothing." I leave open-mouthed kisses across each breast, dipping my tongue between the two to tease the skin. "Just you and me…"

"You and me what?" she hisses when I drag my tongue beneath the edge of her tank and find a nipple.

I take the tight tip between my teeth and pull, sliding my teeth over the sensitive skin as I release her. "We're just going on a little vacation to a secluded island…a few days of fun in the sun and some training. Nothing special."

Twirl pushes me back to look at my face with a perfect brow raised. "You said what now?"

"Vacation starting—"

"When do we leave?"

"Six hours."

"Are you serious?" She's wiggling beneath me to slip away, but I lower my body fully atop hers. Lips to lips and chest to chest, I'm pinning her to the mattress. "Can you move?"

"No." My hands grab her legs and wrap them around my waist. "Not going anywhere."

"But we need to pack." Twirl tries to sound stern but fails miserably when it comes out a low moan.

"No, we don't." Flexing my hips, I let her feel me. How hard I always am for her. "I have everything you'll need already packed, sweetheart. My personal shopper took care of everything with Mariah's help. No need to rush. Just let me feel you a little."

THIS PLACE IS AMAZING," Twirl squeals, rushing up the coral-carved stairway that leads to the main house of this tropical oasis. She walks from the entrance to the living room with one goal in mind; she stands at the veranda with both hands holding onto the wood and takes in a deep, cleansing breath.

The warm sun, tropical trees, and the salt air will soothe even the most savage beast.

The place is huge and very private. Open space, the main house is made to blend the inside with nature—no windows or doors—just the cooling breeze and the sounds of waves crashing below surround you.

This luxury retreat is ours for the next five days. Just the two of us.

No outside distractions or problems.

No worries outside of how to entertain ourselves.

The staff here signs an NDA with each new renter that books, and they're to be off the island by sundown unless otherwise told to. They cook, clean, take care of setting up activities and disappear to a smaller island a short boat ride away that houses their accommodations.

It's the perfect vacation.

The de-stressor we need.

Where I plan to make her mine.

"I'm glad you approve." Walking up behind her, I wrap my arm around her waist. It's still early, and the warm waters of the Atlantic look inviting. "Care to take a swim with me?"

"Don't we need to unpack first?" There's a hint of a pout in her tone and I almost laugh. Almost.

"You're right. We should." My other hand travels lower, down to the edge of her short khakis with a side-tie that make me want to bite her. Kneel before her and undo the small knot holding the almost-indecent piece of clothing in place with my teeth. "It's the responsible thing to do."

"You're right, Malcolm. Adult first and play later?" Twirl pushes her ass against my front, grinding just a tiny bit. She's tempting me. I know she's craving—almost desperate for my touch—but I have other plans for us.

So, I grit my teeth and let her. Let her feel me. How I throb for her and her alone.

And when her arm reaches back to embed her fingers in my hair, I pull back. Release my hold a few seconds before the woman that cleans wheels our luggage toward the master suite. She doesn't look at us, just takes the pathway below us down toward a private bungalow.

"That was mean."

Ignoring her question, I reach back and pull my T-shirt off. Lay it on the back of a chair near us. "Did you bring a swimsuit in your backpack like I told you to?"

Blue eyes narrow. "Yes."

"Then hurry up and change in that bathroom beyond the wall. You have twenty minutes, or I come to take you with me as is."

"And if I say no?"

"Try me."

"I'm going to get you back for this," she huffs and walks past me, shaking those luscious hips while leaving the room. Walking over to the intercom by the wall, I press the number two for the kitchen and wait for someone to pick up.

"How can I be of service?" the voice of an older woman says as the clanging of metal on metal comes through the speaker. "Would you like something prepared for lunch? A snack, maybe?"

"Something light will do. We're going to take a swim and just need something to hold us over until dinner."

"Understood, sir. I'll work on that now and it'll be ready shortly." She pauses for a moment, and the sound of a door closing follows. "Any requests?"

"Surprise me." I remove my belt next and empty my pockets, putting the items on a coffee table. The shorts I have on will have to do. Looking for my trunks at the moment is a waste of time. Time I could be kissing her instead. Feeling her pliant flesh beneath my fingertips. "However, dinner needs to be followed to my every last detail. Do you have the menu?"

"Yes, sir." London walks out then wearing a tiny, itty-bitty little scrap of fabric that doesn't cover much and I find decadent. My eyes eat her up, cock hardening as she struts past me and down the stairway that leads down toward the beach and the rest of the island. Those hips tell me to follow. Her small giggle tells me she knows exactly what she's doing to me. "We have our instructions. Preparations are set to begin early this evening while you and your spouse ready yourselves for dinner. Once you are served and dessert finished, we'll vacate and be a call away if we are needed for any reason."

"Perfect. Thank you." I press the end button and before my slip-on Adidas are off, I'm rushing after her. When I make it down to the long stretch of beach on this side, she's facing the water with her soft skin glistening under the high midday sun. There's a hint of sweat on her with the scent of coconuts from the lotion she's applying on her arms.

Fuck, she bends down to get her legs, and that's the last straw for me. Before Twirl can make a run for it or evade me, I grab her by the hips and toss that tight, curvy body over my shoulder. She screams. Wiggles in my hold.

It's not a deterrent.

On her next shriek of laughter, I toss her in the water and then follow. I swim up to her when she rights herself, pushing her wet hair back and away from her face. Her eyes narrow while my smile grows.

"That wasn't very nice, Mr. Asher."

"Neither is your teasing." She goes to open her mouth, but I pull her in close and steal a quick kiss. "Besides, you looked in need of a cool off. What kind of a man would I be if I didn't take care of your every need?"

"CHRIST, THAT WAS AMAZING." London sits back, patting her nonexistent stomach. For the past ten minutes I've been watching her, ignoring my slice of the key lime pie so I can focus on how sinfully she ate hers. Those sweet, low moans. How she drags the spoon past her berry-colored lips after swallowing.

The way that tiny pink tongue peeks out to swipe the excess sweetness she missed.

It's been torture while I nurse my fifth of gin.

"I'm glad you enjoyed dinner, sweetheart."

Twirl smiles at me, pushing a wayward curl out of her face. "It's not just dinner, Malcolm. The entire day has been incredible...you're almost too good to be true."

"But I am, London." Bringing the glass to my lips, I drain the rest before placing it down. "I'm right here, and there's nowhere I want to be but with you."

"You're nothing like I thought you would be." Azure eyes twinkle in the candlelight as she leans forward a bit, showing me more of the cleavage that's teased me all evening. The flowing white maxi dress with a halter-style neckline is both sexy and innocent.

It fits her perfectly with just a high enough slit over her right leg to keep me hard all night.

She's the entire package. My version of perfection.

My little love.

"That's because you're the only person in this world that will ever see this side of me. Just you."

A touch of pink grazes her cheek as a smirk curls up at her lips. "Is that so? Why am I so special?"

"Because you are mine." Pushing my chair back, I hold out a hand for her to take. "Now, take a walk with me."

Chapter 33
MALCOLM

M ALCOLM," SHE SIGHS, LEANING her head back against my chest while taking in the scene in front of her: The lone bed sitting in the middle of the white sandy beach with gauzy drapery flowing in the breeze. The lit candles on a small table holds a bottle of chilled wine and chocolate-dipped strawberries. How the waves crash upon the shore a few feet from where we stand and the million and one stars that cast a soft light on us. "How? When?"

"I want you, London. Every piece of you for as long as I have breath in my body," I croon, lips skimming the fragrant skin of her neck. My hands explore lower, down her stomach to her hips where I grip her. Pull her to me. "You've changed my life. You're my everything."

"I feel the same way. You own me."

"Do I have your heart? Your trust?" I pause and wait. Needing to hear her say the words we've been holding in. Because I know she does.

It's in her eyes. The smile she gifts me. How she constantly finds a way to tell me what she hasn't with her actions.

Cooking a meal. Making my coffee and bringing it to me while I shave.

Accepting my family without preconceived notions or judgments.

By choosing me. Choosing to let me in.

"I do," she says, a low whisper in the wind, but I hear them. Loud and clear. They also make me think of a future where I tie her to me in all the ways a man can. "It's fast and our lives are crazy, but Malcolm, I…" Twirl takes in a deep breath and then lets it out slow "…I love you."

At that moment, my life began.

Everything prior was a warm-up. A build up to what—the man I could be.

Because her love is what makes me a man. I'm worthy of her.

Her love. Devotion. Trust.

Everything else could go fuck itself; she's what matters. Her opinions of me are what matter.

"I love you, too. So fucking much, London." Turning her around, I wrap my arms around her and lift her off the ground so we're chest to chest. My lips hovering over hers. "You're the only thing in my life that matters, and I'll spend the rest of my life showing you this. No matter what the future brings, what obstacles life may throw our way, my love for you will never be in question."

Watery eyes meet mine with so much emotion that my heart clenches. "Thank you."

"Never thank me for what I was born to do. Loving you is a gift."

"I love you," she says against my lips and on her next pass, I take possession of her mouth. Kiss her with every bit of my love—with the uncontrollable fire that burns within for the beauty writhing in my arms. She's hungry for me, fighting for control of this kiss as our teeth clash and tongues taste.

Her hands are in my hair as I undo the knot at her nape holding the dress up. It falls to the ground and I reach for her thighs once more to hoist her up. Fingertips roam her skin, down her back, and over her ass, where I find nothing.

I take a step back, much to her protest, but I want to see her like this. Naked and in the moonlight with the ocean behind her. *Fuck*, my Twirl is flawless. Beautiful.

"Like what you see?" she says while looking at me from beneath her long lashes. A coy look that's sexy, but it's the sassy bite behind the questions that makes her dangerous. At this moment, this singular second, I'm her prey as I take in her silhouette.

Those luscious curves and the dip between her thighs. The perkiness of her round breasts and the tightness of her nipples.

How there's a slight sheen on her upper thigh letting me know she's turned on. Needs to be fucked.

That I will be the only man to ever take her. Bring her pleasure.

"I love what I see. What I own." My voice is rough—deeper—and doing a horrible job at masking the mounting desperation. Hands clenching and unclenching, I take a moment to breathe and calm myself down enough to be rational. This is her first time, and I need to prepare her for my size. The pain is inevitable, but I'll do what I can to minimize it.

"You're wearing entirely too many clothes, Mr. Asher."

A chuckle slips at her words. "Am I, now?"

"Yes. Lose it all."

"Impatient little thing." Not caring for the shirt one bit, I tear it open and pull it off, sending the buttons across the sand. It's unimportant and in my way. My shoes and belt meet the same fate as they land somewhere, but my pants stay on for the time being with the button undone. She devours me with hooded eyes where she stands, a slight tremble in her body. "Now, can you do something for me, sweetheart? A little favor, if you will."

"Anything." It's a plea. A whimper.

"Good girl." On her next breath, I'm on my knees in the sand and holding a thigh up. "Take your leg and hold it high. Show me my pretty little pussy."

She does as I ask and pulls the leg I'm holding up to her head. The perfect vertical split.

It takes her a few shifts to steady her equilibrium, but when she does, this dancer is beyond graceful. London is perfection. A temptation I plan to bring to heel.

Bringing my face against her core, I take in a deep inhale and groan. My first lick is slow, a gentle flick over her slit, but that changes quickly when her taste invades my senses. I'm gone. Hungry. A beast giving in to his nature as I bury my face between her thighs.

My cock is hard and throbbing—rubbing against the fabric of my pants as I devour her pussy. I'm like a man possessed. Starving. Lost to his baser instincts as I lose myself in her taste.

It's uniquely hers and with a hint of honey. This come-inducing flavor that I can't get enough of.

Need more. All of it.

Swiping the flat of my tongue through her labia, I groan against her core as another rush of wetness coats my tongue. Each drop is sweeter than the last. She's my nectar of the gods.

Sucking those tender lips into my mouth, I take every last drop and pull back. Take in the rapture on her face above me. The light sheen of sweat and the perfect O of her mouth.

London's eyes are closed but snap open after I stop. "Don't. I'm so close."

"Close to what, Twirl? Tell me." It's a growl. An angry hiss as I slip a finger to the first knuckle inside, and her opening clenches.

Her thigh in this position trembles. "Fucking tell me what you need, and I'll give it to you."

"Please!"

"Please what?" I pull it out, only to push in a little deeper. Slowly, I work her opening in short strokes until her hips begin to move of their own accord. She's using me, and I let her for a few more pumps—stopping when she doesn't answer. "Say the words."

"Make me..." the leg that's by her head drops a bit, and I use my free hand to smack her clit with two fingers "...shit!"

"Keep it up there or I stop." Another direct tap, harder, and her juices splash my face. Just a little. She hasn't come but is soaking wet. All soft and swollen.

"Please let me come. I can't...it's...oh God," she cries out as I add a second finger. I'm building her up. Want her tears and screams of frustration. Want her crazy. As lost to this powerful need as I am.

"Give it to me. That's it." Another rush of wetness escapes, and I am quick to lap her, finger-fucking her to an almost orgasm. Her body seizes, leg slipping just as her knees begin to give out.

I stop. Pull back as she's on the brink, and stand.

"No!" There are tears in her eyes, anger in her expression at my denial. However, I don't pay attention to either and swoop her up in my arms, carrying her to the bed as she whimpers.

Without a word, I place her in the middle and part her legs—silently dare her to move as I remove her wedged shoes and then my pants. Our eyes remain locked as I crawl between her thighs, stroking my cock a few times over her sex.

With the blunt head I rub her clit, mixing my pre-come with her wetness. She's slick and needy, arching herself toward me in invitation.

"Whose hungry little cunt is this?" I tap her trembling bundle of nerves with the head twice, and she throws her head back. That won't do. Two more slaps, and she screams. "Answer me."

"Do it, Malcolm. I'm yours...*fuck!*" Her orgasm comes fast and hard, stealing the breath from her lungs. Twirl shakes beneath me, head thrown back as the cries get caught in her throat.

"That's it, baby." I position myself at her entrance, sliding across her slit a few times to wring out every ounce of pleasure from her sensitive pussy. "Let me feel you."

"Malcolm...what...oh my God," she screams as another tremor rocks her. That's what I've been waiting for. This lost feeling. Her innocence coming to the forefront as she loses herself to the pleasure I gift her.

And on her next helpless whimper, I slam in, taking her cherry. "Son of a bitch," I grunt, grinding my teeth while trying not to move. To fuck her like my body demands I do. "So tight. Motherfucking wet heat."

Her walls pulse—hold me tight, yet I don't move. Now my focus is on her. Soothing her from what I know has to be painful. My hands stroke her sides and down to her thighs, helping to loosen the tightness in her muscles.

My lips are kissing any part of her I can reach. Saying *I love you* over and over again as she adjusts to my length.

After a few minutes, she cups my chin to look at her. "Malcolm, this...it hurts, but feels so right. You're right for me." A few tears roll down her cheeks, and I'm quick to wipe them away. Twirl turns her face into my palm and presses her lips to the center. "It's as if all this time I've been waiting for you."

"We were destined to meet. To love each other." Bringing my hand to her nape, I bring us closer and slant my mouth over hers. Just kiss her. No rush. This time I take my time and savor every sigh. How she hums in the back of her throat when I massage my tongue with hers.

The longer I kiss her, the more she relaxes. Melts under me.

London gives a minute shift of her hips, testing the feel of my cock inside her cunt with a few clenches. There's a hiss from her into my mouth, but it's not full of pain.

Tenderness? Yes, but a little pleasure too.

It's the same sound she made when I added a second finger earlier. Adjusting, but not averse to it.

"Move."

I press my forehead to hers. "Are you sure?"

"Yes." She arches against me, sliding a bit off before taking me back to the hilt. "I need this just as much as you do."

"You're my heart, Twirl." With her eyes on mine, I pull out and hold just the tip inside. Her opening squeezes around the head, clenching—trying to pull me back in as I grab her legs and wrap them around me. "Last chance. Are you sure?"

"I want the real you. Don't hold back," she says, voice steady. Her thighs tighten around my hips, fighting my hold. "Fuck me and cuddle with me after."

"I'll make this up to you." I slam back inside causing her to choke on her reply. My hips ride her hard, pounding into her without mercy.

The sounds of the waves crashing upon the shore and her moans create the perfect soundtrack. Nature and beast; I've given in to my carnal desires. Accept that this beautiful woman with her head thrown back and drowning in pleasure was made for me.

From my rib.

Her heat envelops me each time I thrust inside. My cock glistens with her juices; I can feel the sweet little drips rolling down between us and soaking the sheets. I'm hypersensitive—a thousand minuscule electric shocks dance across my skin at the sight below me.

The obscenity. She's so tiny compared to me.

Finding purchase on those thick hips, I raise her off the bed and gift her five punishing strokes in rapid succession.

"So good. Please don't stop," London cries out, fingernails raking down my chest. She breaks the skin, and I revel in the sting. Love how far gone she is to the pleasure I give her.

"Say my name," I grit out, snapping my hips and burying myself to the hilt as a harsh shiver rushes through her. "Motherfuck, baby. You are my heaven...my nirvana. Squeeze me again."

"Malcolm, I'm—"

"I know. Give it to me," I demand through clenching teeth, holding my own release back as her body lets go. Her orgasm borders on painful as the need to fuck her raw becomes unbearable, and yet, as her warm juices drip between us, I let her ride it out.

She's out of breath and beautiful, face flush and chest rising hard with every breath she tries to take in.

Once she's coming down, when the last of the aftershocks subside, I pull out and flip her onto her stomach. She yelps, but it soon turns into a wanton moan when I grip her hair in my fist, spread her thighs just a bit, and mount her from behind.

With her body flat to the bed, I fuck her. Pounding into her tight little body as my body covers hers from head to toe.

Fingers tightening in her hair, I tilt her head toward me. My lips leave open-mouthed kisses on her jaw before I lick her from cheek to neck. "You feel like perfection. Like *my* perfect little cock slut."

Son of a bitch, she's clenching around my dick in the most delicious way. Tighter like this, and in my next thrust, I force my way back inside.

"What's happening to me? Am I...*fuck!*" London arches, pushing against me as another orgasm rocks her, and I follow. With one more punishing thrust, I bury myself deep and let go.

"Fuck, yes, Twirl. Milk my cock," I grunt out, balls drawn up tight as I release the first stream of come deep inside her cunt. Three more leave me and mix with her own, creating a sticky, beautiful mess.

The sheets below are soaked.

She's panting with her eyes closed while I watch her.

Enjoying this moment of calm as my body settles beside her on the bed, I tuck her beneath my chin with the blanket half over us. London is pliant in my arms, all soft and sweet with her head on my chest and a leg thrown over my hip.

There are no words said, but I feel them. Those three simple ones that, put together, are worth more than all the money in the world: I love you.

With her, I'm happy.

At peace.

She's my queen.

Chapter 34
MALCOLM

"AGAIN, LONDON. THIS TIME, close your fist like I taught you yesterday. Keep your thumb on the outside and over your pointer and middle finger. Never under." I'm holding a trainer's punching pad up toward her, expecting the next hit to be full of frustration. She's tired, sweaty, and looks hot as fuck out in the middle of this beach wearing a pair of yoga pants and a sports bra. "You'll break it if you don't position it right."

"I should kick your ass for this," she grunts, landing a mid-kick into the pad instead. It has some power behind it, and I let out a grunt when she lands five more in rapid succession. "This is supposed to be a vacation, Malcolm. Fun in the sun and naked times...sex on the beach and all that jazz."

I heard this yesterday too, but with only another two days left on the island, this is not up for negotiation.

I'll cuddle the fuck out of her afterward. Spend the rest of the day with my tongue in her pussy while feeding her my cock. Making her choke on my girth as I bring her to orgasm multiple times like I did last night.

"Good. Harder." As I say this, I follow the path of a few stray beads of sweat as they gather at the edge of her bra. My mouth waters, and I swallow hard as the fight to lick her becomes almost unbearable. Her nipples are hard. Pressing hard against the thin fabric. "Higher."

"If I knock you down, can we stop for the day?"

"You can try." At that, London throws a jab that misses when I step aside. "Missed."

"Why are we doing this? What aren't you telling me?" Another combination: jab, jab, cross.

"The house is yours, and they've been evicted."

"W-what?" She falters mid throw, and both hands fall to her sides. "Say that again, and slowly. I feel like I heard you wrong."

"You won, sweetheart. Everything they took is either in a new bank account or portfolio. The house, bonds and stocks...your mother's wedding ring that I found in a pawn shop on the South—" I'm cut off by her body hitting mine as she jumps into my arms. The pad falls from my hands and I catch her mid-air, falling back into the sand and taking the brunt of the impact.

Then she's straddling me, and it doesn't matter. Her supple body covers mine, pussy to cock, and she gyrates. Strokes me through the thin fabric of my board shorts. I'm hard for her, throbbing against her core, but it's the smile on her face that holds my attention.

It's the look of a woman in love. Happy. Carefree.

"Thank you," she breathes out, her sweet breath on my lips. Her mouth hovers over mine and her hair falls around us like a curtain.

Fuck, she's beautiful. "I just don't know how I'll ever repay everything you've done for me. For my mother's memory."

"You never need to thank me, Twirl."

"But I do, Malcolm." She kisses me then, a slow and sweet gesture that I feel down to my bones. I can taste her devotion. Feel her love. London pulls back after taking my bottom lip between her teeth, and she bites down hard before letting go. Blue eyes stay on green. "It's because of you that I'm alive and in love. You're my person, something I never thought I'd find. Love wasn't on my radar until you came along, refusing to let me go, and I'll forever be in your debt for doing so."

Tangling my hand in her hair, I hold her in place and return the kiss with a fervent one of my own. Its quick but full of passion and want. Of my adoration for her. After a minute, I slow us down to a few soft pecks. She whines at the back of her throat and undulates her hips, however, with it being so early and with the staff on the grounds, I stop us.

It hurts to do so, but I do. Stop her before she teases and gets fucked with a possible audience watching.

That would ruin this short vacation.

A dead body wouldn't be fun.

"Kiss me," she demands, fighting my hold.

"No."

London sits up then and narrows her eyes on me. "No? Explain that one."

"One; we aren't alone, and no one sees your pussy milking my cock but me." Immediately a light blush sweeps across her cheeks, and she gives me a sheepish look. "And second; you need to finish the last three sets. Faster you do, faster we get to play with some of my favorite toys."

"Sex toys?"

I can't stop the laugh that escapes me. It's loud and she moves to get off, but I just wrap her in my arms to keep her above me. Not being able to slip inside her tight, wet heat at the moment is one thing, but I love having her like this.

Close. In my arms. Feeling her warmth over my cock through the two thin layers of clothing separating us.

"No," I chuckle, laying a tiny kiss to her chin and then the tip of her nose. "Those we'll go shopping for once we get back. You want it, and I'll buy it. Nothing is off the table."

"Okay, then what?"

"Guns, London. I have a couple of my favorites here to play with."

"Seriously?" Excitement rushes through her, and she wiggles in my lap. At my groan, she rolls her eyes and pushes against my chest to be let go. "Come on, lazy. You're slowing me down."

"What happened to this being boring and hard and not vacation-like for you?"

"That's before you mentioned guns. I've always wanted to play with one."

"You shoot, not play."

"It qualifies if it's role-play. I plan on you bending me over before the day is through."

Chapter 35
LONDON

THE FEEL OF A gun in my hand is comforting.

Its weight is an extension of my hand, and the power I feel as the bullet discharges from its chamber cannot be put into words. It's freeing. I feel powerful.

Another shot, and I hit the target in the chest—the vibrations move through me, and I won't deny to feeling a thrill, arousal from his appreciative looks as I fire again and again.

The empty shells fall all around me as I empty this clip and then restock, all the while holding in the needy sound building within my chest.

SIN

Ever since Malcolm put that first Glock in my hand back on the beach, things have changed within me. That fear I've hidden behind disappears with each praise. My confidence grows—my hunger for him has become my life force.

The reason why I am living life my way for the first time.

As I raise my arms up, locking my elbows, he comes up behind me—presses the length of his thick cock against my ass. "How many times can you…" his breath skims my ear as those strong arms encircle my waist "…hit the bull's-eye on its head. Give me a number, Twirl."

"I-I can't—"

"Concentrate. Never let anyone or anything pull you from what matters. The possible threat." This time he leaves a kiss on my neck, then a quick nip. "Clear your mind and focus. I know you can… you're a natural with my gun. Just need a bit more practice."

"You're not being fair." It leaves me on a low moan as I lower my arms, leaning my head back to give him better access. "I can't resist you, Mr. Asher."

"Is that right? Are you wet for me?" His right hand skims down until reaching my core, slipping beneath the thin fabric of my tights to cup me. "Fuck, London. What made you soak your panties, sweetheart—the gun, or the idea of my cock slipping inside from behind as you pull the trigger."

"Do it," I whimper, bringing a hand up to wrap around his neck. "Take me."

The luxury of being with a man like Malcolm Asher is that this gun range is on his property. At the very back and near a secluded path, there's a small structure holding one room, a divider with a small counter for the occupant to place its weapon, and a pulley system that goes back enough to challenge the shooter. That's it. At the most three people fit inside comfortably, and the cameras inside go to his computer, not to the staff. No one but those he trusts the most practice here, and only with permission.

"You want my cock, little Twirl? Want me to fuck you?"

275

"Please." My back arches, rubbing my ass against his length.

"Please what?" His fingers part my folds, rubbing against my entrance before moving to tap my clit. "Fuck you or let you shoot this gun? Make you come if you can hit the target between the eyes?"

"Both?" There's no hesitation. Every time I think about him inside me, my heart speeds up and my pussy aches, but add a gun to that equation and it's downright perverse. "Should we put it to the test?"

"Is that a challenge, love? You think you can handle both?" I don't even have a second to sass him when his other hand loops the waistband of my pants and pushes them down over the swell of my ass. "Tell me."

"I can."

"Such a naughty little slut." His hands press on the small of my back, leaning me over the railing. "Grab the gun and fire the first shot."

"What do I get if I hit?" My hips gyrate once against him and I grab the Glock, cocking it. "Challenge me." There's something so dirty about this, and I want to push him. I want to be taken rough and quick.

The next thing I register is the sting of his palm on my right ass cheek and the heat that follows. "Concentrate, Twirl. Shoot." My body reacts before my mind catches up and my finger pulls the trigger. I miss the target completely. "Again."

The sounds of his belt coming undone fill my ears as I line the sights of the gun up. I try to push out the feel of his hand spreading me, of the hot head of his cock rubbing against my slick slit, but it's futile when his low groan—that almost feral sound rumbles through him.

"Oh God...please!"

"Come on. Shoot." I blow out a breath and fire just as Malcolm slams into me. I choke on my own breath at the overwhelming feeling of him. So good. So perfect. "Motherfucking perfect," he says, echoing my thoughts. "Just think of it as an exercise of shooting from a moving car."

"What?" I ask before he pulls out and slams back in, setting up a quick pace that jostles me. My arms go lax, head falling down as I get caught up in the pleasure. A hiss leaves me when his hand tangles into my hair and he pulls.

"You're not concentrating." I try to line the gun up again as his hips rotate, hitting an explosive part of me. "Hit the target and I'll give you the release you need."

"Fuck!" I fire, missing again, hitting the rotator chain. It ricochets, bouncing somewhere, but I'm not aware of my surroundings anymore. All I know and feel is him, his cock and his hold on me, his heavy breathing and the moans he utters in my ear.

"Again, baby. Focus or I'll finish over your ass." The next flex of his hips is fast and deep, stealing the very air from my lungs. "It'll be a win for me. I love to see you wearing my seed."

"Don't you dare," I grit out, focusing just long enough to empty the chamber. Every shot fires off in rapid succession, and I toss the gun away. Adrenaline pumps through me, my skin tingles with excitement—I'm trembling beneath him.

I'm so close. So close.

And it's his next words that throw me over the edge.

"Good girl."

That's it. Two words and I clench around him while closing my eyes. I'm lost to him, to the feel of his every ridge rubbing my walls as he slams in a final time and comes deep within me. Spurt after spurt coats me—mixing with my own release as I slump forward.

Breathing is hard. Moving impossible, and yet, I still look at him from over my shoulder with a cheesy grin that matches his. "Best shooting lesson ever."

Leaning forward, he catches my lips in a quick and harsh kiss. "You hit the target twice. Congrats, baby."

"YOU'RE GOING to get us into trouble, kid," Gina says from beside me as we head toward the mansion where I met Malcolm. She's driving the large cargo van I convinced Carmelo to lend me with the promise that it's all to surprise his boss.

And technically, I'm not lying. This is all for him. Us.

To play a little. To pay him back for everything he's done for me.

My Malcolm is a voyeur, and as such, gets off on watching. So tonight, after he gets home, I want those gorgeous green eyes on me while I touch myself. Make myself come with nothing but the sound of his voice and my fingers.

Something I never thought I would do or want to try with anyone else, but with him I want to experience it all. The sexy. The perverse. The dirty and even illegal.

Jesus, a lot has changed since that first dance. Since his fingertips dug themselves into my hips and he told me to twirl for him.

The setup at the club—the small stage and his throne—isn't going to be hard to move. And I'm hoping that once I tell Liam what it's for, he'll be very receptive to letting me take it home with us. I'm sure someone there can load it up and one of the guards at the house can get it down.

"How much trouble?" I ask, taking a sip from my latte.

"Depends on how good of a mood he's in later. They've been too quiet since being evicted, and that worries everyone."

I've thought about this too. Why haven't they tried to reach me? Show up and demand I give back the house and everything they had power over.

While on the private island, I learned the final judgement from the judge dealing with my case. I won. Everything is mine again, and they had to vacate before we returned to Chicago.

Since then they've gone underground. Hiding from everyone.

Yet I have a feeling that my man knows more than he lets on. That he's biding his time before he strikes.

"We'll make it quick. In and out mission here." That appeases her as we pull up to the back of the house where the employee parking lot is. There's usually one guy watching the lot at all times, but this one I've never seen before. He waves us in without asking to see our IDs.

"I take it you don't know him?"

"No." My eyes stay on his as we pass, trying to decipher my gut reaction of distrust. "Let's just get this over with."

"Works for me." Gina parks near the back entrance and waits for me to get out. Together we walk inside and head straight for Liam's office. A few of the girls I met while here wave and I do the same, trying to ignore the naked state of their bodies. The tiny red welts one of them has down her arms and legs came from what I assume was a demonstration.

They're heading back into the main lounge area, leaving just us alone back here. The door is slightly ajar when I reach it, and Stacy's giggle meets my ear.

"You stop that," she says, and all that follows is his grunt. It doesn't sound like they're having sex, but I look at Gina and tilt my head so she enters first. "Oh my God, Liam!" More laughter. "Keep those hands to yourself."

"Knock, knock," Gina calls out while tapping her knuckles on the door. "Can we come in, and are you decent?"

"Baby, go see who that is." Liam's voice is rougher than usual.

"Coming!" It's hard to hold in my snort, but I do while Gina rolls her eyes. It doesn't take more than a minute for Stacy to peek her head out, but when she spots me her polite smile turns into cheesiness. "Get your butt over here and give me a hug, stranger."

"Hi to you too!" I laugh, walking in for the tight squeeze. "How have you been?"

"We're good except for Liam. He's a bit cranky after getting a root canal earlier today."

"Am not!"

"Yeah, he is." Stacy takes my hand and pulls me in behind her, leaving Gina to close the door. My eyes take her in then and notice this is the most clothing I've ever seen her wear: slacks, a cardigan, and a thin scarf around her neck. Like this, she looks like the average girl next door. When I look at her face again, she's smirking. "Shut it. I had to drive him to and from his appointment. Tassels and a thong would be frowned upon by the uptight trolls out there."

"Who are you...hello, Miss London." Liam smiles at me and stands, coming around his desk to shake my hand. "How have you been, sweetheart? That Malcolm being good to you?"

"He's perfect."

He eyes me for any deceit and when he finds none, he gives me a nod to sit down. "Good. That makes me very happy, kid."

I take the seat directly in front of his desk. His eyes are on mine as I take in a deep breath and let it out slowly. "First, I want to thank you for hiring me. For helping me the only way you knew how, Liam. My contract wasn't like the rest of the employees here, and I appreciate that."

"None needed." He waves me off. "You're one of the good ones, and while I knew the men here would salivate and it'd bring me money, I made sure it was at your pace. Your call to—"

"You didn't have to," I interrupt, because while he isn't one hundred percent noble, his chance saved my life. Gave me an out. A path to leave or, how fate played it out, toward Malcolm. "I know money was involved, but knowing who my brother and father are, you stuck your neck out for me, and nothing in this world could repay that. Thank you."

"Forget it." He levels me with a look that says I won't win. "Now, what can I do for you?"

"How hard would it be for you to gift me the items in Mr. Asher's private room? For me to pick up my costumes?" I ask, sitting forward toward him. "I'm trying to surprise the man—"

"Done."

"Thank you...oh my God!"

There's blood everywhere. On me. On the walls. Oozing from the bullet hole in Liam's head. Another three shots ring out and I throw myself to the ground. The person on the other side is hell-bent on emptying their clip before coming inside.

Screams come from what sounds like every direction. Stomping —it sounds like a scared herd of wildebeest racing through the mansion. Everyone here is running for their lives while this person continues to give us everything his weapon has.

My eyes find Gina's and she's reaching for her gun. "When I say the word, you duck behind his desk and don't come out. Got it? No matter what, stay hidden."

"What about you?"

"Don't come out." The fact she ignores my question fills me with dread—more so than the bullets flying throughout the room.

A shriek rents the air, and Stacy's body hits the ground. She's been hit in the shoulder and bleeding profusely. I crawl to her, ignoring Gina's curse or the way she tries to block me with her body as best she can.

"Look at me," I whisper to her, taking the loose scarf around her neck and using it to put pressure on the wound. "We need to get you with me behind his desk. Help me get us back there."

"It hurts to breathe. I can't."

"You have no choice, or we all die." My fingers are bathed in her blood. It's dripping down my wrist as I hold the fabric in place. "We don't have time to lose. Crawl and I'll follow."

Stacy takes ahold of the scarf and turns to crawl when the door is kicked open. Wood splinters and flies around the room. More shots are fired as Gina takes the first man down with a bullet to his neck. The one that follows manages to respond, but his shot barely misses her, and the flesh wound on her arm pisses her off.

The sound of empty shells falling fills the room and when all is said and done, the man is dead and so is the attendant from the employee parking area. He didn't have the chance to shoot.

"London, we need to go now."

"I can't leave her here by herself!"

"I'll be okay. Promise." My eyes snap back to Stacy who's

already in motion; she's unsteady but moving aside a discrete area of wall behind Liam's dead body. It opens to a small cupboard-like notch in the wall where a human can hide inside. A tight fit, but she's small enough to be comfortable. "Get out, sweetie. Listen to her and go."

"Are you sure?" Adrenaline is pumping through my system. I'm jittery yet hyper alert.

"Go," she urges, already slipping inside. "Save yourself."

Those are Stacy's last words; they slip past her lips mere seconds before another round of bullets comes from the direction of the other room.

I'm scared, shaking as I look over at Gina, but as soon as she mouths *run...*I do so.

Chapter 36
LONDON

THE WORLD AROUND ME dissolves into chaos.

Noise and destruction as I run out of the house with the unadulterated sense of fear lodging itself in my throat. Feet follow me—run behind me—but I can't tell who it is.

It might be Gina.

Might be worse.

All I know is that I don't look back. I run.

Run until the door opens with force, slamming against the outside concrete wall as I pass the threshold, and still I don't stop.

All I know is that it's not safe. That I must continue moving.

"Head to the car, London. Don't look back and get inside." Her words are comforting, give me hope as I hear the lock click on the van up ahead. The lights flash, and I extend a hand out to open the door.

I'm so close.

Just a little bit more…

The sound of screeching tires meets my ears, and the loud sound of a crash follows. From my periphery something—a large mass moves and falls to the ground, and it takes everything in me not to confirm my fears. In my heart I know it's Gina.

"Don't stop. Just don't stop," I mutter to myself, but the reaction is automatic, and I do so. She's there. Just there. Lying a few feet from me and to the right, unconscious and unmoving. A sob catches in my throat and I turn toward her, wanting to help or make sure she's breathing, when I am taken from behind.

Whoever bumps into me tackles me to the ground, and the hard pavement digs into my flesh. Breaks the skin.

A hiss escapes as pain shoots through my body and I buck my hips, try to wiggle out from beneath him. Because of that, there is no doubt.

It's a man. A large man at that, and his scent is familiar.

Oh God. Please help me.

Panic churns within, and I scream.

"No one left to hear you, little sis. Yell all you want…it only excites me." That's the last thing I hear as he covers my mouth with a dirty rag, and all goes black.

———

HUSHED WHISPERS and the feel of the car I'm in meeting a large pothole awaken me. I have no idea how long I've been out or where we are at this point, and I pray that we're still in Chicago. Darkness surrounds me, my body lying awkwardly on a bench seat inside of what I think is a van or truck, as I try to open my eyes.

I can't. There's something covering them, and my hands are tied behind my back.

Whatever road we're on is in bad shape. In need of repairs, and with the areas that Alton likes to frequent, that could be anywhere.

He likes the dirty and dangerous. Where no one will bat an eye and calling the police is forbidden.

Criminals don't snitch. They don't involve themselves with what doesn't concern them.

I'm a dead duck unless...

I wiggle a bit, just a discreet shift as to not draw attention to myself, and the low clink of my chain follows. It's small, but I feel the locket move across the thin chain, letting me know it's there.

That Malcolm has a way to find me.

I have to believe that.

That Stacy is alive and calling everyone she can. She knows Malcolm. The office must have his number somewhere. The fact that we won't be home soon is also a reason to come looking.

He will find me. Everything will be okay.

It becomes my mantra as I'm driven God knows where and with whom. Because I know Alton's not alone. The voices are a bit muffled, but I can pick apart his and Brittany's. Not that it surprises me; she's a piece of work and his follower. A sick individual.

But then again, sick fucks attract compatible individuals.

The car comes to a sudden stop then, and two doors open. A cool breeze fills the inside of the car's cab and with it, I get a hint of water. That specific scent that comes from a large body of water. Fresh and clean with just a subtle hint of fish.

"Lake? But which one?" I mutter under my breath, but then go slack again when another door opens. This one is near my feet, and I'm taken out like a sack of potatoes. Swallowing my yelp takes heroic effort, but more so my grunt when I'm thrown over a shoulder that digs into my abdomen.

"Take her inside," Alton says, and the man holding me tenses, his hand on the back of my ankle, clenching. "Go on. Wake my darling little sister up and secure her to the pole near the back."

"I'm not your puppet or employee. Watch it, or I pull the plug on everything." *Agent Hayes? What the hell?*

"My apologies, Agent. No reason to be so sensitive."

Another car pulls up, tires screeching, and this time I'm not able to hide my automatic response. If Hayes notices my body tensing, he doesn't say anything, but his tap to my leg is enough to make me still.

There's no yelling. No demands to let me go. No shot being fired.

Instead, I hear a voice that sounds familiar, but I just can't pinpoint. The person has heavy footsteps, clomping on the pavement until coming to a stop near where we stand. "As you predicted, the authorities are all over that place and no one has reported the girl missing. I've gone around the perimeter twice now, and it's empty. No sign of Mr. Asher yet."

"Good. Very good," Alton says, and then Brittany giggles at something. "Let me know when he gets within the property line. I want her to watch me kill him."

And then we're moving.

The bones of his shoulder hurt, pressing into me as we cross a threshold. We go from dark and fresh air to dank and cold. The place is freezing.

"Be quiet and behave, London. I don't want you to get hurt in this." Hayes walks deeper into the room and stops to lower me, his hands gripping my arms to steady me. "It'll be over soon."

"Why are you doing this? Do you have any idea how crazy Alton is? What he's going to do to me?" My breathing gets choppier as my chest gets tight. I have no weapon and my hands are tied. How the hell can I defend myself? "Please, I'm begging you...let me go."

"Now why would he do that?" An arm wraps around my midsection as the blindfold is taken off. Alton is behind me and Hayes in front. "His eggs are in this basket, Lola. The love of his life was killed by the asshole you've given yourself to, and he wants revenge.

A man in love without his woman will go insane." His lips kiss my temple before he licks a path from cheek to chin, nipping my jaw hard before pushing me toward the agent. "Tie her up and gag her."

I stumble into Hayes but turn my head to glare at the man who was never really my brother. My enemy.

He looks like shit. Dirty. Still wearing a cast, but like the rest of him, it's filthy.

Nothing like the vain man I knew.

"You're not getting away with this, Alton."

"Want to make a wager on that, dearest?" His slimy grin causes my stomach to churn. The disgust must be visible on my face because his eyes narrow. "Something you want to say?"

"I hope he kills you—"

His hand meets my cheek, knocking me over, and I'm caught by his accomplice. Hayes pushes me behind him. "Keep your hands off her. Hurt her, and we're done."

"Fine. Just shut her up." Alton walks away, leaving me with another man that I see as a monster.

I don't say a word as I'm taken to the very back and my hands are secured to a metal post. Agent Hayes doesn't use handcuffs and I'm thankful for that, but the thin zip tie in his hand isn't going to be easy to escape either.

"Stay." His voice is gruff, and the look he gives warns me not to defy him. He doesn't go far and grabs a small metal chair by the only doorway in this place. It's a large room. Empty, and with a few dozen boxes stacked against the opposite wall of where I am. There's a second floor, but it's all dark and the windows are too high for me to reach except for one right across from the metal stairs. They look unstable but will have to do.

"Count of three," I mumble and take a step forward, ready to make a run when Hayes grabs my arm. "Let go."

"I wouldn't do that if I were you."

"Do you really expect me to sit here and wait for him to kill me?"

"He won't hurt you, London. I won't allow it."

At that I laugh, the sound rough and sardonic. "Really? You're going to stop him?"

"You have my—"

"Your word means jack after helping a criminal kidnap me to use as a pawn. The fact that you're willing to go this far for what? Revenge for a woman that didn't love you?"

"Shut the fuck up," he spits out, grabbing my wrist in a hold sure to leave a bruise. Hayes pulls me toward the pole, a hand on either side, and wraps the tie around them. It's tight, hurts a bit, but plastic isn't metal. "If you want to get out of here unscathed, I suggest not pissing off the only person here that cares if you live or die. To them, you're just the dessert after a gory main attraction. Remember that next time you open that slick mouth of yours, kid."

He walks away, kicking the chair toward me on his way out of the room. The heavy door clanks against the metal frame as it closes, leaving me alone.

With the toe of my shoes, I kick it closer and take a seat. Think.

The glass above me shows some light, so it can't be that late. Maybe four or five.

"How do I get out of this mess?" Leaning my head against the metal pole, I close my eyes for a minute or two, trying to remember this video on Facebook I once saw about self-defense and what to do if you're tied with zip ties.

You have to tighten them, leaving no space between the hands.

Extend your hands out with the palms facing each other.

Then you pull back as hard as you can.

Easy peasy.

"You seem lost in thought, Lola. Want to share with the class?" My eyes open and snap toward the sound of Alton's voice. When did he come in? Why didn't I hear him?

He's standing a few feet away and watching me with that same creep-tastic look in his eyes. The same one that's always made me wary of him. That he's not right in the head.

SIN

"Why can't you just let me be?" I ask, trying to buy myself a bit of time. He's a talker. Get him going, and he might not notice my actions.

"Because you're mine." He says it so calmly, so emotionless. Alton takes another step toward me, his hand reaching out, but instead, he drops it and turns around, giving me his back at the last second. His good hand is at his hair and pulling. His breathing is becoming agitated. "You just had to fuck him, didn't you? Had to give away the one thing that was going to make me enough money to disappear. He took your cherry and everything else that mattered in my life."

While he talks, I take the end of the zip and pull, tightening the cord. But as his words sink in, I pause and sit straight. "What do you mean, disappear?"

"Dad wanted to sell you to an overseas trafficker. That, or whore you out, while I want to keep you."

"You two are sick," I whisper, but it's not low enough and before I can turn my face, his fist connects, sending me back. The force is enough to break the hold of the plastic, my body landing hard on the cold concrete.

Blood drips from the cut at the corner of my bottom lip, and my head feels woozy. It takes a moment for me to regain complete visual of him, and even then, there's a ringing in my ear that's distracting.

He's angry. Visibly shaking as he lowers himself over me.

Trapping me against the floor so I can't escape. My legs kick out, but it does nothing to dislodge him. Instead, it makes him laugh, a hot, panting chuckle against my neck. He's hard, and I'm disgusted. Acid-like-bile rises up my throat as panic sets in.

No one is here. No one to stop him.

I want to yell. Scream, but the words won't come out.

"Even if you did, no one will hear you. This building is completely soundproof." His good hand wanders over my rib and higher, skimming over my breast before wrapping around my neck. Squeezing hard. Painfully so as to block my airways. "I'm going to

289

fuck you as Malcolm Asher bleeds out in front of you, London. I'm going to break you, pass you around to anyone willing to pay for your used cunt, and then have you train my next whore while I spend every last dime your mother left you. You'll pay for your betrayal."

"You'll never get away with this," I manage to wheeze out, clawing at his hands to let go.

Alton laughs, the sound psychotic. "Did you know that Dad killed your father years ago by cutting his break line? That he planned—used your mother to gain access to Julian's wealth?" Another laugh, his face hovers over mine. Pure evil reflects in his stare. "However, I did something so much worse. I'm the one that killed Amelia, Lola...I pulled the trigger and now I'll own their little girl."

"You—" I don't get to finish as the door is kicked in and multiple guns are cocked.

Chapter 37
MALCOLM

TWO AND A HALF HOURS AGO...

T HE DOOR TO MY office is thrown open and as I reach for my gun, Javier comes into view. He's angry. Full of agitation as he clenches and unclenches his hand, one that has blood dripping from the center knuckle.

"What's going on?" I'm already standing and making my way toward him. The man never reacts—he's calm and collected at all times—knows better than to barge in here like this unless it's an emergency. His expression makes me pause as I reach him, my stomach churning as the worst case scenario plays out. "Where's London?"

"She's been taken. They're holding her at a warehouse attached to a power plant on Lake Michigan just outside of Milwaukee," Javier answers, and I nod. Take a moment to breathe as a rage the likes of which I have never experienced surges through my veins. It's sudden. Maddening as I grit my teeth and fight to not give in to the emotion.

Emotional reactions lead to mistakes. Bad calls of judgement.

She can get hurt in this process if I don't play my cards right. They don't want to hurt her, not when she comes with a price tag, but will to save themselves. Especially Marcus. He's been shopping her innocence—the one she gave me so sweetly—to the first son of a bitch with the right amount of zeroes at the end.

They know I'm coming but will never guess which route I'll take. How far I'll go to save her.

"Alton, Marcus, and Jimmy." It's not a question, but a statement.

"No Marcus, but we do have one Shawn Hayes assisting." This one surprises me, but then again, after what he said to London about Karina, I've been waiting for him to strike. Finding out she was his ex was the easy part. A few clicks and the world's your oyster; the internet has its pros and cons, and this is the perfect example.

A man in love with an old social media account from his days in college that he hasn't closed. That he hides from his job along with a creepy fascination for women who look like Karina. Photos of the couple. Declarations. The last post on his wall is of the day she left him.

It's a personal purging. Dark and full of bitter rage.

Yet it's the last line that stood out for me.

I'll kill him for us.
Take his everything and place it at your feet.

"Where were they, and why the blood?"

"At Lake Forest, and I punched a wall."

My brows furrow as I focus on the first part of his answer. "Why the fuck would she—"

"London wanted to surprise you and they went to pick something up." *What could she possibly want from...that dirty girl. I'll turn her ass a nice shade of red for this after I kiss her stupid.* "They were in his office when shots rang out, killing Liam, injuring a girl named Stacy, among other patrons."

"And Gina?"

"Run over trying to get London out and into their car. She has a flesh wound and a broken leg but is otherwise fine. I have someone with her and Stacy at the E.R. for precautions."

"Who?"

"Carmelo."

Nodding, I scratch my jaw. "Where's Marcus Foster? One doesn't go far without the other."

"We have a tail on him. He's out by the pier and seems to be waiting on someone."

"He's not to leave." Not a request and at once, Javi pulls out his phone and sends out a few messages. Pings follow as I walk back around my desk and remove a black and white drawing of The Asher building given to me as a gift by a customer. It's large and heavy in its expensive casing, and the perfect size to hide the access panel behind my desk.

Placing my entire palm over the screen, I wait for the scanner to skim my hand and the section of wall to unlock. It does with a loud click, and I pull it open, entering my private collection of weapons here.

Javier follows me inside and grabs two assault rifles with silencers while I remove my suit jacket and hang it from a hook on the wall. I'm a man that appreciates the nicer things in life, and my holster is leather-made and one of a kind. Tailor made by an old

Italian man in a shop where a billfold will run you a few grand easily.

Taking the upper-body holster, I slip it on and secure the strap across my midsection before taking my Desert Eagles from their place inside a drawer. There are a few magazines beside them, six to be exact, with nine bullets each, and I take those too.

I want them to hear each shot.

To see the gleam of polished silver as I empty a round into each body.

Once we're outside the weaponry room, I close the door and when the click signals it shut, I turn and open my top desk drawer. Atop a stack of papers is my favorite knife and I grab it, too, before walking out.

Mariah is at her desk when we do, and she's just as angry. Her eyes are cold, and no words are said as I walk up, kiss her forehead, and continue straight back and toward a door that no one uses here.

The private elevator will take me straight to my garage, opening the door mere steps from the car I keep on site. I open the door and enter, turning to look at my cousin who's already on her way to make my office appear as if nothing has happened.

Our eyes meet and she gives me a nod which I return, then looks at her boyfriend for the same.

Today, their blood will cleanse the streets of Chicago.

"I DIDN'T KNOW." Marcelles greets me near the pier's entrance with a serious look on his face. He's holding his hands up, taking a step back as I tower over him. Friend or enemy, everyone around me runs the risk of my wrath at the moment.

Blackness—that dark manifestation of my soul is clawing its way out and wanting to play. For every second they have London, I'll repay the world with my maelstrom of vengeance.

"Where is he?" My voice is cold, hand on the handle of the knife inside my pocket.

"Down below and not alone." Beads of sweat form at his brow, and he wipes them away. "He's with that officer you told me to look out for—"

"Bristol?"

"Yes." His phone rings, but he doesn't answer. Instead, he keeps his gaze on mine. "Marcus seems desperate, Malcolm, while the Lieutenant kept assuring him about some buyer. Those two are deep into some fucked-up shit, and I'll take them out if you need me to. Just say the word, and it's done."

"These two are mine. They all are." Agent or not, Shawn Hayes ran his luck and lost. There is no coming back from this.

"Understood. My loyalty has always been with you and our family, my career be damned."

"I know." And I do. Marcelles has been with us for years and has never betrayed that trust. He's an honest man, a hard-working agent, but loyal to only those in his family. He's my mother's cousin and went to school with my father and Director Monahan.

All sides interconnect and watch out for the other.

He's not a traitor. Neither is Monahan.

However, Shawn Hayes has proven to be more than a nuisance. He's a danger to society.

A rogue.

"The press release will go out to all major networks in three hours. There will be a manhunt."

"I'll make every second count." I turn and walk around toward the pathway below, when I pause and look at Javier. "Who's watching them now if Marcelles is up here?"

"Michael. The kid wants to prove himself and atone for his sins."

THREE MEN now stand right where Marcelles said they would be, talking in hush tones and with hands thrown up in the air as they argue over something. They don't see me or the others with me, and I use it to my advantage.

A moment to test one of my own.

Grabbing Michael by the collar of his shirt, I pull him beside me and hand over my gun. "How good of an aim do you have?"

He gives me a thumbs-up, mouthing *good* while taking my Eagle.

"Three men, and one is young," I say while waving a hand in front of us. "Shoot the one to the left in the chest, and I'll forgive you. Get a bullet in his head, and I'll welcome you back with a forgiven debt. You have one bullet…make it count."

We step back slowly, and he takes his stance. Michael raises his hands and aims with elbows in a locked position. His hand trembles a bit and he shakes his head to rid himself of the mounting nerves. The finger on the trigger twitches, but on his next breath he pulls, and Bristol falls to the ground.

The men turn our way, and Marcus pales but is smart enough to stay quiet as I walk over to inspect the shot. I'm impressed with Michael's accuracy and balls to take this risk when he still looks in pain himself. I can respect that. Forgive but never forget.

"Center of forehead and clean exit by the puddle beneath his head. Welcome back, kid."

Michael makes a humming sound, and I look back to see him place a hand over his heart. He's a good person that made a mistake. He paid for those crimes with blood and the removal of his tongue, took it like a champ, and I'll repay him for proving his loyalty when all is said and done.

"Who the fuck are you, and what do you want?" the older man beside a quiet Marcus asks. "This is a private sale. I've already paid for that cunt to suck—" He doesn't get to finish as I pull my knife out, flip it open, and slide it across his throat. The cut is deep enough to kill, and it splatters across myself and Marcus, ruining my white dress shirt.

I'll never know his name. If he has a family.

None of that matters when his intentions were to hurt the one I love the most in this world.

Blood flows from the open wound and he weakens, dropping to his knees in front of me. Fisting his hair, I yank his head back, stretching the torn skin, prompting more of his life's force to drip onto the wet ground below.

"Please," he cries, a gurgling sound as he begins to choke. "Please get me help."

"She's mine." His eyes widen at my words before I slide the blade once more, cutting his aorta. I drop him and let him bleed out while I turn to face Marcus fucking Foster. "Anything you want to say? Explain?"

"You can have her," he says, holding a hand out as if to keep me from advancing. It didn't. "All I need is five million dollars and two tickets to Mexico. Give me that, and you'll never see Alton and me again."

"Really. Just five?" Wiping the dirty blade on my pants, I bring the gleaming steel between us. "Why not ten? Fifty, even?"

"That would be very generous of you. I'd be forever—" The back of my hand cuts him off, the force of the blow causing him to stagger back and fall.

"I'm going to enjoy every single second of your death, Marcus." Standing over him, I place the sole of my shoe on his chest. "However, before that can happen, I have a promise to fulfill. I told you you'd have a front seat to Alton's end, and I'm a man who keeps his words."

Chapter 38
MALCOLM

PRESENT

FUCKING IDIOTS.

We're about two hours from The Loop and on Lake Michigan standing a little way down from a power plant outside of Milwaukee. London is here. Being held here. Her locket is pinging with a signal and coming from a run-down warehouse toward the east side of this property.

It could be storage.

Could be a structure that they've been meaning to tear down and haven't.

Could be that after the workday is done and employees go home to their families, someone has been letting criminal activity take place on the premises. Someone, like the balding fuck currently slumped over his desk chair inside the central office.

However, I will thank the man for having the CCTV live system off and the recorder looping through footage from last week. Saves me time.

> Ready and in position. ~Javi

> Hold ~Malcolm

My eyes scan the surrounding buildings and the lone structure where they hold London. No one seems to be on high alert. Monitoring the entrances. They're doing a shit job at surveillance.

Overconfidence is a disease many people suffer from. Too cocky. Too stuck within the *it'll never happen* mind frame, and this reeks of it.

Of narcissism on a level that is dangerous.

They're lazily watching the front and back, and yet, the few assholes Alton put together as guards are laughable. Incompetent. Five in total and spread out, the men all imbibing. High. Too busy snorting coke and playing with the cheap guns given to notice they're surrounded on all sides.

"Boss," Carmelo speaks low beside me, looking through a pair of binoculars toward the entrance. He left the hospital to join me after I sent Michael to take his place. "We have movement. Hayes and Jimmy are outside talking, and Alton has gone inside."

"And the whore?"

"Getting high as a kite inside of Alton's car." The car in question, a blue Mustang, begins to inch forward and then stop. It does this three times until Brittany lowers the window and sticks her head out, yelling out something to Hayes.

The man ignores her.

Jimmy ignores her.

She doesn't like it and pulls away from them to do a reckless donut between the building and a few old trees. The rubber burns on the asphalt, blowing smoke around the car as it spins. Any other time, I'd watch the idiot kill herself all day, but right now, I'll need her to stay alive long enough to become a scapegoat.

"How much did her supplier gift her?" Looking at my phone, I send a message to Javier.

Now ~Malcolm

Carmelo chuckles. "Enough to kill a bull."

"Good. Make sure she doesn't leave the property." Adrenaline pumps through my veins and I take my gun out, checking the magazine and cocking it. My body is vibrating with excitement. With anger.

The demon I keep hidden within wants blood and vengeance. To kill. To make them pay for every single minute of fear my Twirl has lived through.

I count to ten and crack my neck, watching as the guard walking close to where I stand hits the floor with two bullet wounds to the chest. My eyes close, and I wait for Javier's signal. For confirmation that everyone but the three main culprits are dead.

Two minutes pass and my phone vibrates. My eyes snap open to read his one-word reply.

Done. ~Javi

Good. Have them clean up and set the stage. ~Malcolm

Already on it. Meet you in ten. ~Javi

I pocket my phone and walk through the lot toward the entrance casually. Carmelo is already with Brittany, turning off the vehicle and pulling her out. She's screaming and throwing punches while Hayes and Jimmy scramble to grab their guns.

My steps don't falter as I raise my gun and fire three shots at Jimmy. The first misses by a hair, but the second and third lodge themselves deep into his chest. He staggers and I fire another two, this time hitting his stomach.

Blood drenches his shirt as his body falls. It pools all around him, staining the ground as he takes his last few breaths.

From the corner of my eye, I see Javier making his way to me with another two men.

"You're a dead son of a bitch," Shawn yells out as a bullet flies by my head. He fires another and again misses. I return the favor and don't, hitting his hand with the Glock. "Fuck!"

It falls to the ground and I put my own away, preferring to use my knife on him. "You want me? Come get me."

"Karina was too good for you, asshole." He charges toward me as I flip the blade out, his body colliding with mine as we hit the ground. Hayes is quick to mount me, throwing a punch that lands on my jaw. It cuts my lip, and I return the favor by embedding the blade of my knife deep into his thigh and twisting it.

His screams are loud. Like the bitch he is.

I'm quick to buck him off and stand up, leaving the blade in his possession. "Did that hurt, Agent? Need help?"

"You ruined everything." He follows me up to his feet, putting the bulk of his weight on the opposite leg. "We were going to be happy together. Had plans to elope."

"Quit lying to yourself. You never had the means to keep her happy."

"Shut the fuck up," he growls out, his hand on the handle of my knife. With a quick yank, he pulls it out, gritting his teeth as the shock of pain travels through his body.

But I don't. I taunt. Push every single button he has.

I begin to circle him, walking just close enough for him to reach if he dares. I'm counting on his rage. "She was a selfish and greedy whore that deserved all ten bullets I put into her body."

I'm ready for him when he lunges, and with a quick turn of my arm flip him over my shoulder. Shawn lands hard on his back but has enough mind to lash out when I turn, cutting my arm. It's not deep, but burns, and I punch him twice in retaliation.

His nose cracks, a sickening sound as blood gushes from the nostrils. "I'm going to kill you." Again, he makes a slicing motion, and I grab his wrist easily, bringing the knife toward his throat. He fights it, tries to push me off, but I use the momentum of my body weight to move the point of the blade to right below his Adam's Apple.

"Accept your fate with dignity," I grunt, adding pressure as the end pricks his skin. His mouth opens to reply, but before he can spew some other bullshit, I shove the blade straight through his neck.

Shawn's body goes limp after a minute and I stand, leaving the knife where it is for now.

"We have an hour between a tip being sent to the police and their arrival. Marcelles and Monahan will be shortly behind since this involves one of their own." Carmelo catches up with me as I pull out my gun with the full magazine and walk toward the door. "She's almost comatose and not going anywhere. Weapons are ready and with her fingerprints. Clean-up crew is staging the rest...let's get them out, and fast."

"Agreed." I don't waste another minute and kick the door in when I reach the entrance. Every gun beside me cocks, but it's my bullet that dislodges when I find him over her body on the floor. It hits his side, causing him to scramble off and land on his back.

London's eyes are wide and full of panic, yet behind that choking fear I see her relief when she spots me by the door. Without another conscious thought, she pushes herself off the floor and runs to me, jumping into my arms and holding tight. Every part of her wraps itself around me.

Tight, not a single inch of space is left between her body and mine.

Her entire form is shaking. Mumbling something that I can't quite make out, but when I try to pull her back a bit, she refuses to move with a shake of her head.

"I'm here, sweetheart. It's going to be okay."

"Not until he's dead." Twirl's voice comes through then, monotone and ice cold. "They have to die."

"Alton Foster was never going to make it past the end of this week—"

"Now." She shudders, a sob catching in her throat as she pulls back to look me in the eye. Those sweet lips I love tremble, tears rushing down her cheeks as I take in the bruise forming on her skin. How pale she is from the shock and trauma.

A million deaths wouldn't be enough for this fucker.

"Tell me how I can make this right for you. Whatever it is, it's done." My men move around us, Carmelo and Javier sending London sad looks. Alton is picked up from the floor and forced to sit in a chair near a pole. My guess is that's where he kept her—tied her to—by the broken skin of her wrist. "Seeing you like this is killing me, love."

"He killed her, Malcolm. They fucking killed my parents."

Motherfuck, he told her. "I know."

"You did? When…why didn't—"

"My investigator looked into their deaths, and the results of his findings were inside my email this morning. I'll show you the time and date if you need me to, London."

"I'm s-sorry, I—"

"Shhh, none of that. I'm not looking for an apology, and you've done nothing wrong." Lowering her to the ground, I wait until she's on steady feet and pull back. Force her eyes on mine with the tip of my finger. "Just tell me how I can make this right."

She nods and squares her shoulders, coming to terms with whatever decision she's made. "No one can, but you could lend me your gun."

"My gun?"

"Yes." Her eyes flick toward a groaning Alton, and that darkness I've seen glimpses of comes to the forefront. The tears stop for the moment, and her lip curls over her teeth in a snarl. The pain is there, but that need for retribution is growing by the second, and I understand it. Her. "Give it to me, Malcolm. No more questions."

"As you wish." I hand over my Eagle and watch as she gauges the weight. Admires its power.

Twirl looks at me then from under her long lashes, those beautiful blue orbs full of love and appreciation. "I love you." That's all she says, making her way toward her step sibling with slow and sure steps. She doesn't pause or so much as blink. Her arm doesn't shake when she raises it, nor does her finger twitch.

One pull. One bullet.

The kickback is stronger on this gun, but she manages to keep it steady somehow. Then again, the human body is capable of miracles when a person is determined.

At close range, she blows his skull in with no remorse. No tears. No screams.

Instead, she watches as his head flies back and the wall behind him is a work of art—eccentric splatters of blood and other matter.

He's dead, and she's safe.

One more to go after I adjust the crime scene. I'll take what I need and leave a high—overdosing Brittany behind to take the fall for both murders.

"ARE YOU READY, LOVE?" I ask, coming to a stop behind London. She's in our bathroom putting on a pair of diamond earrings I gave her for this occasion. The dinner downstairs is in her honor and with a very special guest.

She's a vision in her white dress. A Grecian inspired.

An elegant yet sinfully sexy white lace dress with a deep V at the front and a long skirt. It's tight. Perfectly molds against every dip and curve with a side split that I plan to rip later and fuck her while she wears the tatters.

"Pervert." Her eyes meet mine in the mirror. Those ruby red lips and soft brown curls accentuate the cerulean of her eyes. How bright they are. How devilish she is.

Because while this little girl will always hold a certain air of innocence about her, she's no longer pure. London's taste are ever changing. Morphing. As the week since her kidnapping passed, she has come into her own.

She wants this life. With me.

Craves the darkness I control.

There isn't a single ounce of remorse for what she did, and I'm proud of her. Have let her lead when it comes to how the Foster story ends.

"For you? Always." My hands skim down her spine, and she shivers. Over her ass, and she lets out the sexiest kittenish sound. "Ready to play?"

"With you? Forever." She turns around, and in her heels almost reaches my chin, which she bites. "Now, let's go celebrate."

As we descend the stairs, the noise of conversations infiltrates and her smile grows. My family is here, and she loves them as much as they do her.

The formal dining room is full when we enter. My mother and father, Javier and Mariah, and lastly Marcus, sit around our table. All dressed to the nines, while the last, like he's been inside of a padded cell and is seeing the light for the first time in years. He's skittish. Afraid. *Pussy.*

"Evening." All voices cease as we enter, walking to the front where I pull out London's chair and she waves to the room. A whimper comes from the opposite end, but we ignore him as we take our place at the head.

"You two look rested," Mariah comments, bringing her glass of wine to her lips and taking a sip. "Playing hooky looks good on you."

"Best nap of my life," I reply, winking at my cousin while the others chuckle. Magda comes in then; her dress is all black and for mourning. She walks around the room in silence and places a plate in front of everyone with a domed lid. Every plate is empty except one.

His.

A starving Marcus that hasn't eaten in over three days.

"May I?" comes from where he sits, a low and meek voice that resembles nothing of the man he once was.

"You may, but first I have an important question for you, *sir*." I stand and walk across the room to where he sits and pull a chair out beside him. Sit and wait for him to have the decency to address me. "Aren't you curious?"

The position I have him in is the perfect vantage point for the cameras recording this, a live feed that Thiago is watching from his home in Miami. Because while he understands the cause and effect —the rapid pace in which Alton was killed or how it came to be—for this one he wants front row seats to the show. Something London agreed with wholeheartedly when I explained.

Was actually her idea that we find an encrypted server through the dark web. Something that with money isn't hard to do.

"Where's Alton," he asks, instead, hands clenching atop the table. "Where is my son?"

"You'll see him soon enough." A giggle escapes London, and Marcus looks at her. His eyes turn hard, cold—the hate toward her is palpable.

"Sorry." I know her, and she's anything but. "Just remembered something I heard a few days back."

SIN

"Behave, love," I chuckle and look back at an angry shell of a man. A man that can never hurt her again. Whose last minutes on this earth will be spent in total misery. Because for as much of a piece of shit as Marcus is, the asshole did love his son. Is going to die because of his innate ability to see no wrong in him. "Marcus, the reason I brought you here today is because I'd like to ask you for London's hand in marriage. I promise to always take care of her. Spoil her. Place the world at her feet because she deserves that and so much more. I love her."

He doesn't say a word. He's fuming in his silence.

"Oh, honey!" my mother exclaims from across the table, clapping her hands together in excitement. "I'm so happy for you both. She's perfect for you and this family."

"Welcome to the family, London." This time it's my father who talks, and he raises his glass in a toast they all follow. And still, no response from the man who raised her.

"See how happy she is? How fucking beautiful?"

"Bring me to Alton. I need to see my son."

"Of course. But first…" I lift the lid of his dome where a decent-size portion of a filet sits in a reduction sauce. Specially prepared for him. "Bon appetite."

"I'll wait until after—"

I slam a hand atop the table, tipping his goblet of water over. "Pick up that knife and fork before I shove the entire plate down your throat."

All eyes are on his as he does what I ask, picking up the utensils and cutting into the medium-rare piece of meat. His hand trembles as he brings the small bite to his mouth and chews. There is no savoring. No appreciative noises.

Almost as if he knows…

"Can I see him now?"

"Another bite."

"Please, I just—"

"Two more."

Marcus nods, picking up the next piece and practically swallowing. A dry swallow at that. Then another, larger this time. When he finishes, he pushes his plate away and looks at me with hopeful eyes.

"What?" I ask, not understanding the perplexity of his expression.

"Can I see him? No more games, Malcolm." He's near tears. Beyond desperate. "Just let me see my son."

"You already have. He's been here the entire time." I've never seen the world come down on a person's head before, and the interpretation in front of me is amusing. The look in his eye—the retching that follows as the tears pour from him—it's nothing compared to what they were willing to do to an innocent woman for monetary gain. Leaning forward, I meet his stare with a devilish grin. Neither conforming nor denying his worst nightmare. "Make of that what you will."

"No. NO!" He shoots up from his seat, his blazing eyes set on London. "This is all your fault. I'll kill you, bitch!"

"I pulled the trigger, too." Twirl taunts, her grin matching mine. "My face was the last one that sick bastard saw."

"After everything we did for you? How we took you and that cunt—" He doesn't get to finish his sentence as London shoots him square in the chest, creating a domino effect. My gun follows, as does every person inside this room. A bullet for each member, and then two more for her parents.

Marcus Foster bleeds out in my dining room, a mass of failure. A product of greed.

"Thank you," my girl says then, pulling my attention to her gorgeous eyes. They are happy. Full of relief. "And the answer is yes. A thousand times yes."

"It wasn't a question, sweetheart." Taking her hand in mine, I slip the large princess-cut diamond ring I've carried with me all day onto her ring finger. Where it will stay until we leave this earth. "You're mine, and I am yours. Fated."

"Still saying yes." She's admiring it. How perfectly it fits.

"Never though you wouldn't." I pull her out of her chair, leaving the others to receive my cleaning crew. While we celebrate out tonight with family and friends, they'll take care of the man that'll soon become a distant memory. Leave nothing behind like his son.

"So cocky, Mr. Asher."

"Look at me..." she does, and whatever she sees in my expression melts her against me "...I love you." It's my vow. A promise. My truth. There will never be anyone else for me. No one would ever compare to the perfection in my arms.

"I love you, too."

My lips come down on hers then, and the world fades away. Her taste overtakes my senses, and I let her. She's the only person in this world with the power to destroy me, and yet, I know that my home will always be at her temple.

My tiny dancer.

Epilogue 1
LONDON

SIX MONTHS LATER...

"**Y**OU LOOK BEAUTIFUL, cousin. The bracelet from Grandma Isadora looks perfect," Aurora says from behind me as I stand in front of the mirror adjusting the Swarovski tiara Malcolm insists I wear. He didn't want a veil or anything to cover my face because his queen never hides. Even this dress; with the sweetheart neckline and mermaid-style bodice in lace —how the bottom curves over my behind, accentuating one of his favorite places to grab—was bought with him in mind.

To please him. See his eyes shine with hunger as he takes me in. That man. *Christ.*

He's changed my life in the best of ways. Completely.

I'm no longer afraid. I'm no longer running.

Because of him I have a family, love, and a chance to be anything and everything I want to be. No rush. No expiration dates. He supports me.

Like my wanting to find Aurora and tell her immediately who I am. To build a relationship when she could've easily told me to disappear. It's because of him that I didn't chicken out. That I have someone from my side of the family to walk with us down the aisle of this beautiful cathedral.

Just like Earl and Mary give us their blessing on my mother's behalf.

"Thank you so much for coming, and for this." I lift my wrist and inspect the delicate tennis bracelet with diamonds and sapphires throughout. It's my something borrowed and blue. "Having a piece of the family to wear today means more than you'll ever know." Turning to face her, I take in her appearance in the elegant little black dress I chose for her and Mariah. Take in our similarities. Like our high cheekbones and skin tone. The plumpness of my lips that seems to come from my dad's side. "It means a lot that *you* could make it. That *you* wanted to do this."

"I'm going to flick you if you thank me again, chica. Stop it."

"Ass," I mutter, but she hears and smacks my arm.

"Dork."

"You bruise me, and you'll deal with Malcolm." In the last few months since we connected, if I say something like that she laughs and hits me again. Our relationship feels like what a sibling one should be—what I've missed out on. However, this time she gets a pensive look instead. "What gives? What's with the look?"

"How well do you know his groomsmen?"

"Which one?"

"British and a complete lying asshole."

"Casper?" I ask, thrown off by the change in her demeanor. "Did he do something to you?"

"Other than exist?" At my nod, she lets out a huff that's full of annoyance. "We don't click."

"Why?" Because I get the feeling there's something she isn't saying. "Do I need to involve—"

"No. It's me." Now she's petulant, almost looks close to stomping her feet, and I've never seen her so out of sorts. Like she…

"Do you like—"

"I'm coming in," Malcolm calls out through the door a second before barging in. His eyes fall on me immediately, hungry and calculating. "Aurora, we need a moment before the ceremony. Please find Casper and let him know I'll be down soon."

For a second, I shift my stare toward her and see that she's fluffing her hair a bit. "Of course. Just behave, kiddos. Leave the fun stuff for the after…"

The second the door clicks behind her, he's on me. Turning me around to face the vanity, he lowers my zipper carefully and then pulls the dress down. Lets the expensive gown pool at my feet as he takes in my nakedness.

"No panties, Twirl. Such a beautiful little slut." His filthy words cause a moan to slip from my lips, for my thighs to rub together. The way he's looking at me. How hungry he is…

"Your slut. All yours."

He hums in the back of his throat as two fingers slide over my slit, rubbing my clit in firm strokes. "He likes her, you know. Acting a bit like me when I met you."

"*Fuck*, I know. She's interested." It's a whimper. A plea for more. "I'll hook them up later."

"Much later," Malcolm growls out, burying two fingers deep as my body bows into the pleasure. They move in and out of me at a face past, bringing me close to the edge so fast my knees almost give out. "Hold onto the edge, sweetheart. This is going to be rough and fast."

My knuckles dig into the edge of the counter, trembling as he lowers his zipper. The bulbous tip skims my opening and I clench, needing him inside. "Please, Mr. Asher. Take care of the ache you…fuck!"

He slams in, grabbing my hips to hold me up as I begin to fall forward. His hips are punishing, taking me with fast strokes. "Quiet, London. You don't want the priest to hear your moans. How much of a dirty little girl you are."

I nod, hearing the threat in his voice.

My Malcolm is possessive of me.

Will kill anyone who so much as looks and lingers, something I secretly love.

How protective he is of the women he loves. How he treats me like his most prized treasure.

He shifts my loose curls over my shoulder and kisses the base of my neck where his tattoo is. A tiny owl that mimics his, just cuter. Bold and wise; a symbol of how I see him.

"I need you, baby. All of you."

"Always." He knows my body. What makes me clench, tremble with pleasure, and on his next stroke angles his hips to hit that spot inside me. Each of his thrusts is precise, hard with an edge of pleasurable pain that I crave.

Those fingers on my hips dig in, bruising me, and I welcome the marks. Live for them. They're a reminder of our passion. This nearly psychotic need we can't control.

Malcolm brings a hand to my neck and squeezes. The hold is tight—another way to show his dominance over my female form. I love it. Him. How those fingers wrap around my throat and pull me back to his chest, deepening each thrust.

"Oh, God," I whimper, my mouth going slack as his breath comes to my ear, a harsh, panting groan against my skin before licking the shell.

"Come on me, Twirl. Mark me."

"Malcolm," I yell out, standing on the tip of my toes as a rush of warmth flows through my limbs. Building in its intensity. Pulsing until breathing is obsolete and I come with a brutality that brings forth his own release.

"Son of a bitch," he hisses, burying himself to the hilt as his cock pulses within my core. Rope after rope filling me—running down my thighs as I try to regulate my breathing. And yet, as I find the will to move, my eyes remain watching him through the mirror.

How he tucks himself back in and then fixes his shirt.

How he runs a hand through his perfect mess of hair.

He acts like nothing just happened, while I'm out of breath and with blushing cheeks.

My simple makeup isn't ruined. My hair just needs to be fluffed a bit.

However, one look at my bright eyes and smile, and you'll know.

"You did that on purpose." It's the first thing that comes out after a few minutes. Malcolm is kneeling at my feet now, pulling my dress up and zipping the back. He stands to fix my breasts next, lifting each one into the built-in cup with no shame on his handsome face.

Like he didn't just set me up to walk down the aisle with his come drying on my thighs.

"You look beautiful, by the way," he says, stepping into my space once more after deeming me ready. His smile is boyish. Happier than I've ever seen him. "Breathtaking."

"You clean up well yourself." I fix his lapel, straightening the slightly crooked rose inside his breast pocket. "My Prince Charming."

"More like a beast, but I'll take it." He dips his face to kiss my lips. Just a soft peck. "Cold feet, or burning on a hot sandy beach?"

"I'm toasty warm and ready to become Mrs. Asher."

"Well then..." he steps back to offer me his arm "...let me walk you down the aisle toward your forever."

I giggle at that. Crazy man. "Is that even allowed?"

"My wedding. My woman. My rules."

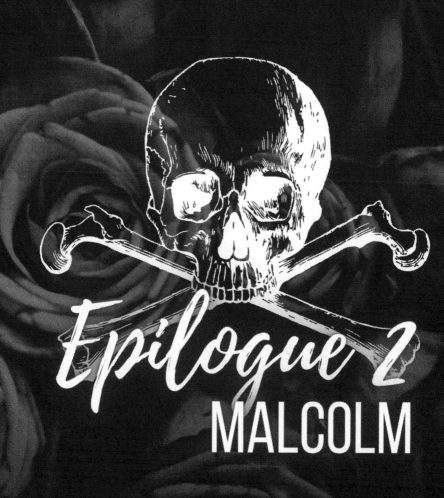

Epilogue 2
MALCOLM

THREE YEARS LATER...

LONDON STANDS WITH our little prince in her arms as our family surrounds them. My parents, Aurora, Mariah, and Javier are all here with their little one, Charlotte—a baby girl born almost nine months to the date after their wedding, and who owns Javi wholly.

Beside them is Stacy, who now runs the club for me as the majority shareholder as per Liam's will. Even being the bastard that he was, he made sure to take care of her the only way he knew how. He left everything to me that had to do with the club, making sure she wouldn't be out of employment.

She's a good employee who's proven herself loyal, has become a good friend to London, and who Carmelo adores.

A group of adults varying in age, and they're standing there watching the kids in action. One sleeping and being an angel, while mine is the center of attention.

But he was like that during the pregnancy, too. Kicking and shifting—keeping her up at night—but London always had a smile. So happy and grateful that we were starting a family after months of negative test results.

I knew it was the stress. That once her body began to relax and accept that her nightmare was over, it would happen.

And it did with the biggest blessing.

Maximus is awake now and clapping in that adorable way only toddlers can, with a cheesy grin, a head full of dark brown curls, and an enthusiastic disposition that has everyone in attendance eating out of the palm of his tiny hand.

Future dictator that he is.

Kids are brutal. Demanding. Lovable in that you-do-what-I-say-or-there'll-be-mutiny until I get my way. Like father. Like son.

And I want another one.

He reminds me of myself. Even at two years old, he's observant. Likes order and for his rules to be followed without complaint.

Makes me motherfucking proud while his mother just rolls her eyes. Tells us to chill or the one who runs the house will let us starve. My staff fears her more than me.

It's a beautiful thing.

London is kind and generous, but that kitten has very deep claws when it comes to how our home is run. She likes to be hands-on. Cooks and cleans, only asking for help if it's too high or her attention is needed elsewhere.

Over the years, I have learned to not fight this. A happy wife means a happy life, and I like getting my dick wet every night.

"Congratulations, bloke," Casper says, walking up to me from the crowd and giving me a hug. He's smirking at me, while his eyes stray every few minutes toward a giggling Aurora. She's ignoring him while making faces at my son, and you can see how frustrated he is by her refusal. Something happened between them while we were on our honeymoon, yet neither wants to explain. "Not many have the guts that you do, Asher. Out in the open like this..."

"Interpol can look but can't touch. Not in this country, at least." With the success of my Shanghai location, I've built two more in major Asian cities. The ribbon-cutting ceremony today for the Hong Kong building in the middle of their financial district is my largest. My customers here include a few syndicates, but the main source of transactions come from the counterfeit market: the purses, shoes, and clothing that are sold in the States and in a massive quantity.

Those items are produced all over Asia, but they come to this location to secretly deliver deposits. China would be too obvious for those following the paper trail, and it doesn't hurt that the government here loves me.

Love my business motto and the money I bring to the country's economy.

If they thrive, no one asks stupid questions. Cheeks turn while they shake your hand.

"You have my respect."

"And money. Don't forget that." My eyes scan the large crowd, and I spot a few of my other clients milling about, each with their families and happily celebrating out in the open with no fear of repercussion. My success is to their benefit.

As my empire grows, so do the risks. However, the rewards outweigh them.

Money rules the world, and I dominate the market.

That's what sets me apart. The fact that I have no fear.

"Very true, and I also think it's time our families grow. Unite."

"What do you have in mind?"

"Is London still looking to sell her childhood home?" Once more his eyes flick toward my wife's cousin.

I raise a brow and nod. "Yeah, why?"

"Is Aurora still working at the foundation with her?"

"Yes."

"Then Chicago is about to become my permanent home base."

Two warm hands wrap around my midsection then, interrupting, and a head sneaks under my arm. "Hello, gentlemen."

"Hello, Mrs. Asher." Her smile is wide, so fucking sweet each time I call her that. "Ready to go?"

"Just about. I'm waiting for Aurora to leave with Sam—"

"Who the fuc...fudgesicle is Sam?" Casper corrects himself quickly, shooting us an apologetic look. "Where is she going?"

"Aurora?" She's playing coy, and I narrow my eyes.

"Yes," Casper grits out, his eyes on the woman standing a few feet from us and talking to a couple from the new office here.

"She said something about a prior engagement with Sam. Not sure if it's the guy, or..." And just like that, Casper stalks off in her direction. We hear the gasp that follows, a curse or two, and then the crowd laughs as he throws her over his shoulder and leaves. Not that Aurora put up much of a fight. Even from her upside down position, I can see the sly grin she's fighting back.

The same one her cousin isn't.

"Who was the mastermind?"

"I have no idea what you're talking about, husband. I'm an angel."

Wrapping my arm around her waist, I pull her in close and lean down just enough to nuzzle the soft skin of her neck. "I'm going to punish you for that lie. Make you choke on my cock as you beg for forgiveness."

"Promise," she mewls low, smiling out into the crowd. "Are you going to make it hurt?"

"Where's Maximus?" My lips kiss the shell of her ear.

"Your parents are taking him. Giving us the night off to explore the city."

"Is that so?" Her nod is my reply. "Then head upstairs to my office and strip down, Twirl. You're going to dance for me like that first night before I split you in two. I want us to explore the option of baby number two and make it a reality."

"I don't think that's necessary." The tone she uses makes me pause and pull back enough to look into her eyes. The radiant blue is glistening with unshed tears while her bottom lip trembles. In that moment as reality hits me, I fall in love with her all over again and thank God for putting her in my path. For gifting me the privilege of loving her. "I found out a few days ago, Mr. Daddy. Asher baby number two is already on its way and growing strong."

"I love you so much, London. So fucking much." Without giving a single fuck about the people around us, I lift her into my arms and leave the stage toward my building. I don't stop until we're alone and locked away at the very top overlooking the city.

Not until her clothes and mine lay in tatters somewhere by my desk.

Not until I feel her bare skin against mine and I'm buried deep inside her against the floor-to-ceiling windows. Her back to my chest.

Because this is where I find my heaven. The temple I repent to.

I love her slowly. Tenderly.

Thanking her with every kiss for giving me my babies. For trusting me with her heart.

I pour my heart out to her with every thrust. With every moan I draw from her shaking body, and when she reaches her peak and turns to look at me from over her shoulder, I whisper, "I love you," into her mouth as we break apart and come together again.

My life is crazy. Thrives on danger and moments of chaos.

Yet with her I find my balance.

The reason to be a better man.

And I'll spend the rest of my life ruling this world so I can gift it to her every single night.

She will always be my Twirl. My best friend. My queen.

The End For Now...

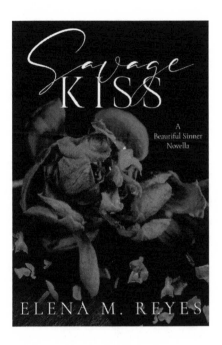

🌷 NOW LIVE 🌷

I've been watching. Patient.

Building an empire worthy of her while moving every piece—our enemies—into position. And while she lived in peace, I killed to protect her. I've picked off every single threat, one by one, but the last laugh will be hers.

It's what the KINGS owe her.

An apology.

Because it all ends today.

No more running. No more hiding.

I will never spend another night without Willow in my arms.

My bunny will never leave me again.

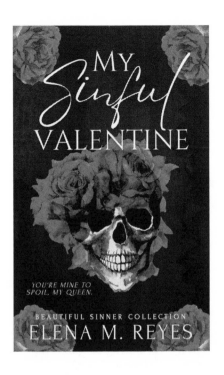

The only thing that can crumble a KING is disappointing his QUEEN. So what do my Beautiful Sinners do on Valentine's Day for their women? They spoil and lick and eat...

Worship: Malcolm and London
Say My Name: Casper and Aurora
One More: Thiago and Luna
You've Been Bad: Javier and Mariah
Pretty Doll: Alejandro and Solimar

Buy LINK: MY SINFUL VALENTINE
https://books2read.com/u/bprv29

BEAUTIFUL SINNER SERIES

BEAUTIFUL SINNER SERIES
Each book is a standalone.
Now Live!

SIN (#1)
COVET (#2)
MINE (#3)
YOURS (#4)
RISQUE #5
OWN #6

Beautiful Sinner Spin-Off
CORRUPT
MY SINFUL VALENTINE
SAVAGE KISS

NEW DARK ROMANCE

LITTLE LIES

https://books2read.com/little-lies

I AM DARKNESS.
I AM SIN.
I AM YOURS.

A truth imprinted onto my skin—its sharp vines digging into my flesh as our bond strengthens with each shallow intake of breath my love takes. Her life is intertwined with the devil, a man who hungers for depravity and death, and yet, I bend my knee for her.

Only her. Always her.

She is mine and I will kill to protect. Kill to own her.

Gabriella Moore will never leave me. Not by choice or circumstance.

ABOUT THE AUTHOR:

Elena M. Reyes was born and raised in Miami, Florida. She is the epitome of a Floridian and if she could live in her beloved flip-flops, she would.

As a small child, she was always intrigued with all forms of art—whether it was dancing to island rhythms, or painting with any medium she could get her hands on. Her first taste of writing came to her during her fifth-grade year when her class was prompted to participate in the D. A. R. E. Program and write an essay on what they'd learned.

Her passion for reading over the years has amassed her with hours of pleasure. It wasn't until she stumbled upon fanfiction that her thirst to write overtook her world. She now resides in Central Florida with

her husband and son, spending all her down time letting her
creativity flow and characters grow.

Website: https://www.elenamreyes.com/

Find My Books Here:
https://www.bookbub.com/authors/elena-m-reyes

Email: Reyes139ff@gmail.com

FB Reader Group:
Elena's Marked Girls. Come join the naughty fun.
Link: https://www.facebook.com/groups/1710869452526025/

facebook.com/ElenaMReyesAuthor
x.com/ElenaMReyes
instagram.com/elenar139
bookbub.com/authors/elena-m-reyes
amazon.com/Elena-M-
Reyes/e/B00E3E26X8/ref=dp_byline_cont_pop_ebooks_1
tiktok.com/@elenamreyes

ALSO, BY ELENA M. REYES

FATE'S BITE SERIES

LITTLE LIES

LITTLE MATE

HALF TRUTHS DUET

HALF TRUTHS: THEN

HALF TRUTHS: NOW

OMISSION PART 1 & 2

COME TO ME (2024)

THE HUNT (2024)

TERO (TBD)

BEAUTIFUL SINNER SERIES

Each book is a standalone.

Now Live!

SIN (#1)

COVET (#2)

MINE (#3)

YOURS (#4)

RISQUE #5

OWN #6

Beautiful Sinner Spin-Off

CORRUPT

MY SINFUL VALENTINE

SAVAGE KISS

ONE RULE

(BOOK #2 LIONEL TBD)

(Marked Series)

Marking Her #1

Marking Him #2

Scars #2.5

Marked #3

(I Saw You)

I Saw You

I Love You #1.5

Teasing Hands Duet

Teasing Hands #1

Taunting Lips #2

SAFE ROMANCE:

Taste Of You

Doctor's Orders

Back To You

STANDALONES:

Craving Sugar

Stolen Kisses